MY ENEMIES, MY FRIENDS . . .

CLEMENT ARCHER—The Director. He had two weeks to prove his friends were loyal Americans . . . or ruin their lives.

FRANCES—The Star. She picked up her radical politics in bed. Now she knew all the tricks of seduction . . . and survival.

STANLEY—The Comedian. He was black, bitter, and very funny—and that was enough to make him "guilty."

MANFRED—The Musician. A Jewish refugee—for him the investigation was a nightmare he'd lived before.

ALICE—The Aging Actress. She'd lost her looks, her husband, her dreams. Now the investigation could destroy whatever she had left.

VIC—The Leading Man. He was rich and famous enough to manipulate anyone and anything—even his friends.

Books by Irwin Shaw

NOVELS

Voices of a Summer Day
The Young Lions
The Troubled Air
Lucy Crown
Two Weeks in Another Town
Rich Man, Poor Man
Evening in Byzantium
Nightwork
Beggarman, Thief
The Top of the Hill
Acceptable Losses
Bread Upon the Waters

SHORT STORY COLLECTIONS

Sailor off the Bremen
Welcome to the City
Act of Faith
Mixed Company
Tip on a Dead Jockey
Love on a Dark Street
God Was Here, but He Left Early
Irwin Shaw Short Stories: Five Decades

PLAYS

Bury the Dead
The Gentle People
Sons and Soldiers
The Assassin
Children from Their Games

NONFICTION

In the Company of Dolphins
Paris! Paris!

IRWIN SHAW

The Troubled Air

A DELL BOOK

Published by
Dell Publishing Co., Inc.
1 Dag Hammarskjold Plaza
New York, New York 10017

TO MARTIN

Dell ® TM 681510, Dell Publishing Co., Inc.

ISBN: 0-440-18608-0

Reprinted by arrangement with Random House, Inc.

Printed in the United States of America

One Previous Dell Edition

March 1987

10 9 8 7 6 5 4 3 2 1

WFH

1

The clock on the acoustically perfect wall moved toward nine-thirty, nibbling at Thursday night. The scarred Negro in the cashmere jacket peered through his glasses at the pages in his hand and drawled a line that had seemed funny to everyone in the studio at rehearsal. Fifteen million people laughed. Or were supposed to laugh. Or perhaps didn't laugh. There would be repercussions from this later in the year.

In the control room, Clement Archer, behind the sound-proof glass, waved his arm to indicate that time was running out. Loyally, on the floor in front of the microphone, the next actor, Victor Herres, spoke a little more quickly than usual and bit crisply into other people's cues and the lost seconds were won back from the electric clock.

Momentarily victorious over Thursday, Archer leaned back in his chair and squinted at the actors on the other side of the glass. Eloquent fish in a clear aquarium, they swam on the element of time up to and away from the nourishment of the microphones, their voices and the sound of musical instruments from another room blended delicately by the ear-phoned engineer who sat at the control board next to Archer.

The music swelled slowly and the conductor was putting more trumpet into it than Pokorny, the composer, had wanted. Archer was certain that Pokorny, sitting behind him on the edge of a chair, would make a face at this point. He turned and looked. Pokorny was making a face. Pokorny never hid anything. The loose fat jowls, the little pale eyes behind the European glasses, the pink bow mouth immediately reflected every thought that passed through Pokorny's head. Right now he was making a complicated face, in which he was trying to announce to the world that he was not responsible for the sounds that the butcher of a conductor was drawing from the orchestra, that American musicians were too loud, that he had warned everyone, had fought and as usual lost, because he was a foreigner.

Archer smiled and turned back to the program. He liked the music. He rubbed his bald head reflectively. He had lost his hair by the time he was twenty-five and in the process had developed a nervous habit of touching the top of his head, as though to confirm the bad news a dozen times an hour. The disaster was now twenty years in the past and confirmation was history, but the sorrowful investigating movement remained.

The music died down and the closing scene of the program swept smoothly toward the finish. Across the studio, in a small gallery behind another window, the sponsor and O'Neill, the agency man, sat quietly. The sponsor had a dignified expression on his face. He didn't look happy, but he didn't look restless. I will settle for dignity, Archer thought, and listened to Herres making the long final speech.

The scene ended, the music swelled up, Pokorny made another, less complicated face, the announcer praised the product generously, but with decorum. The sponsor looked dignified; the closing theme roared up and faded; the engineer twisted a dial. A pleasant silence filled the control room for a few seconds. Archer blinked and stood up as the actors in the studio broke away from the microphones and started to talk among themselves. Archer patted the engineer's shoulder. "You were lovely, Johnny," he said. "Never, in many long years of listening, have I been so moved by an engineer. Such delicacy with the left hand, such virility with the strings, such control with the American Federation of Radio Artists."

Brewer, the engineer, grinned.

On the floor, Herres was looking up at Archer in the control room and invitingly lifting his hand as though he had a glass in it.

"The actor is making a significant gesture," Archer said, nodding to Herres. "Would you say that was beer or bourbon in his hand?" He started out of the room, passing Barbante, who was still sitting slumped in his chair, tapping a cigarette on a heavy gold case. Barbante was the writer for the program and, as usual at these moments, he had a derisive and challenging look on his face. He was a small, thick man with a long dark head. He dressed like a diplomat and always exuded a musky smell of expensive toilet water. Archer liked to avoid Barbante after a show.

"The script worked out very well," Archer said, sniffing the perfume distastefully. "Didn't you think so, Dom?"

"Oh, I thought it was peachy," Barbante said. "Just peachy. Sir Arthur Wing Pinero just twirled twice in his grave in envy."

"All personnel," Arthur said, staring down at Barbante, disliking him, "are hereby advised that, as of this date, all scripts are to be scorned on the writer's own time."

"You asked me, amigo," Barbante said, smiling up, "and I told you. I thought it was peachy. So sad, so funny, so brainless. I may ask for a raise next week."

"Mr. Archer, Mr. Archer." It was Pokorny, struggling into a trench coat behind him. Archer recognized the warning wail of complaint in Pokorny's voice and sighed as he turned to face him. Pokorny had on a long wool muffler and a stiff, reddish tweed suit with trousers that were too long for him. The trench coat was almost pink and was stained with grease over the round bulge of Pokorny's stomach. With it, Pokorny wore a black velour hat, snapped down all around over his long, thin gray hair. Fully dressed, he looked as though he had been turned out by a demented governess who had an uncle who played in a military band. He came very close to Archer and grabbed his arm. "Mr. Archer, in the most respectful terms, it is necessary to talk about the insolence of the conductor." He had a singing Viennese accent and he never blinked his eyes and Archer always had the feeling that he wanted to sit on your lap when he talked about his music.

"I thought the score was fine, Manfred," Archer said mildly, being polite and using Pokorny's full name because he knew Pokorny hated to be called Mannie.

"Of course, it is probably not in my place to say," Pokorny gripped Archer's sleeve more tightly. "But I feel it is my duty to tell you that every value was one hundred percent wrong." Pokorny's mouth quivered moistly. "I merely put myself on record. The conductor refuses to talk to me, so I advise you—it should be sharp, it should be hard like diamonds for the proper values. And what do we get—a flood of sentimentality, a Niagara of whipped cream, a Rhine of molasses."

Archer smiled. Gently he withdrew his sleeve. "I know, Manfred. You're right. I'll do something about it for next week. Depend upon me."

Pokorny bowed. "I am in your debt," he said formally. He picked up a briefcase stuffed with musical notepaper, and went out. Talent, Archer thought, watching the retreating, righteous back, sometimes assumes alarming shapes.

He went through the door and into the studio. Barbante followed him, holding a soft black overcoat over his arm. Barbante strode purposefully over to Miss Wilson, who was the prettiest girl on the program and who had been with them for only a week. She was talking in a corner to a character woman, pretending not to be waiting for Barbante. That size, Archer thought with a flick of envy, that face, you'd never think they'd wait so anxiously for him. Barbante, the fragrant bachelor. There must be something about him that only women can detect. At any distance up to a mile. And they do it on instruments when the visibility is bad. Archer watched the girl's nervous, surrendering smile as Barbante came up to her, and turned away, feeling unpleasant.

Alice Weller approached him and he arranged his face. You had to be gentle with Alice because she was unlucky and because in the last two years she had suddenly lost her looks.

"How was I tonight?" Alice was asking softly, peering nearsightedly at him. She was wearing a terrible hat that sat on her head like a breadboard. "Did I do what you asked in the second scene?" she asked in her low, rescued voice.

"You were wonderful, darling," Archer said. "As usual."

"Good." Alice flushed and her hands moved with aimless pleasure over her bag. "You are nice to say that." Then, trying to keep the pleading out of her voice, "Is there a chance you're going to need me again next week, Clement?"

"Sure," Archer said heartily. "I'm almost positive. I'll give you a ring. Maybe we'll have lunch."

"Oh," Alice said, "that would be awfully nice. I look forward to it . . ."

Archer leaned over and kissed her cheek. "Good night, darling," he said, and she flushed again as he walked away.

"Gambling," Herres was saying as Archer approached him, "gambling is the curse of the working-man." He was matching quarters with Stanley Atlas. "I'll be with you in a minute, Clement. I have him lined up for the knockout now."

"Stanley," Archer said to the Negro actor, who was digging into his pocket for more coins, "you were slow again tonight."

Atlas took two quarters out. "Was I?" he asked mildly.

"You know you were," Archer said, irritated with him. "You're milking laughs to death."

Atlas grinned. The scars on his cheek looked like grayish quotation marks when he smiled. The scars were surprising on him. He had a quiet, secret face and it was hard to think of him going any place where people would be likely to fight with razors. He seemed slight in his well-cut clothes, and his speech, unless he affected an accent, was clear of any trace of his Tampa childhood. "My public expects it, Clem," he said, playing with the quarters. "The voice of the dark, lazy South. The sluggish rivers, the willows on the bank, the mules on the dusty roads . . ."

"When was the last time you saw a mule?" Archer asked.

Atlas grinned again. "1929. In a moving picture."

"Anyway," Archer said, annoyed with the neat dark face over the white collar, "from now on, when I ask you to go faster, go faster."

"Yassuh, Boss," Atlas said. "Yassuh, Boss, you bet, Boss." He turned back to Herres and lost the two quarters.

O'Neill came through the door, buttoning his overcoat. O'Neill's coat was lined with mink, the gift of an actress wife who had a lot of money. He sometimes wore a derby hat. Archer admired O'Neill's courage in wearing a mink-lined coat, especially with a derby hat. Right now, O'Neill had his serious face on, which was incongruous, like a beard on an alderman.

"Ah," said Herres, "the mink-lined O'Neill."

"Hello, Vic," O'Neill said. "Stanley, Clement. Nice show tonight. The sponsor was pleased."

"Tonight," said Archer, "we die happy."

"Clement and I're joining my wife for a drink," Herres said. "Come along with us?"

"Thanks," said O'Neill. "Not tonight. I'm busy." He turned to Archer. "Clem, can I talk to you for a minute?"

"Be with you in a minute," Archer said to Herres and followed O'Neill across the studio to a corner. The studio was almost empty now and the sound man was seated at the piano, idly playing scraps of songs. *La Vie en Rose*," the sound man played, forgetting the noises he was paid to make professionally, the sound of rain, the sound of footsteps on a gravel path, the sound of auto accidents. Then he switched to a song about a warm, non-existent island in the southern ocean. He didn't play well, but he played with feeling, and you could tell the sound man longed for distant, quiet and melancholy places.

O'Neill stopped and turned toward Archer. "Listen, Clem," O'Neill whispered hoarsely, "there's a little party somebody's giving the sponsor and he wants you to come."

"Sure," said Archer, wondering why O'Neill had to cross the room and whisper this information. "We'll just go to Louis' and pick up Nancy Herres and we'll come along later. What's the address?"

O'Neill shook his head. "No," he whispered. "Herres isn't invited."

"Oh," said Archer. "Let's skip it, then."

"The sponsor said he'd like to talk to you."

"Any time from nine to five," Archer said. "Tell the sponsor I'm an unpredictable artist after business hours."

"OK," said O'Neill, visibly controlling his temper. "I'll tell him you've got a headache."

"Lies," said Archer, "are the foundation of all decent

social relations. You'll make somebody a wonderful hostess some day, Emmet."

O'Neill didn't answer. He was staring at Archer, his dark blue eyes baffled and friendly. He reminded Archer of a bulldog struggling to communicate with the human race, walled in by the lack of language.

"I'm sorry, Emmet," Archer said. "But I promised Vic."

"Sure," O'Neill nodded vigorously. "Don't worry about it. Will you drop into the office tomorrow? There're a couple of things I have to talk to you about."

Archer sighed. "Friday's my day of rest, Emmet," he said. "Can't it wait?"

"Not really. It's important. Say eleven o'clock . . ."

"Eleven-thirty. I expect to be sleepy tomorrow morning."

"Eleven-thirty," O'Neill said, putting on his hat. "And don't call me up and say you can't make it."

"O'Neill, you're an exploiter of labor." Archer peered at O'Neill curiously. "What's so important about it?"

"I'll tell you tomorrow." O'Neill waved and went out without saying good night to Herres or Atlas.

The sound man sat at the piano and worked at a complicated arrangement of "Some Enchanted Evening." He made it sound mournful, as though every time he had been in love he had been jilted.

Archer shook his head, dismissing O'Neill and his problems until eleven-thirty the next morning. He picked up his hat and coat and went over to Herres, who had taken all of Atlas' quarters by now and was reading a newspaper, waiting.

"OK," Archer said, "the barroom detail is ready for action."

"Mercy killing is the question of the day," Herres said, tapping the newspaper. He got into his coat and they started out of the studio, waving good-bye to Atlas, who was waiting for a friend. "Doctors with air-bubbles, husbands with breadknives, daughters with police revolvers. You never saw such violent mercy in all your days. It opens up completely new fields of saintliness. At the trial of the war criminals after the next war, the euthanasia society will conduct the defense. The hydrogen bomb was dropped in a temporary access of pity. Saved whole populations from the pains of cancer and living in general. Airtight. What jury would convict?"

Archer grinned. "I knew that finally somebody would prove how dangerous air can be," he said. "Memo to all radio executives—treat air with caution."

They got into the elevator and plunged twenty stories in a low howl of wind.

Outside the building, New York was deceptively clean and shop windows glowed down the dark avenue. Taxis swept past in the light traffic and you could almost taste fine crystals of salt from the rivers in the air. It was still early and Archer felt that there was a great deal that might be done with the evening.

He started walking uptown, with Herres striding beside him. They were both tall men, and although Archer was almost ten years older than Herres, he walked briskly, with a healthy, solid way of planting his feet. Their heels echoed in rhythm against the shut buildings and they had the street to themselves as they went north, into the wind.

They walked in silence for a block. Then Herres said, "What's wrong with O'Neill? He looked as though he'd been bitten in the ass by an ingenue."

Archer grinned. You had to be very careful with Victor. He didn't seem to be noticing anything, but he took everything in, and was barometer-sensitive to the slightest changes in the emotional climate. "I don't know," Archer said. "Maybe the sponsor sneezed during the commercials. Maybe a hatcheck girl rubbed his mink the wrong way."

"Mink," said Herres. "The Class A uniform. To be worn for parades, court-martials and when leaving the post. Do you think O'Neill'll vote Republican now that he's so warmly dressed?"

"I doubt it," Archer said gravely. "The entire O'Neill family suffers from tennis elbow from pulling so hard and so long on the Democratic levers on the voting machines of a dozen assembly districts."

"For he's a jolly good fellow," Herres said, "with his balls in a sponsor's sling."

Archer smiled, but he felt the click of criticism in his brain. Ever since Herres had come back from the war he had salted his speech constantly with barracks images, no matter who was listening. Archer, who felt uneasy when he heard profanity, had protested once, mildly, and Herres had grinned and said, "You must excuse me, Professor. I'm a dirty man, but I got my vocabulary in the service of my country. Patriotism is a four-letter word. Anyway, I never say anything you can't find in any good circulating library."

This was true. It was also true that most of the people Archer knew spoke loosely, in the modern manner, and Archer always had an uncomfortable sense of being spinsterish and old-fashioned when his inner censor made these private objections. But he had an undefined sense that when Herres spoke in front of him in the tones of a sergeant's mess, a hidden flaw in their friendship was being momentarily exposed.

Archer shook his head, impatient with his reflections. Probably, he thought, it's some hangover from the schoolroom, the inextinguishable core of schoolteacher in him, everlastingly herding phantom students into proper channels of deportment. Consciously, he resolved not to allow himself to be annoyed the next time.

"I had a thought," Archer said, "while watching you tonight, Victor."

"Name it," said Herres. "Name the thought."

"I thought you were a very good actor."

"Mention me in dispatches," Herres said, grinning, "the next time you go up to Division."

"Too good for radio."

"Treason," Herres said gravely. "Biting the hand that murders you."

"You never have to extend yourself," Archer went on seriously, looking into a bookstore window. The window had a display of books from the French, all celebrating despair in bright, attractive covers. Collaboration, guilt and torture, imported especially for Madison Avenue, at three dollars a copy. "Everything's so easy for you, you win every race under wraps."

"Good blood lines," Herres said. "My sire was a well-known stud in Midwestern stables. His get took many firsts. In the sprints at second-class meetings."

"Aren't you curious to see what you could do against tougher competition?"

Herres looked thoughtfully down a side street. "Why?" he asked. "Are you?"

"Yes," Archer said. "On the stage. Where you could be fully used. You're a good type. You're still young-looking. And you've got a simple, open face, with the necessary touch of brutality in it for the older trade."

Herres chuckled. "Hamlet, 1950," he said, "wearing his major H."

"Listening to you reading Barbante's silly lines," Archer said, "I get a sense of waste. Like seeing a pile driver used for thumbtacks."

Herres smiled. "Think how comfortable it is," he said, "for the pile driver to be asked only to handle thumbtacks. Last forever and be as good as new a hundred years from date of sale."

"Think about it, dear boy," Archer said, as they turned down Fifty-sixth Street.

"Dear boy," said Herres. "I won't."

They smiled at each other and Herres held the door of Louis' bar open for him. They went in, out of the cold.

The first drink was fine, after the day's work and the brisk walk. Nancy hadn't come yet and they sat at the bar, on the high stools, rolling the cold glasses in their hands, enjoying watching the bartender handle the bottles and the ice.

Woodrow Burke was sitting by himself around the curve of the bar, staring into his drink. He looked drunk and Archer tried to keep from catching his eye. Burke had been a famous correspondent during the war. He was always being spectacularly caught in surrounded towns and burning airplanes and because of this specialty his price had gone very high in those days. Since the war he had become a news commentator on the radio and his washboard voice, hoarse with criticism and disdain, had for awhile been the disturbing incidental music at dinner tables all through the country. He had been fired suddenly over a year ago (his enemies said it was because he was a fellow-traveler and he said it was because he was an honest man) and since that time had sat in bars, deciding to divorce his wife, and announcing that free speech was being throttled in America. He was a fattish pale young man, with bold, worried dark eyes, and with all that weight he must have landed very hard the time he had to bail out of the airplane. During the war he had had a reputation for being very brave. He had grown much older in the last year and his tolerance for alcohol seemed to have diminished seriously.

He looked up from his drink and saw Archer and Herres. He waved and Archer saw the gesture out of the corner of his eye, but pretended not to. Carefully, Burke got down from his stool and walked, steadily but slowly, around the curve of the bar toward them, holding his drink stiffly to keep it from spilling.

"Clem, Vic," Burke came up behind them, "we who are about to die salute thee. Have a drink."

Archer and Herres swung around in their chairs. "Hi, Woodie," Archer said, very heartily, to make up for the fact that he was sorry Burke had come over. "How's it going?"

"I am sinking with all hands on board," Burke said soberly. "How's it going with you?"

"Fair," Archer said. "I'll probably live at least until the next payment on the income tax is due."

"Those bastards," Burke said, sipping his whiskey, "they're still after me for 1945. The Vosges Mountains," he said obscurely. "That's where I was in 1945." He stared gloomily at himself in the mirror. His collar was rumpled and his tie was damp from spilled whiskey. "Were you there?" He turned pugnaciously on Herres.

"Where?" Herres asked.

"The Vosges Mountains."

"No, Woodie."

"Old Purple-Heart Vic," Burke said, patting Herres on the shoulder. "You were a good boy, they told me. Never saw for myself, but I heard you were a good boy. But watch out now, Vic, the Big Wound is coming up now."

"Sure, Woodie," Herres said. "I'll take good care of myself."

"The wounds of peace," Burke said, his prominent eyes angry and troubled. "Jagged and with a high percentage of fatalities. Invisible bursts at treetop level on Fifth Avenue. The Big One. No medals for it and no points toward discharge, either. Watch out for the big one, though."

"I sure will, Woodie," Herres said.

"How about you?" Burke swung his head and aimed it at Archer.

"How about me what?" Archer said mildly.

"Where were you?"

"No place, Woodie," Archer said. "I was a continental limits man."

"Well," said Burke, generously forgiving him, "somebody had to stay home." He sipped his drink noisily. "My big mistake," he said, "was not being kicked out of Yugoslavia when I had the chance." He nodded, confirming himself.

Archer kept silent, hoping that Burke would notice that he was not being encouraged to talk. But Burke was now on his nightly subject and refused to stop. "I left of my own free will," Burke went on, "instead of being invited out, and I didn't write that Tito raped a nun every day before breakfast, and the hand of suspicion was laid on me. I said what I had to say as an honest man, and the bastards got me. Powerful agencies at work, Archer, throttling the means of communication. Sinister and powerful agencies," he whispered over his glass, "weeding out the honest men. Don't laugh, Archer, don't laugh. Somewhere, somebody has your name on a list. Treetop level." He drained his whiskey and put the glass down on the bar. He looked shabbier and more lonesome without a glass in his hand. "Archer," he said, facing around, "can you lend me a thousand dollars?"

"Now, Woodie . . ." Archer began.

"OK." Burke waved his hands. "No reason for you to lend me any money. Hardly know me. Barroom bore, with his credit running out, always telling the same old story of everybody's life. Forget it. Shouldn't've asked. It's just that I happen to need a thousand dollars."

"I can let you have three hundred," Archer said. He was surprised at the figure as he said it. He had meant to offer a hundred, but three hundred came out.

"Thanks," Burke said calmly. "That's nice of you. I need a thousand, but three hundred helps, I suppose."

Herres turned his back on them, and said something to the man on his left, delicately trying not to overhear Burke.

"You couldn't let me have it now, could you?" Burke peered uncertainly at Archer. "Tonight? I could use three hundred in cash tonight."

"Now, Woodie," Archer said. "I don't carry money like that on me. You know that."

"Thought I'd ask," Burke mumbled. "No harm in asking. People carry all kinds of things on them these days. Inflation, maybe, the general feeling of insecurity, always being ready to cut and run if necessary."

"I'm not running any place," Archer said.

"No?" Burke nodded soberly. "Who knows?" He put his face closer to Archer. "Maybe you have it at home," he whispered. "In the old safe behind the picture on the dining-room wall. I'd be happy to go downtown with you and wait. Pay the taxi myself."

Archer laughed. "Woodie, you're drunk. I'll put the check in the mail tomorrow morning."

"Special delivery," Burke said.

"Special delivery."

"You're sure you can't make it a thousand?" Burke asked loudly.

"Woodie, why don't you go home and get a good night's sleep?" said Archer.

"The minute a man lends you a buck," Burke said angrily, "he begins to give you advice. Traditional relationship of creditor to debtor. Archer, I thought you'd be above that. I'll go home and go to sleep when I'm damn well ready." He turned and started back toward his place at the end of the bar. After he had gone two steps, he stopped and reversed himself. "You said special delivery, remember," he said threateningly.

"I remember," Archer said, trying not to be angry.

"OK." Burke turned again and walked, without swaying, back to his stool. He sat down, very straight. "Joe," he said to the bartender, "Bell's twelve-year-old. Double. With water."

That's a hell of an expensive drink for a man to order in front of somebody who's just loaned him three hundred dollars, Archer thought. Then he heard Herres whispering harshly at him, "Why did you give that scrounging windbag that money?"

Archer shrugged as he swung around to face Herres. "I don't know," he said honestly. "I'm as surprised as you are."

"You'll never get it back," Herres said. "He'll never

get a job again, and he'll be too drunk to hold one if he does."

"Why, Vic," Archer said, "I thought he was a friend of yours."

"The only friend he has is Haig and Haig. You've just kissed three hundred bucks farewell," Herres said. "I hope you can afford it."

"Mr. Herres." It was the headwaiter, standing behind them. "Mrs. Herres is on the telephone."

"Thanks, Albert," Herres said, swinging off his chair. "Probably she wants to say she will only be three days late for drinks." He followed the headwaiter toward the phone in the back room.

Archer watched his friend stride easily and gracefully past the tables. He noticed with amusement that, as usual, two or three ladies looked away from their escorts to examine Herres as he passed. One hard-faced woman in a veil got out her handbag mirror and surreptitiously followed Herres' progress over her shoulder. What went on in women's minds, behind those weighing faces at a moment like this? Archer wondered. Better never to know. A bald man, he thought ruefully, is in no position to speculate on this subject, just as a starving man could not judge a banquet. He looked at himself in the mirror on the other side of the bar. Gold-tinted in the soft light above the bottles, his face stared back at him. I have lost weight, Archer decided, and I look a lot better than I did five years ago. The prime of life, he said to himself, smiling at what he thought was vanity, the prime man. Good for another five years without refrigeration.

Herres came back and Archer looked away a little guiltily from the mirror. "Nancy on her way?" he asked.

"No," Herres said. He seemed worried. "Young Clem woke up yelling, with a hundred and three fever. She's waiting for the doctor."

Archer made the usual face of the adult confronted

by the report of the wanton and inconvenient illnesses of the young. "That's too bad," he said, hoping it wasn't polio or meningitis or a psychosomatic symptom of a mental disorder that would send young Clement to a psychiatrist twenty years later. "But you know how kids' fevers are. They don't mean anything."

"I know," said Herres. "But I'd better get home."

"One more drink?"

"Better not." Herres started to leave. "I'll call you tomorrow." He stopped. "Oh," he said, reaching for his wallet. "The bill . . ."

"Forget it." Archer waved him away.

"Thanks." Herres strode swiftly out of the bar.

Archer looked after him for a moment and asked for the check. Nearly four dollars, nearly five with the tip. He felt the recurrent twinge of extravagance as he paid. Some day, he thought, for the hundredth time, I am going to keep an account of what I spend in bars for one month. Probably be scandalizing. We live to support the Scotch. And three hundred dollars promised to Burke, staring at his twelve-year-old whiskey down the bar with a cold, unthankful eye. That shiver you feel each month is your bank balance opening and closing.

He got his coat, regretting the necessity of tipping the girl a quarter, and went out. I really should go by subway, he thought, standing in the dark wind, feeling tired and economical, and looked for a taxi.

Then he heard his name called. "Clement . . . Clement . . ." It was O'Neill, bulky in his coat, hurrying up the street toward him. "Wait a minute."

"I thought you were going to a party," Archer said as O'Neill came up to him.

"I have to talk to you," O'Neill said.

"We have a date for tomorrow at eleven-thirty," Archer reminded him.

"I just saw Hutt and the sponsor," O'Neill said, "and I have to talk to you tonight." He peered at the dark fronts of the buildings, broken here and there by a restaurant's lights. "Where can we go?"

"I just came from Louis'," Archer said. "I guess they'll take me back."

O'Neill shook his head impatiently. "No," he said. "Someplace quiet. Where nobody knows us. I don't want anybody barging in."

"What's the matter, Emmet?" Archer asked as O'Neill took his arm and started toward a little Italian restaurant on the other side of the street. "The police after you? Have they finally got you for double-parking?"

O'Neill didn't smile, not even politely, and Archer wondered whether he had had time to get drunk since the program went off the air. The radio business, Archer thought resignedly, as O'Neill held the door open for him; everything is treated as though it's a matter of life and death.

2

In the restaurant, which was small and dark and smelled of dried cheese, O'Neill picked a table in a corner. He waited until the bartender had put their drinks on the table and gone off before he said anything. He took a quick sip of his whiskey, looked briefly at Archer, then kept his eyes down, staring at his fingers.

"The party I went to," he said, "wasn't really a party. It was more of a conference. Hutt and the sponsor." Lloyd Hutt was the president of the agency that put on University Town. "They thought it would be better if I got to you tonight."

Archer watched him, puzzled, but didn't speak.

"The program tonight," O'Neill said officially, keeping his eyes lowered, "was well liked."

Archer nodded. University Town had stayed on a comfortable, even keel for more than four years now, but it was pleasant to hear that the individual show had done well.

"And the next two scripts have gone through mimeograph and been approved," O'Neill went on. Archer could tell he was slowly getting himself ready to say something disturbing. "But . . ." O'Neill picked up his glass, looked at it absently, and put it down again. "But, there's a . . . a feeling that this is about the time to . . . make some changes, Clem." Suddenly O'Neill began to flush. A deep plum color tided into his cheeks and forehead. Only the skin around his lips remained pale and looked surprisingly white.

"What sort of changes, Emmet?" Archer asked.

"Well," O'Neill said, "the general impression is, maybe we've been using the same people a little too much. Too familiar, maybe. Not enough variety. The music, too. Maybe it's a little too modern," O'Neill said lamely.

"Now, Emmet," Archer said, annoyed with him, "you just said the program was fine. What's the sense in tampering with it now?"

"This might just be the time to do it. Not wait until it starts to slide. Keep ahead of it, in a manner of speaking. Shake it up. Not rest on our oars."

"Emmet," Archer said, "did I hear you say, 'not rest on our oars'?"

"Yes, you did," O'Neill said angrily. "What the hell's wrong with that?"

"What're you practicing to do—make speeches to conventions of vacuum-cleaner salesmen?"

"Cut it," O'Neill said. He was redder than ever. "Save your jokes for the program."

"Look," Archer said. "You're embarrassed. I can tell that. You're passing on somebody's message and you don't like the assignment. OK. You don't have to be delicate with me. Let's have it."

"I'm not passing on anybody's message," O'Neill said loudly. "I'm representing a general consensus of opinion." His voice had the same unaccustomed rhetorical falseness in it. "We want to make some changes. What's so damned curious about that? An agency's entitled to improve a radio program from time to time, isn't it? You don't have any feeling we're putting Holy Writ on the air every Thursday night, do you?" The flush was receding now that he was getting angrier and arguing himself into righteousness.

"All right," Archer said. "What changes are you thinking of? Specifically."

"First of all," O'Neill said, "the music's been getting more and more highbrow every week. We've got to remember that we're working in a popular medium and our listeners like to hear a little melody once in a while and at least one resolved chord a week."

Archer couldn't help smiling. "OK," he said cheerfully. "I'll talk to Pokorny."

"The feeling is," O'Neill said slowly, "we want somebody new. Get rid of Pokorny."

"You want my opinion?" Archer asked.

"Of course."

"Pokorny's music is the best thing on the show."

"We've discussed it," O'Neill said, "and we decided Pokorny is too European."

"What does that mean, for the love of God?" Archer demanded. "Every other writer of incidental music steals it all from Tschaikovsky. Where do they think Tschaikovsky comes from—Dallas, Texas?"

"We want someone else to start doing the music for next week's show," O'Neill said stubbornly.

"What else?" Archer asked. He would argue about Pokorny later, he decided, when he heard the whole story.

O'Neill stared at him for a moment. To Archer it seemed as though O'Neill were begging for something with his eyes, and again Archer thought of the baffled bulldog.

"We want to drop certain actors," O'Neill said. "For the time being." He waited for Archer to say something. But Archer remained silent. "Stanley Atlas . . ."

"Now, Emmet," Archer began.

"Alice Weller," O'Neill went on quickly. "Frances Motherwell." He stopped and took a breath. Then, in a low voice, he said, "Vic Herres."

He took a long gulp of his whiskey.

"You're kidding," Archer said. "Now tell me the joke."

"It's not a joke, Clement," O'Neill said, his voice troubled. "We're dead serious."

"First of all," Archer said, speaking slowly and with exaggerated reasonableness, "my arrangement with the agency is that I'm in complete control of hiring and firing. Right?"

"It has been, Clement," O'Neill said. "Up to now."

"You mean that's changed," Archer said. "As of today."

"Not really," said O'Neill. "Only in the case of these five people."

"Also," Archer looked squarely at O'Neill, who was opening and closing his mouth in a nervous half-yawn, "whoever made up that list happened, by luck, to include the most valuable people on the program."

"That's a matter of opinion," O'Neill said. "Maybe you're a little too close to them and your judgment's been influenced. Vic Herres is your best friend. And the truth is you've been carrying Alice Weller for a long time." He stopped uncomfortably. "I'm sorry, Clem," he said.

"All right," Archer said. "Let's leave Herres and Weller out of it for a moment, although you could ask anybody around radio for a list of the five best actors in the business and Herres would be named every time. As for Alice Weller," Archer went on, evenly, "she's no Duse, but she's a good solid type and she does a decent, dependable job every time out. And you'll never get anyone one-tenth as funny as Stanley Atlas, and you know it. A funny man, a really funny man like Atlas is a rare thing, Emmet, and I treasure him. I don't like him, but he makes me laugh. And he makes everybody else laugh. A good proportion of the people who listen to your show turn on their radios to hear Stanley Atlas and taking him off is deliberate sabotage and I want to know who wants to sabotage the program and why you're willing to let it happen."

O'Neill opened his mouth as though he wanted to say something. Then he closed it again and uneasily slid his hand along the table.

"Now we consider the case of Frances Motherwell," Archer went on, professorially. "As they say at the cocktail parties, Frances Motherwell is one of the most exciting young talents in the country." He waited for O'Neill to oppose him, but O'Neill still didn't say anything. "In two or three years she's going to be one of the biggest stars in the country and you've told me that yourself, haven't you?"

"Yes," O'Neill said miserably. "I did."

"And yet you want me to fire her?"

"Yes," O'Neill said. It was almost a whisper now.

"You insist," Archer went on, methodically, like a lawyer delivering a charge, "that I fire all five of the people."

"We insist," O'Neill said.

"In that case, Emmet," Archer said pleasantly, "I fire myself too. See you in a bar somewhere." He started to get up.

"Clem!"

Archer stopped.

"Sit down, please."

Archer hesitated.

"Sit down, sit down," O'Neill said impatiently.

Archer dropped slowly back into his chair.

"Clement," O'Neill said, "I think you're going to be sorry you made me explain."

"What did you expect?"

"I expected you'd make me explain." O'Neill smiled wanly. He rubbed his hand over the back of his head and the bristly hairs stood up aggressively. "You're right," he said. "We're not asking you to get rid of those people because they're bad performers." He paused. "Clement," he said soberly, "will you take my

word for it that it'll be better for your peace of mind
to stop inquiring right here and let me handle it for
you?"

"I don't know what the man is talking about," Archer said.

"OK," O'Neill said. "Here it is. All of them are accused of being Communists. The sponsor wants them
off the program. Immediately, if not yesterday."

Archer blinked and felt that he had been sitting with
his mouth open. I must look stupid, he thought irritably. Then he turned to O'Neill. "Once more, please,"
he said.

"They have been accused of being Communists,"
O'Neill said without expression, "and the sponsor
wants them off the program."

"O'Neill concurring?"

"Hutt concurring," O'Neill said. "O'Neill just works
here. He is not asked to concur or not concur."

"Still," Archer persisted, "O'Neill must have an
opinion."

"O'Neill has the opinion that he likes to collect his
salary every Friday," said O'Neill.

"What would you say my position was?"

"The same as mine." O'Neill moved uneasily in his
chair. "Exactly the same as mine."

"Thursday is a tough day," Archer said pettishly.
"I'm tired on Thursday. You might at least have waited
till tomorrow."

O'Neill didn't say anything and Archer knew he
would have to collect himself, do something, immediately. He rubbed his hand across the top of his head,
staring at O'Neill's broad tweed shoulders and unruly
hair.

"Item one," Archer said finally, thinking, That's it,
get it down in mathematical order, "Item one, who says
they're Communists?"

"You ever hear of a magazine called *Blueprint*?"

"Yes," Archer said. He had seen copies of it several

times lying in radio producers' offices. It was a belligerent little magazine, financed mysteriously, dedicated to
exposing radical activities in the radio and movie in-
dustries. "What about it? I haven't seen anything about
us in it."

"Not yet," O'Neill said. "Come close." He glowered
suspiciously at the bartender across the room. "I don't
want to shout this."

Archer hitched his chair a little nearer O'Neill.

"They sent a letter to the sponsor last week," O'Neill
said wearily, "saying that in their next issue, three
weeks from now, they would expose the Communist
connections of five people from our program. They
also wrote that if before presstime they could have
proof the five people had been released, they'd hold
the story."

"That's blackmail, you know," Archer said, "in a
very plain form."

"They don't call it that," O'Neill said. "They say
they don't wish to hurt the sponsor or the industry with
bad publicity unless they're forced to. Anyway, the
editor once worked for Hutt and he did it as an act of
friendship."

"Who appointed them to the job of referee in this
game?" Archer asked. "Why don't they mind their
own business?"

"People have a right to fight against Communism,"
O'Neill said patiently. "In any profession. Maybe
they're fanatic about it, but it's the temper of the time
and maybe you can't blame them too much."

"Did you see the letter?" Archer asked.

"Yes."

"What sort of connections did they say our people
had?"

"All of them are mixed up with the usual list of
fellow-traveler organizations," O'Neill said in a low,
guarded voice. "You know. The Attorney-General's
list of subversive societies and committees and some

California group's separate little honor roll. Plus some that the magazine has given the red star on its own hook."

"They could be wrong you know," Archer said. "They've had to apologize before this."

"I know," said O'Neill. "But they've been right an awful lot of the time, too. And they're awfully strong. They've wrecked two or three programs already. And I don't know whether you know this or not, but they've been responsible for getting about twenty people quietly dropped from jobs throughout the business in the last year or so. Some pretty big people, too."

"Has anybody said that University Town is Communistic?" Archer asked. "The program itself?"

"Not yet." O'Neill lit a cigarette. He did not look as solid and as staunchly entrenched as he had earlier in the evening. "There've been a few letters. Cranks, I suppose. Too many stories about poor people, not enough religious feeling in some of the episodes . . ."

"Oh, God, Emmet."

"I'm just telling you what we've already gotten," O'Neill said. "But if the story comes out . . ." He shrugged. "They'll need six extra mail carriers for the letters. And they'll say everything. From telling us we buy our time with money direct from the Kremlin to accusing us of selling atomic secrets to the Russians."

"What a business we're in!" Archer said.

"Well, we're in it." O'Neill grinned palely. "So far."

"Well, what do you think?"

"I think," O'Neill said slowly, "that we've been a little close to the edge a couple of times. That Barbante's such an irreverent bastard, and he makes fun of everything and who knows what little tricks and hints he slips in without our catching him?"

"Now, Emmet . . ."

"Now, Clement." O'Neill imitated Archer's tone, harshly. "You don't know. You're protected. You work at home, you come into the studio once a week and you pull out and nobody bothers you. I sit there eight hours a day and I get it all thrown at me."

"From now on," Archer said coldly, "do me a favor. Stop protecting me. Let me know what's happening."

"Anything you say." O'Neill suddenly looked weary and he dug his fingers into his eyes. "But don't think you're going to be any happier when I do."

"Listen," Archer said, "do you think we have the right to fire people from their jobs even if they *are* comrades?"

O'Neill took a deep breath. "We have a right to fire any unpopular actor," he said flatly.

"Unpopularity," Archer murmured. "New grounds for capital punishment."

"What do you want me to say to that?"

"Nothing," Archer said. "Not a thing."

"Don't make me the heavy here," O'Neill said. "I'm paid to sell a sponsor's product. If I deliberately hurt the business, I'm out on my ear in a week. If the American people decide they don't want to listen to a certain actor, all I can do is go along with them."

"The American people," Archer said. "Who knows who they are and what they want? Do we take the word of one little magazine on the subject?"

"This year, Clement," O'Neill said, "I guess we do."

"And we take their word that whoever they call a Communist is a Communist?"

"The sponsor says we do," O'Neill said. "This year."

"The sponsor is willing to see the program crippled? This year?"

"I suppose he is."

"And, later on," Archer continued, "if somebody says I'm a Red or you're a fellow-traveler, or Barbante, the sponsor will fire all of us, too?"

"I guess so."

"What do you feel about that?"

"It's a tough world, Brother," O'Neill said. "So put your money in the bank."

"And the people we fire won't get any other jobs, either, will they?"

"Probably not," O'Neill said.

"Conceivably, they'll starve to death."

"Conceivably," O'Neill nodded. His eyes were glazed now and he answered stubbornly and automatically.

"And, even if we grant that Communists should not work on radio," Archer went on evenly, "still, we do not permit the people who are accused to defend themselves?"

"No."

"It doesn't occur to you that that's a little bit on the filthy side, does it?"

"It occurs to me," said O'Neill. "A lot of things occur to me." O'Neill played with his glass. "I get paid $18,000 a year because I have such a fertile mind. Next year, they put my name on the door."

"If there's still a door."

O'Neill nodded agreeably. "If there's still a door."

"Now, as for the question of technique," Archer said, pleased with the fact that he was doing this so calmly. "What am I supposed to say to the five people? Do I say, You're Communists, or, We think you're Communists, or, The editor of a throwaway magazine is of the opinion you're Communists, kindly leave and starve in another section of the city?"

"That's up to you," O'Neill said. "I suggest it would save trouble to do it as quietly as possible."

"Quietly." Archer nodded reasonably. "Be so good as to walk, not run, to the nearest exit when you discover your throat is cut. Something along that order? Maybe Mimeograph will run off a form."

"It was felt," O'Neill returned to his earlier oratorical style, "that the best way would be merely to say nothing. None of them has a contract. We don't have to tell them anything."

"I see." Archer pursed his lips thoughtfully. "Do you suggest that that's the way I do it to Vic Herres, for example? Is that what you would do with your friend Herres, Emmet?"

The plum surge of blood showed in O'Neill's face again. "Please, Clement," he said, "what do you want me to do?"

"I don't know about you, Emmet," said Archer, feeling his hands trembling, "but I can't do it this way. Maybe I can't do it any way, but this is out. So I'll quit now, and you find somebody else who knows how to handle these things better."

"You can't quit," O'Neill said. "Your contract runs another sixteen weeks."

"Mr. Clement Archer," said Archer, "the not very eminent radio director and producer, was last seen entering a private nursing home, suffering from a nervous breakdown due to overwork. Before he went in, he issued a statement regretting his inability to fulfill his obligations due to reasons of health. He was assured by his lawyers that this was sufficient legal justification for laying down his contractual burdens."

O'Neill listened unhappily. "All right," he said, "what do you want? Within reason."

Archer thought for a moment. "First of all," he said, "I want time. You sprang this on me without warning and you can't expect me to make up my mind in fifteen minutes. Is that within reason?"

"How much time do you want?"

Archer considered. "Two weeks, anyway."

"You won't help Herres in two weeks," O'Neill said.

"Maybe not." Archer smiled. "But maybe I'll help myself. I'm a slow thinker, and if I was smarter I wouldn't be in radio, but in two weeks there's a chance I can get one or two things settled, anyway. For one thing, I might even find out whether these people *are* Communists or not."

"How'll you do that?"

"In a very novel way. I'll ask them."

O'Neill laughed harshly. "Do you think they'll tell you?"

"Who knows? Maybe they will," Archer said. "The world is full of people with a sickly leaning toward the truth."

"What if Frances Motherwell tells you she's not a Communist?"

Archer considered for a moment. "I won't believe her," he said quietly.

"What if Vic Herres says he's not a Communist?"

"I'll believe him."

"Because he's your friend."

"Because he's my friend," Archer said.

"Then what'll you do?" O'Neill demanded. "After the two weeks are up?"

"I'll tell you then." Archer noticed that his hands had stopped trembling.

"All right," O'Neill said. "You have two weeks. I don't know what I'll say to Hutt, but I'll stall him off."

"Thanks, Emmet," Archer said, feeling pleased with O'Neill.

"Yeah," O'Neill said. "I'll probably be on my ass by next Friday. Here . . ." He reached into his pocket and took out a folded piece of paper. It was a galley sheet. "Maybe you'd like to read this." He put it on the table in front of Archer.

Archer opened it and glanced down at it. It was the article from the magazine. It looked badly printed and harmless on the flimsy paper.

"Do you mind if I read it?" he asked.

"Go ahead," O'Neill said. He waved to the bartender for two more whiskies.

"Of all the programs on the air at this time," Archer read, "one of the most flagrant and cynical offenders against loyal and patriotic Americans is University Town, sponsored by the Sandler Drug Company, prduced by the Hutt and Bookstaver Agency, and rected by Clement Archer."

"Water or soda?" the bartender asked, standing beside Archer's chair. Archer folded the galley automatically.

"Soda," he said. He watched the bubbly water fill the glass. The bartender went away and Archer opened the galley again. He read hazily, not being able to focus very well without his glasses and too lazy to take them out for half a column of print.

The article was written in the aggrieved prophetic style with which people air their views on Communism in the newspapers. There were some pugnacious metaphoric generalities about the necessity of clearing the American air of the termites who inveigled their way into the middle of the American home and then charges that Stanley Atlas, Frances Motherwell, Alice Weller, Manfred Pokorny and Victor Herres were either Communists or sympathizers. It offered some twenty organizations on the Attorney-General's list in which the actors were alleged to hold membership, lumping them all together and making it sound as though all the people who were accused were equally culpable. Pokorny, according to the article, was soon to be brought before the Immigration authorities, with a view toward deportation. The article closed with a blunt hint that if the sponsors of the program did not take action, appropriate steps would be instituted by the American people.

Archer sighed when he finished the article. Except for the names, it was so familiar, and by now, so boring. He was always surprised at the freshness and vigor with which the crusaders of the press could stir up the old names and the old charges. Even if a man felt that they were true and he was serving his country nobly by repeating them, it took a special imperviousness to boredom to roar them over and over again like that. Power, he glimpsed dimly, is finally in the hands of those who find a geometrically increasing pleasure in repetition. The equivalent among saints would be a man who merely said, "God, God, God," ten thousand times a day. I am probably a weakling, he thought, because I demand novelty.

"Dandy, isn't it?" O'Neill asked. He had been staring at Archer's face as he read, studying it for hints of what Archer was feeling.

"Delicious prose style these fellows have perfected," Archer said. "Can I keep it so I can study it?"

"Sure," O'Neill said. "But burn it when you're through with it."

"You're jittery, Emmet," Archer said. "Maybe you ought to join Alcoholics Anonymous."

"Yeah," said O'Neill. "I'm jittery all right. And I don't join anything."

"Thanks," Archer said, "for the two weeks. I hope it doesn't cost you your job."

"Who knows?" O'Neill stared at him sourly. "You marked me lousy tonight, didn't you?"

Archer hesitated. "A little, maybe. Around the edges."

"It's always nice to have honest friends." O'Neill let his breath out in a long, sighing sound. He looked truculent and embarrassed, like a boy who has just been taken out of a football game by the coach for allowing himself to be blocked out of a play. "Honest friends," he said ramblingly, "in this day and age . . ." He put his head in his hands.

Archer stood up. "I'm going home," he said. "I've had enough fun for one night. Can I give you a lift?"

"No," Emmet said, still with his head in his hands. "I'm going to stay here and drink. I'm having a fight with my wife and I'm waiting for her to fall asleep." He picked up his head. "Sometimes," he said unsmilingly, "I wish I was back in the Marines. On Guam."

"Good night," Archer said. He patted O'Neill's shoulder lightly. Archer went out. O'Neill, sitting alone in the dark and empty restaurant, ordered a double Scotch.

3

Fifteen minutes later Archer opened the door of his house. He saw that there were lights on upstairs and he knew that Kitty was awake.

"Kitty," he called from the hallway, closing the door behind him. "Kitty, I'm home."

"Clement." Kitty's voice floated softly down the stairwell. Even in merely calling his name, there was the private tone of pleasure and welcome with which she always greeted him. "I'm in bed, darling."

"Do you want anything?" he asked, throwing his coat and hat over a chair in the hall. "Before I come up?"

"Well . . ." He could picture her sitting in bed, pursing her mouth, slowly making up her mind. "Well . . . There're some fresh cookies in the jar. And a glass of milk. Half a glass."

"On the way up," Archer said. He went through the living room to the kitchen. There were some freesias in a bowl, a tropical, summer scent, and the maid had fixed the room before she had left for the night and all the cushions were crisp and perfect on the couch and chairs. The room was a pleasant hodgepodge of furniture styles, with some early American tables and Victorian chairs in bright silk upholstery and you could tell that an interior decorator had never been allowed past the front door. Home. Archer thought comfortably, home. He could feel himself relaxing, forgetting O'Neill, forgetting the program, forgetting the folded galley sheet in his pocket.

When he entered the bedroom, carrying the milk and cookies, Kitty was sitting up in bed, the pillows piled behind her, her head in a blue bandana, because she had washed her hair during the evening. She looked absurdly young with her bare, full shoulders and the brilliant handkerchief tied in a bow around her hair, like the pretty girls driving through vacation towns in the summertime on the way to the beach. Archer put the tray down and leaned over and kissed her shoulder. "That's for lying in bed half-naked," he said.

"Ummm," Kitty said, patting the bed beside her, indicating that she wanted him to sit there. "The service in this establishment is getting better every day."

Archer took off his jacket and tossed it over a chair and opened his collar and took off his tie before he sat down on the bed. Kitty sipped her milk, looking like an obedient little girl at early dinner. "I'm gluttonous," she said. "I've been lying here all night, thinking of food. You know what I kept hoping?"

"What?"

"I kept hoping somebody would have a flash of inspiration and go into Schrafft's and buy a pint of ice cream. Coffee ice cream."

Archer laughed and patted her knee under the quilt. "Tomorrow," he said. "I promise tomorrow."

"I kept using mental telepathy," Kitty said, crunching on a cookie. "I said to myself, Now he is walking down the street and he is passing Schrafft's and the message stops him in his tracks. 'I hear a voice,' he says to himself. 'It says coffee-flavor.'" She giggled. "I'm going to weigh three hundred pounds before this is over."

"Don't worry about it," Archer said. "You never looked better in your whole life."

"I'm ashamed of myself when I go into the doctor's office and he puts me on the scales." Kitty took another cookie. "I can tell from the way he looks at me, he thinks I'm a woman without any self-control."

"That's exactly the kind of wife for me," Archer said. "Without self-control."

"You're perfect," Kitty said complacently. "You're the absolutely perfect husband."

"Did you have a good day?" Archer asked. He got up and began to undress.

"I stayed in bed most of the time. I'm getting real lazy. I didn't read. I didn't sew. I didn't answer the telephone. I didn't tell Gloria what to order for dinner. I didn't think a single thought. Are you ashamed of me because I'm so lazy?"

"Uhuh." Archer took off his shirt and held it indecisively in his hand for a moment.

"In the closet," Kitty said warningly. "Hang it up. I can tell you're deciding to throw it on the chair."

Archer grinned as he went into the large closet, with his clothes hanging on one side and Kitty's dresses a row of colors on the other. "Some day," he said, as he hung up his clothes and put on his pajama bottoms in the closet, "you're going to go too far with your mind-reading act."

"Isn't it infuriating?" Kitty agreed complacently.

Archer came out of the closet, putting on the pajama jacket.

"What a nice thing," Kitty said, watching him.

"What a nice thing?"

"You have no belly. The first sign I saw of a belly, I'd have to leave for Reno. And I'd hate that. And be careful of your neck, too."

"There's nothing wrong with my neck," Archer said, defensively, feeling it with his two hands.

"All I said was, be careful. I hate the way some men's necks jut out past their ears."

"My," Archer said, buttoning his pajamas and looking down at her, smiling, "you're a hard woman to live with."

"I want you to be beautiful," Kitty said. "That's not much to ask for, is it?" She put the empty glass on the table, sighing. "Oh, those cookies are sinful," she said. "Was it nice out in the world today?"

Archer hesitated. No, he thought, what's the sense in telling her?

"OK," he said, sitting on the edge of his bed, a table's distance away from Kitty's. "Did you like the program?"

"Oh, darling," Kitty said guiltily. "I forgot to listen. I was just dozing here and I forgot. Will you forgive me?"

Archer chuckled. "Just don't tell the sponsor."

"I'm getting so rattlebrained," Kitty apologized. "I never remember anything. I guess becoming a mother at such an advanced age is a drain on the brain. I just lie here thinking whether I want the child to have blue eyes and whether he's going to be bald by the time he's twenty-five." She put out her hand and touched Archer. "Am I offending you, darling?" she asked.

"I'm going to my club," Archer said gravely. "Please have my mail forwarded."

"You're perfect, Clement, you know that," Kitty said. "But it isn't really disloyal to hope the boy keeps his hair, is it?"

"No," Archer said. "How do you know it's going to be a boy?"

"The way he kicks. He marches up and down all day like a company of Marines. When I had Jane she just used to give me little ladylike nudges from time to time. Oh—Jane's coming down from school for the weekend. A boy is taking her to the theatre, but we have to give them dinner tomorrow night because the boy is poor, Jane says. If I'm feeling tired, do you think you can manage it by yourself?"

"If the boy doesn't patronize me," Archer said, "like

the last one she had here. The organic-chemistry boy."

"Oh," said Kitty, "she's through with him. He did something boring at a dance. Isn't it nice, Jane's not being ashamed of having a mother who's pregnant?"

"Now, Kitty," Archer said, "that's preposterous."

"She's so grownup and modern, Jane," Kitty said. "Everything amuses her, even her parents. I know if my mother had started to swell when I was eighteen, I'd have hidden in the corner of the church for days."

"You were pregnant yourself by the time you were nineteen," Archer said. "Let me remind you."

"That's an entirely different matter," Kitty said primly. "Aren't you going to wash your teeth before you go to bed?"

Archer rubbed a finger reflectively over his front teeth. "No," he decided.

"Why not?"

"My mouth tastes so good," he said. "All the nice food I've had, all the good liquor. I like to wake up during the night and run my tongue around my teeth and remember how well I've eaten all day. Instead of that miserable peppermint and disinfectant flavor."

"You're a dirty man," Kitty said. "I'm married to a real dirty man. Isn't this nice?" she said. "Isn't this the best part of the day—just sitting here gossiping like this at night?"

"Yes, dearest," Archer said gently.

"I think I'm going to stay in bed most of the time now," Kitty said. "I get tired when I walk around and I don't want anything bad to happen. And I'm not interested in anything else. I just want to lie here and doze and wait for you to come home."

"You ought to take up something," Archer said. "Knitting, needlepoint, something. A hobby."

"I only have one hobby," Kitty said.

"What's that?"

"You."

They chuckled together.

Archer reached over and put out the light.

"You coming in here for awhile?" Kitty's voice was elaborately arch in the darkness.

"I can't sleep that way."

"But I can." Kitty giggled, as Archer got into bed beside her.

She lay on his outthrown arm and kissed his neck. "Clement, Clement," she whispered, then stretched out on her back. "I feel so good today," she said. "This is the first day I felt really good. I could even bear the taste of the lipstick today and I tried smelling my perfume and there were actually two bottles I could stand." Her voice rambled off and in a moment or two, close beside him, she was asleep.

Archer listened to her breathing and the domestic rustle of the curtains at the window. No wonder women live longer than men, he thought. They know how to sleep.

Conscientiously, he closed his eyes and pretended to himself that he was drowsy. I mustn't think about it now, he thought. I'll be up all night and then, tomorrow, when I really have to make decisions, I'll be uncertain and exhausted. Not now, he thought, not now. O'Neill. Pokorny, Weller, Atlas, Motherwell, Herres. Archer. Herres. Keep your eyes closed. You have two weeks. Take ten deep breaths and put your hands flat on the blanket. Archer. Herres. What do you really know about your friend? Is accuracy possible after the blunting years of habit and affection? Who knows his friend? Who dares to add up the facts of fifteen years, the jokes, the conversations at night, the journeys, the parties, the crises and disasters, and say at the end— "Here he is. This is what he is like . . ."?

Archer had first seen Vic Herres in History 22, Europe from the Renaissance to the Congress of Vienna,

Required for Degree. An Indian summer afternoon, with the windows of the classroom all open and the trees still deep green and everybody a little sleepy after lunch. Fifteen years ago, with the old creased map of Europe in 1600 hanging from a hook behind Archer and the smell of the lawn and all the girls with bare brown arms. The academic year lurking ahead like a beartrap. Everybody dreamy and still attached to the memories of summer and wishing they were swimming or taking a nap in the sun or walking through the woods. Everybody resentful of Europe from the Renaissance to the Congress of Vienna. Archer, thirty years old, fiddling with his notes on his desk, waited for the bell to ring and the year begin, glancing surreptitiously out over the class, wondering what they were thinking of him. Especially the girls ("Why he's *bald*! A true, historic, ancient, old crock.") He must remember, Archer thought, waiting for the bell, and regarding the class with hostility, not to keep rubbing the naked top of his head. Keep that ammunition, at least, out of the hands of the remorseless imitators in the class.

Then a tall boy wearing a bow tie had sauntered in, holding hands with a pretty girl. That was Herres. The boy and girl had seated themselves in the last row of chairs, on the end. They were expecting to talk about a lot of other things besides history for the next five months, that far away from his desk, Archer thought grimly, and looked at Herres closely. Flunking material, he decided. Then he saw that the boy had a big raw bump on the bridge of his nose and a black eye. Unreasonably, he was annoyed with the boy, as though it was deliberately rude to approach Louis the Fourteenth and Robespierre with a black eye. Also, he was wearing a better suit than Archer. And rather than disfiguring him, the swelling on his nose and the purple lines around the eye socket gave him a dashing and mocking appearance. A wealthy rowdy, Archer judged, probably with an open roadster of his own, and a big hand with the campus girls and the waitresses down-town. And thick straight blond hair, cut very close, to crown it all. And the girl next to him looking up at him as though she was ready to melt into her seat at a kind word from him. The secret stresses that instructors were exposed to, that no course on education ever took into account.

Then the bell rang and the year began and Archer called the roll. Herres answered with a clipped, "Here" and Archer remembered the name. Quarterback on the football team, another mark against him. Probably there'd be a hearty, embarrassed visit from Samson, the coach, in a month or two, with a plea to keep the boy eligible until Thanksgiving, even though he cut half his classes. Not this time, Samson, old boy, Archer resolved in advance, not for this particular young hero in a bow tie. He can come in with both eyes closed and swinging on crutches after scoring twenty touchdowns on Saturday afternoon, but I won't give an inch.

That was how he saw Vic and Nancy Herres, who was then Nancy MacDonald, for the first time.

"Ladies and gentlemen," Archer had said, after reaching Zimmerman on his alphabetical list and ascertaining that Mr. Zimmerman was present and ready for knowledge, "ladies and gentlemen, we are all the captives of history. In a double sense. First, we are all here in this room on this pleasant afternoon, when we would prefer being someplace else, because this is a required course and autumn has officially begun." There had been the usual tentative polite chuckles, although not from Herres or his girl, and Archer went on. "And second, because, here in the middle of America, in 1935, all our actions are in some measure the result of certain decisions made in Paris in 1780 and certain books written by dead foreigners in the early part of the nineteenth century . . ." Well, it was all banal enough, but you had to begin somewhere, and every teacher of anything had his own standard openings to lead the way into the routine of a term.

Herres had surprised him. He cut no classes, listened carefully, whispered very seldom to the pretty girl at his side while others were talking, seemed to take no notes, but answered swiftly and easily in his cool, confident voice, was witty on occasion without being a clown, and obviously had read a great deal more on the subject than anyone else in the class. Archer was first surprised, then suspicious, and finally grateful to have someone like that in his class. He began to look forward to History 22 and prepare it more thoroughly than any other of his courses and allow many more digressions and tangential debates because the whole class seemed to learn more quickly and interestedly because of Herres' lead. When, in the middle of the season, Herres came up to his desk and in his casual and offhand manner offered Archer two tickets for the next football game, he was pleased and said he'd be delighted to go, although he had been religiously devoting Saturdays and Sundays to writing a play on Napoleon III that he had high hopes for.

The stadium was really nothing more than two sets of field stands with a wooden fence around them, but there was a gala air about it, with the stands filled and the bands playing during the pre-game practice and the flags snapping in the raw October breeze. Herres had given Archer tickets high up in the stands, saying, "It's the only place you can make any sense out of a football game. Down low, it'll just look like a mob of ruffians beating each other over the head for two hours." Seated in the last row, between Kitty, who had bought herself a yellow chrysanthemum for the occasion and who looked younger than most of the students this afternoon, and Nancy MacDonald, who was playing hostess in a grave, adult manner, Archer could see over the fence through the bare trees, down the hill to the buildings of the college. They looked peaceful and solid in the gray afternoon and for a moment he felt deeply attached to them and glad that he was spending his life here.

"That's Vic," Nancy was saying, her voice betraying nothing. "Number 22. He's throwing passes now, but he doesn't do much of that in the game."

"He looks so large," Kitty said. "It doesn't seem fair, letting such a large boy play with some of those poor little undernourished ones."

They had all laughed and Kitty's eyes had been dancing and lively. Kitty loved parties, dances, events of all kinds. Watching her out of the corner of his eye, Archer felt a little guilty, because he kept her so close to home all the time. He himself disliked noise and group hilarity, and stayed at home whenever he could and Kitty, although she sighed from time to time when he made her refuse an invitation, loyally smothered all complaints.

He looked for number 22. He had brought a pair of binoculars and he put them to his eyes. Vic Herres emerged from the circular blur of the glasses. He did look enormous, with the shoulder pads and helmet, as he took the pass from center and ran back easily and threw with a jumping, flipping motion. He seemed bored but relaxed, in contrast to the tense excitement of the other boys around him. His hips seemed very narrow, sloping in from the spread of the shoulder pads and his legs, tight in the silk pants, were thick and long. When he moved, Archer realized what sports writers meant when they talked about the way an athlete handled himself.

"Mr. Archer," Nancy said in a low voice and Archer put down the glasses, "I have something here for the cold."

Archer looked down and saw that Nancy was holding a silver flask, keeping it low on her lap, and partially covered under a plaid blanket. He must have looked a little surprised, because Nancy said hastily, "It's Vic's. It's his whiskey, too. He said not to press it on you, but to be quick with it if you showed unmistakable signs of exposure." She smiled and Archer decided that he liked her very much.

"Kitty," he said, turning to his wife, "we're being tempted with spirits by the younger generation. Look."

Kitty bent over and saw the flask. She looked at him doubtfully. "Here?" she whispered, with a quick flick of her eyes for the students and faculty members and alumni and parents crowded below them.

"Vic said that's why he got you tickets in the last row," Nancy said. "There's nobody around you and everybody's looking the other way."

"Victor Herres is probably the most thoughtful man playing collegiate football this year," Archer said. "He has my vote for All-American right now." He took the flask and offered it to Kitty.

Kitty giggled as she took the flask. "Gilded youth," she said. "I feel illegal and dissolute. As though Prohibition were still on." She unscrewed the top, which had a little silver chain, and drank. She looked mischievous and boyish, with her head tilted back from the collar of her old fur coat and Archer thought vaguely and pleasantly of the time when he first met her. She took a long drink, and made a little satisfied pursing sound with her lips as she passed the flask back to Archer. "Some day," she said, "I'm going to investigate whiskey more completely. Scandal on the campus. Faculty member's wife found looping in chapel-tower every Saturday evening."

Archer smiled at her, pleased that she was having such a good time. Then he offered the flask to Nancy.

Nancy shook her head soberly. "Vic gave me explicit instructions not to," she said.

"I won't tell the man," Archer said. "Mum as the grave."

"No," Nancy said. "He says I get silly on one drink and he's right."

"Does Vic drink much?" Archer asked curiously.

"Yes," Nancy said, without criticism. "I've had to carry him into his fraternity house twice so far. He weighs a ton, too, and he's dangerous when he's drunk. He'll do anything. The last time, he walked across the water pipe over the gully near the lake. In the middle of the night. Somebody dared him. It's a twenty-foot drop and he wouldn't listen to any of us when we tried to stop him. He knocked out Sully, that's number 17, the center, because Sully stood in his way. And Sully's his best friend."

The history student, Archer thought dryly, does other things with his time, too, I see. And there's more to little Nancy MacDonald than you can see with the naked eye across six rows of chairs in a classroom, too.

He lifted the flask and drank. It was Bourbon, very smooth and strong. Another thing about the quarter-back, Archer thought appreciatively, he does not serve inferior spirits to his elders.

The game was about to begin and Samson, the coach, was hanging onto Herres' arm and talking earnestly into his ear. Herres kept nodding again and again impatiently and trying to walk away from Samson, as though he had heard everything that the coach had to say and was bored by it. Archer watched through the binoculars as the players gathered into a pre-game huddle, exhorting each other, shaking hands and clapping one another on the back, their faces strained and tense. Archer noticed that Herres stood quietly on the edge of the group, his hands on his hips, taking no part in the fervent little ceremony, looking on almost tolerantly, like a grownup watching children playing. When a man whacked him encouragingly across the shoulders, Herres shrugged, as if he were annoyed. And when, just as the knot of players broke up, number 17, Sully, kneeled swiftly and crossed himself, Herres' face, calm and soldierly-looking under the golden helmet, showed amused disdain.

"He shouldn't do that to Sully," Nancy said. "Vic always makes fun of him when he crosses himself and he knows it hurts him. He keeps telling Sully that's taking God too cheaply, pulling Him in on athletic events. He says if God spends His Saturdays watching football games, He must be neglecting more important work somewhere else."

"Oh, that's unfriendly," Kitty said. Kitty came from a religious family and treated anyone's observance of ritual with worried respect. "I should think it would make Mr. Sully hate him."

"Oh, no," Nancy said, seriously. "Sully loves Vic. He goes to Mass and prays for Vic's safety every Saturday morning. It makes Vic furious."

Watching Herres trot out onto the field to line up for the kickoff, Archer had the feeling that there was no necessity for praying for the boy's safety at any time. He moved with calm assurance and didn't jitter around the way the other boys did and his long powerful body seemed to be under easy control at every moment. Yet, when the game got under way, Archer was surprised. Herres played with cold recklessness, backing up the line on defense and throwing himself at charging blockers with insane disregard for what Archer, who was a sedentary man, would have felt were the most rudimentary rules of self-preservation. Archer used his glasses almost all the time and found himself following Herres rather than the game. Herres hurt people when he hit them, brushing through blockers with his hands swinging cruelly and tackling savagely, even when a ball carrier was stopped by other men or herded against the sidelines so that a mere push would have sufficed to throw him out of bounds. And when his team had the ball he blocked the same way, with that ferocious, cold tenacity, knifing into tacklers' legs with long, lunging dives or driving them with his shoulders, his helmet bobbing up into their chins, hitting, it seemed, harder and harder as the game wore on. And when he carried the ball, he barely deigned to twist or dodge, but plunged disdainfully and with furious power into tacklers, knocking them over, trampling on them, carrying them on his back as he plowed on. Without knowing much about the game, Archer understood that Herres was an unpleasant and discouraging man to play against.

There was something curious about the way he played, different from the rest of the boys on the field. He seemed to do everything impersonally. When the others would congratulate a man after a play or cheer each other on, he remained out of it. Between plays he stood by himself, his hands on his hips, not seeming to listen to the other players or notice them. And in the time outs he walked off by himself and got down on one knee to stare placidly at the crowd.

"He shouldn't do that," Archer heard Nancy say during one time out, when Herres as usual, went off toward the sideline, and with his back half-turned from the men on his team grouped around the waterboy, knelt and played with a blade of grass at his feet.

"Shouldn't do what?" Archer asked.

"Go off by himself like that all the time," Nancy said. "The other boys don't like it. They think he's stuck-up."

Archer smiled at the childish phrase.

"It's not so funny," Nancy said. "Sully's come to me to ask him to change. They don't like him, really. They think he's making fun of them all the time. They won't elect him captain for next year, Sully says, even though he's the best player on the team."

"Did you tell him?"

"No," said Nancy.

"Why not?"

"Because nobody can tell him anything," Nancy said soberly. "Especially not his girl. That's the wonderful thing about him. Do you want another drink?"

Archer looked at her gravely. There was a lot more here than just two children holding hands on the way to a history class. Archer had the feeling that if he asked if she were Herres' mistress she would answer, surprised at the question, "Of course. Didn't you know?"

"Yes," Archer said, "I'd love a drink."

"Don't leave me out," Kitty said, from the other side, her cheeks bright from the cold and the chrysanthemum shedding its petals in a yellow shower over her coat. "I'm numb." She drank from the flask. "Oh, glory," she said, "I'm going to become a sportswoman. You're so lucky, Nancy, to have a man who gets you out into the open air every week."

I'm not so sure, Archer thought as he took the flask, I'm not sure at all how lucky she is.

Just before the end of the game a fight broke out on the field. The visiting team was behind by three touchdowns and felt punished and humiliated. Their tempers were touchy and when one of the defending backs was knocked down after the play was over he got up swinging. In ten seconds there was a melee around the two players, with fists flailing among the helmets. Almost all the players, including the substitutes on both benches, rushed to the scene and joined in. Only Herres, who had not been in on the play, remained aloof. He stood twenty yards away, smiling amusedly and shaking his head. When a substitute from the opposing bench ran past him, Herres mockingly put his hands in the position of prizefighters in old-time prints. The substitute stopped running and looked at Herres puzzledly, and the crowd laughed. Oh, no, thought Archer, you will not be elected captain this year, young man.

The officials broke up the fight quickly and the game continued. It was over two minutes later and the crowd wound onto the field, darkening spots of color on the dark green grass in the autumn dusk.

"I have to go now," Nancy said. "I have to wait for Vic outside the field house and he's always the first one out. He never hangs around after the game." She put the flask to her ear and shook it to see if there was any left. She smiled as she saw Archer and Kitty watching her. "Vic likes a good long slug after a game."

"Does the coach know about this?" Archer asked.

"I'm sure he does," Nancy said. She shook hands with Kitty. "Good-bye," she said. "This has been so nice."

"Tell Mr. Herres," Kitty said, "that he had an ardent admirer in the top row. Under the influence of liquor all through the second half."

"I certainly shall. I know he'll be glad to hear it."

"Do you think he'll get drunk tonight?" Archer asked, although he knew he shouldn't.

"I suppose so," Nancy said lightly. She folded the blanket she had brought with an intense and suddenly childish look of concentration on her face.

"Well," said Archer, "have a good time tonight."

"I'm sure we will, Mr. Archer," the girl said, and went carefully down the creaking wooden aisle, with her blanket and her flask and the long slug of Bourbon for the boy who was now taking off his sweaty jersey in the field house. She walked away, happy, her hair shining in the dull evening light, young and not innocent. As he watched her, Archer had the feeling that the generations were filling in behind him.

He walked home slowly through the dusty-smelling trees, holding Kitty by the arm. He kissed her when they got to the shadow of the porch, without knowing exactly why he did it. Kitty's face was cool from the wind and her skin smelled of the chrysanthemum, autumnlike and healthy when he kissed her. "I feel nineteen," she said as he held her. "I really feel only nineteen years old."

Archer thought that he knew why Kitty felt that way. But he knew he didn't feel nineteen that afternoon.

When they went into the house and Kitty started calling for Jane, to give her supper, he went into his study and put on the light. He sat down at his desk and picked up the act and a half of the play about Napoleon III. He read it through. It seemed empty and dead, deprived of all the life he had thought it had as recently as eleven o'clock that morning.

He sat in the limited light of the desk lamp, thinking how pleasant it would be to get drunk that night.

After that, Archer went to see all the games, allowing Napoleon III time off on Saturday afternoons. Herres always played the same way, remotely, savagely, and with amusement. He was involved in a small scandal when he refused to attend the rally on the eve of the last game with the season's traditional rival, and Nancy told Archer that there was a great deal of resentment on the part of the other boys on the team, especially when Herres told them he had just gone to a movie that evening. And as Sully had predicted, he was not elected captain for the next year.

But the real scandal came the following season, when Herres was a senior. By that time, he and Archer were friends and both Herres and Nancy were dropping into the house casually, playing with Jane, who had given herself to Herres on sight, and helping Kitty with the dishes when they had dinner together. At Kitty's request, Herres dragged Archer off to ice skate during the winter and play tennis when the weather got warm. Kitty was afraid Archer was getting too fat and was always after him to exercise, but until Herres came along to root him out with imperious good nature, Archer had placidly sat in the easy chair in his study, allowing his wife's scolding to flow unremarked over his head. Herres was a good tennis player, too, hitting the ball hard and volleying deftly, and Archer, who was physically a clumsy and untrained man, was no match for him. But Herres didn't seem to mind, good-naturedly playing with him three or four hours a week, coaching him mockingly, putting the ball from one cor-

ner of the court to the other, for Kitty's sake, as he
said, to make Archer run the fat off.

Then Herres joined the Dramatic Society and got
the leading part in the spring play.

"Now what did you do that for?" Archer asked him
one night. It was a surprising thing for Herres to do.
Aside from the football team, he paid no attention to
the extra-curricular life of the campus. And he had no
friends besides Sully and the Archers and steered away
from all group activity. Even in his fraternity he lived
alone, more like a guest at a hotel than anything else.
"I didn't know you thought you had any talent."

"I probably haven't." Herres grinned at him. "But I
want to keep an eye on Nancy." Nancy was the star
of the Dramatic Society and was talking about going to
New York and trying to get on the stage. "I don't like
her walking home at one o'clock in the morning with
the leading man, after rehearsing love scenes all night.
So now I'm the leading man and she's trapped."

It had started as frivolously as that. But just before
the play was to go on, Herres had come to him with
tickets and had said, very seriously, "Now, listen, Clement, I want you to watch me carefully. Don't drink
too much before you go and watch me as though you
weren't my friend. As though you were a critic on a
tough newspaper and you didn't give a damn for anything."

Archer had watched conscientiously. The play was
The Hairy Ape, and while Herres, with his close blond
hair and aristocratic face had seemed somewhat too
polite for the part of the tortured, gorilla-like stoker,
there still was evident enough of the competence and
self-assurance with which Herres always conducted
himself to keep it from being hopeless. Later that
night, Archer had told him this, Herres listening intently, nodding and agreeing when Archer had pointed
out crudities and amateurishness, and shaking his hand
with unaccustomed emotion when he left and saying,

"Thank you. It's just what I needed to hear. Thanks for being so honest."

In bed, with the lights out, Archer said to Kitty, "That Vic is a queer one. Acting now. The last thing in the world you'd expect from a boy like that. And really concerned about it."

"Don't worry about Vic Herres," Kitty said. "All he has to do is lie down under the tree and the fruit falls into his mouth."

That summer, Herres and Nancy got a job in a summer theatre in the East, working fourteen hours a day, playing small parts, attending classes and painting flats just for their keep. That was the summer Archer finished the play about Napoleon III and threw it away.

The scandal came after the second game of the football season and Archer never got over the feeling that he was partly responsible for it. Herres showed up one evening after practice, played for awhile with Jane, then asked if he could have a minute alone with Archer. In the study he had seemed uncharacteristically ill at ease and Archer had fiddled elaborately at cleaning and filling his pipe to allow Herres time to gather his forces.

"I want to ask you a favor," Herres had begun.

Oh, thought Archer, he's in trouble with Nancy and he's come to an older man for the name of an abortionist.

"I'm in the new play," Herres went on, gravely. "They gave me the lead. And we've been rehearsing two weeks. And I want you to come to the runthrough tonight and watch me. And then I want you to be as honest as you were last spring. I've worked hard all summer, but I'm still not sure. I want you to tell me whether you think there's any hope for me as an actor. You're the only one I know I can trust. And it's very serious. After you tell me, I'll explain why."

"Sure," Archer said, relieved and ashamed of himself, thinking, I must stop reading all these realistic novels. "I'll be there right after dinner."

"And the truth," Herres said, staring somberly at Archer. "Right out of the feed box. If you kid me, I'll never forgive you as long as I live, Clement."

"That's an unfriendly kind of thing to say," Archer said, troubled and annoyed.

"I mean it." Herres got up. "Eight-thirty sharp," he said as he went out.

Seating himself later in the rear of the empty auditorium, Archer realized he still felt resentful about Herres' warning, and tried to clear it out of his mind so that he could judge fairly as the curtain went up. The play was Sidney Howard's *They Knew What They Wanted*, and Herres had the role of the tough young wandering ranch hand who seduces the waitress-wife of the Italian farmer. Nancy played the wife and was astonishingly good, simple, pathetic, sensual, and finally pitiful. Archer refused to make up his mind about Herres until the play was over.

When the curtain was lowered, Herres and Nancy came out from backstage almost immediately. They had not been in costume and Herres came down the aisle pulling on his jacket.

"Let's get out of here quick," Herres said as Archer stood up. "Before that idiot Schmidt decides he has some new gems for us."

Schmidt was the director. He had, so he said, once worked for Reinhardt in Germany, and was given to long, philosophical analyses. Herres also called Samson, the football coach, an idiot. Generosity toward his elders, especially the ones who attempted to teach him anything, was certainly not one of Herres' strong points, Archer reflected, as they hurried out of the auditorium. For a half-second Archer wondered what Herres said about him after a dull Wednesday afternoon history class. The trouble was, Herres was accurate. Schmidt and Samson *were* idiots, or the academic equivalents of idiots.

"Nancy," Archer said, when they were safely outside, and walking away from the building, "you were awfully good tonight."

"The second act," Nancy said. "I wasn't bad in the second act."

Archer smiled. That girl, he thought, is practically a member of Equity right now.

"Nancy," Herres said, when they came to Sorority Row, "this is where you say good night to the people and go home."

"I don't want to go home," Nancy protested. "It's early yet."

"Home," Herres said quietly. "Clement and I have some things to talk about. Men's talk."

"I hate men," Nancy said, coming as near to a pout as she could manage. "I think men ought to be abolished."

"Yes, darling," Herres said, and kissed her, domestically, not paying any attention to the fact that Archer was watching. "Run along now."

"Aren't you even going to walk me home?" Nancy sounded aggrieved and Archer realized that she was still wound up and excited by the evening's performance and wanted to continue sharing the excitement as long as she could.

"No, darling," Herres said.

"I hope you're miserable with each other," Nancy said. But she went off down the street, her figure slim and docile under the shedding trees.

Handling women, Archer thought enviously, watching her, is a talent you're born with. Either you have it or you never learn it. He could never get Kitty to do what he wanted except on the gravest and most crucial matters.

"I want a beer," Herres said, starting toward the inn. "Acting is thirsty labor."

"What if Samson hears of it?" Archer asked, swinging into step beside him. "In the middle of the season? Won't he be hurt?"

"Screw Samson," said Herres, and Archer reminded himself he meant to talk to Herres about his language. Ten years later he actually managed to do this.

They didn't mention the performance until they had settled themselves in the corner of the barroom and had their beers in front of them. Herres drained off half a glass in one gulp, then put the beer down and said, "All right. Let's have it. And remember—" again the warning "—no pulling punches. You've lived in New York and you've been seeing shows all your life and you know the difference between an actor and a performing seal. I worked hard all summer but I don't know whether I'm a bum or John Barrymore. You can save me a lot of grief by telling me the truth tonight. Here's what I want from you," he said bluntly. "I want you to tell me whether you think I have a chance to make a career in New York on the stage."

"Now, Vic," Archer protested, "nobody can tell you that. There are a thousand accidents that might happen and . . ."

"Don't sound like an article on what's wrong with the American theatre," Herres said harshly. "I know all about the accidents. They don't interest me. For one thing, I'm lucky, and if there are going to be accidents, the percentage is in my favor."

What conceit, Archer thought, what useful, happy conceit! To believe, in 1936, at the age of twenty-one, that you're lucky and the percentage is all in your favor.

"What I want to know from the professor's mouth," Herres said, staring at him coldly, "is whether the professor thinks I have enough talent to go to New York and earn my living on the stage. A simple, clear yes or no, from an enlightened member of the audience."

"The usual way people decide this," Archer said mildly, "is if they feel they can't help themselves. If that's the only thing they want to do or think they *can* do with themselves."

"I don't want to do anything," Herres said flatly. "And I *can* do a lot of things. So let's rule that out."

"All right," Archer said, feeling bludgeoned, "I think you can do it. I think you have a lot of talent and you've improved enormously over the summer and your looks are on your side and I think there's a good chance you'll be the darling of all the Wednesday matinees."

"Good," Herres said calmly. He finished his beer. "I'm going to New York in June. Watch for my name in electric lights." He grinned and for the moment looked boyish.

"Now wait a minute," Archer said. "Don't just take my word. It's your whole life and I . . ."

"Don't worry, Professor," Herres patted his arm and smiled. "I won't blame you when I wind up in the old actors' home."

"Now," said Archer, feeling unpleasantly that he was being condescended to, "maybe you can tell me what's behind all this."

"Sure," Herres said as he waved to the waitress for two more beers. "Nancy MacDonald. She's going to live in New York after she graduates and there it is. My father has a job for me with General Motors, but that's in Detroit and Nancy won't live in Detroit. And I don't want to be separated from her for a couple of years, while she's going around with all the pretty boys in New York and finally climbing into bed with them and forgetting her gentleman friend at the Buick plant in the West. And I want to have her with me every day and take our vacations together and see each other for dinner every night."

This man, Archer thought, is a fanatic on the subject of monogamy. A freak. A post-war, pre-war freak. "Wait a minute," he said, "have you talked to her about this? About marrying her and living in Detroit?"

"Yes," Herres said soberly. "Nothing doing. She won't even say we're engaged if we live so far away from each other. She won't be tied down, she says, her first time in New York, just by an idea. That's what she says a man a thousand miles away is. Just an idea."

"And because of that," Archer said wonderingly, "you decide that you're going to be an actor for the rest of your life? Just like that?"

"Just like that," Herres said. He drank off half his second beer. "Anyway, I like the notion of New York. And I don't like the notion of Detroit. I know Detroit. So I figured out all the ways I might earn a living in New York, pronto. And acting came up on top. I don't care what I do. I'd just as soon act as make Buicks. Don't look shocked, Professor. Nine-tenths of the population of the United States don't really care what they do. They just kid themselves. You teach history," he said challengingly. "Is that what you really want to do?"

Archer sipped his beer. "I don't know," he said slowly.

"I know I want to do one thing," Herres said. "I want to live with Nancy MacDonald the rest of my life. That's my ambition. Complete. Maybe I'm a disgrace to my family and to the Constitution of the United States, but that's the way it is. So here's to marriage and grease paint." Herres lifted his glass mockingly. "In that order."

"David Garrick is screaming in pain," Archer said. "Wherever he is."

"Let him scream." Herres smiled. "Let the old faker yell his lungs out. Wherever he is. Visit us in New York on your sabbatical."

Then, the next day, the scandal broke. Herres walked up to Samson just before afternoon football practice was to begin and told him that he was quitting.

As of that minute. To devote all his spare time to the
Dramatic Society. Poor Samson, who had had his
troubles in years of coaching, who had had boys flunk
out on him and turn up drunk at practice and contract
gonorrhea on road trips, had never heard of anything
like this before. He didn't believe it and almost wept as
he pleaded with Herres to think it over for another
week, play just one more game. . . . But Herres had
been pleasant but firm, had given Samson just five minutes of his time, and walked off the field.

The school paper had come out the next day with
the story on the front page under their biggest headline
of the year, "HERRES QUITS," and there was an editorial on the inside page, in which Herres was called a
betrayer of trust, as though he had been caught trying
to burn down the Science Building or selling signals to
Ohio State.

Samson had come to Archer's home, feeling in his
dim, athlete's way that Archer was in some manner
mixed up in this, and had talked ramblingly about a
sense of mutual responsibility, and the old school, and
the fact that there wasn't another quarterback on the
squad who could be depended upon to throw a block
or call for a kick on fourth down, and had ended by demanding that Archer influence Herres to go back.

"Now, listen," Archer told Samson, annoyed with
him and with Herres, too, for putting him in this absurd
position, "my job here is teaching history. I wasn't
hired to recruit athletes. And even if I wanted to help,
which I don't, there's nothing I can do with Herres.
You ought to know him well enough to understand
that by now . . ."

"He's ungrateful," Samson said, mournfully. "He's
a boy without spirit. He has no team feeling. He's a
God-damn intellectual."

"Then you ought to be glad he's quit," Archer said,
"before he infects all the others."

"Yeah," Samson said, running a huge, sorrowful

hand across his battered face. "Yeah. He's doing this, right in the middle of our best season, because he doesn't like me. Personally. He looks down on me. Don't shake your head, Archer. The sonofabitch looks down on me. I'm twice his age, but sometimes he treats me like I was his backward nephew. I took it. I'm willing to take it some more for the sake of the school. But I need some help. I got nobody else. There's O'Donnell," Samson rambled on, continuing a bitter reverie that had obviously begun the moment Herres had broken the news, "but he hasn't blocked out a tackle since he was in high school, and besides he's got a trick knee. And there's Shivarski, and he couldn't outrun my mother in a hundred-yard dash. And when it comes to calling signals . . ." Samson looked up tragically to heaven. "It's like giving a Swiss watch to an ape in the trees."

"I'm sorry, Samson," Archer said. "There's nothing I could do."

"You could try to talk to him," Samson said. "Just try. The boys say he likes you. The boys say you're the only one on this whole God-damn campus that cold-blooded sonofabitch gives two cents for," he said bitterly. "You could *try*."

"He's made up his mind," Archer said. "You better find another quarterback by Saturday."

"Yeah." Samson stood up. He laughed hollowly. "Just like that." He picked up his hat. "I'm surrounded by enemies on this campus," he said darkly, going out. "Waiting for me to fall."

Even the Dean of Men had called Herres into his office and tactfully attempted to persuade him to go back. Herres had been polite, crisp and unyielding, and he left the Dean of Men shaken and wondering if he was losing touch with the younger generation.

* * *

"That demented editor came to me," Herres said to Archer a day after Samson's visit. "He said he wanted to be fair. He said he wanted to give me space in the paper to defend myself. He wanted me to explain what he called my disloyalty to the school, by giving my real reasons for quitting."

"What did you say to him?" Archer asked.

Herres grinned. "I told him I was considering becoming a fairy and the boys on the team were not my style. I wouldn't be a bit suprised if he prints it. Give a man a couple of columns of print to fill up and he loses touch with reality. Loyalty!" Herres snorted. "What the hell loyalty do you owe a school? I pay my tuition and keep my grades above passing and refrain from punching the instructors. Aside from everything else, I got bored with playing football. The games're all right, but the practice is a nuisance. And if the team loses a game or two because of me, what the hell do I care? Or for that matter, finally, what the hell does anyone care? There's one boy, Sam Ross, a tackle, who cries in the locker room every time we lose a game. Twenty-three years old, weight two hundred and seven, blubbering away for fifteen minutes at a time. He ought to be put away. In a home for expectant mothers. Once he wanted to fight me because he heard me whistling in the shower after we lost by two touchdowns. Character building! You know what aspects of my character I built up playing football?"

"What?" Archer asked curiously.

"Cruelty, sadism, duplicity, pleasure in destruction," Herres said slowly. "I figured it out before I quit. The reason I enjoyed playing was because I like to knock people down. I broke a man's leg in a game last year and I walked alongside the stretcher pretending I was upset, but I was pleased with myself all the time. Looking down at him, yelling on the stretcher. Clean-cut American boy, building a sane mind in a sound body every Saturday afternoon." Herres peered mockingly at Archer. "Do you think I ought to put all this in a letter to the editor?"

"Even so," Archer said, although he was not surprised at what Herres had told him, remembering the savage way he drove into opponents, "even so, you might write a tactful letter to the paper to calm everybody's feelings."

"Let them boil," Herres said carelessly. "It's none of their business."

"Vic," Archer said slowly, displeased suddenly with the boy, "there's a point up to which arrogance in the young is understandable, even engaging. It gives evidence of independence of spirit, courage, private confidence. But after a point—it shows vanity, cruelty, a disregard of the people around you. It's the sin of pride, Vic, and maybe that's the worst of the lot."

Vic grinned. "I didn't know they had compulsory chapel on this campus any more," he said.

Archer restrained his anger. "I'm not talking as a preacher," he said. "I'm speaking as a teacher and friend. There's a certain minimum of decency you owe whatever society you find yourself in. When you do something that seems strange or harmful or unfriendly to the people you've been working with who depend on you for one thing or another, it seems to me you owe them some kind of explanation. You have to live with them and they have to live with you, and they have a right to be able to locate you in a general sort of way."

"The band will now play the college anthem," Herres said. "I don't owe anybody anything. If I find anybody locating me, I'll move. If I'm suffering from the sin of pride—" He lifted his eyebrows mockingly. "I'm delighted. Thanks for your interest, Professor. Want to see the game with me tomorrow?"

When he left, Archer sat staring into the empty fireplace, troubled, obscurely oppressed. Ah, he thought, I'm taking this too seriously. I mustn't forget he's only twenty-one years old.

* * *

The parade in front of the stands the next day with Herres and the slow climb up the aisle to their seats was one of the most embarrassing experiences Archer had ever lived through. People fell silent in groups as they approached and others, farther off, stood up and stared, all faces cold and full of suspicion. Archer, who wanted people to like him at all times, felt rejected and lonely at Herres' side, but Herres seemed oblivious of what was going on. He talked easily, nodded to acquaintances who barely acknowledged the greeting, chuckled at a joke of his own making, and as soon as they were seated, not in the last row this time, took out his flask and offered it to Archer. Archer, conscious of a thousand eyes upon them, refused to drink, feeling cowardly and exposed. This is going to make me real popular all over the campus, he thought glumly this afternoon. Herres drank, not very much, and without ostentation, and put the flask away.

All through the game, especially when the team failed to move the ball, or was scored against, their neighbors would stare accusingly at Herres, but he still paid no attention. He explained plays to Archer, pointed out where men were missing assignments, predicted where plays were going, and drank from the silver flask, not too heavily. Either this boy is completely encased in armor plate, Archer thought, admiringly, or he is one of the great actors of our time. In a reckless gesture, during the fourth quarter, Archer took a drink himself, staring coldly, mimicking Herres, at the disapproving faces around him.

"The silver flask award," Herres whispered, grinning, after Archer had drunk, "for Mr. Clement Archer, for extraordinary courage in the face of heavily concentrated disapproval."

It was a joke, but Archer knew Herres well enough

to see that Herres was very pleased with him. I must watch that boy carefully, Archer thought, I can learn a lot from him.

After the game was over (the college lost by two touchdowns) Herres and Archer walked through the crowd, little hushed, resentful eddies marking their progress, and without hurrying, made their way toward Archer's home. Suddenly, Herres began to chuckle. Archer, who was feeling spent by this time, looked at him curiously. "What're you laughing at?" he demanded.

"The big moment," Herres said. "The moment of decision. When you finally took the drink and stared everybody down. Caesar watching the gladiators in the arena on a slow afternoon. You came through, Professor. I was testing you all day, and you came through like a lion. You're solid, Professor, rock-solid, and I admire you."

He's too perceptive, Archer thought, he knows too much for a boy his age. But mixed with this was a feeling of warm accomplishment and pleasure in Herres' praise. Herres was not free with his approval and this was the first time he had ever explicitly given it to Archer for anything. As they walked, more swiftly, toward home, Archer thought, I'm going to miss him when he graduates in June. This place is going to seem awfully empty next year.

A gust of wind made the shade rattle under the curtains at the window and Archer blinked and almost sat up in bed at the sudden noise. Kitty was sleeping without moving, the sound of her even breathing almost a snore in the dark room. The luminous dial of their bedside clock showed that it was after three o'clock. Archer shook his head, thinking, I'll be in great shape in the morning.

He got out of bed quietly and padded barefooted over to the window. He parted the curtains and looked out over the neat backyards. The moon was out and made the thin trees look as though they were made of bare silver.

He dropped the curtains and looked at Kitty. He shook his head, trying to make the dark room and his sleeping wife more real than the lost autumn evening in Ohio. He felt melancholy, and the two figures disappearing down the streets of reverie seemed wonderfully young and hopeful to him, as though they were better at that moment then they would ever be again. The cleaner time, when you could prove yourself to your friend merely by lifting a silver flask to your lips even though the Dean of Men was only two rows away.

He stood silently in the space between the beds, looking down at Kitty. He leaned over and kissed her gently on the forehead. She stirred a little in her sleep, moving her head slowly on the pillow.

Archer got into bed and closed his eyes.

When I wake up, he thought, I'm going to call Vic.

The phone was ringing on the table next to him and Archer kept his eyes closed, hoping someone else would answer it. The phone kept ringing. He opened one eye and squinted at the instrument. The clock on the table said ten-thirty. Automatically he calculated, three to ten-thirty. Seven and a half hours. I am not tired. He opened both eyes and saw that Kitty was not in her bed. The phone kept ringing. Archer reached over and took the instrument off its rest and put the receiver against his ear on the pillow.

"Hello," he said.

"Clement," O'Neill's voice said crisply over the wire. He always sounded very much like an executive on the telephone, as though he had taken a course somewhere in sounding forceful at a distance and had never forgotten the rules. "Are you up?"

"Just," Archer said, "Is anything wrong?"

"Have you got a cold?" O'Neill asked.

"No," Archer said, puzzled. "Why do you ask?"

"You sound funny. Very deep."

"I'm lying down," Archer said. "I sound sexy."

But O'Neill didn't laugh and Archer knew it was serious. "I thought you had a cold," O'Neill said. "Listen, Clement, I'm sorry I have to reneg, but I had a talk this morning with Hutt and he's blazing."

"Now, Emmet," Archer began, "you said . . ."

"I know what I said. Let me finish, please, Clement. It isn't as bad as you think."

"Oh." Archer waited.

"Hutt hit the ceiling, but he came down. Most of the way. He'll give you the two weeks because I promised."

"Well," Archer said, "that's all I asked for."

"He'll give you the two weeks on everyone," O'Neill said, "except Pokorny."

There was a silence on the wire while O'Neill waited for Archer to respond to this. But Archer said nothing.

"I argued with him until I was blue in the face," O'Neill said, "but he won't budge about the musician. He's ready to fire everybody tomorrow, Clement," O'Neill said harshly, "including you and me, if we insist about Pokorny."

"How about next week's show?" Archer said. "The music's already in."

"He'll take that," O'Neill said. "Then farewell."

Archer looked up at the ceiling, allowing the phone to fall away from his ear a few inches. The ceiling was beginning to flake near the window. It will need a new coat by October, Archer thought.

"Clement," O'Neill's voice seemed small and forlorn in the distant receiver on the pillow. "Clement! Are you still there?"

"I'm here," Archer said.

"Well?"

"I'll call Pokorny," Archer said slowly, "and tell him for the next week or two we won't need him. Temporarily."

"Good." O'Neill sounded relieved. "I think that's the sensible thing to do."

"Yes," Archer said. "Very sensible."

"After all," O'Neill said, "Hutt's being decent about the others."

"Thank Mr. Hutt in my name," Archer said.

"He wants to see you," O'Neill said. "Today at four o'clock."

"I'll be there," Archer said.

"Clement . . ." O'Neill was hesitant, and didn't sound like an executive now. "I did what I could."

"I know," said Archer. "I'm sure of it, Emmet."

"Well," O'Neill said uneasily, "till four."

Archer hung up. He stared at the ceiling again. Question—is it better to talk to Pokorny before or after getting out of bed? Which is healthier at the beginning of the day? Is pleasure to be found in action or delay? Do you start or end breakfast with dismissal? How much easier it would be to call O'Neill back instead and tell him he was resigning as of that moment. Except that then four other people would be lost without a fight. Resignation, Archer told himself, would be irresponsible. Pokorny, he thought, reaching for the phone, you are temporarily expendable. You are the rear guard covering the main body's strategic withdrawal and we hope to redeem you later when prisoners are exchanged. Be brave among the trumpets.

"Hello," Pokorny's voice was saying. "Who calls?" He sounded shrill and worried, as though the telephone invariably damaged him.

"Manfred, this is Clement Archer."

"Oh, Mr. Archer, I am happy you called," Pokorny said in a rush. "I have been wishing to apologize. Last night, I went beyond the boundaries of my position, if

you understand me. About the conductor. I was excited. I used language that was extreme. It is a bad
habit of mine, my wife is constantly pointing it out to
me. . . ."

"That's OK, Manfred," Archer said. "You were perfectly right."

"Oh, thank you, Mr. Archer. I couldn't sleep, I was
so . . ."

"Don't worry about it," Archer said. "I called about
something else." He paused, wondering how to say it.
"Look, Manfred," he said, "we're making some changes
on the show. Experimenting. . . ."

"Oh, yes, of course," Pokorny hurried on, wishing to
agree with everything in advance, "that is always necessary in such fields of . . ."

"For the next week or two, Manfred, we're going to
try something different in the way of music."

"Anything. Anything you say," Pokorny said shrilly.

"I mean we're going to try someone else," Archer
said. "Another composer." There was a breath on the
other end of the phone. "Temporarily."

"Yes," Pokorny said flatly. "Yes, of course."

There was the sudden clicking of the phone being
put down at the other end, then the ghosts and murmurs of the wires. Archer hung up. It was easier than I
figured, he thought, and got out of bed and began to
dress.

4

"I am not going to be angry," Hutt was whispering. "It is not my intention to be arbitrary. I believe O'Neill exceeded his authority in telling you you could have two weeks, but it has always been my policy to allow my account executives to make their own decisions. If, finally, I do not approve of those decisions, I do not reverse them. I fire the executive."

Hutt smiled bleakly. He had a face like a wedge, sharp, pale and formidable, and had a tendency to talk in sonorous and legal-sounding paragraphs. He always whispered. Whether it was because he mistrusted his larynx or whether he had discovered that it made people pay more attention to him, Archer didn't know. But you always had to sit on the edge of your chair and strain forward when you had any dealings with Hutt. He was a man of about fifty, slender and short, in an expensive suit. His graying hair was always brushed tightly around his head and looked, in some lights, like a clipped fur cap. He had been an important figure in the Office of War Information during the war, and he had many contacts high in the Government and in the Army, whom he was always mysteriously calling, in whispers, on long distance. He got drunk on week-ends, but always appeared on Monday mornings clear-eyed and straight-backed, carrying himself like a divisional commander. He was a man who clearly had confidence in himself and his own opinions and who gave orders naturally and was accustomed to being obeyed. Archer saw him only on rare occasions and always felt uncomfortable with him, although Hutt's manners were correct and friendly and he sometimes took Archer to lunch. His office was cold and unadorned and reminded Archer of surgery.

Just now, O'Neill was sitting glumly in a corner in a leather chair, almost lost in the blunt shadows of the winter afternoon. Archer sat on a padded chair close to Hutt's desk, listening silently.

"Only on the question of Pokorny," Hutt went on, "I must beg your indulgence and depart from my usual routine. I must insist that he go immediately. That isn't really too bad, is it? One out of five?" He smiled frostily. "You couldn't call me overbearing and meddlesome for that, could you, O'Neill?"

"No, sir," O'Neill said from the shadows.

"I have very good information," Hutt said, "that Pokorny perjured himself when he applied for entry into this country in 1939 and that the Government is certain to deport him. Also, some rather important people in the music world vouched for him at that time and their names will give the story notoriety in the newspapers, so that there would be no possibility of its being done quietly."

"What if Pokorny proves he didn't perjure himself?" Archer asked. "At his trial or hearing or whatever he's going to have? What do we do then?"

"Then, of course," Hutt smiled gently at Archer, "I would be delighted to take him back."

"Then why can't we wait until the Government decides?" Archer asked. "Why do we have to deport him in advance?"

"I'm going to say something ugly," Hutt whispered,

smiling again, the wedge momentarily splintering, "and I hope you don't hold it against me. We can't afford it. Radio, as you two gentlemen know, is not at the moment in a strong position. In fact, it is not putting it too vigorously to say that the medium is fighting for its life. A new form of entertainment, television, is gaining enormous momentum, capturing our clients and our audience; the economic situation of the country is uncertain and advertisers are retrenching everywhere— the old days when we could do anything and get away with everything are gone, perhaps forever. We are teetering on the edge of the cliff, gentlemen—and it might take only the slightest push to send us off into space. Mr. Pokorny and his particular problem might prove to be just that push. He is not a citizen and I think it will be proved shortly that he violated the laws of the country to get in here. He is not famous enough to be forgiven his lapses by the public—and perhaps in these days no one is—and, personally, he is not a completely attractive figure at best . . ." Hutt smiled apologetically. In the wan light, his face looked as though it were planed out of bleached wood. "I'm afraid, as far as Mr. Pokorny is concerned, the decision, is, as of this time, final."

Hutt fell silent for a moment. Archer watched him light a cigarette. He used a long black holder that had been given to him by an admiring lieutenant-general during the war. He looked fragile, aristocratic and dangerous behind his bare desk. Poor Pokorny, Archer thought, matched out of his class this winter.

"As for the others," Hutt went on, in his low, soft voice, speaking through the smoke of his cigarette, "I will, as I told you, respect O'Neill's promise to you. I will not hide the fact that I, myself, would have made no such promise. Also, practically, I don't really see what you hope to gain by delay . . ."

"I told O'Neill," Archer began.

"I know," said Hutt. "O'Neill has explained it to

me. I hope you won't take offense, Archer, but I think you're being naive."

Why don't I just stand up and get out of here? Archer thought.

"I'm afraid," Hutt was saying, his voice even and hard to follow across the desk, "that you haven't really looked into the background of this affair, Archer. As you know, I'm acquainted with quite a few people in Washington . . ."

"I know," Archer said.

"And," Hutt said, measuring Archer's voice for irony, "as a man who deals in the molding of public opinion, I have been called in from time to time to make suggestions and also—and this is important—to receive suggestions. Democracy," he said, allowing more volume into his voice for the first time, "is not completely a one-way arrangement."

Ah, thought Archer, his training in the OWI is paying off—he can now generalize on Democracy.

"It is not enough," Hutt said, "merely to pass on instructions to our political leaders. We must from time to time expect our leaders to pass on instructions to us. Does that sound reasonable?"

"Yes," Archer said, grudgingly. "That's reasonable enough."

"Also, if I'm not mistaken," Hutt continued, "you voted for the Administration. Or, at least," he nodded pleasantly, "during the elections you voiced your approval, quite strongly, of Mr. Truman."

"Yes," Archer said, puzzled, wondering what Hutt was driving at and whether it would mean a trap, and also how Hutt knew what his sympathies had been. "What has that got to do with us now?"

"So, in effect, the Administration is partly your doing and represents you quite accurately. Am I fair in saying that?"

"Roughly, yes."

"Now, if I were to tell you that quite recently, last

week, to be exact, it was hinted to me by someone high in the Government that the time had come to clear out Communists and Communist sympathizers from all fields of communication and public opinion, it would not be too far-fetched to say that that particular hint was actually an expression of *your* will."

"I am with you," Archer said sourly, feeling clumsy and unprepared. "Part of the way."

"I, myself," Hutt said, smiling, "happened to vote Republican. So, actually, it is you who are telling me what to do in this matter, rather than the other way around."

"I don't think it's necessary to go into the freakishness of representative government," Archer said, knowing he was coming off badly. "Just now."

"Quite the opposite," Hutt said, waving his cigarette gaily. He was clearly enjoying himself. "This is just the time. We have a problem. We are opposed. We are co-workers and we are necessary to each other. We are both, I hope, reasonable men. Even O'Neill," he said with a fatherly chuckle, "may be supposed, for the purpose of discussion, to be a reasonable man."

"I'm nothing," O'Neill said from the corner. "Leave me out of this. I'm a primitive idiot. I'm going into the business of handmade arrowheads."

"As reasonable men we try to reach some ground for agreement. To do that we have to advance our arguments, listen to each other, weigh, as honestly as we can, the other man's position. And we must see the whole matter in the round." This was one of Hutt's pet phrases. He was always talking about seeing matters in the round, even when it was just a question of launching a campaign for a new washing machine.

"In the round, what is the situation?" Hutt asked, Socratically. "If we get away from our particular small sphere of activities, from our little problem of four or five unimportant artists, what do we find? We find a divided world. We find that this country is threatened by an enormous and expanding power—Russia. Are you with me up to now?"

This, too, was another pet punctuation of Hutt's speech. It made him sound gracious and reasonable and he used it as a kind of packaging device for certain portions of his argument, wrapping up one section in his listener's approval and going on neatly to the next. The only trouble was that Archer, for one, had never heard anyone tell Hutt, when asked, that he was not with him up to now.

"I am with you," Archer said, "up to now."

"We are engaged in what the newspapers have turned into a cliché," Hutt said, "the cold war. That doesn't make it less dangerous. It is possible to be destroyed by a cliché, even if it bores us. And I assure you, Archer, I am bored by the whole matter. But that doesn't relieve me or you, for that matter, or any citizen of this country, from responsibility to the agencies in the Government who are fighting this particular phase of the war, just as the fact that we might have been bored in 1942 and 43 and 44 did not relieve any one of us from responsibility to the Army in its war against the Germans and the Japanese. I hope I make myself clear."

"I am with you," Archer said. "Up to now."

Hutt stared at him coldly, fractionally. Then he went on, without emotion. "The Russians," he said, "are using a variety of means to defeat us. Military action in China, strikes in Italy and France, speeches in the United Nations, subversive activities in our own country by deluded or treasonable Americans. As the military analysts used to say during the war, they are trying to impose their will upon the enemy. And the enemy is us, although until now they have not fired a shot at us. So far, this is a fair estimate of the situation, isn't it?"

"Yes," Archer said, thinking, one thing I never imagined was going to happen this afternoon was that

I was going to get a lecture on international affairs.

"Now," Hutt went on, "I think of myself as a loyal American. My family arrived here in 1710. Ancestors of mine have been in Congress from three states."

"My grandfather," Archer said, absurdly, "fought in the Civil War." As he said it he was ashamed of bringing the dead old man into the conversation.

"Good," Hutt said generously, posthumously, decorating the hero of Cold Spring Harbor with his approval. "So I take it, you are as devoted to preserving this country as I am."

No, Archer thought, I am not going to keep yessing him, parading my patriotism and the patriotism of my grandfather to please him.

"The Secretary of State," Hutt said, "has invented a phrase to describe our defensive activities in this period. Total diplomacy." Hutt licked his lower lip, relishing the words. "Total diplomacy means exactly what it says—it means all the powers of this country, all the strength of its citizens, are combined in this single effort. Nothing," Hutt said slowly and gravely, "and nobody is left out or exempt. Not you or me or O'Neill or the five ladies and gentlemen we are being forced to release. In total diplomacy, Archer, as in total war, we must be ready to discipline all citizens who give aid and comfort to the enemy . . . or," he took the cigarette holder out of his mouth, with a definite, emphasizing gesture, "any citizen who *potentially* might give aid and comfort to the enemy."

Here, Archer thought, we reach the crucial ground. "I am not convinced," he said, "that Pokorny or Herres or any of the others are giving or will give aid and comfort to Russia."

"You are making an individual judgment," Hutt said pleasantly, "that does not coincide with the stated policy of the Government of the United States. These people all belong to organizations which the Attorney-General has declared to be subversive."

"I may disagree with the Attorney-General," Archer said.

"I do not," said Hutt crisply. "And what's more—if I may say so without offense—your agreement or disagreement is not of very great importance. During the war, when the Army ruled that a certain area of a town was out of bounds—say the Casbah in Algiers—the fact that the individual soldier saw no harm in the Casbah did not prevent him from being picked up by the MP's and punished if he was found there. Even in the freest society, Archer, the opinions of the individual are finally limited by the decisions of authority."

"You're talking about a wartime situation," Archer said, "when certain rights have to be put in abeyance . . ."

"We live in a curious age," Hutt said, smiling warmly, "when grown, sensible, well-educated men and women cannot agree whether they are at war or not. Once more, forgive me if I look to authority in this matter. The Government, and remember, again, Archer, it is a government which you helped put in power, the Government says we are at war. In 1941, when the Government said we were at war, you believed it, didn't you?"

"Yes."

"Before December 7, 1941, you would not have dreamed of firing a shot at a Japanese soldier, would you? And, after August 14, 1945, you would again refrain from firing at such a soldier. But in between, if you happened to be where it was possible to do so, you would have killed as many soldiers of the Japanese Army as you could, wouldn't you?"

"Yes," Archer said helplessly, thinking, this gentleman must have gone to Harvard Law School.

"So, as you agreed," Hutt said, lighting another cigarette, "in this field you forego the right to make personal decisions. What was true in 1941 cannot be any less true in 1950."

"Let's drop that angle for the time being," Archer said, feeling cornered, "and let's look at the people themselves."

"If you insist," Hutt said regretfully.

"I insist," Archer said. He stood up and started to walk around the office, trying to break out of the grip of Hutt's logic. "For one thing—we don't even know whether they belong to those organizations you mention."

"I know," Hutt said.

"How?"

"I've read the article accusing them and I've been in touch with the editor and I'm satisfied."

"You haven't asked the people themselves, have you?"

"I don't think that's necessary," Hutt said.

"I do," Archer said.

Hutt smiled and shrugged. "Each one to his taste," he said. "I am deferring to yours to the extent of two weeks."

Archer rubbed the top of his head nervously, then pulled his hand away, fearing that Hutt, who missed nothing, would realize that it meant he was uncertain of himself. "Also," Archer said, striding up and down in the bare office, over the thick cold rug, "the organizations aren't all the same. It's one thing to belong to the Communist Party, although I won't even admit that that's grounds for punishment yet, and another to belong to the League of Women Shoppers."

"The Attorney-General," Hutt said, "does not draw quite so fine a line."

"I am annoyed with the Attorney-General," Archer said.

"A good Democrat," Hutt grinned. "An appointee of your friend, the President."

"Again," Archer said, staring at O'Neill, who was slumped deep in his chair, with his eyes closed, "there is the question of time and the question of intention.

It is one thing to have joined the Friends of the Soviet Union in 1943, when they were our allies, and another to join it in 1950. And it is one thing to join an organization for the purpose of promoting peace, say, and another to join for the purpose of promoting revolution."

"Those are theoretical differences," Hutt said, "and practically, I'm afraid they diminish every day."

"I'm interested in theory," Archer said. "I'm a very theoretical man."

"It's a luxury I wish I could afford," Hutt whispered. He smiled agreeably up at Archer, standing before his desk. "Unfortunately, I am in a position in which I can only afford to be interested in results. In a way, Archer, I find your defense of these people admirable. No . . ." he waved his hand as though to dismiss Archer's remonstrances, "I really am. It springs out of two admirable qualities, loyalty to your friends and an abstract sense of justice. If you want to know the truth, I'm a little ashamed of myself that I cannot indulge fully in those qualities. There are certain classes of people who for one reason or another find themselves, in certain situations, indefensible. That's harsh—but it does no good to pretend otherwise. Actors, radio actors especially, are members of that class. They are like the old gladiators in the Roman circus. If they please the public and the emperor by their performance, they are spared when the sword is at their throat. Thumbs up. But if they, for any reason whatsoever," Hutt said deliberately, "displease the public and the emperor— thumbs down. I understand O'Neill explained this to you."

"O'Neill explained it," Archer said flatly. "Without the classical allusions."

"Now, actors are terribly vulnerable," Hutt went on evenly, "because their art is personal. It is their bodies and their voices and their personalities that they must make agreeable to their public, directly. So, if I were an actor, I would be most careful to remain politically neutral at all times. That is," Hutt smiled thinly, "if I intended to pursue my career fully. I would realize that I could not afford to antagonize any section of my audience. Each man must look realistically around him and mark out the limitations of his personality and profession, and content himself with working within them. If he doesn't . . ." Hutt shrugged. "He must not be surprised when he is hurt. Like crime, unreality does not pay. And actors, for another reason, should be discouraged by their friends from entering the political arena. Actors, almost by necessity, must be rather childish, undeveloped, emotional, unstable, irrational . . ." Hutt looked obliquely up at Archer to see how he was taking this. "And politics demand reason, stability, coldness of outlook. You can almost be certain that any actor who engages in politics, on any side, is going to wind up by behaving like a damn fool. At other times, when the general atmosphere was more relaxed, they could be forgiven. Today, we are too pressed to be in a forgiving mood. Today, Archer, and please remember this, because you will finally have to make certain choices yourself, we are living in a fearful, vindictive, unforgiving time. The rules of the game are being changed. One strike and out."

"Don't you think the players should have been warned about the new rules," Archer asked, "before they got up to bat?"

"Perhaps," Hutt said carelessly. "But that isn't the way it works. In this field, the rules are always made behind closed doors and on the spur of the moment. And you're likely to find out that they've really been in existence, secretly, for ten years, and that your side has actually been retired a long time ago, although you've been permitted to go through the motions of competition again and again."

"That's horrible."

"We live," Hutt said gaily, "in a horrible world. Now

—I'm going to ask you—just once—and without trying to apply any pressure—to waive your two weeks
and release those people immediately."

"No," said Archer. "I can't do it."

"Just exactly what do you hope to accomplish?"
Hutt asked.

"On my terms," Archer said, sitting down again,
because he felt it would help him overcome his increasing nervousness, "I may find out that all five of the
people are innocent. And even on your terms, I may
be able to prove that one or two or three of them
deserve to be spared."

"I can assure you," Hutt said, "that there is almost
no hope of that. They have been accused and that is
just about enough. I don't say that means that they are
all equally guilty—but I do say that it means that they
are no longer—" he paused, "—useful."

"I'm sorry, Mr. Hutt," Archer said, "I can't go
along with that. I can't accept a blanket indictment.
They're five different, individual people I know and
I've worked with, with five different histories, five
different crimes or five different alibis."

"Once again," Hutt said, "let me go back to the
premise that you keep avoiding. The premise that we
are at war. In a war, actions are approximate, not individual. When we dropped bombs on Berlin, we did
not carefully pick out SS colonels and members of the
Nazi diplomatic corps as our targets. We dropped them
on Germans, because Germans were, in general, our
enemies. We never managed to kill Hitler, did we, although we killed thousands and thousands of women,
children, and old men who were, I suppose, by peaceful standards, quite innocent. Become modern," Hutt
said cheerfully. "Learn to be approximate."

"That's a disease," Archer said. "I prefer not to be
infected."

"Perhaps you're right," said Hutt. "But remember
that it's a disease that the Communists started. Not us."

"I'm also opposed to the theory," Archer said, "that one must always embrace the enemy's sickness. Look, Mr. Hutt, maybe we're just wasting each other's time . . ."

"Oh, no," Hutt whispered hastily, "I've found this most interesting. We never have gotten a chance to really talk seriously about things, Archer. And I must confess I'm not as sure as I sound. And this little conversation has helped clarify quite a few matters for me. I hope it has done as much for you. And for O'Neill."

"I was out late last night," O'Neill mumbled, in his corner. "I'm sleepy. Nothing is clear to me except that I must go to bed early tonight."

Hutt chuckled, indulging his lieutenant. "Perhaps," he said gently to Archer, "perhaps we may have to resign ourselves to an unhappy fact. Perhaps we live in a time in which there are no correct solutions to any problem. Perhaps every act we make must turn out to be wrong. You might find some comfort in that, Archer. I do. If you're resigned in advance to knowing that you can't act correctly, no matter what you do, maybe you will be relieved of some of the burden of responsibility."

"I have not yet reached that austere height," Archer said, "and I doubt that you honestly feel that you have, too."

Hutt nodded. "You're right. Not yet. Not yet."

"I have to ask you one thing, Mr. Hutt. And I expect an honest answer." Archer saw Hutt's face stiffen at this, but he continued bluntly. "I want to know if anything can change your mind about any of these people. If I can prove that some of them are *not* Communists or fellow-travelers, and are, in fact, anti-Communist, would you still say they have to be fired?"

"As I said before," Hutt said, "I don't believe you'll be able to prove that."

"If I *can* prove it, will it make any difference in the way you act?"

"It's all so conditional, Archer . . ."

"Because," Archer said, interrupting, "if not, I'd rather know it now."

"Why?"

"Because I'll quit now. This afternoon." He felt his hands begin to shake and despised himself for the fluttering weakness. He stared coldly at Hutt. Hutt leaned back in his chair, looking at the ceiling, the cigarette holder at a jaunty angle in the corner of his mouth, the well-made suit creasing easily across his shoulders.

"There's no need to do that," Hutt whispered finally, his face pointed toward the ceiling. "I'm open." He swung back to face Archer and smiled. "Not very open. But enough."

"Good," Archer said. "Now, may I ask you another question?"

"Of course."

"What about the sponsor? Does he know about this?"

"Unfortunately, yes," Hutt said. "He was sent the article and a letter from the magazine the same day I was."

"What is his reaction?"

"He called me that morning and told me to fire the five people immediately. Really, Archer, you can't blame him."

"I'm not blaming anyone—yet," Archer said. "Now —what if I went to the sponsor with absolute proof and he . . . ?"

"That would be quite out of the question," Hutt said coldly. "It is the policy of this office to keep all problems about the programs within the organization. You may speak to the sponsor only at his request, when he wishes to invite you on social occasions. On all other matters I am his one and only contact. I hope that's perfectly clear, Archer. Two years ago, on a much smaller matter, I was forced to release an account executive who broke this rule and out of misplaced enthusiasm went over my head to talk to a sponsor. You understand what I'm saying?"

Archer nodded, registering the threat. He stood up. "Well," he said, keeping himself calm, "that does it for now, I guess."

Hutt stood up politely. "I wonder," he said, with uncharacteristic hesitancy, "if I might deliver a small warning, Archer. For your own good."

"Yes?" Archer said, putting on his coat and picking up his hat.

"Be careful. Don't be hasty," Hutt said earnestly. "Don't expose yourself. Don't be quixotic, because the world doesn't laugh at Quixote any more; it beheads him. Be discreet in your methods and in your choice of friends whom you wish to defend. Don't depend too much upon reason, because you are being judged by the crowd—and the crowd judges emotionally, not reasonably, and there is no appeal from an emotional conviction. Avoid the vanguard because you will attract attention up front, and it is hard to survive attention these days. You're a valuable man and I admire you and I don't want to see you destroyed."

"Wait a minute," Archer said, puzzled. "I haven't done anything. Nobody's accused me of anything."

"Not yet," Hutt came around from his desk and put his hand lightly and in a friendly manner on Archer's elbow. He seemed dapper and insignificant standing up, away from the cold bulwark of his desk. "But if you become known as a partisan of an unpopular group—for whatever innocent reasons—you must expect to have the searchlight put on you. Your reasons will be investigated—everything about you will be investigated. People you've forgotten for ten years will come up with damaging misquotations, memories, doubtful documents. Your private life will be scrutinized, your foibles will be presented as sins, your errors as crimes. Archer, listen to me . . ." Hutt's voice sank even lower and it was hard for Archer to hear him even though he was standing next to him. "Nobody can stand investigation. Nobody. If you think you can you must have led your life in deep freeze for the last twenty years. If there were a saint alive today, two private detectives and a newspaper columnist could damn him to hell if they wanted to, in the space of a month." Hutt dropped his hand from Archer's arm and smiled, to show he was through being serious. "There is a motto," he said, "I am thinking of putting up over the doorway here—'When in doubt, disappear.' "

"Thanks," Archer said, shaken and disturbed because he saw that Hutt was really trying to help him and that Hutt actually did like him—or liked him as much as he could like anyone. "I'll keep all this in mind."

"It was very good of you to come up this afternoon," Hutt said, moving to the door and opening it. "I've enjoyed our little talk."

"Good-bye," Archer said. He waved to O'Neill. O'Neill grunted in the darkness as Archer went out of the office. Hutt closed the door softly behind him.

5

Archer got out of the elevator in the lobby of the tall building in which Hutt had his office and went over to a phone booth in an alcove to one side. He sat down on the little curved bench and stared at the instrument before him. There were four people whom he would have to call some time within the next week and he wondered if there was some particular order which would be most profitable. He felt incompetent and shaken. The two weeks that he had to work in seemed ridiculously short and inadequate. I have a hard enough time deciding what I believe myself, he thought. How can I ever find out what four other people believe in only fourteen days? This is the year, he thought, for a man to be ignorant, confident and rich.

A fat little woman in a sealskin coat came up to the closed door of the booth and stared accusingly at Archer, seated reflectively inside, with the phone on the hook. She stood very close, every hair on her coat impatient for conversation.

Archer put a nickel in the slot and called Vic's number.

"Hello. Hello." It was Nancy's voice, and he could tell from the hurried tone that Nancy was busy with her children. She had a special way of answering the phone when the children were distracting her.

"Hello, Nancy," Archer said.

"Clement." Nancy's voice was welcoming, as always, but he could tell she was keeping a weather eye on a son. "How are you?"

"Great," Archer said. "Just great." In the radio business, you got into the habit of saying that, even if you had just been told you had to have an operation, or if your wife had left you or you were suffering from the year's most important hangover. "How's young Clement?" he asked, remembering the night before.

"Oh, Clement," Nancy wailed, "he's got the measles. And I'm watching Johnny like a hawk, waiting for spots to come out on *him*. And we have guests coming for dinner, and I don't know what to do. Did you ever have measles, Clement?"

"At the age of five, Doesn't everybody?"

"No," Nancy said. "And that's what's so awful. Vic didn't. He's never had anything. Clement, is it measles or mumps that make you impotent if you get them when you're grownup?"

Clement grinned in the phone booth. "I think it's mumps."

"You're not sure, though?"

"No."

"I forgot to ask the doctor when he was here and now his nurse can't get hold of him and I've got to know in time to warn off the people who're coming to dinner, if it's measles," Nancy rushed on. "There're four grown married men coming to dinner, and how would I feel if . . ." Her voice trailed off.

"Is Vic there?"

"No," Nancy complained. "He rushed off. You know him when anyone's sick. He despises them if they're still sick after a half hour. He was horrible to young Clement. Should I tell him to call you when he gets in?"

"No," Archer said carefully. "Never mind. It's not important. Tell him I'll give him a ring tomorrow."

"Young Clement wants to say something," Nancy said. "Hold on. I'll carry the phone in to him."

"Hi," the childish bold voice said over the phone, after a moment.

"Hello, Clement," Archer said. "Are you in bed?"

"Yes," the boy said. "I have spots. And I have fever. And Johnny can't come into the room. He's waiting for his spots. He can only talk to me from the door. I have a hundred and two. If you come here you can come in my room. You can tell me a story."

"Maybe tomorrow, Clem."

"OK. I have a new puzzle. I worked it four times already."

"You're getting real smart, aren't you?"

"Yes. I only have trouble with the yellow pieces. The doctor said I could have ice cream. Good-bye." The boy banged the receiver down before Nancy could reach the phone.

Archer was smiling as he came out of the booth and onto the street again. Somehow, as he walked, he felt less baffled and alone, because a small, yellow-haired boy with measles had invited him to come to the familiar sickroom and tell him a story while his brother waited at the door for his own spots to turn up. In a curious way, too, it made the whole situation seem less forbidding. Comfortingly, it seemed absurd to be accusing a man whose four-year-old son was in bed with such a homely disease and whose wife was worrying about whether her male dinner guests would be made impotent from exposure to an infant's measles of plotting the overthrow of the Government of the United States by violence. Perhaps that was the true purpose of the everyday annoyances of life, to insulate us from the naked damage of theory.

And young Clement was his namesake and godson and he had stood at the altar, holding the child as it

"How?"

"Writing for radio."

Archer chuckled.

"Don't laugh. You never listen, you have no idea how easy it is. A two-headed Zulu could do it. As long as you can type fast enough, you have nothing to worry about. Look, Clement," Herres said gravely, "I've talked to a couple of people about you already and they're willing to read some of your stuff. You'll make more money than you'll ever make here, you'll live in a city you like, you'll be near us, and you'll have a lot more time to work on anything of your own you really want to do. . . ."

"I haven't the faintest notion of where to begin," Archer said, although the idea was already beginning to sound reasonable, attractive.

"I'll show you," Herres said. "By now I've seen enough of them to qualify. Though for anyone with an IQ of over 70, it shouldn't really take more than fifteen minutes. I have a lot of time on my hands, especially in the summer, and I'm available for a full course of instruction. . . ."

"Ex-student pays election bet," Archer said. "Teaches ex-teacher how to earn living in big city in only seventeen years."

"I tell you you can do it," Herres said. "I guarantee. And if you need any dough for the move, my bankbook's yours," he added carelessly. "Pay me back out of the first million."

As it turned out, it took more than a thousand dollars out of Herres' bankbook before Archer finally got started. And Herres, Archer knew, was far from rich. His father had died the year before and what small money had been left in the estate went to support Herres' mother. But the money had been offered almost automatically, as though it was inconceivable that it should not be offered. To Archer, whose family had always been poor, the quick and generous proffering of money had always been the touchstone of friendship. "Either you're prepared to put your money to a friend's service, without a blink," his father had said, reversing Polonius, "or do not invite the scoundrel to your house."

And it all had had the added charm of coming out well. Herres had persuaded the producer of a five-a-week serial to give Archer a trial, had tactfully coached him over the first three or four weeks, when the issue was in doubt, and had helped celebrate when Archer was signed to a twenty-six-week contract, at three hundred dollars a week. The program was about an immigrant girl with vague and secret royal connections in the old country, an equally vague stretch of territory somewhere in Northern Europe, and required a steady flow of sentimental invention, as the young lady, with an uncertain accent, fought off seducers, temptations of all kinds, misunderstandings, brushes with the police brought about by the work of jealous older women, poverty, and a large assortment of diseases, many of them fatal everywhere else but on a noonday radio serial. It was murderously hard work for Archer. "My natural prose style," he told Herres, "is something of a cross between Macaulay and the editorial page of the New York *Times*, and my idea of how people should behave in fiction comes mostly from James Joyce and Proust. And I never had Bright's disease and I never tried to seduce a twenty-year-old immigrant, and I actually believe that the innocent always suffer and the evil always prosper in real life. So I can't say I feel boyishly confident about my equipment on a Monday morning when I sit down and know I have to write five fifteen-minute heart-breaking episodes before Friday night. Still, I can be as sentimental as the next man on a six-month contract. I have a lovely idea for next week. Little Catherine (the name of the program was Young Catherine Jorgenson, Visitor from Abroad) is going to California and she's going to get caught in an earthquake and be arrested for looting when she goes into a burning building to rescue an old miser in a wheelchair. Ought to be good for ten programs, what with the arrest, the examination by the police, the meeting with the cynical newspaper reporter who is reformed by her, and the trial."

He could joke about it when he was with Herres, but sitting alone in the narrow room at home, facing the typewriter, was another matter. He wrote frantically, then found himself staring blankly at the wall for days, hopeless and disgusted with himself. He began to drink too much, snapped at Kitty and Jane, had trouble with his stomach, slept badly and woke feeling listless and hot-eyed. He went to a stomach specialist who gave him pills, but told him they wouldn't work and advised long vacations. He wrote his last play during this time, working heavily on the week-end on it, and then quit that.

Then, when the war came, Herres had gone in early and had been sent out to a camp in Texas, and Nancy, now with an infant son, had gone to join him there. Catherine Jorgenson, the Visitor from Abroad, seemed worse than ever, with the disasters from the battlefields on every page of the newspaper. In 1943, Archer presented himself for enlistment, looking old and uncertain among the young men in the Sergeant's office. He was not surprised when the Army rejected him, but when he went out of the office he felt defeated and useless. He had to drive himself to his typewriter and there was one morning when he sat staring at it without moving for two hours, then felt himself beginning to weep. He wept uncontrollably in the small, cluttered room, frightened, hoping that Kitty wouldn't come in, wondering if he ever would be able to stop. He thought of going to a psychiatrist, but he was frightened of that, too. What would a psychiatrist say? he asked himself defensively. Find more congenial work, take seconal at night, tell me if you hated your father, win the war . . . Besides, he couldn't afford a psychiatrist.

The letter from Vic, in Texas, came soon after that.

"Nancy and I have been worrying about you," Vic wrote, "in between field problems. Before we left you were showing signs of radio-writer's disease. In engineering it's called metal-fatigue. When there's been too much strain for too long a time on a piece of steel, the molecules rearrange themselves, and whoops! there goes the bridge. We don't want your molecules rearranged, please. We want you to be nice and sound and ready to support us when I come home waving my bloody stumps and telling everybody how I won the war. So we applied ourselves to the problem. 'What job is there in radio,' we asked ourselves, 'that entails absolutely no strain on the brain?' One minute later, we came up with the answer. 'Director!' And, naturally, directors get paid more than anyone else, too. Actually, it was Nancy's idea, and I kissed her for you and told her she was a bright girl, even if she was a second lieutenant's wife. I took the liberty of writing about you to a man I know, name of Hutt, dreary man, but with a lot of jobs in his pocket. Hutt and Bookstaver. You know the bastards. I gave him pitch number one, how sensitive you were, how intelligent, how cleverly you handle people, other interesting inventions. He's a muck-a-muck in the OWI, but he gets up to New York from Washington at least once a week to count his money, and he'll expect your call. Don't wear your Phi Beta Kappa key when you go to see him. He's a big man for the common touch. If you get the job send me a can of Spam as my commission. Notice the APO number at the bottom of this letter. The Army is arranging for me to travel. I never felt so kindly disposed to Germans, Italians, Hungarians, Japanese in all my life.

Dig in, men, the bastards are using live ammunition.
                                        Love,
                                        Vic."

When Archer got the job, at more money than he had ever made before, he bought a pair of topaz ear-

rings and sent them to Nancy, because Nancy had
pretty ears and wore rings in them whenever she could.
He took to the work easily and got a raise and a more
important show six months later and after awhile he
forgot that there ever was a morning when he had sat
before his typewriter and wept.

The noise of an automobile horn made him jump.
He blinked and looked around him. He had been
walking aimlessly and automatically and he saw that
he had wandered over to Fifty-third Street. The entrance to the subway was across the street and he decided to go home. He bought a newspaper and went
down the subway steps.

As the train moaned along the tunnel, he looked
through the paper. In Washington, congressmen were
accusing people high in the government of treason and
espionage in favor of Russia. In Europe and Asia,
trials were being conducted against dozens of men who
were said to be spying for the United States. In various
places the execution of traitors was announced. Treachery was widespread on this winter day and you could
be hanged or jailed or deported or denounced in many
localities. Perjury, also, was general. In the second section there was an article quoting a City Commissioner
who had said that all sirens should be taken off fire
engines, police cars and ambulances, so that when the
people of the city heard a siren it would mean only that
enemy planes were approaching and the citizens must
prepare to be bombed. Peace, the Commissioner said,
would slide into war at a speed greater than the speed
of sound. Archer turned to the sports page. A prize-
fighter had been killed the night before, in the eighth
round. Sport, too, was betrayed, death paying the
amusement tax. The subway, Archer thought, was the
only place to read today's newspapers. Underground,

in a bad light, at a raised fare, with all the riders
fearing the worst about each other. Everyone suspecting the man next to him of preparing to pick a pocket,
commit a nuisance, carry a lighted cigar, pinch a girl,
ask for a job, run for a vacant seat, block the door at
the station at which you wanted to leave the train.
Archer put the paper down and looked around at his
fellow passengers. They do not look American, he
thought; perhaps I shall report them to the proper
authorities.

At Fourth Street, Archer got out. People were buying candy and flowers and long loaves of French bread.
Across the street, in front of the women's prison, a
police van was unloading a batch of prostitutes. Everything was normal on Sixth Avenue, now called the
Avenue of the Americas, although a report had just
come out in which it was stated that several of the
countries for which the avenue had been named were
plotting invasion of several other good neighbors. A
thin tree, which had been planted in the concrete by
Mayor LaGuardia, since dead, waited for spring among
the cold gasoline fumes, its buds closed and secret and
admitting nothing. The heads of families bought newspapers on the corners, folding them under their arms,
dutifully taking the poison home to be distributed
equitably among the generations. There was the smell
of Italian cooking from a restaurant, garlic on the
foreign air. In Italy, there were riots and ceremonial
funerals for the victims of the police, and the Pope
mourned publicly for convicted priests to the north and
east. A girl in black slacks came out of a drugstore,
having just had breakfast at four-thirty in the afternoon.
She looked sleepy and as though she were going back
to her room and her unmade bed to wait for the telephone to ring. There was a narrow rift in the clouds to
the west and the sun appeared there in the green and
red sky, falling fast, and making the building fronts

look like water colors. The city trembled on the brink of evening, waiting for the first drink.

How is it, Archer thought, walking slowly, that we do not all commit suicide?

6

Standing in front of the door to his house, Archer hesitated. Uncertain at his doorstep, he knew he had to decide, now, whether or not he was going to tell Kitty what had happened in the last twenty-four hours.

At another time, there would have been no question about it. He'd have told Kitty exactly how matters stood and gone to her for comfort and advice. But Kitty had had a very bad time for the first three months of her pregnancy and the doctor had privately warned Archer that there was danger both that Kitty might lose the child prematurely and that the birth, if the pregnancy went the full period, might be very hard. He had warned Archer that Kitty was not to overtax herself physically and to be disturbed as little as possible emotionally for the next few months. Archer had smiled wryly at the doctor's naive faith that a mere husband could keep a grown woman serene in the middle of the twentieth century, but Kitty, surprisingly, had accomplished serenity by herself. She had been sick in the beginning and her face had become bony and exhausted, but after the third month she had retreated, out of some instinctive sense of self-preservation, into an artificial and beneficial childishness. She had refused to see people who were any drain on her, had stayed in bed most of the time, attaching herself almost solely to Archer, but being playful and easily moved to tears and laughter, like a little girl, and avoiding talking to him about anything serious or unpleasant. Archer understood that Kitty was protecting herself and her unborn child by purposely drifting away from the adult woman of thirty-eight she really was into a warm, artificially reconstructed, self-pampered adolescence. And Archer had gone along with it and noticed with satisfaction that it had worked. She was blooming now, full-fleshed, healthy and in high spirits. When she had the baby, Archer did not doubt she would return to her real self, as mature and reliable as ever.

But not now, Archer decided. Not yet. He would tell her nothing. Marriage, among its other aspects, sometimes entailed the duty to lie.

Fumbling in his pocket for his key, Archer experimented with his face. The object, he thought, is to achieve an expression of contentment. Not a permanent one, just a nice fifteen-minute expression to cover the necessary hellos and the small talk before he could escape to his study. Reject worry, fatigue and twilight desolation, but beware a fatuous and incredible grimace of happiness, which any wife would recognize as counterfeit in the space of the kiss of greeting. It took delicacy and a light touch. Talent is required to go through a door. Half-satisfied with what he thought his face looked like, Archer went into his home.

There were voices coming from his study and the clink of cups. Archer listened as he hung up his hat and coat. Jane and Kitty. Friday night, he remembered, an early dinner because there was a boy coming to take Jane to the theatre. Archer groaned inwardly as he thought of entertaining a shy young man that evening at the table. He fixed the expression firmly on his face and went through the living room into the study.

They were having tea, seated side by side on the old

sofa, with the silver teapot and a ravaged chocolate cake in front of them.

"It's gruesome to have to admit this," Jane was saying, "but I think store cake is so much more exciting than anything you can bake at home." She giggled. "And the cheaper the better. I couldn't resist this little horror when I saw it in the window." She waved at the remnants of the cake on the coffee table. "I suppose my taste is just depraved."

"Hi, girls," Archer said. He went over and kissed Kitty.

Jane stood up and kissed him, hugging him hard. She was a tall, solid girl, with what she despairingly called private-school legs, robust and muscular. She had blond hair that was growing darker and which she constantly threatened to bleach. She had eyes like Archer's, large and deep blue, but youthfully alert and questioning, and a wide, vigorous, pretty mouth, at the moment several shades of red because she had chewed the lipstick off with the chocolate cake. She smelled scrubbed and young and her arms around Archer held him with enthusiastic strength.

"Daddy," she said, "we saved you a piece of the goo . . ." she gestured toward the cake, "at great personal sacrifice."

Archer grinned, as he sat down in an easy chair, facing his women. "Thank you, no," he said. "You overestimate my stomach." He turned to Kitty, who was smiling at both of them, the teacup balanced neatly on the swell of her loose skirt. "How is it today?" he asked.

"I threw up twice this morning," Kitty said, "but I've been eating ever since."

"I like the way George Bernard Shaw has it arranged," Jane said, sitting down, with her legs under her and taking up with her cake again. "Back to Methusela. Come out of the egg at the age of seventeen, speaking several languages.

"It's easier on the stage," Archer said. "As you'll find out some day."

"I would have come out just one year ago," Jane said. "Tapping on the inside of the shell and studying Greek. I suppose it has its disadvantages."

"Did you go out today, Kitty?" Archer asked.

"No," Kitty said. "I decided I was going to languish today. I stayed in bed until Jane came home and I'm going to have dinner in bed, too."

"I thought Jane had a friend coming for dinner," Archer said.

"Bruce," said Jane carelessly. "I flunked him. He came up to see me last night and I decided he was weary-making."

Archer winced at the phrase. There were now about two dozen boys on whom Jane had made that pronouncement who no longer were met, blue-suited and rigidly shaved, in the Archer living room.

"He's too yearny," Jane went on. "He wants to marry me. Too utterly sticky."

Good God, Archer thought, what are the English departments of our women's colleges doing to the language?

"You're awfully cold-blooded, darling," Archer said. He was unpleasantly disturbed by the news that anyone wanted to marry Jane, but he had sense enough not to bring up the subject.

"Mother understands," Jane said. "Don't you?"

"Yes, dear," Kitty said placidly.

"Anyway," Jane said, "I gave him a life preserver. I told him if he wanted to take a chance he might drop in for an hour later. If he promised not to yearn."

"Some day," Archer said, "some man is going to make you pay for this."

"I dare them," Jane said coolly. "I just dare them."

"Oh," Kitty said. "Dominic Barbante kept calling all afternoon for you, Clement. He wants you to call him."

"I'll call him," Archer said. "Later."

"He said to call him as soon as you came in," Kitty said. "He sounded impatient." She looked inquiringly at Archer. "Is anything wrong?"

"No," Archer said. "Nothing."

"You looked tired," Kitty said. "Did you have a bad day?"

"No, not at all," Archer said. "I just wandered around."

"Why don't you take a little nap?" Kitty asked. "You really look dreadfully tired, Clement."

"I'm not tired," Archer said, his voice louder than he expected it to be. Women, he thought, are convinced that one way of showing a man they love him is by telling him how badly he looks from time to time. "I feel fine."

"Dad," Jane said, putting down her scraped plate reluctantly, "what are the distinguishing characteristics of a thirty-year-old woman?"

"What?" Archer looked at her puzzledly.

"I want to know how a thirty-year-old woman acts," Jane said. "In all situations."

"Why don't you wait and find out?"

"I can't," Jane said. "I have to know next week."

"She's in a play at school," Kitty explained. "And she has to be aged for it."

"Oh," Archer said. "What's the play?"

"*The Male Animal*," Jane said. "I'm the wife of a professor."

"Why don't you watch your mother?" Archer said. "I guarantee she's thirty years old."

"Don't be ugly," Kitty said.

"I thought about that," Jane said candidly. "I've been watching her for an hour."

"Well?"

"She just acts like everybody else. Anyway, she's just Mother, I can't make head or tail out of her."

"I'm mysterious," Kitty said. "I'm an enigma in a dressing gown. I'm a pregnant enigma."

Archer grinned. "I understand your problem, Jane," he said gravely. "I wouldn't be able to describe the way the old lady acts myself. And I'm in the business."

"What makes it worse," Jane said, "is she's supposed to be funny. It's a comedy and she's supposed to make you laugh."

"Act very serious," Archer said. "That'll have them roaring."

"I have to act exactly twelve years older," Jane said soberly. "It's not easy."

"No it isn't, darling," Archer said. He felt touched and curiously moved as he looked at his daughter, sturdy and troubled on the sofa next to his wife, pondering on the problem of seeming exactly twelve years older than she was, reaching uncertainly out to capture the signs and portents of maturity. "Well," he said, "I'll try to help. Before you go on the stage," he said reflectively, "consider your troubles, because that's what makes people thirty years old. Think of how hard it is to make both ends meet on a college instructor's salary. Think of how differently your husband acts now, after so many years of marriage, from the way he did when you first met him. Worry about his complexion and if he's getting enough exercise and if he remembers to wear a coat in the springtime when the weather is changeable. Look in the mirror before you go downstairs for dinner and search for wrinkles and wonder if the wife of the chemistry professor who's coming to dinner is prettier than you. Worry about what you said to the dean's wife at the last Community Chest meeting and whether she was offended. Be annoyed at the dress you have to wear because it's the year before last's and the length of the skirt isn't right. Go into the nursery and look down at the baby and wonder if he's coming down with the measles and if he is going to grow up and be bored with you and if he's going to be killed in the next war . . ."

"Clement!" Kitty said sharply. "Don't be morbid."

"I'm sorry," Archer said, displeased with himself for allowing his mood to expose itself this way. "I was just running on."

"But, Daddy," Jane wailed, "none of this is *practical*."

"I suppose not," Archer said wearily. "I'll try to think of something better over the week-end."

"I'll call Vic," Jane said. "I'll bet he'll have dozens of hints."

"I bet he will." Archer stood up slowly. He peered at his daughter. "You're not planning to become an actress, are you?"

"Oh, no," Jane said carelessly. "It's just to break the utter boredom. Why? Would you object?"

"Yes."

"Clement," Kitty said warningly. She had nervous theories about allowing children to develop themselves.

"Why?" Jane asked.

"Because one person who depends upon the ups and downs of public favor is enough for one family," Archer said.

"Don't worry, Dad," Jane said. "I intend to marry and have four children. Let my husband worry about the ups and downs of *my* favor."

"Excellent," Archer said. "I approve. Now I'm going to go upstairs and try to nap."

"Will you call Barbante?" Kitty said. "I promised him faithfully."

"I will call Barbante," Archer said. "Faithfully."

He went out of the room.

"I'm going to have just one more insignificant, imponderable piece of cake," Jane said as he left.

Archer lay down on one of the twin beds. He closed his eyes. The lids felt weighty and hot. The hell with Barbante, he thought. I'll call him tomorrow. I've done enough for the radio industry today.

He fell asleep quickly, as though he had been exhausted for a long time. He began to dream. Jane was in the dream, in a short, little-girl's dress, smudged with chocolate cake. There were many boys around Jane and she had a lot of papers in her hand. The papers were like the ones that Archer had marked term grades on when he was teaching in college. Jane had a fountain pen in her hand and she began to mark the papers. Zero, she put down on sheet after sheet, zero, and boy after boy disappeared. Then Jane was a woman of thirty, in a mink coat, looking like Frances Motherwell, and there were grown men around her. She was still marking papers. The faces of the men swam into the dream. O'Neill, Hutt, Pokorny, Atlas, Herres, Archer. "You're too yearny," Jane was saying, and she marked zero, zero, on the papers, dropping them on the floor. One by one the men vanished. Archer was the last one left. "You're utterly weary-making," Jane said and put a zero on Archer's sheet. Archer dissolved in the dream. Zero.

"Clement. Clement." It was Kitty, bending over him, and shaking his shoulder softly. "Wake up."

"Zero," Archer mumbled, blinking.

"What?" Kitty asked.

Archer shook his head to clear it. "Nothing," he said. "I was dreaming."

"Mr. Barbante's downstairs," Kitty said. "I said you were sleeping, but he said he'd wait."

Archer sat up. "Have I been asleep long?"

"A half hour," said Kitty.

"How long has Barbante been here?"

"Twenty minutes. I told him you were tired and I wouldn't disturb you for awhile. If you don't want to see him, I'll tell him you're not feeling well."

Archer swung his legs over the side of the bed. "I'll see him," he said wearily. He went into the bathroom and rubbed his face with cold water, waking himself up.

He put on his jacket and went downstairs, leaving Kitty in the bedroom. Kitty was standing in front of the mirror, staring speculatively at herself.

7

Archer went toward his study, from which he heard the sound of Jane's voice.

"Soda or water?" he heard Jane say and then Barbante's voice, very precise and actorish, answering, "Water, please. I always take water." He opened the door. Barbante was sitting in the big chair, fluent in a dark suit, tapping a cigarette on his gold case. The bottle of Scotch in Jane's hand seemed, to Archer, incongruous and vaguely disturbing.

"Hello," Archer said, coming into the room.

"Daddy," Jane looked up from the bar. "I'm entertaining for you." She finished mixing the drink.

"Hello, Clement," Barbante said, getting up politely. "She's doing it handsomely, too."

Archer shook hands with Barbante. "Glad to see you, Dom," he said, trying to sound as though he meant it.

"I was passing by," Barbante said, seating himself again, balancing his glass on the arm of the chair. "And I thought I'd take a chance and drop in. There're one or two things I have to talk to you about."

Archer sat down, conscious suddenly of the heavy smell of Barbante's toilet water in the room. God, he thought, that man leaves a trail wherever he goes. "I'm sorry I wasn't here," Archer said, "when you called . . ."

"Perfectly all right." Barbante waved graciously. "It gave me a chance to become acquainted with the charming member of the family."

"Daddy," Jane said, "can I make you a drink?"

"No, thank you," Archer said. He really wanted one, but he preferred not to have the scene too cosy and friendly.

"I think I'll have a Martini," Jane said. She looked obliquely at Archer, half-daring him to object. She had been permitted to drink for the last two years, but only a little wine before and during dinner, and this, as far as Archer knew, would be her first Martini.

"Here," Barbante said, standing up and going over to the little bar, where Jane was irresolutely facing the collection of bottles, "let me make it. I have an objection to lady bartenders. Old family prejudice. Roughens the hands and coarsens the female spirit. You just get a glass, Jane," he said easily, "and sit down and leave the rest to me."

My, Archer thought, putting up a cloud of smoke, he really makes himself at home fast. Twenty minutes and he's taking over the bar, ordering the child around . . . Archer watched Barbante deftly mix the drink, his large gold cuff links flickering expensively over the shaker. Jane brought him a glass and Barbante rewarded her with one of his slow, enigmatic, ambassadorial smiles. Jane sat down on the couch near the bar and watched him seriously.

"There," Barbante said, giving Jane the brimful glass. "Salut."

"Salut," Jane said self-consciously. "This is an utterly delicious Martini."

How would she know, Archer thought resentfully; why does she have to put on these grownup airs?

"I was telling Jane about my father's ranch, before you came in," Barbante said, seating himself with his glass. "In California. About the roundup in the spring when the range begins to go dry and the drive up to the pastures in the mountains for the summer . . ."

"He's a cowboy, Daddy," Jane said. "He can rope a steer."

"That must come in very handy," Archer said, "at the Stork Club."

Barbante laughed easily.

"You'd never guess he was a cowboy," Jane said. "He looks so urban."

"Dom," Archer said, "what is it you wanted to see me about?"

"Oh, yes," Barbante said. "Jane," he turned familiarly to the girl, "don't you think you'd better go up and dress? You can finish your drink while you're doing your face."

"I'll be down in a flash," Jane said, standing obediently, subtly flattered at the conception of herself among the company of women who did their faces with the aid of alcohol.

"Are you going out?" Archer asked.

"Yes, Daddy," Jane said. "Mr. Barbante has two tickets for the ballet tonight and he's invited me. And he's going to give me dinner. Isn't he a nice man?"

Barbante, the ever-ready man, Archer thought, roaming the world with two tickets to something in his pocket at all times, always ready for any emergency.

"Didn't you have a date for tonight?" Archer asked, not looking at Barbante. "With Bruce?"

"We left it up in the air," Jane said carelessly. "I'd rather go to the ballet, anyway."

Poor Bruce, Archer thought.

"Look," Barbante said, "if your boyfriend—what's his name . . ."

"Bruce," Jane said, standing at the door.

"If Bruce shows up," Barbante went on, "why don't you leave a message for him? Tell him to meet us for a drink after the theatre. Say, the Oak Room of the Plaza, about eleven-fifteen."

"Daddy," Jane said, "if Bruce happens to call, will you tell him?"

"I'll tell him." Archer nodded. "The Plaza. Eleven-fifteen."

"I'll just be a minute," Jane said, starting out of the room, carefully holding her drink.

I'll bet she pours it down the drain, Archer thought, as soon as she gets upstairs. "Darling," he said, "will you tell your mother we'll be alone for dinner?"

"I'll pass on the happy news," Jane said. She went out, leaving Archer vaguely annoyed at her flippancy. She wasn't flippant with him at other times. Young people, Archer thought, turning to Barbante, invariably pick the most unpleasant techniques of appearing adult.

"A delightful child," Barbante said, making it sound like an official proclamation. "So fresh and unspoiled."

"Yes," Archer said bleakly. "You said you had one or two things to talk to me about . . ."

"Oh, yes." Barbante rolled the ice around in his glass. Say, listen, amigo, what's this about Pokorny?" He looked curiously at Archer.

"What about Pokorny?" Archer asked carefully, trying to figure out instantaneously how much to tell Barbante.

"He called me today," Barbante said, "and I went down to see him. He's sick in bed."

"What's the matter with him?" Archer said, stalling for time.

"Cold, grippe, general dissatisfaction with life," Barbante said. "Viennese weltschmerz."

"I'll call him tomorrow," said Archer, "and see how he's doing."

"He's really in bad shape," Barbante said. "Not only from the cold."

"I'm sorry to hear that."

"He told me you fired him," Barbante said. "Is that true?"

"Not exactly," Archer said. He filled a pipe and took a long time lighting it, conscious of Barbante's eyes on him, critical through the thick lashes. "We're trying someone else. Temporarily."

"Who?"

"We haven't decided yet," Archer said.

"Amigo," Barbante said, pretending to be hurt, "you are going into the old agency double talk. I never thought I'd live to see the day."

I wish he'd stop calling everybody amigo, Archer thought, resenting the short, richly dressed, self-confident man with his gold appointments and his familiar manners. We all know he comes from California and his family is of old Spanish stock; he doesn't have to remind us in every sentence.

"Actually, Dom," Archer said, keeping his voice friendly, "Pokorny is a big grown man. He can take care of his own problems."

"Actually, amigo," Barbante mimicked Archer's tone, "Pokorny is not a big grown man. He's a naked, unhappy child and he's been through a lot and he has a tendency to fall to pieces over his problems, as you call them."

"Still," Archer said stubbornly, angry with Barbante because everything Barbante had said was true, "I don't see where you come into the picture."

"Well," Barbante drawled, getting up and pouring himself some more of Archer's whiskey, "for one thing, I'm his friend, if he can be said to have any friends. For another thing . . ." Judiciously he dropped a cube of ice into the glass and poured a few drops of water on top of it ". . . it's to my advantage to see that the show does as well as it can." He smiled agreeably at Archer. "From a purely crass, materialistic basis, you understand. When the rating goes up, I buy my hardware at Cartier's. When the rating goes down . . ." He shrugged and seated himself once more, crossing his legs deliberately, exposing a gold buckle on his garter. "I might have to start handling cattle again."

"Don't give me that, Cowboy," Archer said shortly. "You're one of the top writers in the business and you'll do all right, no matter what."

Barbante chuckled. "Don't sound so gloomy about it," he said. "You don't begrudge me my sordid little success, do you?"

"Of course not," Archer said hastily. He looked at Barbante. The expression on Barbante's face was cold and amused. He would gladly do me harm, Archer thought, if he had a little more ambition.

"I have a more personal interest, too," Barbante said, veiling his eyes. Fleetingly, Archer wondered if Barbante, too, was mixed up in Pokorny's politics. Oh, no, he thought. I mustn't start *that*. "Pokorny and I," Barbante said, "are collaborators."

"I know you are," Archer said. "After all, I got you together."

"I don't mean only on University Town. We're writing a musical comedy together. In the spare time we steal from the air waves."

"I'd like to hear it when you get through with it," Archer said politely. "I'm sure it will be very good."

"Maybe." Barbante smiled deprecatingly. He took a long drink. "It's about the West." His smile continued into a chuckle. "You'd be surprised how Western your friend Pokorny can be. The spirit of Texas, New Mexico and Nevada in every bar. And he's never been past Buffalo."

"He's a very talented man," Archer said.

"He certainly is," said Barbante. "That's why I'm curious about his losing his jobs."

"What do you mean jobs?" Archer asked, noting the plural.

"He had one other job. With Crowell and Hines. He lost that this morning, too. Temporarily." Barbante put a mocking emphasis on the last word. "They suddenly felt the need for changes in their program, too. Isn't the world full of coincidences this year?"

"I don't know anything about that," Archer said, sorry for Pokorny. "Why don't you ask Crowell and Hines?"

"I intend to," Barbante said. "But I thought I'd ask you first. Since we're such old friends and since we've worked together so happily for so many years." His voice was flat and artless and he stared candidly at Archer as he spoke. "You're not particularly fond of me . . ." Barbante said surprisingly.

"Now, Dom," Archer began to protest.

"You're not particularly fond of me"—Barbante waved his hand to silence Archer—"and I know it, but I've never heard that you've double-dealt anyone else, either. You're a bloody monument in the radio business, Archer. You have to be seen to be believed."

"Thanks," Archer said. "I'll put it in my scrapbook." But he felt uncomfortable and tongue-tied.

"I want a square shake now, Clem," Barbante said soberly, "for Pokorny. He's on the verge of breaking up. He's defenseless and he feels persecuted. What the hell, he *is* persecuted. God persecuted him in the beginning when He made him look like that and made him a Jew in Vienna in the twentieth century."

"Now, don't bring *that* up, Dom," Archer said, grateful that at least on this charge he could feel righteous. "You know that has nothing to do with his being dropped for awhile."

"I don't know anything." Barbante drank again. "And Pokorny doesn't know anything. And he fears the worst. Pokorny is a man who automatically fears the worst all the time, because up to now, the worst has almost always happened to him. At least if he finds out that he's been rejected now for one speicfic sensible reason, he can localize his depression." Barbante smiled a little at his own phrase. "He won't feel that it's a general, nameless attack on him from all points of the compass. Do you understand what I'm talking about?"

"I understand," Archer said.

"Now," Barbante said, "are you going to tell me that Pokorny is being dropped, 'temporarily,' just because you think some vague changes ought to be made in the program?"

"Yes," Archer said, after a little pause, "that's what I'm going to tell you."

Barbante finished his drink. He stood up and went over to the bar and put the glass down. It made a little damp click on the chromium surface. "You're not leveling with me, Clement," Barbante said gently. "For the first time. I regret it."

He turned and faced Archer silently. He looked serious and intelligent and friendly and there was a sense of reserved emotion in his dark face. For the first time, Archer got an inkling of what it was in Barbante that made him so attractive to women.

"I'm sorry, Dom," Archer said quietly. He stood up and made a task of knocking his pipe out. "In a few days," he said, knowing as he said it that it was unwise to promise anything, "in a few days maybe I'll be able to tell you more."

"I'll be around," Barbante said more lightly. "With questions. Never fear."

"Here I am." It was Jane, at the door. "Wasn't I fast?" She came into the room, presenting herself a little uncertainly in her grownup black dress for Barbante's approval.

Barbante looked at her gravely. "You look very tasty," he said.

Archer glanced sharply at the writer. That's a stupid thing to say to an eighteen-year-old girl, he thought, in front of her father. But Jane was smiling widely, delighted with what she obviously took as a compliment. The dress was cut low, Archer noticed, and showed

quite a bit of bosom. Jane was quite full in front and
for the first time Archer realized that it was not just
the healthy robustness of a child that was being displayed there. Who the hell picks her dresses, he
thought. I have to have a conversation with her mother
on that subject.

"Do you like the dress, Daddy?" Jane asked, coquetting. Disagreeably, Archer thought. "It's new."

"It's all right," Archer said.

"Aren't you *glum*?" Jane said, pouting.

"It's beautiful," Barbante said. "You look as gay as
a florist's window. Never listen to fathers about things
like that. Fathers don't know anything."

"It's very pretty," Archer conceded, feeling that he
had to compete with Barbante for his daughter's good
will and hating Barbante momentarily for it. Jane did
look very pretty. She had swept up her hair and put on
a lot of lipstick and her eyes were glistening, very blue
and deep, at the prospect of the evening. The dress
made her look slender and graceful. She had borrowed
two of Kitty's rings and her hands glittered when she
moved them. She might have been anything from eighteen to thirty, Archer decided, examining her. Girls
these days, he thought resentfully, are impossible to
classify. They all look as though they might be any
age, of any virtue or experience. What has happened
to the ideal of the virgin? Every child looks knowing,
wicked, and cynically gay. If he saw her walking on
the street beside Barbante, and didn't know her, he
wouldn't have any notion whether she was the man's
wife, his mistress, the wife of a friend committed slyly
to adultery . . . He looked down at Jane's feet and saw
that she was wearing low-heeled shoes. Usually, when
she went out, she wore the highest heels she could manage. But Barbante was small and Archer knew Jane
was surrendering, that much, in advance. Even so,
Archer noticed with sour satisfaction, she's taller than
he is, even in low heels. But he was annoyed that his

daughter had decided to alter herself in this tiny but significant way for Barbante's pleasure.

"Make sure," he said, kissing her on the forehead, smelling her perfume, "not to come home too late."

Barbante chuckled. "The cry of the parent," he said, "is heard in the land."

But Archer saw Jane's mouth stiffen in resentment, although she said, obediently, "Yes, Dad." She pulled away and started toward the door. "Will you help me on with my coat, please, Mr. Barbante?" she said.

Barbante looked at both of them, knowing what was happening, silently amused. "Good night, amigo," he said.

"Good night," Archer said. They didn't shake hands. In a moment, Archer heard the door open and shut. He stood in the pleasant, rumpled little room, smelling the mixture of perfumes. Then he went to the window and opened it wide.

The night air came in with a cold rush. Across the gardens he could see people sitting down to dinner at a table that was lit by candles. In the next garden a collie dog sat on its haunches, muzzle pointed to the sky, howling deep in its throat at an airplane that was crossing high above the city, its lights winking against the stars.

Archer shook his head and slowly mounted the steps to his wife's room.

Kitty was sitting up in bed, wearing a pale yellow bedjacket with ruffles around the throat. She was reading a fashion magazine and she had her shell glasses on.

"You look impossibly secretarial tonight," Archer said.

"I'm examining all the fashions," Kitty said, waving the magazines, "and plotting to spend a great deal of your money once I get out of bed."

"That reminds me," Archer said, seating himself on

the chair near the bed. "Who bought that gown for Jane?"

"It wasn't expensive," Kitty said hastily, "it only cost . . ."

"I'm not complaining about the cost."

"Don't you think it's pretty?" Kitty asked.

"It's pretty all right," Archer said. "Only I think it's too . . . too . . ." He searched around for the word. "Too advanced." It sounded lame, but it was the only word he could think of.

Kitty giggled.

"Don't laugh," Archer said, annoyed that Kitty was taking his opinion so lightly. "She's just a child, and it's ridiculous for her to go traipsing around looking like one of Louis the Fourteenth's favorites . . ."

"You think it's cut a little low?" Kitty asked doubtfully.

"I think it's cut a damn sight too low."

Kitty chuckled again. "She's very nicely built," she said complacently. "Isn't she?"

"All right," Archer said, exasperatedly. "I'm stuffy. She told me that, too."

"Girls have to make themselves look nice," Kitty said mildly. "You ought to be thankful she's so pretty."

"I'm thankful," said Archer. "I'm delighted. It's working out fine. It's working so well she's out tonight with one of the most notorious men in New York."

"Notorious!" Kitty pretended to be shocked. "Heavens!"

"Now, Kitty," Archer shouted, "will you please stop being so damned tolerant for a minute or two?"

"I haven't heard a man called notorious," Kitty said, "since our preacher ran off with the telegraph operator's wife, and that was in 1923."

"You know what you are?" Archer asked, resigned to the fact that he had already lost this battle.

"What?"

"Slippery. I have what your daughter would call an utterly slippery wife."

"Don't take it so hard, darling," Kitty said. She leaned over and patted his hand comfortably. "I think Mr. Barbante is very nice."

"He is the most thorough woman chaser in the city," Archer said gloomily. "He's at least thirty and has the morals of a Turk."

"I'm sure Jane will behave very well," Kitty said primly. "I'm not at all worried about her."

Archer knew that this was meant as a rebuke for his lack of faith. "Neither am I," he said quickly. "Not really."

"It's all good experience for a girl," Kitty said. "Let them see the whole line early so they won't be surprised later in life."

"If I weren't so tired," Archer said, "I would be shocked."

"Why don't you try to take a cold shower before dinner?" Kitty asked, instantly solicitous.

"I don't want a shower. Also—she put on a whole batch of disgusting airs with him and she wore low-heeled shoes because he's a midget."

Kitty smiled. "Girls have to grow up sometime," she said. "You've got to try on an air or two when you're eighteen years old to see what the effect is. And I always wore low shoes myself when I went out with a short man. Don't be so stern."

"Anyway," Archer said, with grim satisfaction, "I told her to come home early. From now on, I'm going to take over Jane's instruction, and I hope that that one"—he pointed to Kitty's stomach—"is a boy."

"My," Kitty said, wrinkling her nose, "you must have had a bad day. Did you have a fight with O'Neill?"

"No," Archer said. For a moment, he thought of telling Kitty the whole story. It would be a relief to unburden himself, get someone else's advice, share the painful interior monologue of the last twenty-four hours. He regarded her thoughtfully. She looked fragile, childish and helpless in the pillowed bed. Then he de-

cided against it. Not now. Not yet. Not until it couldn't
be avoided. He would leave Kitty's protection intact as
long as he possibly could. "No," he said, "I didn't have
any trouble with O'Neill. Just the regular routine," he
said carelessly. "I spoke to Nancy on the phone.
Clement has the measles. I told him I'd come up soon
and tell him a story."

Kitty looked at him strangely. "You don't plan to
go into the room, do you?"

"Of course I plan to go into the room. You can't
tell a four-year-old child a story by coaxial cable, can
you?"

"Oh, Clement . . ." Kitty looked at him reproachfully. "Measles're so catching."

"I had the measles," Archer said, "when I was five
years old. And I've known young Clement since before
he was born and I'm his godfather. What do you expect
me to do—stand at the doorway and make him feel
like a leper?"

"Now you're angry at me," Kitty said. Her voice
began to tremble. She had developed an unhappy tendency toward tears in the last few months. "You think
I'm unfeeling toward the child."

"I despise the idea of being frightened of sickrooms,"
Archer said. "It's so cowardly and . . ."

"You despise me," Kitty began to sob.

Archer put his arm around her to comfort her. Her
shoulders felt frail and young under the frilly bedjacket.
"Now, darling" he kissed her neck, "I don't despise you
at all. You know that."

"It's not for me," Kitty said. "Or even for you. But
even if we don't get it ourselves, we can carry the
infection and then when the child is born. . . ."

"I know, I know," Archer said. "Don't worry about
him. He'll be enormously rugged. I guarantee."

"I feel so queer these days," Kitty said wetly into
his shoulder. "You have to forgive me."

"Of course I forgive you."

"It's not like when we were young. I *knew* nothing bad could happen then. . . ."

"Nothing bad is going to happen now. And we're not so old," Archer said. "Stop making us sound as though we're both ready to fall apart."

"I don't have any confidence any more," Kitty whispered. "I have such terrible dreams. . . ."

"Don't cry. Kitty, darling, please don't cry," Archer whispered, holding her. "And from now on, whenever you have a bad dream, wake me up and we'll put on the light, and you can tell me about it if you think that'll help, or we'll just sit up and read. . . ."

Kitty stifled her sobs and rubbed her face against his coat. She kissed him. "I'm all right now," she said. She smiled wanly. "Isn't it dreadful, weeping like this? I'm ashamed of myself."

Archer stood up. "Don't worry about it," he said. "You cry all you want for the next four months."

"The perfect husband." Kitty even managed a chuckle.

The phone rang on the bedside table and Archer leaned over and picked it up. "Hello," he said.

"Clement." It was Vic's voice. "I heard you called."

"Yes." Archer glanced at Kitty, moist and inquiring on the bed below him. It would be impossible to talk now. "I wanted to see you."

"I'm afraid it'll have to wait a few days," Vic said. His voice was sober. "I'm having a little trouble."

"What's the matter?"

"I just got a call from Detroit. I'm taking a plane for there now. I'm leaving in ten minutes. My mother's had a stroke and the doctors're being gloomy."

"Oh, I'm terribly sorry, Vic."

"Well," Vic said calmly. "She's a pretty old lady. Maybe you'd better have somebody standing by for me next Thursday, in case I can't get back in time."

"Sure," Archer said. "Don't worry about it." He was unhappily conscious that he was annoyed with

Vic's mother for deciding to have a stroke at just this time. For a moment he thought of telling Vic he'd see him at the airport. Then he thought better of it. Vic had enough trouble for one night. "Is there anything I can do for you here?" Archer asked.

"You can come up and pat Nancy's hand from time to time."

"Of course," said Archer.

"What did you want to see me about?" Vic asked. "Anything important?"

Archer hesitated. "It'll have to wait," he said, "until you get home. I hope your mother . . ."

"I know, Clem," Vic said gently. "Give Kitty my love."

Archer put the phone down slowly. Kitty was looking up at him inquiringly.

"Vic sent his love," Archer said. "He's leaving for Detroit. His mother's had a stroke."

"Oh, I'm so sorry," Kitty said. She put out her hand and took Archer's, as though the threat of death, even though to an old lady far away whom she hardly knew, had made her seek for obscure reassurance in the touch of her husband's healthy and robust flesh.

But the news cast a pall on the evening. They hardly spoke through dinner, and Archer wandered restlessly around the house the rest of the night, looking at the clock again and again, thinking of Vic crossing the night sky toward his stricken mother, and wondering where Jane was at that moment and what she was doing. He was unnecessarily brusque with Bruce when he appeared at nine o'clock. He gave Bruce Barbante's invitation at the door and didn't invite the boy in for a drink and was irritated with the forlorn, hopeless expression on the boy's face.

He sat up drinking by himself and resisted going to bed. He didn't want to dream. Zero, he thought. Zero.

8

There was always something disturbing about Frances Motherwell's voice, even on the telephone. It was low and a little hoarse and suggested, at all times, hidden invitations. "What that girl has," the agents said, accounting for her success, "is Sex, from Coast to Coast."

Just now, on this Monday morning, the voice, with its constant undercurrent of energy and excitement, was merely saying, "Clement, darling, I just have to see you. *Tout de suite.*"

"Sure," Archer said. He had been caught by the telephone's ringing in the hall, just as he was about to go out. He thought for a moment. He had wasted Sunday, tired and lying around and reading the papers, until it had been too late to call Pokorny, as he had planned. Frances Motherwell would do for a starter, he thought grimly. Might as well eat the bitter pill first. "I'm at your service. How about lunch?" Coat the pill with food and drink and keep everything friendly, at least in the beginning.

"Sorry, lover," Frances said. "I'm waiting for a call from California from a semi-forgotten man. Could you come up to my place?"

"Of course."

"You have the address, don't you?"

"Engraved on my heart." Elephantine gallantry, Archer thought coldly as he said it, brought on by embarrassment. Frances embarrassed everyone. She embarrassed women because they felt that she could take any man in the room from them and she embarrassed men because they couldn't help wondering if it was true.

"I live on the fourth floor. Can you make the steps?"

"I'll have a cardiogram and see," Archer said, displeased that the girl thought he was so old.

She laughed. Her laugh was a little wild, as though there was something in her that was out of control which revealed itself in her laughter. "Don't be angry, lover," she said, as Archer winced at the word. "I just want to preserve you for better things. Say a half-hour?"

"A half-hour," Archer said.

"Promise not to mind how I look. I just got up and my face is folded together."

"I'll wear rose-colored glasses," Archer said. "See you soon."

Frances lived on a street in the East Fifties. The house was an old mansion converted into small apartments. Archer always got the feeling of transience from these streets. Actors lived there on subleases, ready to go to Hollywood at the first offer; readers for publishers lurked in polite cubby-holes, prepared to switch to larger quarters the day after they were made editors; newly married couples shared a few cubic feet of space, sleeping on daybeds, until the advent of the first child made them move to the country. Still, it was a pleasant street, especially today, with the air clear and the sun glinting on all the windows and making the thin row of winter-bare trees in front of the buildings very black against the clean pavements. Young women strode purposefully out of the gaily painted front doors, carrying their bags slung over their shoulders, like military messengers carrying important information to a higher headquarters. And hatless young men, who had jobs that permitted them to sleep late, strolled back from breakfast at the corner drugstores, their heads bent as they read the morning *Times,* giving a false, week-end air of leisure here in the middle of the busy city.

Archer rang Frances' bell, wondering how he would begin with her. Conducting a conversation with Frances was difficult at the best of times, because she had a jumpy, quick mind and went imperiously in her own direction in any company. It's too nice a day, Archer thought resentfully, staring back at the sunlit street, for a job like this.

Then the buzzer rang. He sighed and went in. He climbed the dark, genteel steps, past a door from which the smell of frying bacon wafted out, and another door behind which someone was practicing a run from the Brahms Second Concerto on the piano. Frances was waiting for him on the top floor, looking over the banister. He tried to disguise the fact that he was panting as he said hello.

"Oh, you poor darling," Frances said as she closed the door behind him and took his coat, "I just must move someplace where there's an elevator. Your dear little bald spot is perfectly purple. Sit down and don't say a word."

Archer grinned weakly as he seated himself in a narrow modern chair that made him feel as though he had been captured. He felt that he was already at a disadvantage and that he would never recover from it. "You have a very nice apartment here," he said, looking around him at the tiny room and spacing the words between gasps. "Although at this altitude I advise the use of oxygen."

"My lair," Frances said carelessly, glancing at the dark-brown wall above the white fireplace. "It's all right if you don't try to get more than a hundred people in at any one time."

The phone rang in the next room and Frances said,

"Oh, damn it, there it goes again. Excuse me." She rushed into the bedroom and picked up the phone. "Motherwell speaking," she said crisply, sounding like an officer in the Army. Archer noticed the business-like affectation and was displeased by it. Actresses, he thought, if they're any good, never can persuade themselves to sound like normal human beings. He could see her through the doorway, one knee up on a chair, frowning into the phone and poking a pencil at her hair. She was a striking-looking girl and her face didn't look folded together at all, he noticed. Her hair was pulled back severely to show her high, bold forehead. She had a nervous mobile face, with large gray eyes that were a little too flat in her head, so that they seemed over-prominent. She was slender and had good legs and Archer could see she didn't need a girdle and wasn't wearing one. She was dressed in a sweater and a closely fitting green skirt, simple and finely made and reminded Archer of his daughter. Give Jane another six or seven years, Archer thought, and she'll probably look very much like that.

"It's perfectly sweet of you to ask me, lover," Frances was saying into the phone, causing unknown tremblings on the other end of the wire, "and I'd adore coming. Just let me look in my little book and see what it says about Tuesday." She put her hand over the mouthpiece and made a grimace at Archer. "Bore Number One of the Winter Season," she whispered hoarsely. She didn't open the book on the table. She waited an acceptable amount of time, then took her hand off the mouthpiece. "Darling," she said, her voice freighted with regret, "the little book says I'm spoken for on Tuesday. Isn't it damnable? I'm so sorry. Do remember to ask me again, won't you?" She nodded impatiently several times and took the phone away from her ear and hung it over her shoulder as the voice on the other end made several diminishing remarks. "That's sweet," she said briskly, putting the phone to her ear again. "We must get to-

gether. But *real* soon. Thanks so much for calling."
She hung up, looked briefly at herself in a mirror and
came back into the room.

There ought to be a law, Archer thought, regulating
the conduct of pretty women over the telephone. The
Federal Communications Commission. And they do it
brazenly in front of you, confident of the absence of
solidarity among men.

"Poor dear," Frances said. "He's such a lump. And
he never catches on. Do you mind if I go into the
kitchen for a second? I was just getting myself a goodie
when you rang."

"Go ahead," Archer said. "I have all day."

Frances swept into the kitchen. She moved in swift
bursts, brushing past the furniture in the crowded room
with a dancer's precision. Archer heard her rattling the
door to the refrigerator. "Can I get you anything?" she
called in. "I see I have five oranges, a quart of milk
and a half pound of pâté."

"No, thanks," Archer said, smiling at the menu.

"Oh," she called again. "I saw your daughter two
nights ago. At the Ruban Bleu. With Dom. She looked
heavenly. She's a true mankiller, that girl."

"Is she?" Archer said loudly, wondering uneasily if
in the language of the day that was a compliment.

"She will devour them by the dozen," Frances said.
"Mark my word."

She relapsed into silence as she pushed glasses into
the sink. Archer looked around the room curiously.
There were red and white candy-striped draperies at
the windows, an abstract painting that looked ugly,
authentic and expensive above the fireplace and, surprisingly, a whole wallful of books. When does she
get time to read? Archer wondered. Helplessly he felt
himself staring at the books, searching for the titles. A
great many current novels and one whole side devoted
to poetry. Dobson, Donne, Baudelaire, Eliot, Auden.
What message was hidden there for him? Or for the

poor lump who had asked for Tuesday on the phone?
Off to one side, in a neat pile, was a group of magazines.
The top one was a small literary magazine that was
put out by avowedly Communist writers. Archer leaned
over and read some of the names on the cover. Two
of them he recognized as being leaders of what the
magazine itself often referred to as left-wing thought.
He sat back feeling distaste for himself. Before this,
he had, as a bookish man, always glanced curiously at
his hosts' books when he was invited anywhere. Until
now he had done it thoughtlessly, without any sense of
guilt. Now, he seemed to himself to be looking at
bookshelves through the eyes of a potential informer.
Perhaps, he thought, I will never be able to pick up a
friend's book innocently again. The curtailment of
pleasure, brought about by secret dislocations in attitude. Guilt was not in the act, but in the conception of
the act. Archer had an old-fashioned sense of hospitality
and he could not help but feel that judging your host in
his own home was a betrayal of friendship. I wonder,
he thought, how detectives square their consciences
after a fruitful day's work.

Frances came back into the room carrying a tall glass.

"What's that?" Archer asked.

"Chocolate milk," Frances said. "I'm queer for it.
Wonderful after a rough night. Want some?"

"Lord, no. I haven't had a rough night since
1940."

"Lucky man," Frances said. She sat down on the
sofa across from him, putting her leg under her. She
sipped at the milk. "Heaven," she said.

She has decided, Archer thought, that today she will
be girlish and is putting in the proper strokes unerringly.

"Clement, dear," she said, staring at him over the
rim of her glass, "I'm sure you're wondering why I
dragged you up here like this."

"Well . . ." Archer began.

"I've always been meaning to invite you up," she
said swiftly. "You and your wife. For a little party. I'd

never invite your daughter." She smiled widely. She had a disturbing habit of licking her lower lip in darting little movements of her tongue. "Not after the other night. Things're bad enough around town as it is without bringing the competition to your own fireside. Dom was all over her."

"Was he?" Archer asked, not reassured.

"You know Dom. He never means any harm—except to women." She grinned and Archer smiled woodenly back at her, confused and wishing she'd move on to another subject. "He never looked at me once," Frances said. "And we've been friends for a long time. Though to be perfectly truthful, Dom is too fleet of foot for my tastes."

Dimly, Archer remembered that Frances and Barbante had been seen together for a short period. But then Barbante had been seen with almost everybody for a short period. Frances, he knew, had been involved with quite a few men. She was not promiscuous, but she was—well—restless. She fell deeply in love, made no bones about it, displayed her love proudly and publicly, was furiously attached to one man for a time and then suddenly, finding him lacking in one way or another, ditched him without ceremony, usually in public, and went on to the next. At every party she went to there would be several men who watched her warily and a little regretfully from corners, carefully keeping out of her way. She had a rough, ironic tongue and in her trail there were several limp markers where she had left lovers permanently demolished.

"In a better-regulated society," Frances was saying briskly, "you could hire Dom by the night, and send him out in the morning before the maid arrived to see how naughty you'd been."

"Now, Frances," Archer said uncomfortably, "Dom is a friend of mine."

"He's a friend of mine, too," Frances said cheerfully. "I say all these things right in front of him. He loves it. He thinks it's a compliment."

"Frances," Archer said desperately, "you started to say . . ."

"Oh, yes." She took another sip of her chocolate milk. "Clement, I'm afraid I have some dreadful news for you. And I wanted to tell you in advance before . . ."

The phone rang again. "Oh, damn it," Frances said, putting her glass down. "I'm going to have the number changed." She got up and went to the phone, patting Archer's cheek as she passed him. "Motherwell speaking," she said impatiently. "Yes. I see." Her voice became guarded and she glanced involuntarily at Archer. He felt out of place and superfluous, knowing that she wanted privacy for this conversation. He wondered if it would be discreet to go and lock himself in the bathroom for awhile.

"Yes," Frances said. "That's quite clear. Look— where are you? You'd better call me back. In about thirty minutes. Right." She hung up. "Sorry," she said, as she resumed her seat. Archer glanced obliquely at her face, but nothing was revealed there.

"You said you had bad news," he said gently.

"Well," Frances said, "maybe I'm just being egotistic when I say that. Maybe you won't mind at all."

"What is it, Frances?"

"I want to quit the program." She peered at him with her head to one side. The sun caught her cheek and lit up her hair and she looked young and morning-like. "Have I broken your heart?"

Archer sighed. A dozen sensations flooded through him, jumbled and contradictory. He didn't try to sort them out. Now, he thought, is the time for me to be very careful. "Why, Frances?" he asked.

"I've been offered the lead in a play," she said. "The most beautiful part. And Cowley's directing and he's on fire to have me. It's too good to be true." She laughed, again a little out of control. "I even have to go mad at the end of Act Three."

Listening to her laugh, Archer realized why the director had picked her for that particular scene.

"It's the chance I've been waiting for ever since the war," Frances said earnestly. "I couldn't let it pass, even though it's going to cost me quite a bit of money. I have to give up all my radio jobs, but I think it's worth it."

"When would you have to quit?" Archer asked, guiltily feeling that luck, for this day at least, was running his way.

"Well," Frances said, "rehearsals don't begin for another ten days. But I thought if you'd be a love and said it was all right for me to quit right now, I'd go skiing for a week and get that clear-eyed young look back on my face before rehearsals."

"You don't have a contract," Archer said. "There's nothing to keep you—legally."

"I know," Frances said. "But you've been such a dear, I couldn't bear to leave you in a hole."

"Where're you going skiing?" Archer asked.

"The Laurentians," Frances said. "But only if you say OK."

The suspects, Archer thought, may be found at all the winter resorts, coming downhill at thirty dollars a day.

"Sure, Frances," Archer said. "I wouldn't want to stand in your way." For a moment, Archer was almost ready to leave it at that. Telling her what he had to say seemed almost gratuitously candid. And Frances, as she had proved again, always made out all right. If you were that young, that attractive, that talented, nobody had to worry about you finally. And besides, she had a rich family back in Texas or somewhere, to complete her luck. Pokorny was a different matter, Alice Weller . . . That's where the truth would be necessary, on those gloomy, unlucky grounds. It was almost silly to insist upon having your bad half hour with a girl like Frances Motherwell. Archer wrestled himself out of his chair, ready to go.

"Good luck, Frances." He extended his hand formally.

She jumped up and came over and kissed him. Even for a sisterly, congratulatory kiss like that, she provocatively threw her body, wiry and soft in the soft sweater, against him. As he kissed her, Archer thought reprovingly, somebody ought to tell her not to do that with older men. He stepped away. Her eyes were shining, almost as though she were holding back tears, although of course, with a girl like Frances, you never really could tell whether it was talent or emotion, and probably she couldn't either.

"You're the nicest living man," Frances said. "Some day I may fall in love with you."

Archer chuckled falsely, rubbing his bald spot and pretending to be older than he was. "I couldn't stand the strain," he said. He almost left then. He took a step toward the door. Then he stopped. How far could you let expedience push you into cowardice? How would he feel when Frances heard of the accusations against her, and what the agency had planned to do to her? And there was no doubt about it, she would find out. And probably very soon. At the top of a snowy hill in Canada, feeling young and healthy, racing down the slope in her nervous excited way because she had been told that a telegram awaited her below and all news these days was good news . . . How would she feel about him then, remembering this afternoon? The nicest living man . . . He stopped and turned toward the girl.

"Frances, darling," he said. "Please sit down. I have something to say to you."

"You're not going to change your mind, are you?" There was alarm in her eyes and a flicker of stubbornness.

"No. Now sit down. This is awfully serious."

He watched her seat herself, erect now on the sofa, her hands crossed, looking up at him puzzledly.

"Frances," he said, standing above her, "I hardly know where to begin. I was going to try to see you today even before you called. I want to ask you some questions. You don't have to answer them, because, actually, they're more to help me than to help you . . ." He shook his head. "No," he said, "I'll start over again. I'll tell you the facts and then, if you want, you can give me some answers. . . ."

"You look so uncomfortable," Frances said. "Maybe you'd be better off if you sat down."

"If you don't mind," Archer said, "I'll stay on my feet." He began to pace slowly back and forth in the room. "Look," he said, "here it is . . . Three days ago I had a conference with O'Neill and was told that I had to fire a certain number of people from the program." Archer avoided looking at the girl. "One of the people was you." He stared at the painting on the wall. There seemed to be two or three heads that ran together, with a profusion of eyes and noses, all done in purple and black, with ominous touches of red.

"The reason I was asked to fire you is that you're supposed to be a Communist," Archer said, looking at the painting. "I was told that it would be advisable not to give you the correct reason, but to let you drop quietly."

"You're not doing that," Frances said flatly.

"No. I didn't think I could."

"No," Frances said, "of course not."

Archer turned and faced her. She was thoughtfully finishing her glass of milk. For one of the few times in her life, her face was expressionless.

"Did you come up here to tell me I was fired?" Frances asked, putting her glass down.

"No," Archer said. "I got the office to give me two weeks' grace."

"What for?"

"For my own amusement." Archer smiled wryly. "To conduct my own little investigation, I guess."

"Whom are you investigating?"

"Myself, mostly." Archer smiled again. "Anyway,

for you, this has become something of an academic question—since you're quitting anyway."

"I don't think it's academic," Frances said coldly. "Not at all academic. Who said I was a Communist?"

"Did you ever hear of a magazine called *Blueprint*?"

"Yes," Frances said. "A lying, Fascist sheet."

Archer sighed, displeased with the quick slogan. "I don't know," he said mildly. "I rarely read it."

"Take my word for it," Frances said. "And just because a dirty little rag makes an accusation like that, I'm scheduled for the axe?"

"That was the idea," Archer said. "Actually, you won't be hurt. The piece isn't coming out for several weeks—and since you're going into a play, and you won't be on the program any more—they probably won't print anything about you."

"Isn't that a fortunate coincidence," Frances said bitingly, "for everyone? Did they mention anybody else?"

"Yes."

"Who?"

"I'd rather not say. At the moment."

"Are you going to fire them?" Frances demanded.

"I don't know," Archer said, walking back and forth in front of the bookcase. "The office wants to."

"Are the others conveniently going into plays, too?" Frances asked. "Or would that be too much to ask?"

"No." Archer began to be annoyed with the girl, because her tone was accusing him, making a villain out of him. "I don't imagine they are."

"Did you come up here just to tell me I was being thrown out?" Frances demanded. Her voice was harsh and sounded almost masculine now. "You were willing to climb four flights of stairs, with your aging heart, just to pass the good word onto me?"

"That's a little unfair," Archer said, conscious that the girl was trying to hurt him.

"Then why did you come up here?"

"I wanted to talk to you," he said uncertainly. "I wanted to see what I could do."

"Well," Frances said, "what *are* you going to do?"

"I don't know yet," Archer said softly. "I thought maybe you could help me."

"I don't think so," Frances said. "You're not angry enough."

"I don't know what you mean by that."

"You're accepting it already."

"Now, Frances . . ."

"With regret," she said loudly. The skin over her forehead seemed to be stretched tighter than ever and her face was very hard. "You're a nice man, so you're sorry—a little—but I can see you're ready to do what they ask you to do."

"Well," Archer said, controlling himself, "I think that closes the meeting for today. I'll go now. If you want to talk to me reasonably some time, give me a ring." He started for his coat.

Frances watched him silently for a moment, until he had picked up his coat. "Put it down," she said. "You might as well hear what I have to say." She picked up a cigarette and lit it, with quick, nervous movements, her hands shaking a little, while Archer carefully put his coat back on the chair. Her fingers, he noticed, were stained by nicotine. He walked slowly over to the narrow chair and sat down again, once more feeling his hips being cramped by the hard sides.

"First of all," Frances said, blowing a great deal of smoke straight ahead of her and breaking the match in her fingers, "what do you think about me? Do you think I'm a Communist?"

"Well," Archer said carefully, "I really don't know you very well, do I? Outside the studio, I don't see you more than five or six times a year. And . . ."

"Don't hedge," Frances said flatly. "You think I'm one, don't you?"

"The truth is, Frances," Archer said, "you *do* belong to a lot of organizations, and you're quite outspoken . . ."

"If somehow you were forced to say, one way or another, what you thought," Frances went on, attacking him, "you'd say I was a Communist."

Archer thought for a long moment. "Yes, darling," he said.

"Well," she said, "you're right. I *am* a Communist." She stared at Archer. There was a kind of harsh, religious triumph in her face.

"I'm proud of it," Frances said. She doused her cigarette in an ash tray with jabbing, excessive strength. "I'm not ashamed. I'm not ashamed of anything I've ever done."

Archer was not really listening to her. Now I know about her, he thought, she's told me herself. What do I do about it? What do I do about it if later on I am asked about her? What if I'm asked under oath?

"If it didn't help the bastards so much," Frances was saying bitterly, "I'd take an advertisement tomorrow in the New York *Times* and announce it to the whole world. What do you think being a Communist means?" she demanded accusingly. "Do you really think I've been plotting to kidnap the President and overthrow the Government? Do you think I've been going around picking out churches to burn down when the great day comes? Do you believe that I've been drawing up plans for the nationalization of women?"

"Now, Frances," Archer said reprovingly.

"I don't know," Frances said. "I don't know what you believe. I don't know what anybody believes these days. The way the newspapers talk, you'd think we're all spending our time putting together atom bombs to blow up the water system next week."

"You know I don't believe that."

"I give you three months," Frances said. "Three more months of being exposed to the poison you take in every day and you'll believe everything they want you to believe."

Archer sighed. She sounds like a placard, he thought, in a May Day Parade. In two minutes she's rejected any notion that I might behave with sense or in good faith.

"I don't know what I'll think in three months," he said. "Maybe you ought to wait and see before you make any charges."

"Nobody's hesitated to make charges about me," she said wildly. Her fingers were jumping as she took another cigarette. "And they're using you. You're their finger man. You're their respectable front, waving your conscience, going around and doing their dirty work for them, turning people out to starve because they have an opinion or two."

"Wait a minute," Archer said, stung. "You're putting up a big fuss and you're making it sound as though there was a gigantic conspiracy against you. Actually, nobody's stopping you from working. You're getting a big part in a play, at a damn good salary, no doubt, and if you're any good you'll be a big success in it and make a lot of money . . ."

"And if the play flops," Frances interrupted, "and I have to go back to radio? What happens then? And even if I'm a success, and I get smeared, who'll hire me for another play?"

"Plenty of people. Nobody's said a word about the theatre yet and you know it. For all I know there are three regiments of Communists on Broadway today, and if they're right for a part, they get hired. And no questions asked."

"That's today," Frances said. "Don't be naive about what's happening. If they get away with it on radio, how long after that do you think the theatre'll be left alone? They're smart, they're picking off the easy ones first. All you serious, intellectual fellows think the movies and the radio aren't very important—jokes—

you don't care what happens to them. So you let them get away with it. You think they'll stop. They won't stop. They've got the habit now and they see they can get away with it. They'll keep on going until they have every word that's written or printed or spoken censored in advance and sterile as hospital gauze."

Archer sighed. "Frances, darling," he said, "I didn't come up here to get into a political debate. I'm not a politician, but even so, I can't help feeling that a Communist is the last one in the world to make speeches about freedom of expression."

"Ah," Frances said bitterly, "the poison's got you already. We don't have to wait three months."

"Don't insult me, darling," Archer said, feeling that he really ought to leave, that nothing was going to be decided here in this room with this nervous and fanatical girl. "Maybe I'm wrong, but from everything I've heard about Communism and everything I've heard about Russia—and no matter what good things might be found in the doctrine—freedom of opinion is not included. Don't you realize that to a reasonable person when you ask to be defended on those grounds it sounds like the utmost cynicism?"

"No," Frances said stonily. "Not at all. You don't know anything about it. You're completely confused."

"Every time I've had an argument with a Communist in the last fifteen years," Archer said gently, "he's always wound up by telling me I'm confused."

"Well, you are. You're lazy and you don't investigate for yourself and you believe all the lies they tell you."

Archer nodded agreeably. "I probably am lazy," he said. "And until now I haven't even been really interested."

"You'd better get interested fast, brother," Frances said harshly. "You haven't got much more time before they wipe you out. You're the one they're really after—not me. There aren't enough Communists in this country to make one good swallow for a Congressional Committee. But there are millions like you, thinking you're independent, liberal, working for your living. First they have to get you ready to fight Russia, and after that, if you're still alive, they've got to leave you so scared you'll never dare to open your mouth when they take over."

"When who takes over, Frances?" Archer asked patiently.

"The Fascists," Frances said promptly. "It's the same pattern as Germany. They're even using the same war cries. And they're splitting up the opposition the same way. The Red scare, the Red scare, and you wake up one morning and the police are knocking your door down to take you to a concentration camp because three years ago you were overheard to say you didn't like the Fuehrer's moustache. You used to be a history teacher." Frances' voice rose mockingly. "You ought to crack a book now and then, even though you're out of the field for the moment."

The trouble with all pat, standard, well-worn arguments, Archer thought, is that there is always a great deal of truth in them.

"Do you want to know why I became a Communist?" Frances asked. Her voice was low again and personal and her face had lost some of its rigid tension.

"If you want to tell me," Archer said.

"I want to tell you," she said. She stood up suddenly and walked over to the window and looked out. Outlined against the sunny curtains she looked slender and gilded. "Doesn't it strike you as queer that a girl like me went bad? My family's got a lot of money, I went to the best schools, I'm pretty and men have always chased after me as though I was giving it away free, so I don't have to go to meetings for *that* reason." She chuckled harshly. "I had a happy childhood, Doctor," she said mockingly, "and everybody thinks I'm just wonderful and I'm so rich I have a second mink for

rainy days and in general I'm as merry as a lark. Why
can't I be like the other girls? The only thing they have
to be afraid of if they're investigated is that their husbands will find out that they paid sixty dollars for a hat
or had a slight Lesbian affair when their old school
chum from Vassar came up to the country last summer." She turned and faced Archer. "That's a synagogue across the street," she said. "When I'm bored, I
stand at the window and see if I can pick out the Jews
at seventy yards." She laughed at her own joke, the
laugh shrill, gasping, slightly out of control.

Archer moved uneasily in his chair. Maybe I
shouldn't have gotten in this deep with this girl, he
thought. You never can be sure what she's going to do.

"To continue, Doctor," she said, staring at Archer
with her eyes half-closed, sensing that she had made
him uncomfortable and amusing herself by increasing
his discomfort, "sex is not the trouble, although it says
in the books that dissatisfied women are susceptible to
curious aberrations. I'm not frigid, Doctor, I assure you,
and my orgasms are in charming condition. If you really
must have it for your diagnosis, I will write down the
score on this little slip of paper and you can put it in
your notebook when I've gone."

I came up here to talk about her politics, Archer
thought resentfully; now look where we are. You always
sink deeper than you want to go; everybody always
answers more fully than you desire; you are forever
infinitely implicated after you have asked the first, irrevocable question. The trouble is that people always
regard themselves as wholes, and they never can extri-
cate the one aspect of themselves that you are interested
in for special examination. The mind is swamped by
the abundance of over-available fact. Ask a veteran
where he lost his leg and by the time you're answered
you have a history of a division, a detailed account of
several campaigns, a judgment on his commanding officers and an elegy of the men who fell around him. Ask

a woman a question on any subject concerning herself and she starts at the root of the matter—sex.

"I'm listening, Frances." Archer spoke gravely, in an attempt to get the girl away from the mocking, derisive self-revelation.

"I picked up Communism on my trip abroad," Frances said, her voice still joking and harsh. "In the Red Cross." She came over to Archer and stood above him, her hands on her hips and her legs spread wide. "Are you surprised?"

"I give the Red Cross fifty dollars each year at Christmas," Archer said. "I don't know what they do with it."

"I was stationed at a B-17 base in England," Frances said. "I served doughnuts and wrote letters home to the parents of the dead. I thought I was very patriotic and adventurous and the uniform looked good on me. I teased the men at dances, but I was wholesome as an apple, and slept by myself at night. One boy, he was a bombardier, told me he used to go and make love to an English girl in town after he danced with me, and close his eyes and pretend it was me in bed with him. I told him it wasn't wholesome; that was a big word of mine in the winter of 1944, but he was flying over Bremerhaven and Schweinfurt and he had his mind on other things. Then I met an older man, a squadron leader, he must have been twenty-six, and I stopped being so wholesome."

Archer moved uncomfortably. He felt that Frances was standing too close to him to be talking about things like that.

"He was from California," Frances went on, looking over Archer's head. "One of those big sunny boys they grow out there. He was quiet and cheerful and dependable. The men in his squadron loved him—and I enlisted in the squadron, privately." She paused and peered uncertainly at Archer as though she didn't quite remember who he was or what he was doing in her room. She turned abruptly and sat down on the sofa, her hands between her knees, pulling her skirt in tight lines.

"When you give up being a virgin at the age of twenty-three," Frances said, "it seems like an enormous date on the calendar, and maybe you attach more importance than you should to the man . . ."

Twenty-three, Archer thought, in 1944. That makes her twenty-nine now. I didn't realize she was that old.

"Though I don't think so," Frances said, as though she were arguing with herself. "He was brave, he was careful, he took care of his men as though they were precious. Not precious only as soldiers. Precious as human beings. He took care of me. We were going to get married and live in Santa Barbara if he came out alive." She shrugged. "I'm going to say something funny," she said. "I'm going to use a funny word. He was a saint. Are you going to laugh?"

"No," Archer said. "I'm not going to laugh."

"I don't think it's only because he's dead now that I say that. I felt all this when I saw him every night. After missions and when we went down to London on leave. London . . ." She stopped and looked blindly away, as though she were remembering what the streets looked like and the ruins and what it felt like to come out of a restaurant in the blackout holding onto a dead boy's arm. "He was religious," Frances went on finally, her voice sounding empty and strained. "His father was a minister and he himself had considered, for awhile . . . So he thought about a lot of things that the other boys didn't seem to bother about. They all seemed to be thinking only about getting home alive or finding a girl or getting promoted or not cracking up when things got tough. Maybe I'm unfair to them. I guess they thought about other things, too, only they never happened to tell me. Hank had a . . . a grave turn of mind. He wasn't solemn, but he wasn't a kid any more, and he took the war very seriously, and he had a habit of questioning himself."

Hank, Archer thought. What a name for a saint. Saint Hank.

"I guess he had a lot of time to ask questions, coming back on those long missions," Frances said, "after the bombs were dropped, after watching his friends go down, sitting there on oxygen, with the co-pilot at the controls, and the wounded lying on the floor of the plane waiting for the morphine to take effect. He kept asking himself what it was all for. Whether it was worth it. What the result would be. What it would be like after it was over. Whether it would happen all over again. He was a freak in the Eighth Air Force. He really began to feel that he was fighting for peace, equality, justice. Those words." Frances grinned crookedly. "The son of a minister, and from California besides, they grow them queer. And somewhere along the line, he got the notion that that's what the Communists stood for. Back in college, he'd had a couple of friends in the Party and they'd been very good about Mexicans and Chinese and Jews and Negroes and a living wage for apricot-pickers and things like that. Then, to prove they weren't kidding, they went off and got themselves killed in Spain. And he felt they'd been right about that, too. They'd warned everybody about that and nobody had listened and it had turned out just the way they predicted. So, aside from everything else, he felt they were smarter than everybody else, that they had the inside track on that information, too."

"That was in 1944," Archer said gently. "Do you think he'd still feel the same way today?"

Frances shrugged. "All I know is that he told me that the day after he got out of uniform, he was going to look up the nearest Party headquarters and join up. Should I tell you his name so you can drop him from something, too?"

"Don't take it out on me, Frances, darling," Archer said quietly. "Please."

"His name was Vaness. Major Henry Vaness," Frances went on. "Maybe you could have him dropped out of the American military cemetery at Metz. Conduct unbecoming a dead pilot." Her eyes were glistening, but she didn't cry. She wasn't acting now. Her voice was flat and lifeless. "He was the only complete man I've ever found," she said, "and nobody can say I've been lazy about looking since then." There was sour self-mockery and self-disgust in her voice. "And do you know why he was complete? Because he had love in his heart. Love for everybody. For his men, for his little silly Red Cross girl, for the people he was forced to kill . . . Twenty-one missions and good-bye. Should I tell you what the men in his squadron did for me the day his plane went down? Ah—what for? You're like all the rest. You're more polite and maybe you'll struggle a little longer—but finally you'll be snowed under, too. It'll just make it harder for you if you have to hear that somebody who believed in Communism was a great man and that everyone who ever knew him loved him. I'll make it easy for you," Frances said challengingly. "I'll tell you I was a famished little virgin and I fell in love with a dashing Major and I picked up my politics in bed. Anyway, the day after I took off *my* uniform I went to the nearest Party headquarters and told them I wanted to join. Guilty as charged. That's what you came to find out and you've found it out. Now I must ask you to leave, Clement. I expect somebody up here any minute and I'd rather you didn't meet him . . ."

She stood up. Her hands were clenched at her sides and her face looked drawn. Archer rose from his chair uncertainly.

"Thanks," Archer said lamely. "I want to thank you for being so frank."

"Sure," Frances waved her hand carelessly. "I'll tell anybody anything. I'm famous for it." She started toward the door.

"I'll keep you posted," Archer said, following her and picking up his hat and coat. "Whatever develops."

"By all means." Frances opened the door for him. "Keep me abreast."

The phone began to ring in the bedroom and Frances said, "I'd better answer it. Good-bye." Her tone was remote and cold and as though she had no connection with Archer and her pose at the door was plainly impatient.

Archer wanted to say something gentle, hopeful, persuasive, something that would show he had been moved and that he wanted to be her friend. But Frances looked hurried and forbidding, standing at the open door, and all Archer could manage was, "Good-bye, Frances. Good luck on the play."

Then she closed the door crisply behind him. He could hear her hurrying through the room to the phone as he put on his hat and began to work himself into his coat.

"Motherwell speaking," he heard her say through the thin partition. "Oh. Hello. Yes. I'm alone now." Archer buttoned his coat and started down the stairs. Faintly he heard Frances' voice saying, "How're the measles today?" Then he was out of earshot on the dark stairs. He stopped, reflecting on what he had heard. He realized that he was straining to hear the rest of the conversation, but at that distance there was just the low, indistinguishable murmur of Frances' voice. Then he was ashamed of himself and descended the stairs swiftly. The pianist on the floor below was still working on the same run.

Archer emerged into the sunlight, blinking his eyes a little. No, he thought, it's ridiculous, probably ten thousand families in New York at this moment have a case of measles, somewhere on the premises. And even if, by a wild chance, it was Vic, now in Detroit, who was calling her, what of it? There might be a hundred reasons, all innocent, for such a call. And whatever the reason, it certainly was none of his business. Forget it, he told himself, forget it, it's just because you're so shaky after that weird half-hour with the girl, forget it. But he knew that the next time he saw Vic and Frances together, he would look at them curiously, with new speculation and doubt. He was committed, he began to realize, to an endless task. Once you began to inquire into the fundamental and hidden motives of human beings, you were confronted with an infinite number of clues. And there was never any time off and there was no one whom you weren't ready to suspect. The bloodshot detective within you was on duty twenty-four hours a day, seven days a week.

He looked curiously at the faces of the passers-by, wondering whom they had questioned that morning and who was going to question them that night. He wondered if they felt as trapped and uncertain as he.

He walked slowly across town, grateful for the pale winter warmth of the sun on his skin. Well, he thought, smiling weakly, Interview Number One is over, now where are you? The magazine had been right about Frances Motherwell, at least in calling her a Communist. That had been no surprise. But did that mean they were right about the others? And after listening to her, did he feel she was dangerous, that she deserved to be punished? A neurotic, unstable girl, theatrically given to attitudinizing, making out of her politics a romantic monument to a man she'd loved and who had been killed in the war. Spouting the stalest slogans and the most passionate personal revelations in the same breath, all mixed with a night-club glitter and fashionable vulgarity. A new development in political circles—the elegiac Communist in a cashmere sweater shakily recovering from the champagne of the night before. The unwed widow of the crashed hero, hopefully presenting herself for martyrdom and never finding it because she was too rich, too talented, and too pretty to be picked for sacrifice. The placarded mind under the permanent wave, convinced by a voice from the grave that she was in the vanguard of those who were standing for the equality of men, whatever that was. A liar on the telephone to a desolate suitor, fiercely certain that she was privy to the only truth. A lost prowling girl hunting for a lost boy among later beds, making up with a substitute devotion for what she knew in her heart she would never find. An indiscreet, nervy performer whose hands shook when she lit a cigarette, natural casting for the part of a woman who had a mad scene toward the end of a play, confident that she and her friends formed a solid core of reason and virtue in an insane and villainous world. God help those friends, though, Archer thought, if she ever thinks that they have betrayed her.

She's indigestible, Archer thought; there's no nourishment there for either side. Attack or defend her at the risk of your own confusion. Still, and Archer sighed relievedly as he thought of it, this time I'm sharing in her luck. By a fortunate coincidence, the question of Frances Motherwell need not be debated at the moment. Moving on to better things, the girl had neatly removed her problem to the field of theory. Practically, you could forget about her, knowing that she was above harm. It was too bad the others could not be disposed of as happily. As for the principle . . . Archer shrugged. Time for that, later on, later on. Get the survivors off the wreck now, and bring in the boat at another time, when the water was calmer.

Now—who next? Archer stopped in the middle of the street. Pokorny? Herres? Atlas? Weller? He really ought to see Pokorny as soon as possible, because he was already suffering. But Pokorny was bound to be the most painful of them all and Archer still felt shaken after Frances. Atlas, he thought selfishly, there's the toughest of the bunch; he doesn't give a damn about anything. He'll give as good as he gets and you can check your pity at the door.

Archer went into a phone booth and called Atlas' number.

"Hello, Stanley," Archer said when he heard Atlas' voice. "This is Clement Archer."

was baptized, taking on the responsibility of its welfare if it ever became necessary . . . He remembered how touched he had been that day that Nancy and Vic, who by that time knew all about him, his weaknesses, his failures, had used his name for their second son.

He had come to New York because Herres had made it possible.

"Look, you've got to get out of here," Herres had said the last night of a five-day visit during the Easter vacation, during the year following his graduation. He and Nancy had been in New York about eight months, and while Nancy so far had not landed anything, Herres was already doing fairly well on daytime radio shows. Neither of them had as yet been offered a part in a play. "If you stay on here at the college, hating it the way you do," Herres had gone on earnestly, as they sat alone in Archer's study, "you're going to turn into a sour, garrulous, dried-out old orange by the time you're forty."

Archer had smiled, nervously. "Don't be hard on your old instructor," he had said. "He has his own problems."

"You love New York," Herres went on, simple, logical and young. "You hate this place, you hate teaching. Move on down. It's not so tough."

Not so tough for you, Archer almost said, not so tough for the young and talented and beautiful and lucky. But he didn't say it. "Have you thought about one interesting point?" he asked instead, trying to keep it light. "The little matter of keeping alive, and keeping a wife and child with good appetites alive at the same time?"

"Nancy and I talked about it," Herres said, "and we think it can be managed."

"Yes?" Atlas said, not friendly and not unfriendly.

"I have to see you, Stanley. Today. As soon as possible."

"Oh." There was a pause on the phone and Archer could almost picture Atlas coolly deciding whether to be agreeable or not. "Why?"

"I can't talk about it on the phone."

"Got a nice tip in the seventh at Hialeah you're just dying to give me, Clem?" Atlas asked.

"I've got to see you. Right away." Archer tried to keep the note of impatience out of his voice.

"Where?"

"Well . . ." Archer hesitated. He couldn't ask Atlas to meet him at O'Neill's office for this particular conversation and he didn't know of any place where he could take a Negro in for lunch without a fuss. "Well," he said, "how about Louis' bar?" He had never seen any Negroes there, but he was known there and he probably could arrange something.

"Massa Clem," Atlas began, his voice rich and Southern, "don' you-all know what shade I am?"

"Don't be silly, Stan," Archer said, with false confidence.

"Last time I was in Louis' bar for ladies and gentlemen, Massa Clem, they done break the glass I was drinkin' from after I was finished. I sure would hate to put those nice white folks to any more expense on my account."

The trouble with him, Archer thought, sweating in the cramped phone booth, is that he *enjoys* telling me these things. "OK, Stan," Archer said, "I won't argue with you. Why don't you come down to my house?"

"That's mighty downtown," Atlas drawled. "That there's a long ride on the underground for jes a little spot of conversation."

"Stanley," Archer said loudly, "will you please spare me the carry-me-back-to-old-Virginny dialect? I've got to see you. For your own good. It's important. Now, where'll you meet me?"

"Well," Atlas was still drawling, with the same undertone of malice and amusement, "I got a puffictly nice sittin' room, right up heah in lovely old Harlem. I'll get the hens off the settee and the pig out from under the television and we'll have things just as shiny as a three-hundred-dollar coffin by the time you get heah."

"What's the address?" Archer asked curtly.

Atlas chuckled, victorious. Then he gave Archer the address, in a clear, well-modulated voice that sounded as though its owner had been graduated from Harvard.

9

"So," Atlas was saying, "they have me tabbed as a real red type of feller and they want to retire me from competition, is that it?"

"Just about," Archer said. He had wasted no time in telling Atlas the reason for his visit. Atlas had sat relaxed in a big leather chair, moving a moccasined foot gently back and forth from time to time, listening without a word. Occasionally Archer thought he caught the hint of a smile on the comedian's face, but his attitude had been grave and attentive. The living room was large and neatly furnished in imitation early American pieces. There was a small upright piano with a few photographs of Negro entertainers and athletes on it, inscribed to Atlas. The apartment overlooked a small park and Archer could see scraps of dirty snow still clinging in spots on the brownish earth. Atlas was dressed in gray flannel trousers and a dark-blue wool shirt, open at the collar. He was wearing bright-yellow wool socks and they made little flashes of color when he moved his legs.

"What am I supposed to do now?" Atlas asked, looking curiously, and with a hint of secret amusement at Archer. "Am I supposed to get up and say

I'm just a dirty old colored man and I confess everything and I'll be a good nigger from now on if you don't whup me and I promise to sing the 'Star-Spangled Banner' every night before going to bed?"

"You do whatever you want to do," Archer said.

"Did you take that long ride in the subway just to tell me that, Clem?" Atlas asked. He spoke mildly and he seemed perfectly at ease. The scar marks looked neat and leathery on his cheeks in the cold north light.

"I came up to see if I could help," Archer said. "To see if there was anything you wanted to tell me that might clear this up. We have almost two weeks to work in before . . ."

"Two weeks," Atlas nodded reasonably. "How long have I been working on the program, Clem?"

"You know as well as I do. Three years."

"Going onto four. And now I get almost two weeks to clear this up, like you say. That's what I call real generous of you, Clem."

"Listen, Stanley," Archer said, feeling as he always did with Atlas, at a disadvantage, "I'm not doing this. If it were up to me, this wouldn't have come up at all."

"You mean you wouldn't mind if us Reds took over the Government and razorcut ol' Mr. Hutt and raped all the white girls?" Atlas asked in mock astonishment. "That comes as a real surprise to me, Clem. It surely does."

What a satisfaction it would be, Archer thought grimly, to punch that cool, grinning man right in the nose. "Look, Stanley," he said, fighting to keep his voice steady, "I'm involved in this as much as you."

"They got you marked down in their books, too?" Atlas grinned more widely. "Why, those boys don't miss sparrow drops, do they?"

"No," Archer said, beginning to feel that it was hopeless, "they haven't got me marked down. Nobody's accusing me of anything."

"Jest you wait," Atlas said comfortingly, "you'll be

invited to the party one of these days just like everybody else."

"I'm trying to save the program," Archer said earnestly, trying to break through the shield of Atlas'
mockery. "I'm trying to save as many people as I can.
I'm trying to figure out what kind of position I have
to take."

"I get it," said Atlas. "You didn't take that subway
ride to help me. You came up here to get me to help
you."

"All right," said Archer wearily. "Put it that way."

"Now," Atlas smacked his lips judiciously and
looked thoughtfully up at the ceiling, "let's us see
what we-all can do to help the white folks. Would it
be more convenient for your taste if I call up Mr. Hutt
right now and tell him I am a red, raving Communist
and I get my instructions every morning direct from
the Kremlin? Or would it make it more homey if I
just said I'm just a poor dumb colored boy that just
barely learned to read and write, spellin' out the Eman-
cipation Proclamation we used to have hangin' in the
privy out in the yard back home, and I been duped and
led into evil ways unbeknownst to myself by a lot of
red foreign Jews from downtown? Or maybe it would
be more suitable if I got up on my hind legs and
yelled and hollered and rolled my eyes and said, 'May
Jesus strike me dead this minute if I'm tellin' a lie! I'm
as innocent as a newborn lamb and I hate the Communists like snake poison because they're leadin' us poor
black children into the ways of sin and temptation.'
You just tell me," Atlas said, smiling, "and I'll say
whatever you like, because my aim is to please."

"I don't think you're taking this seriously enough,"
Archer said, hating the man. "You're on the verge of
being fired from every program you've ever played on.
You won't get another job. You'll be finished. You
won't earn a cent. Now, for God's sake, stop joking!"

"Money ain't my primary interest in life," Atlas said

lazily, "so I can afford to joke. I been working a long time and I don't go in for fast motor cars or fast ladies and there's a standing rule around this house that my wife don't buy ermine more than once a year. So I got a cushion. A nice, fat cushion. Just for occasions like this. I own two buildings on Lenox Avenue and I'm silent partner in a very nice bar and I got some bonds that'd look sugar-sweet in anybody's bank vault. So I got what you might call a steady income, Clem, and I don't have to take guff at all. Nobody's guff. No guff from the sponsor, no guff from any white magazine writers, no guff, excusin' the expression, from you. If people get nasty, maybe I'll just pack up with the old lady and take off to France. Spend those francs. I was there during the war with the USO and I was attracted. I even got a running start on the language. *Chérie*," he said, grinning "*je cherche du cognac, s'il vous plaît.* Let them yell all they want about me back here, I'll be reading the Frog newspapers."

"If you run away," Archer said, "without defending yourself people're bound to believe the worst about you, Stanley. Eventually you'll want to come back and work. An actor lives on his reputation, and he's more vulnerable than other people; he's got to be more careful . . ."

"Is that what you believe?" Atlas peered bleakly out of his chair.

"I don't want to believe it," Archer said wearily. "I'm forced to."

"I get the same story from some of my friends," Atlas said quietly. "Only not about being an actor. They're colored and they say a colored man has to be more careful than anybody else. Maybe you're thinking a little of the same thing yourself, Clem?"

"No," Archer said, wondering if he was telling the truth. "I'm not."

"That's good. I don't like people who think colored folks ought to make sure to act like angels at all times, just because we're what you might call unpopular in certain quarters. First of all, it ain't possible. It ain't possible for actors and it ain't possible for blacks. And if it was possible that'd be the worst thing of all, because then people'd have a real grievance against the race, if they went around behaving better than everybody else. They'd be so holy they'd be swinging from every lamppost. And then, as a voting citizen, I'd be against it because it's un-American." He grinned coldly, confident and unmoved, taking his time, lazily enjoying playing with Archer. "In the United States of America, the man says here, everybody's born free and equal. Don't say nothing about black men or actors on the radio or anybody. It just says everybody. That means we all got the equal right to be mean or dirty or obstreperous with everybody else. We got the same license to get into trouble as anyone else. I don't notice no quota system in the jails. Folks who run the jails, they're firm believers in the Constitution, they say, Sinner, you broke the law, we got a spot for you, we don't care who you are."

"Stanley," Archer said impatiently, "we could talk like this all day and never get anywhere."

"I was just lettin' my mind ramble around among the possibilities," Atlas drawled. "I feel playful today. Now, I suppose what you really want to know is—am I or ain't I."

"If you want to tell me," Archer said.

"First, let's us look at the reasons why a colored man might decide it'd be a smart idea to be a Communist," Atlas said, crossing his legs comfortably with a flicker of his yellow socks. "Give us a understanding of the subject," he said gravely, "in case we get asked about it some time."

I'll never get anything out of him, Archer thought; he's got color on the brain; he never thinks about anything else.

"Right off," Atlas said, "the Reds come to you and

they say, "You're as good as anyone else, we don't notice what shade you are. Comes the Revolution, you'll be just like everybody else. They're happy, you're happy. They're miserable, you're miserable."

"That's very likely the way it would work out," Archer said. "You'd be permitted to share in the general misery."

Atlas nodded vigorously, as though Archer had just said something enormously clever.

"Right. I don't doubt for a minute but that you're right, Mr. Archer," he said. "And that's mighty attractive doctrine. We're all in trouble, but it's the same trouble. That's real promising, just to begin with. So then, they set out and prove they ain't just talkin' to stir the wind. They make a big fuss to get colored folks to live in white neighborhoods, they make up committees to see the mayor, they send down nice white girls to explain it to us at cocktail parties, they invite us in to join what they call cells and we can all go out and get our heads knocked in together by cops on picket lines. They send a candidate to the city council and he turns out to be a colored boy, and he's on the National Committee besides. They're not kiddin' at all there, are they?"

"No," Archer said. "They're not."

"Very attractive," Atlas said. "You got to admit that."

"There're a lot of other organizations," Archer said, "that have Negro members and are trying for the same thing."

"Uhuh." Atlas nodded again. "But they're all just a little polite. They sign things, they make nice speeches —but, when it gets tough, they don't really kick up any trouble. And one thing you got to hand the Reds, Clem . . ." Atlas chuckled. "They sure do kick up trouble."

"I hand it to them," Archer said grimly. "They know how to do that."

"For example," Atlas said, "me. I ain't doing bad. At least," he smiled softly, "till today I wasn't doing bad. The dough was coming in; people laughed at my jokes as though they was paid by the company; I got a nice enough house." He looked around at his possessions consideringly. "In the summertime you can look out and see a tree." He indicated the window. "Free enterprise. I got more dough than you and Vic Herres, say, put together . . ."

"I wouldn't be surprised," Archer said.

Atlas shook his head warningly. "You white boys just too rash with yo' dollar bills," he said. "Still, Herres, he lives on Park Avenue; he can walk to the studio if he wants. You live down in the Village, a real agreeable neighborhood. Can you imagine what would happen if I went to the renting man at Vic Herres' house and I said, I work around here, this is real convenient, give me a nice apartment with southern exposure, never mind the rent because I'm loaded." Atlas looked at Archer mockingly. "Can you imagine the reception? And on your block, Clem," Atlas inquired innocently, "you got a lot of colored families as neighbors?"

"There's no answer to that, Stanley," Archer said, "and I'm not going to pretend there is."

"The Reds," Atlas said slyly, provoking Archer, "they say they got an answer."

"Are you trying to tell me that you're a Communist, then?"

"I ain't trying to tell you anything, Clem," Atlas said. "I'm just rustling around among my souvenirs. Anyway, it might be a little hard for me to be a Communist. I'm a capitalist, like I told you. Two tenement buildings and a half interest in a bar. And gilt-edged securities piled up like snow drifts in the vault. You look at my income-tax return some day, Clem, and you'll see how hard it'd be for me to be a Communist. Not impossible, of course," Atlas said tantalizingly. "But hard. And many ways, I'm not so fond of everything they do. They ain't 99 and 44/100ths percent pure themselves. They're out for something of their own and they latch onto us because we got our troubles and they can score some runs off of that particular pitching. They pretend to be a lot more interested in us colored folk than they really are. We are what you might call incidental income on their original investment. Sometimes we get to looking real hard at each other and wondering whether we're using them or they're using us. It ain't as easy to tell as a person might think, looking at it from the outside."

"Stanley," Archer said, "there's more to it than the Negro problem and you know it. They stand for a lot of things and do a lot of things that have no connection with Harlem."

"Foreign policy?" Atlas shrugged carelessly. "Labor unions? I'm too busy to bother. My foreign policy is maybe I'll move to France and take up blowing a trumpet again, like in the old days. And maybe I'll spend a couple of nights at home and have a kid or two. I ain't in the mood for no more colored kids in this country. It don't fit in with my principles."

"Listen, Stanley," Archer said desperately, feeling that he was adrift, "practically, what do you intend to do? Do you want to defend yourself?"

"How do you do that?" For a moment Atlas seemed absolutely serious.

"Maybe one thing you do," Archer said, "is bring a libel suit against the editors of the magazine. Maybe you join with the others who've been accused and do it together."

Atlas grinned. "What is it, Clem?" he said. "You got friends in the legal profession you anxious to make rich? When I was a little boy at my mother's knee, she told me, 'There's only one rule I want you to follow, Son. You can drink corn liquor and you can snuff cocaine and you can sleep with the parson's wife, but never sue a white man.' My old gray-haired Mammy down South. And the way things're going today, half of any jury you could pick'd call you a Red if they found out you voted for Theodore Roosevelt."

"Whom *did* you vote for?" Archer asked. "What organizations do you belong to? Maybe the time will come when we have to go to the newspapers and fight it out there. Have they got anything on you? What can you prove?"

Atlas grinned. "Ain't you nosey, Clem?" he said. "Let them go and find out for themselves. They ain't getting any help from me. Those're white-folks questions. Let the white folks get the answers. Would you feel better if I told you I voted Republican and I belong to the National Association of Manufacturers? Though I ain't guaranteeing any of this is the gospel fact. Would it be bad for me if I told you there was a time I was a runner for a policy racket, or don't that make any difference? You think it'd hurt my fair name if I told them I used to hang around a night club when I first came up from Tampa and go to bed with white ladies for ten bucks a throw? Harlem was lively in those days and there was a surprising amount of traffic in that line of goods."

Archer stood up, defeated. "OK, Stan," he said flatly, "have it your own way. I thought maybe if I got the straight dope from everyone we'd all be able to help each other."

"I ain't interested in helping anyone," Atlas said. "Not even myself."

He sat easily in the deep leather chair, stretching his legs, his bare arms wiry and thick, his eyes steady and baleful, resigned to everything, hating everything.

"All right," Archer said. "I'll call you if anything comes up."

"No need to bother," Atlas said without moving. He didn't show Archer to the door.

Outside, in the hall, waiting for the elevator, Archer sniffed. There was a stale, sour smell of cooking. He was annoyed with himself for noticing it.

10

Alice Weller lived high up on Central Park West, in a building that had at one time been luxurious and genteel. By now it was only genteel. The carpets were threadbare and greenish, if they were any color, and the walls of the lobby were a dim olive stucco. The elevator clanked and groaned as it rattled up the shaft and the operator wheezed as he worked the lever.

"Mrs. Weller," Archer said.

"Fourth floor," the elevator man said. "Does she expect you?"

"Yes." Archer sniffed the mingled odors of oil, dust and age, and it brought back the memory of the pleasant evenings he had spent a long time ago in this house, when Alice's husband, who had been Archer's friend, was alive. Since his death, Archer had visited Alice less and less frequently, salving his conscience with the knowledge that he had found work for her more or less steadily ever since he had become a director, even though there had been times when he had to fight the producers of his shows to do it.

Alice opened the door herself. She was dressed in a ruinously youthful cotton dress that made her look older than she was. Her hair, just out of curlers, was

too tightly bunched over her forehead. She smiled softly when Archer kissed her. "It's nice to see you here
again," she said, without reproach. "It's been so long."

Her hands, Archer noticed, as she hung up his coat,
were cracked and red, as though she had done a great
many dishes very recently. She led the way into the living room, seeming, in the incongruous dress, not ma-
tronly but exhausted.

"Take that chair," she said, pointing. "The one you
used to like has a broken spring."

Archer sat down obediently, feeling guilty that Alice
remembered that he had liked a particular chair. He
didn't remember any of the chairs.

"I think I'll sit me down here," Alice said, folding
into the sofa, which gave off several grinding squeaks
as her weight settled. It was her one affectation, Archer
remembered. She said, I must sit me down, and I must
wake me up and I must take me home. Probably it had
charmed some man a long time ago and she had dimly
clung to the trick, feeling momentarily younger each
time she used it. Archer had always been uneasy when
he heard her talk like that and he realized it still left
him uneasy. She sat stiffly on the stiff couch, as though
she had somehow lost the knack of grace.

"Ralph will be so glad to see you again," Alice was
saying. "He's asked for you often."

"How is he?" Archer asked politely, wondering how
long he would have decently to wait before telling Alice
what he was here for.

"He's grown so tall you won't recognize him," Alice
said, like a mother. "He wants to be a physicist now,
he says. You know, the papers're so full of science
these days, and they have professors down to talk to
them all the time." She laughed softly. If you closed
your eyes and just listened to the gentle melody of her
voice, you would imagine a young, delightful, hesitant
girl in the room with you. "I don't know what's happened to firemen and jockeys any more," Alice said.

"The things the boys wanted to be when I was a young girl."

Ralph was her only child. Her husband had been an architect who had just begun to have his initial successes after years of struggle when he had been killed in an automobile accident in 1942. He had been something of a political thinker and had not believed in insurance. Looking around him at the meager room, with its worn furniture and mended curtains, and its air of being fragile and desperate, as though it was inhabited by people who could not bear another shock from life, Archer thought that it would have been better if the architect had not had such original notions and had taken out a policy or two in his wife's name before he took that automobile ride.

"So many problems come up," Alice was saying. "Just last week I was offered the role of the mother in the road company of *Breakwater*. It's a good part and the money was good and they wanted to give me a year's contract. But it would have meant leaving Ralph alone—sending him to a boarding school. I talked to him about it—he's amazingly grownup, you can discuss anything with him—and he was very brave about it. But at the last minute I told them no." She laughed sadly. "I don't know what I'll do when he grows up and decides to go off and get married. I'll probably behave terribly and get drunk and insult the bride." She waved her hands vaguely, apologizing. "I must shut me up," she said nervously. "I mustn't babble on about my family. What about you? You look very well these days. Very distinguished-looking. I've been meaning to tell you," she said, with a painful, dim echo of coquetry.

"I'm fine," Archer said, because that described it as well as any other one word. "The program keeps me alive."

Alice chuckled self-consciously. "It also keeps me alive," she said shyly. "And Ralph."

That was an unfortunate way for me to put it, Archer thought. The phrase went too deep when you examined it seriously, as Alice was doing.

"You're on it this week, too," Archer said, grateful that he could say that much. One hundred dollars more for the complicated process of keeping Ralph and his mother alive. "Quite a nice part. Not very long, but juicy."

"Thanks, Clement." Alice's hands waved in front of her. Her gratitude, Archer thought, is always uncomfortably naked. "Mr. O'Neill called me this morning and told me."

Archer phoned in a list of people he was going to use each week and O'Neill made the necessary calls each Monday morning. There were going to be some bad Monday mornings for Alice from now on, sitting by the silent telephone, if Hutt had his way. Well, Archer thought, the longer I wait the harder it's going to be.

"Alice," he said, rubbing the top of his head nervously, "I'm in trouble."

"Oh." Alice took in her breath sharply. An expression of concern washed tremblingly over her face. "Can I help?" she asked.

"Something queer has come up," Archer said. "About you."

"About me?" Alice looked surprised, then frightened.

"You know," Archer said, "for the last year or so, agencies have been dropping people from programs because they've been . . ." He hesitated, searching for the least harmful word. "Because they've been accused of being Communists or fellow travelers, whatever that is."

"Clement," Alice peered worriedly at him, "you're not being fired, are you?"

Archer grinned weakly. "No, not at the moment."

Alice sighed with obvious relief. "These days," she said, "it's impossible to tell what's going to happen next."

"Alice," Archer said, determined to get it out without further delay, "the truth is, I've been asked to drop you."

Strangely, she smiled at him. It was a slow, hurt smile, an involuntary twitching of the muscles that had nothing to do with joy, but which, by some trick of mechanics, twisted her mouth upward at the corners. Clumsily, without seeming to notice what she was doing, she lifted her hands and poked aimlessly at the tight curls around her ears.

"But you're not doing it," Alice said. "You just said there was a nice part for me this Thursday. And O'Neill called at ten o'clock this morning . . ."

"Yes," said Archer, "that's right. I got us a period of grace." As he said it he wondered abstractedly why he had said us. "We have two weeks to do something about it."

"Two weeks." Alice's shoulders drooped and her hands dropped again. "What can you do in two weeks?"

"Don't give up in advance," Archer said, annoyed at Alice's quick acceptance of defeat. "We might do a great deal."

"I don't understand." Alice stood up heavily. She walked toward the window, looking stout, hiding her face from Archer. "I don't know where to begin. What do they say about me?"

"Hutt received an advance copy of a magazine article," Archer said slowly and clearly, trying to pierce through Alice's vagueness. "In it you and several others are said to belong to various Communist-front organizations. Do you belong to any organizations that might be—suspect?"

Alice turned and faced him bewilderedly. "I don't know." She seemed distracted, as though she were having trouble focusing her mind on the subject. "I belong to several things. AFRA. Actors Equity. The Parent-Teachers' Association. Then there's a league that my husband used to give money to, for protecting Negroes' civil rights. I sometimes send them five dollars . . . Do you think it might be any of them?"

"Probably not," said Archer. "Is there anything else?"

"Well, I certainly don't belong to the Communist Party." Alice tried to smile. "I'm sometimes pretty vague but I'd know that, wouldn't I?"

"I'm sure you would." Archer smiled reassuringly.

"I haven't done anything illegal." Alice's voice became stronger as she began to get accustomed to the idea that she would have to defend herself and that Archer was there to help her. "I'd know it if I'd broken any laws, wouldn't I?"

"It isn't quite as simple as that," Archer said, "any more." He was unhappy about being the one who was forced to explain the new, melancholy, uncertain order of things to Alice. "Because of the strained relations between us and Russia," he said rhetorically, like a schoolteacher, "because of the tensions that have developed since the war—there's a kind of twilight zone now, in which people are placed without committing any overt acts. It's a zone of—of moral disapproval, I guess you could call it—for certain opinions, certain associations . . ."

"Opinions?" Alice laughed softly and sank into a chair, as though she were very tired. "Who knows what my opinions are? I don't know myself. Oh, dear, you must think I'm an absolute fool. In the last few years I seem to have grown incapable of thinking clearly about anything. I belong in a cartoon—in one of those hats, making a speech to a gardening club in the suburbs."

"Not at all," Archer said, feeling that his voice was too brisk.

"Yes, yes." Alice shook her head ruefully. "You don't have to be so polite. Even Ralph makes fun of me sometimes, and he's only fourteen years old." She picked up a photograph of her son that was on a bookcase and stared at it.

"Last year," Alice said suddenly, "it might have something to do with what happened last winter."

"What's that?" Archer asked, puzzled.

"I got a terrible letter. Printed. In pencil. All misspelled."

"What letter?" Archer tried to sound patient. "Try to remember everything you can, Alice."

"It was anonymous. I only read half of it and I threw it away," Alice said. "I couldn't bear to read it. It called me the most filthy names. You'd be surprised what people can send through the mails. It said why didn't I go back to where I came from if I didn't like it here." Alice essayed a laugh. "I don't know quite what they meant by that. My family's lived in New York for over a hundred years. They threatened me." She looked up at the ceiling, remembering, the sagging skin of her throat pulled tight. " 'We're going to take care of you and your kind,' it said, 'soon. We are forming,' it said, 'and it won't take long now. In Europe they shaved the heads of women like you, but you won't get off just with a haircut.' "

Archer closed his eyes, ashamed for the people he passed every day, unrecognizingly, on the street. "Why didn't you show it to me?" he asked.

"I couldn't," Alice said. "Some of the names they called me you just couldn't show to anyone. I bought a new lock for the door and I had a chain put on." She laughed nervously. "It was really nothing. Nothing happened. I even managed to forget about it until today."

"Have you any idea why that letter was sent to you?" Archer asked, thinking, Now we are entering another field, the field of the anonymous threat to impoverished widows. Live in the big city and expose yourself to all its cultural advantages.

"Yes," Alice said, surprisingly definite. "It was after that big meeting last winter, that peace meeting at the Waldorf. The one that had those Russian writers and composers . . ."

"Were you there?" Archer asked incredulously.

"Yes, I was." Alice sounded defiant.

"What the hell were you doing there?"

"I was on the radio panel. I was supposed to make a speech, but I was too nervous and I got out of it. I was going to speak on the bad effects of the crime shows on children."

Hopeless, Archer thought, listening to the soft, defensive voice, absolutely hopeless.

"You have no idea how evil they are," Alice said earnestly. "Full of people being tortured and killed and hitting each other over the head. It's the only thing I fight about with Ralph. He sits there, listening, getting jumpy and over-stimulated, when he should be out in the open air or doing his homework. I feel quite strongly about it," she said primly, as though she were a little surprised at herself for permitting herself the luxury of feeling quite strongly about anything. "But then, when the time approached, I knew I could never manage to stand up in front of all those important people . . ." She laughed embarrassedly. "I said I had a headache."

"There were thousands of pickets around the hotel all the time," Archer said, wonderingly. "Didn't you realize you were liable to get into trouble?"

"I saw those pickets. They looked like very low types. Very coarse and unreasonable," Alice said, invincibly ladylike. "Just the kind to send a woman an unprintable anonymous letter."

"Was your name on the program?" Archer asked wearily.

"Yes." Alice started to get up. "I think I have it in the desk if you'd like to . . ."

"Never mind. Never mind. Sit down." He stared consideringly at Alice, as she subsided. At least he knew now why the magazine had included her in its list. It didn't take much, he realized grimly. One undelivered speech on the effects of afternoon serials on the minds of growing boys . . . He shook his head, half in pity, half in exasperation. "How did you get mixed up in it, Alice?" he asked.

"Frances Motherwell told me about it," Alice said, "and asked me to appear in the radio section. She said it would focus the attention of the world on the necessity of avoiding a third world war."

Frances Motherwell, Archer thought bitterly, herself almost invulnerable, energetically supplying slogans and disaster to bereft ladies with low bank accounts.

"You mustn't be angry with me, Clement," Alice said unhappily. "I knew a lot of people thought that there was something wrong with the Conference, and the papers kept saying it was a Communist trick. And, really, they didn't seem to accomplish very much. But even if they accomplished just a tiny bit, even if it made people in Washington and Moscow just a fraction more unwilling to go to war, I had to go . . . I suppose a mother, especially if she only has one son, is kind of crazy on the subject of war. Ralph is fourteen. In four or five more years, he'll be just the age . . . My sister, she's older than I am, she lives in Chicago, she sent a son to the last one. He came back—but he was hit in the face, his chin was all shot away. They've operated on him ten times, but he still . . ." Alice stopped. "He refuses to go out. He refuses to see anyone. He sits in his room at the top of the house, all day long. You read the papers and every day they talk about being firm, about delivering ultimatums, about sending soldiers all over the world . . . They keep building new submarines, faster airplanes, rockets, bombs. You look at your son, fourteen years old, sitting in the front room, practicing the cello, and you think they're preparing it for him, all those old men in Washington, all those generals, all those people on the newspapers. They're preparing to have Ralph shot. Blown up. That's what I think every time I read a general's speech in the papers, every time I see new planes in the newsreels. When I get home from the movies I go into Ralph's room and I look at him sleeping there and I think, 'They want to kill him. They want to kill him.' I'll tell you something, Clement," Alice said loudly, "if there was any place to go and I could scrape together the money, I'd take Ralph tomorrow. To the smallest island, the most backward country—and hide him there and stay there with him. Of course there's no place to go. They've made sure of that." There was a profound note of bitterness in Alice's voice that Archer had never heard before. "So I did what I could. I was very brave and I went to a meeting, one afternoon, at the Waldorf Astoria, on Park Avenue," she said with harsh sarcasm. "And I put a chain on my door."

"Alice, darling," Archer said gently, "did it ever occur to you that you were being used?"

"Good," Alice said. "They can use me all they want if it means there's not going to be a war."

"The Communists are for peace today," Archer said. "Tomorrow they're just as likely to be for war."

"All right," Alice said, stonily. "Tomorrow I won't let them use me. Today I will."

Archer shrugged. "OK," he said. "I know how you feel." He took his pipe from his pocket and filled it from his pouch.

"You think I'm wrong, don't you, Clement?" Alice asked, her voice pleading and hesitant again.

"No, I don't think so," Archer said, feeling that the question was too complex to answer in one afternoon. He stood up, holding the pipe in his hand. "I have to go now," he said.

Alice stood, too. "Clement," she said, "what will I do if they won't let me work? How will I live? How will Ralph live?" She looked haggard and old, standing close to him, peering wildly into his eyes, her curls silly and out of place over her drawn face.

"Don't worry," Archer said, because he had to say

something, but knowing as he said it that it was foolish.

"Are you going to let them fire me, Clement?" Her hands clutched fiercely at his shoulders. Her hands were large and very strong and he could feel the nails biting in through the cloth.

Archer took a deep breath. "I'm on your side, Alice," he said. "I want you to know that."

"Are you going to let them fire me?" Alice asked, ignoring his answer.

Archer put his arms around her. She was shivering, and he could feel the small, sweeping spasms going through her body. She wasn't crying. Her body was thick and corseted and the material of the dress felt sleazy under his hands.

"Clement," she whispered despairingly, "are you going to let them fire me?"

Archer kissed her cheek, holding her close. Her skin felt harsh against his lips. "No," he said. "I promise you."

She clutched him convulsively for a second. Then she pulled away. She still wasn't crying. Her lips were quivering, but there were no tears.

"Some day," she said, "I'm going to tell you how grateful I am, Clement." She touched the pipe in his hand. "I'm so glad," she said, "you still like this pipe."

"What?" Archer began, looking down at the pipe. It was an old one that he had picked off his desk that morning because it had no ashes in it from the night before. Then he remembered, Alice had given it to him as a gift after he had given her a job on his first program, back in the years of the war. It was a straight-grain briar and he knew it must have been very expensive. It was a handsome pipe, but for some reason it never drew well and he rarely smoked it. "Yes," he said, "it's one of my favorites."

11

A plump, fifty-year-old woman in shorts was standing on her head on a mat in a corner, her reversed face very red, but her ankles neatly together and her toes expertly pointed. Mr. Morris, the bank-teller, was sitting in the Buddha position, his thin legs wound around each other. He had an intent expression on his face and he was trying to make his stomach touch his backbone. Archer was lying on his back, working on his breathing, looking up at Mrs. Creighton, who was standing above him, shaking her head.

"Your thoughts are congested, Mr. Archer," Mrs. Creighton said. "Your lungs are tense. You are denying yourself the full beauty of oxygen. You are not thinking with your whole soul about breathing."

Mrs. Creighton was an English lady who had lived in India a long time ago. Now she conducted classes in Yogi exercises on Fifty-seventh Street. She was over sixty and she had the face of an exhausted athlete, but her body was as slender and supple as a girl's. Gliding energetically around the city in smart dresses that she bought in the debutante sections of the department stores, she was a glowing advertisement for her system of physical discipline, and her classes were full of ladies who thought they were being conquered by age and by men who had been told by their doctors to give up smoking. There were rumors that she practiced strange religious rites in the room back of her studio and that she intended to retire to the Himalayas at the age of seventy, to achieve oneness with the infinite, but in her day-to-day career she behaved more like a gymnasium instructor than a priestess, and, in fact, reminded Archer of Horace Samson, the football coach at his old college, although Samson rarely used the word "soul" when complaining about the failure of an off-tackle play. Archer had heard about her at a party several years before. It had been during the trying period in his life, when he was suffering badly from insomnia and was ready to try any remedy to defeat the looming threat of seconal. He had met a man whom he knew slightly, and who had been unhealthily fat, with a bad complexion and a stertorous, shallow way of breathing. But in the period of three months, the man had lost at least twenty pounds, had achieved a smooth, rosy complexion, and had learned to breathe quietly and deeply.

"It was a question of my bowels," the man had said earnestly, drinking celery juice, staring disapprovingly at a trayful of canapes. "The center of feeling. Without knowing it, I was being shaken constantly by secret spasms. My body was controlling me, rather than the other way around. Then I went to Mrs. Creighton. I stand on my head fifteen minutes a day now, aside from the other exercises. Now look at me. I've had to get an entire new wardrobe of suits," he said with mournful pride. "My bowels," he said profoundly, "are now my servant."

Feeling a little silly, Archer had gone to Mrs. Creighton's studio. He had never approached the holy reverence of the man with the bowels, and he did not drink celery juice, but he found, after going two or three times a week for a month, that he was beginning to sleep better. Occasionally, when he was feeling ambi-

tious, he did some of the simpler exercises on a rug at
home.

Today, after the session with Alice, he had felt that
a workout would help him. It took a great deal of concentration even to breathe to Mrs. Creighton's satisfaction, and there was no time to reflect on other matters. "Breathing," as Mrs. Creighton often put it, "is
the first function in living. While you're here you must
learn to devote all your attention to it."

So Archer lay on the mat in a sweatsuit, devoting all
his attention to breathing.

"No," Mrs. Creighton said, critically, peering down
at him like a horse-trainer. "Not good. Be fluid. Feel
like a wave. Feel limitless . . ."

Maybe they can feel limitless in India, Archer
thought, trying not to smile, but a man has his work
cut out for him feeling like a wave on Fifty-seventh
Street.

"Mr. Archer, you are retrogressing," Mrs. Creighton
said in her high, English voice, that sounded like teacups being washed in the pantry. "Your concentration
has become faulty. You are divided, and division is the
parent of tension and tension is the father of disease."

Mrs. Creighton glided frostily over to the chubby
woman who was standing on her head and began to
show her how to bend backwards in one sinuous, easy
movement, so that she could touch the mat with the
back of her head. Archer lay on his own mat, doggedly
trying to be undivided, trying to forget everything but
breathing. In the studio upstairs, which was used by a
voice teacher, a contralto was working on scales, the
notes liquid and diminishing. The tone of the voice reminded Archer of Alice Weller's way of speaking and
it became harder to combat division as he listened.

Later, as he was dressing after his shower, sitting on
a stool next to Mr. Morris, who was methodically putting on long woolen underwear, Archer felt better. The

exercise and the cold water had made his skin glow, and he felt younger and more robust as he stood in front of the mirror buttoning his collar and adjusting his necktie. In the mirror, he saw Mr. Morris watching him soberly, shoe in hand. Mr. Morris was a small, sandy man who kept his rimless glasses on even when he was standing on his head. At first glance, he seemed completely innocuous, the sort of man whose name you never remember, although you see him once a week for years behind the gilded grating neatly entering items in your bankbook. But when you looked at Mr. Morris closely, you saw that a wild, harsh fanaticism lurked behind the shine of his glasses. His eyes were dark and full of judgment. Just the sort of man, Archer thought as he pushed the knot of the tie up against his collar, who surprises everybody one day by walking off with fifty thousand dollars of the bank's money and somebody else's wife.

"Mr. Archer," Morris said, "may I take a liberty?"

"Of course." Archer turned and nodded pleasantly to the man in the long underwear.

"I've been watching you," Morris said, "and you ought to lose twenty pounds."

"Yes?" Archer said, displeased with the remark, since he did not feel particularly obese. "You think I'm fat?"

"You are carrying excess weight," Morris said. He bent down and put on his shoe. It was made of dark canvas and had a gum sole, like the shoes that are sold to yachtsmen. "You are over-fleshed."

"Perhaps," Archer said resentfully, putting on his coat and not feeling over-fleshed.

"You eat too much," Mr. Morris said accusingly. "You have too much energy."

"Is that bad?"

"Very bad. Excess energy turns the spirit away from contemplation, from the spiritual to the practical, from reflection toward action. I myself eat one meal a day.

I allow myself to grow hungry and weak in the flesh to reach satisfaction and strength in the spirit." Mr. Morris nodded soberly as he stood up and put on his shirt. "I used to eat heavily, five or six times a day. I weighed twenty-eight pounds more than I do now. I behaved like all the other barbarians in the streets."

"Everyone to his taste," Archer said with false good humor, thinking, Maybe I just ought to join the YMCA and get my exercise there, without lectures.

"And I don't eat meat," Mr. Morris said accusingly. "I eat fruits, nuts and raw vegetables. I do not eat eggs or drink milk, either. I do not live off the flesh of my fellow creatures."

I wonder if the people at the bank know about this fellow, Archer thought, as he smiled fixedly at Mr. Morris.

"Meat eating," Mr. Morris said, putting on his trousers, buttoning them with meticulous, small movements of his fingers, "is at the root of the terror of civilization. It is only to be expected. If we kill daily the harmless and innocent creatures of the field and waters, in person or by proxy, if we get our pleasure from death, if we satisfy our appetites with living agony, what can that do to our moral natures?"

"I suppose," Archer said agreeably, "a case could be made for that argument."

"We become the enemy of all living things," Mr. Morris went on. "The birds dart away at our approach, the deer leaps into the thicket when he sniffs us on the wind. We are the villains in the system of nature, the upsetting element in all of the Infinite's calculation, the unstable and bloody x in God's arithmetic. We represent tragedy and disorder on the stage of life."

"You certainly have a lot of arguments on your side there," Archer said placatingly, putting on his coat and showing as plainly as he could without being rude that he was on the verge of leaving.

"It is the inevitable next step," Mr. Morris said, in

his mournful piercing voice, "to go from killing cattle and fowl and swimming things to killing human beings. The moral restraint is blunted by the act, and the step from the smaller game to the largest game is taken without hesitation, almost without notice. If daily we wage war against the dumb flesh of billions of animals, for the transitory pleasure of our palates, how easy it is to turn our ferocity against our fellow-men and kill them for even more powerful pleasures. The ruins of Berlin and London, Mr. Archer," Mr. Morris said, his eyes glittering madly behind his glasses, "are the only natural result of our stockyards and slaughterhouses. The full cemeteries of the war dead are the final testimony to our shameful indulgence in table delicacies."

"I must go now," Archer said hastily, grabbing his overcoat. "This has been very interesting, but . . ."

Mr. Morris moved swiftly over to Archer and stood in front of him, very close, looking up at him accusingly. "I am going to live to the age of one hundred," Mr. Morris said. "I am going to fulfill my destiny. I am going to decide the day I am going to die and I am going to die in full possesion of my faculties. I am not going to fall into a coma and I am going to make the transition from life to other-life, understanding every moment of the experience. And experience is knowing and knowing is the only ecstasy. Those who die before the age of a hundred, or those who die unconscious of that supreme act, are perishing incomplete. In sin, error and ignorance. Nourished on death, they succumb to death. As you notice," he said conversationally, "I do not wear leather shoes and my belt is made of plastic."

Archer inspected Mr. Morris's costume and saw that he was speaking the truth. "Yes," he said, edging toward the door, "I noticed."

"There can be no temporizing and no compromise," Mr. Morris said, moving imperceptibly with Archer. "There is either the principle of life, which is holy and indivisible, or the principle of death, which is evil. And until now, we have subjected ourselves to the principle of death. We manufacture the pig-sticker's knife and the atomic bomb, two products of the same machine. Because a principle is a machine, Mr. Archer, and can only turn out the same kind of goods, no matter how different they appear on the surface."

"Yes," Archer said, "that's quite logical. I'm sorry but I'm a little late and I'm afraid I have to . . ."

"I understand you deal with the public," Mr. Morris said. "On the radio."

"Yes."

"You reach into millions of homes every week. Homes that reek of the smell of death. You could do incalculable good, Mr. Archer, if you wished . . ."

"Well," Archer said, "I don't really set policy and I . . ."

"The work of enlightenment has to be carried on by all possible means," Mr. Morris said earnestly. "It does not necessarily have to be overt. I know some of the opposition you would face, powerful forces, the meat-packers, the military." His face assumed an unclerk-like and conspiratorial air. "In the beginning you would only be able to introduce hints, suggestions, prepare the ground."

Peace, Archer thought dazedly, is regarded as a conspiracy by everyone, even vegetarians. Nuts and fruits are fraught with peril. Propagandize them at your risk. I ought to introduce him to Frances Motherwell.

"I am working on a document," Mr. Morris whispered, "that I intend to present to the United Nations through the proper channels. I hope to get a million signatures. Will you sign?"

"Well, I'd have to see it first," said Archer, thinking, Everybody wants a million signatures.

"The exact wording is most important," Mr. Morris said. Unaccountably, he winked at Archer. "It's a document of historic importance. I've been working on it for more than a year. It has to be just right before you can expect people to give their names to it. They're afraid of the consequences and you have to make the arguments irrefutable in black and white before you can shame them into signing. I'm going to call on the United Nations to make meat illegal." He smiled triumphantly at Archer. "By solemn compact of the nations of the world. Humanity's pardon of the beasts of the field and the fowls of the air and the fish of the sea. I have great hope for the government of India," he said obscurely, "now that the British are out. After that, peace is inevitable; it is the next logical step. You can forget politics, forget the jockeying for power. Get to the heart of it, the essential crime, the universal moral wound. You can imagine what a bombshell it will be," Mr. Morris said complacently, moving back, away from Archer, "when the document is made public."

"Yes," Archer said, "you must show it to me when you have it ready."

"Of course," Mr. Morris said. He inclined his head graciously, his eyes a glitter of prophetic light. "I know you won't be able to resist signing. It will be ready in a month or six weeks, at the outside."

"I look forward to it," Archer said, opening the door.

"I'll leave a copy of it for you with Mrs. Creighton," Mr. Morris said. "She's helping me."

"Thanks," said Archer. "Good night, Mr. Morris."

"Good night, Mr. Archer. We must talk again." Mr. Morris put on his hat, which was made of nylon, and bowed to Archer. Archer went out hurriedly. The contralto upstairs was singing something from Bizet, her voice sweet and sad. Archer could hear her even after he got in the elevator and started to drop down toward the street level.

On his way home in the crowded subway, Archer found himself chuckling as he thought of the bank-teller who was going to live to the age of a hundred. Then he was conscious that the people around him were watching him curiously, and he arranged his face soberly. There were lunatics on all sides. Peace had its madmen, just like war. No doctrine, however noble, was without its supporters who would be more at home in padded cells than loose on the streets. Death, the principle of evil . . . Well, that wasn't too different from what Alice Weller had been trying to tell him that afternoon in her shabby living room. He wondered if Mr. Morris's superiors at the bank would fire him when he came out with his international proposal of nuts and berries. How far did the zone of moral disapproval extend? Was your money safe with a man who did not believe in killing anything and wore canvas shoes and a plastic belt? Could the State survive Mr. Morris's success? How much leeway could you give a man who challenged the very foundations of society, starting with its basic diet? Especially if he turned up with a million signatures!

Archer smiled again, trying to imagine Mr. Morris as a sinister figure. Still, anything was possible. If Alice Weller could be considered suspect and marked for punishment, why exempt the bank-clerk? Then Archer remembered that he had promised Alice that she would not be dropped. He grew sober again. He had done it out of pity and without thought, but now he was committed to it. Committed. It was a clipped, final, responsible, menacing kind of word. He sighed and tried to assure himself that somehow matters would work out all right. When the train stopped at his station he was annoyed with the people who shoved their way in as he tried to get out of the door. Nobody gives an inch these days, he thought, as he pushed against a large, fat woman in a lynx coat, who charged implacably into the car, searching, iron-eyed, for a vacant seat.

* * *

Kitty was downstairs, in his study, sitting at his desk, working on the monthly bills, when Archer came into the house. She was wearing one of her shapeless, tent-like maternity dresses and her head looked very small and frail over the billowing cloth. He could tell from the expression on her face that she was adding figures. When Kitty had to add a column of numbers, her face grew stern and cross, as if she suspected treachery at every step. Archer went over and kissed her lightly on the top of her head.

". . . three and nine and carry two," Kitty said aloud. "One more minute, darling. Seventeen, twenty-five, thirty, thirty-four." She wrote down some numbers with a dashing gesture and swung around in her chair, smiling. "Actually," she said, "we can't afford to live any-more."

"I know," Archer said. He kissed her forehead and rubbed his hands alongside her cheeks.

"The butcher," Kitty said, "ought to be arrested by the Government."

Archer grinned and moved over to his easy chair and sank into it gratefully. "Man I met today," he said, "is going to present a petition to the UN outlawing meat."

"Tell him," Kitty said, "he has my support."

"Anybody call?"

Each day when he came home he asked the same question, with subdued eagerness, as though he expected, in his hours of absence, some delightful magic to be worked by the telephone company, a sudden honor, a glorious invitation, a surprising windfall to be included in the afternoon's messages, changing the evening and indeed the whole course of his life for the better. Examining his feeling as he waited for Kitty's reply, he knew that this sense of bright expectation marked him once and for all as an optimist. At the age of forty-five, with ten thousand telephone calls behind him, a great many of them announcing sickness, loss, trouble of all kinds, he still connected the ringing of the telephone bell with possible joy. Fundamentally, he thought comfortably, my glands must be functioning well, the bile low, the acid under control, the hormones properly regulated.

"Well," Kitty said, pursing her lips, "let me see. Mary Lowell called to ask us to their house for dinner next Wednesday. Black tie."

Archer made a face.

"Teague Brothers called. Your suit is ready for a fitting. And Mr. Burdick called. He wants to do something with your insurance policy and he wants you to go to the doctor for another examination. Also, he says this quarter's payment is overdue and would you please . . ."

Archer grimaced again. Joy had been absent from the wires this afternoon, at least. Wait for another day.

"A good wife," he said playfully, "would have a better collection of messages waiting for the breadwinner when he got home. That reminds me." He stood up. "I have to make a call. I'll be right back." At the door he stopped. "Vic didn't call from Detroit, did he?" Kitty shook her head.

He went out into the hall, where the telephone was, and dialed Pokorny's number, feeling self-righteous that he wasn't putting it off any longer. A woman's voice answered.

"Hello," Archer said, looking at himself in the mirror, noticing that he had rings under his eyes, "Mrs. Pokorny?"

"Yes?"

"This is Clement Archer. May I speak to Manfred, please?"

There was silence for a moment on the other end of the wire. "What do you want to speak to him about?" Mrs. Pokorny asked. She had a flat Middle-Western accent, cold and unmusical, and her voice was suspicious now and wary.

"I'd have to tell him," Archer said, sighing, and feeling that nothing you did with the musician was un-complicated. "In person."

"He can't come to the phone now," Mrs. Pokorny said. "He's not feeling well."

"Oh, I'm so sorry." Archer tried to inject a tone of sympathy into his voice. "I really must talk to him."

"You could tell me," Mrs. Pokorny said. "We have no secrets."

"I'm sure not," Archer said, laughing falsely, feeling cornered by the resentful prairie voice. "But it's really too long a story to be relayed by anyone else. Actually, I'd like to see him for a half-hour or so."

"The doctor says he can't leave the house," Mrs. Pokorny said, accusingly, as though Archer were to blame. "He has a fever."

Archer thought for a moment. "Would it be possible," he asked, "for me to come and see him this evening?"

"He shouldn't be disturbed."

Pokorny, Archer thought, exasperated, with all his other troubles, is married to a watchdog. "It's really very important, Mrs. Pokorny," he said, trying to keep his voice mild.

"I'm sure it is." Mrs. Pokorny made it sound like a threat.

"I'll make it as short as I can," said Archer. "We really shouldn't delay any longer than necessary. It's about his job."

"What job?" Mrs. Pokorny laughed stonily into the receiver. "He doesn't have any job. You ought to know that. Why don't you leave the man in peace?"

"Please," Archer said, "will you ask him if it's all right for me to come over and see him around eight o'clock? I'm sure he'll want to talk to me."

"I'll ask," Mrs. Pokorny said unpromisingly. She put the phone down hard and the wires crackled in Archer's ear. He waited, conscious that Mrs. Pokorny, whom he had never seen, was his enemy. After what seemed like a long time, he heard her steps, heavy and forbidding, approaching the phone.

"All right," she said curtly. "He'll see you. You mustn't stay more than thirty minutes. He has blood pressure." She hung up before Archer could say anything.

Blood pressure, too, Archer thought. That poor man isn't let off anything. He walked slowly back to his study, wondering what he was going to tell Kitty.

Kitty was studying the movie page of the evening paper when Archer entered the room. "Clement," Kitty said, keeping her finger on a line of print, "there's an English picture in the neighborhood. It starts . . ." she looked down. "It starts at 8:20. I'd love to see it. What do you say we . . ." She stopped, as she looked up and saw in Archer's face that she was going to be denied the treat.

"I'm terribly sorry, darling," Archer said, sitting down. "I have to go out for awhile this evening."

"Where to?" Kitty's voice was curiously harsh and her face showed a sudden suspicion.

"I have to see Pokorny about something."

"Why can't he come over here?"

"He's sick."

"That's convenient, isn't it?" Kitty closed the newspaper and pushed it off the desk onto the floor, childishly angry.

"What do you mean by that?" Archer asked, knowing that he shouldn't argue with her, but angered himself by her gesture of temper.

"I merely mean that it's convenient. That's all. Go out and have a good time with Mr. Pokorny."

"I'm not going out for a good time. I have some work to do with him." Archer rubbed the top of his head nervously, until he remembered that Kitty had once said that she always knew he was lying when he did that.

"Of course," Kitty said. "Of course you have to

work. I suppose you were out working all day, too."

"Actually, I was."

"Actually."

"Now, don't talk like that, Kitty," Archer said, fighting down his annoyance with her.

"I'm not talking like anything." Kitty was staring at him harshly, the whole effect of frailty and youthfulness which her hair and the loose clothing had given her now vanished from her face. "All I said was actually. Actually. Simple, plain little word. Actually."

"I'm sorry about tonight," Archer said, making an attempt to patch things up. "Maybe we can go tomorrow night."

"You might have to work tomorrow night," Kitty said, feigning concern. "I would hate to interfere with your work. I don't think a wife ever ought to interfere with a husband's work, do you?"

"Oh, cut it out," Archer said, letting his impatience show. From time to time Kitty was given to jealous, suspicious moods, and they almost always ended in fights and took days to recover from. Tonight, she was obviously having one of her moods. Archer realized that with her uncomfortable pregnancy, he was more liable than ever to these unreasonable seizures and he knew that he should pamper her. But after the painful day he had spent, he felt the need of pampering himself. "Don't be dreary."

"Maybe I can't help it," Kitty said, her eyes shining dangerously. "Maybe I'm just dreary by nature. I'm a dreary wife. I just sit home here, throwing up and getting jabbed with needles. I'm not out in the big world doing exciting man's work. You have to expect me to be dreary."

"I'm sorry," Archer said, resenting being forced into the apology. "I shouldn't have said that."

"Why not? That's what you meant."

"I didn't mean it." Archer sighed.

"Now we enter the sighing department." Kitty

smiled, her mouth making a brittle grimace. "The poor tired artist after a hard day at the office, or wherever he was, being badgered by his stupid wife."

"Now, look here, Kitty, what do you want? Do you want a minute-by-minute report on where I've been all day?" Even as he said it, he tried to arrange the history of the day plausibly, to account for his time without telling Kitty precisely how he had been involved.

"I'm not interested," Kitty said, essaying grandeur. "Not in the least bit."

"I had to see various people on the program," Archer said doggedly. "Some things have come up that had to be cleared up."

"What things?"

"Technical things. It would take too long to explain."

"Oh," Kitty said brightly. "Technical things. That's convenient, too. I couldn't be expected to know how to understand technical things. That's for big, smart, grownup men, not for backward women who only know how to sit home and have babies."

"Oh, for God's sake, Kitty," Archer said loudly, "stop feeling sorry for yourself."

"And I'm sure," Kitty said, ignoring the jibe, "that tonight there are some more technical things to be attended to. Until what time? Eleven? Twelve? Five o'clock in the morning?"

"I'll be home by ten o'clock."

"Well, thank you, Mr. Archer," Kitty said in a high, artificial voice. "Don't trouble yourself on my account. I've been home alone all day and I'm sure I can keep myself amused all night. Look, Clement," she said evenly, "I'm not blind. I've been able to see that something's happening. You've been locked in yourself for days now. I haven't been able to connect with you at all. If that's the way you want it, that's all right with me. Only don't lie about it."

"I'm not lying," Archer said desperately. "I had to

see Motherwell today, and Atlas, and Alice Weller, and I went to Mrs. Creighton's for a workout."

"Motherwell and Atlas," Kitty nodded, pretending to be reasonable. "You've been doing the program for four years and seeing them once a week, on Thursday, and now you have to spend the whole week with them."

"It isn't the whole week," Archer said wearily. "And something special has come up."

"What?" Kitty challenged him.

"Nothing important." Archer started to sigh and checked it. "It's too boring to talk about."

"Too boring. Of course. How good of you to spare me!"

"Please," Archer said. "I'm tired and I'd like my dinner. I have to be at Pokorny's at eight o'clock."

"You're hiding something from me," Kitty said loudly. "I can tell. Something bad. You don't have to tell me. I don't want to know. I just want you to know that you're not fooling me."

"I'm not trying to fool you. I . . ."

"You're pushing me out," Kitty went on, her voice rising and bitter. "You're building a wall and putting me on the other side. You're mixed up in something, and I'm helpless here, stuck in this house, sick, looking like this . . ." She stared down bitterly at the ungainly swell of her skirt. "My skin's bad and my hair is awful and I look terrible, and you're escaping."

Then he knew he would have to tell her. He went over to her and gently took her hands. "Kitty, darling," he said, conscious that she was keeping her hands limp and unfriendly within his, "listen carefully. You're right. I *have* been hiding something. I *am* mixed up in something. I tried to keep it from you because I didn't want to upset you. I'm sorry I was so clumsy about it and made you worry."

Slowly, the hard, suspicious expression on Kitty's face was dissolving and Archer could feel her hands gripping his now as she looked into his eyes.

"It's about the program," Archer said, choosing his words thoughtfully. "It has nothing to do with you or me." Then he told her what had been happening, starting with the conversation with O'Neill on Thursday night. He spoke calmly, trying to make the situation sound annoying and unpleasant rather than dangerous, and he didn't tell Kitty about his offer to quit his job. She listened intently as he told her of his interviews with Motherwell, Atlas and Alice Weller.

"I haven't been able to speak with Vic yet," Archer said, "and I don't want to make any move until I do. In the meantime," he smiled ruefully, "when you see me sitting in a chair and staring at the ceiling, you'll know I'm reflecting on Karl Marx and not about blondes or redheads."

Kitty smiled, too, but grew sober immediately. "Thank you for telling me," she said. "You be as quiet and as moody as you want. If you want to talk about it to me at any time, I'm here. If you'd rather forget about it when you're home, I'll understand. And whatever you decide to do about it finally is OK with me. Whatever it is, I know it'll be right . . ."

"Kitty . . . Kitty . . ." Archer said softly. "Imagine a wife saying that to her husband after nineteen years of marriage!"

Kitty kissed him swiftly. "I mean it," she said soberly. "I mean it absolutely."

"I hope you're right," Archer said. "Oh, God, I hope you're right."

He pulled her to him and kissed her, hard. They were standing that way when Gloria came in and said, "Dinner's ready, Mis' Archer," and they moved apart, laughing a little embarrassedly, because people didn't kiss like that in front of the maid after they had been married nineteen years.

12

Archer sat across the table and watched Pokorny eat. Luckily, Mrs. Pokorny wasn't home, and Archer could not help glancing at the clock, hoping to get the discussion finished before she returned. The tendency to look away from Pokorny was strong, anyway. He was dressed in a bright orange rayon dressing-gown and had a rumpled towel around his neck. The dressing-gown was stained with old food, and as Pokorny brought up his spoon from the soup bowl before him, holding the spoon with all his fingers, his knuckles fist-like and clumsy over the handle, new drippings were added to the collection on the dressing-gown with each mouthful. Pokorny also ate very noisily, making avid sucking sounds as the liquid went in over his false teeth. With the soup he ate thick slices of bread, filling his mouth incessantly, as though he weren't sure he would ever eat again. He needed a shave and his skin was greenish and lumpy under his uncombed gray hair. He kept shuffling his carpet-slippered feet constantly, in a hasty rhythm, in time with the shovel-like motions of the spoon.

How much easier it is, Archer thought, as he talked, to pity a man with good table manners.

He had been brief, frank and thorough with Pokorny. Deception, he had decided, which might be kindlier at the moment, would be more painful in the long run. "So," he said, concluding, "Hutt was absolutely firm about you. He says he has information that you perjured yourself to get into the country and that the Immigration Department is going to call you up on it. And to save the others, I had to agree about you."

"Yes. Of course." Pokorny made a particularly wet noise with a spoonful of soup and a damp lump of bread. "I understand. It is necessary to try to save the others. You are my friend. I am convinced." His teeth seemed to slide moistly behind his wet bow lips. Archer found himself looking away, fixing his attention on the carved cuckoo clock on the wall, trying to make no judgment on the unprepossessing face across the table. "It is good of you to tell me the truth. The others—the other agency—they didn't tell me anything. Just goodbye. No explanation." He took out a handkerchief and wiped his mouth. "That is not polite. I worked for them for three years. I deserved better than that. And I knew the Immigration was investigating me again. They went to friends of mine, asking questions, and my friends called me." Pokorny resumed the nervous, greedy rhythm of his eating. "I thought there was a connection, but I wasn't sure. Mr. Hutt is my enemy."

"No," Archer said gently. "It's not that. He's being careful, according to his lights."

"He is my enemy," Pokorny said. "I know. I have seen the way he looked at me. I know how it is when people look at me like that."

Archer tried to remember if he had noticed any special expression in Hutt's face when he talked to Pokorny. "That's the way he looks at everybody," Archer said, trying to make Pokorny keep from feeling singularly persecuted. "He has a cold manner."

"Very cold." Pokorny nodded vigorously. "Very special for me. Also—the conservatory where I teach.

Harmony and counterpoint. They are dropping me too for next term."

"I'm sorry," Archer said, looking at the grand piano, messily covered with music sheets, that made the living room seem small and crowded.

"I expected it," Pokorny said. "When it begins to happen bad, everything goes bad."

"Don't be too downhearted, Manfred," Archer said, trying to sound hopeful, and forcing himself to look directly at the composer. "It's not over yet. If you get a clean bill of health from the Immigration authorities, I'm sure you can come back and . . ."

"I'm not going to get a clean bill of health from the Immigration authorities." Pokorny leaned over and filled his plate again from the heavy crockery tureen in the middle of the table. "My wife. My ex-wife. She has been talking to them. She's out of her mind. She walks the streets, but she is out of her mind. She hates me. I know some of the things she tells the Government. Finally, she will be happy. I'll be sent back to Austria and she will be happy."

"Don't be so pessimistic," Archer said, annoyed at Pokorny's quick surrender to despair. "I'm sure you'll get a chance to give all the facts."

"All the facts." Pokorny tried to laugh, but his eyes, behind his glasses, misted over by the steam from the soup, were frightened and sober. "Why do you think that all the facts will do me any good?"

"The truth is, Manfred," Archer said, as Pokorny bent low over his plate, "the truth is I've known you a long time and I've never heard you say anything that anyone could possibly hold against you."

"Yes," Pokorny said. "Maybe you will come and say that to the Inspector."

"Of course," Archer said, feeling uneasily that he would rather not. "Anytime you need a witness."

"Oh, I will need a witness. I will need hundreds of witnesses. Let me advise you something, Mr. Archer.

Be careful. Don't be too good a friend to me. You will be hurt, too."

"Nonsense," Archer said sharply. "I won't tell any lies. I'll just say what I know about you."

"What do you know about me?" Pokorny looked up from his soup, his mouth quivering. "If I may beg your pardon, you know nothing. What have we ever said to each other? We work on the program, you say, 'Manfred, I need fifteen seconds of music here. The music last week was good. Or the music last week was just so-so, let's make it better next week . . .' You're polite to me. You listen to me even when I am unreasonable and I talk too fast. You make a little fun of me, how excitable I am, the way I dress, when I am not there . . ." Pokorny spread his hand and shook his head as though to forestall denial. "No, no. I don't care. It is without malice, because you are not a malicious man, Mr. Archer. It is friendly, it is a human comment on my personality. But more fundamentally, have we ever touched? This is the first time you have ever been to my house. You have not met my wife. I have been to your house only to work once in awhile, and after the work is over, we don't know what to say to each other. I wait for five minutes and I leave. Now, all of a sudden, you find yourself involved in my troubles. I wouldn't blame you if you said, 'What is that funny little man to me? He is a machine I take out of the closet every Thursday night. The machine is now out of order, I will get another machine.'"

"That isn't the way it is at all," Archer said quietly.

"No," Pokorny said. "Of course not. I know it isn't. All I was saying is that I wouldn't blame you . . ."

"I came up here, Manfred," said Archer, forcing himself to look at the wild-haired little man, bent over the plate, inaccurately spooning up soup, "to help you if I could."

"Why?" Pokorny sat up, spoon caught in midair, and looked challengingly at Archer.

"Because I admire you as an artist. Because you wrote music for me conscientiously and well for three years," Archer said, feeling that this was only a small part of the truth, if it was true at all. "Because I know you. Maybe that's it."

"Would you still want to help me," Pokorny asked, bending down again, "if I told you that Mr. Hutt was right? If you knew that I *did* perjure myself to enter the country?"

Everybody is guilty of everything, Archer thought sinkingly. Nobody is innocent of any charge. Describe a crime and I will find a friend to fit it. "That would depend," Archer said, feeling that he was being evasive, "on all the facts."

"All the facts." Pokorny pushed the plate away from him. He took out his handkerchief again and wiped his mouth, not quite catching all the leakage. "If I give you all the facts, will you keep them secret?"

"I can't promise anything. Don't tell me anything you feel it would be harmful for me to know."

"Then you would feel I was hiding something from you," Pokorny said, peering near-sightedly at Archer. "You would begin to believe everything you heard about me, because you could not check. I would be a question mark in your brain. 'Pokorny,' you would say, 'he is a doubtful character. He must have plenty to hide.' All right!" Pokorny stood up abruptly, the orange robe swinging open to reveal a pudgy, pale, hairless breast. "I will tell you everything. What's the difference? I can't lie, anyway. I don't have the temperament to hide anything. My face is my own lie-detector. The portable model. Ask me a question, I get nervous, in a minute I give the answer, even if I know I should keep quiet. It's the way I am. I am like the radio networks—I am on the air twenty-four hours a day." He laughed weakly at his own joke, then padded over to a library table on which there was a plate of grapes. He offered the grapes to Archer. "Would you like some? In the middle of the winter. The American way of life. Refrigeration. From the Argentine." He stuffed five or six of the grapes into his mouth, tearing them off the main stem with his teeth and chewing them, seeds and all. "Tasteless," he said thickly, carrying the plate with him and coming back to the table and sitting down. "I eat all the time. It is a disease. I feel that there is a hollow in me. The doctor says I am overweight. The arteries are undecided. They do not know whether they should continue working for me or give their notice." He chuckled again, morbidly, as he put some more grapes into his mouth. "The doctor says I must lose twenty-five pounds or he cannot be responsible. I tell him I don't like to be responsible for my arteries, either, but the doctor doesn't laugh, he doesn't enjoy the European type of humor in the medical field. The calories, he says, are disastrous, he predicts a stroke. I tell him about the hollow inside me, but he says it is all psychological. He is young, very modern, he is always saying 'psychosomatic.' When I die, he will try to perform an autopsy, I'm sure. He looks at me and I can see it in his eye. He is bothered already he will have to cut through so much fat. He will investigate and write a paper on the psychosomatic hollows in Viennese composers with blood pressure. See—I finally have found I can have a conversation with you. Trouble—it loosens the tongue, gives you subject for discussion. The facts." Pokorny ran his tongue around his teeth, sucking at grapeskin. "I promised the facts. And you promised nothing. It is my kind of bargain. That's what my wife would tell me. She is a woman who does not have any illusions about me. You will meet her later, but please do not take everything she says too seriously. She is disappointed in the world —for my sake. She thinks I am neglected and she hits back. Ah—I see you are moving your feet. You are impatient. You are saying, he is a disorderly fat man. Why doesn't he come to the point?"

"Take your time," Archer said carefully, recognizing that Pokorny was nervously postponing the moment when he would have to expose himself. "I have nothing else to do tonight."

Pokorny pushed the plate of grapes away from him. "Don't tell her that I had grapes. She is scientific, too, she knows all about sugar content and fat deposits in the blood vessels. All Americans are scientific, there are amazing articles every Sunday in the New York *Times*. She is opposed to my having a stroke. She calls the doctor on the phone and informs on me. She says, 'He had two rolls and a quarter of pound of butter for breakfast.' She tells me if I have a stroke and I am paralyzed I will have to find another wife. She is trying to frighten me into being young and healthy. She is very fond of me. She sits and listens to me play my compositions on the piano and she closes her eyes and cries. She has no more ear than a camel, but she cries just the same, out of loyalty. The doctor said sex was dangerous, too. He is very modern, he calls it relations. The strain on the heart muscles. Everything is dangerous these days, grapes, your wife, writing music for the radio. It's the times we live in. When I was younger, it never occurred to us—food, love and music might be fatal." Pokorny sat hunched over the table, restlessly playing with the stained towel around his throat, opening it, pulling it closer, talking more and more swiftly, as though his thoughts were rushing to his tongue, as though the necessity of talking on one subject to a man he had barely spoken to before this had freed a flood of other information that had to come out, in an eruption of confession. Archer tried to keep his face impassive. He listened carefully, attempting to catch and remember the word here and there that was useful in the spate of revelations. Conscientiously, he tried to keep himself from being disgusted or critical or pitying.

"My wife is at the root of my troubles," Pokorny said. "It sounds ungallant, not the sort of thing an artist

from romantic Vienna ought to say. But I love her, so
I can be ungallant about her. She is at a meeting tonight, but she will be home soon. She'll look at the
soup and tell me I had too much and she'll threaten me
that she won't bring white bread into the house any
more. She's always at meetings. She's a Communist.
She's very important; it's surprising how they listen to
her. That's why they're getting after me, the Immigration, they see my wife's name on everything. I will get
deported because I married an American lady who was
born in Davenport, Iowa. Love is upside-down too.
When there was the strike on the waterfront, she
brought a boy here with his head split wide open.
Another quarter of an inch and you could have seen
his brain. The police were looking for him and we hid
him. He slept in our bed and we put a mattress on the
floor in here for ourselves. She would walk through
blood for her ideas. She would be very dangerous if
she got the chance. She should never be put in charge
of anything. If I get deported, she will lead a parade to
the dock, with signs about the war-mongers. I would
never recover from it."

"Look, Manfred," Archer said, dazed by the com-
plexity of the life he was uncovering and feeling that
he had to interrupt and warn the man, "you don't have
to tell me anything about your wife. That has nothing
to do with the program or with you."

"I beg your pardon, Mr. Archer," Pokorny said
formally, "that is where you're wrong. It has everything
to do with it. She is well known. She is extreme. She
draws attention to me. I cannot bear attention. I had
one hope—to be quiet, to be anonymous. My wife has
a file in the FBI this thick . . ." Pokorny's pudgy hands
indicated ten inches in the air. "What does it say in the
file? Mrs. Manfred Pokorny, married to a refugee, who
entered this country on an alien's permit in 1940.
Never took out citizenship papers. Now working on the
radio. Next step, Mr. Hutt. Next step—good-bye. I tell
you all these things about my wife because it doesn't

make any difference. It's all known. And even if it isn't, all they have to do is ask me. I'm excitable, I'm weak, I'm afraid of prison. The only time I'm calm is when I am composing music. Even when I eat—you noticed—it is like a whirlpool."

"Still," Archer said, almost successfully hiding his dislike of Pokorny's voluble terror, "you haven't told me anything that would warrant deporting you."

"No," Pokorny said, automatically reaching for the grapes again, "not yet. So—in 1940—I made out my application for entering the United States. I was in Mexico. I was living on seven dollars a week. I had a violin, a good violin, a Guarnerius, and I sold it. It was the last thing I had to sell. The Mexicans were getting ready to put me out of their country. My wife—my first wife, I married her in Vienna in 1921—kept telling me she was going to kill herself if we were pushed out again. We had been in France, in Morocco, in Santo Domingo. Some musicians in America—people who had played some of my music—I had a little vogue before the war—in the style of Schoenberg—they vouched for me. On the application they asked me—was I ever a member of a communist party, anywhere . . ."

He hesitated. Archer watched him intently. Pokorny was sweating, little rivulets sliding down the loose rolls of fat on his neck.

"What should I say?" Pokorny asked. "I have seventy dollars in my wallet. I am a Jew. My mother and father are already dead in the crematoriums . . . it sounds calm when you say it like that. It almost sounds natural. Neat. But when you remember what your mother looked like, standing over the stove, cooking dinner. Dressed up for Sunday in a black lace dress. When you remember going to hear your father in the symphony orchestra . . . He played the flute. He never was very good, really, speaking as a musician, now, not as a son . . ."

Pokorny's mouth, stuffed with grapes, was trembling

and Archer realized that the composer was on the verge of tears. "Look," Archer said gently, "you don't have to tell me anything more just now. You're feeling badly tonight, your wife told me you had a fever. You probably ought to be in bed. Maybe this is too painful for you. I don't have to hear it now. I'll come back some other time, Manfred, when you're feeling better."

"What do you put on the application?" Pokorny said, ignoring Archer. "America is just over the border. Twenty miles away. Everybody is being kind. Everybody is being sympathetic. Everybody wants to help. If you say yes . . ." He shrugged. "You vanish. You sink. You are obliterated. If you say no—two little scratches of the pen—you're alive, you're a musician, you exist . . . Yes or no. On a form, the questions sometimes are too simple. Whatever you say is the wrong answer. A man's life can't be described sometimes in yes or no. In Vienna, in 1922, I joined the Austrian Communist Party. There. Now you know. But does yes or no tell anybody what it was like in Vienna in 1922? Inflation, strikes, starving, speeches, promises—can you put that in yes or no? And I quit two months later. Even my wife will have to admit that, and I know she's told the Immigration about me, because she said she would, when I divorced her and married Diana . . ."

Diana. Archer felt himself being hypnotized by the name. Diana and Manfred Pokorny. Names for the low-comedy servants in a musical comedy. It was almost impossible to assign them to tragic parts. Diana Pokorny, with a cornbelt accent, commissar for the waterfront regions. Parents, Archer thought, must have more respect on the day of christening, for the mortal possibilities lying in the future for their children.

"She's crazy," Pokorny said. "My first wife. She is always coming up here making scenes. She brought a pistol once, but it didn't have a hammer on it, but we didn't find that out until later. I give her sixty dollars a week in alimony, but she's always sick and she always keeps trying the most expensive medicines. Now it's cortisone. She knows a doctor who wants to experiment on her, but it costs three hundred dollars for a treatment. And she went to an analyst for six years."

Archer felt a grin pulling at his mouth and turned his head so that Pokorny wouldn't see it. It was heartless to smile, he knew, but the complexities Pokorny had brought about in his life by his choice of women were, considered at all objectively, melodramatically ludicrous. And somehow, and Archer was displeased with himself at the realization, Pokorny with all his agony did not touch him. Perhaps, Archer thought, if he combed his hair and stopped stuffing his mouth with Argentine grapes . . . If he has to go before the Immigration board, Archer resolved, I will make him go to a barber first, and make certain he puts on fresh linen.

"I quit because they were idiots," Pokorny was saying. His voice had become tired and he was resting his head in his hands, his elbows on the table. His skin was flushed now and he looked as though his fever were mounting. "The Communists. They began to tell me what kind of music to write, what kind of music I should listen to, what I should applaud, what I should not applaud. Politicians who didn't know the difference between a sonata and a bugle call. I was writing an opera then and I found out the librettist had ten thousand collaborators. They didn't listen to an opera with their ears—they listened with a copy of Lenin's collected pamphlets. I figured if they were that wrong in my field that I knew about, they were probably almost as wrong in other fields that I didn't know about. So I drifted out. I wasn't important, I was twenty-three years old—so they didn't bother me and I didn't bother them . . . I tell Diana, but it will take an explosion to change her mind. She says I'm an unreliable intellectual." Pokorny essayed a wan smile. "She's half-right, anyway. Still—sitting in that hot little room in Mexico, living off the last of the violin, what do you do when you see the question, 'Were you ever a member of any communist party in any country?' Yes or no. How truthful do you have to be? Who do you hurt? What does a man do to survive? How much are you expected to suffer for two months of your life seventeen years before when you were twenty-three years old, in another country? Now . . ." Pokorny shrugged helplessly. "They will produce the paper. They will say is this your signature. They will say is everything written on this paper true. My first wife will be sitting there, looking at me, hating me, knowing all about me. My advice to you, Mr. Archer, is keep away from me, don't try to help me. Deny you ever knew me. Say that the music was delivered by an agent and that he told you it was being written by a man called Smith. Say that you didn't know I was a Jew."

"Now, Manfred," Archer said, remembering that Barbante had warned him about this, "that's unfair. Whatever else is behind this, it has nothing to do with being Jewish."

"Yes, it has," Pokorny spoke softly, but stubbornly. "It always has."

Archer stared exasperatedly at Pokorny. Atlas, Pokorny, comedian, composer, both remote, untouchable, lost in their private dementia. No matter what food was served them, they always tasted the same single, bitter flavor.

"You say that Mr. Hutt wants to fire four other people, too," Pokorny was saying, using logic to torture himself. "But with the others he is willing to give them a chance, wait two weeks. But with me—" He smiled unhealthily. "I have the honor to be particularly chosen. I am treated promptly. There is no waiting on line for me. The others, now, they are not Jews, I gather?"

"No." This is the worst so far, Archer thought. I knew it would be.

"Why do you think I get this personal service, Mr.

Archer?" There was even a small smile of triumph on Pokorny's face, as though he were delighted with his success in debate.

"I don't know," Archer said.

"I do," said Pokorny, almost in a whisper. "Mr. Hutt hates the Jews."

"Oh, God, Manfred," Archer said, "that's outlandish. I've never heard him say a word."

"He doesn't have to say a word. He looks. When he looks at me, I see the same expression on his face I used to see on the Nazis in Vienna. Waiting. Hating. Confident. Five years later they pushed my father into the furnace."

"You're out of your mind," Archer said. "And that's not just a way of speaking. I mean it. You're demented."

"Maybe." Pokorny shrugged. "I hope you're right. I don't think so. I have had experience. You couldn't know, Mr. Archer. You're an intelligent man, but you haven't had the experience. Also—you're too good. There's nothing in your character to answer to that look—to understand it even. And do you know what the worst thing is?"

"What?" Archer asked, wearily feeling that he might as well get the whole thing out now, get it done once and for all.

"When I see Mr. Hutt look at me like that, even for a minute, even just passing him in the hall, I suffer from a trick. It makes me see myself with Mr. Hutt's eyes. I look at myself and I'm dirty, my face is ugly, my voice is bad, my accent is unpleasant, I am too anxious to please one minute and I yell too loud the next minute. I am not nice to have sitting at the next seat in the theatre or in a restaurant and I understand why it is impossible to allow me into a good club or a hotel. I'm a miser, worrying about money all the time. I'm extravagant, wearing diamonds, throwing my money around. I'm a plotter, I can't be trusted, I understand the necessity for the furnace . . ."

"That's enough, Manfred." Archer stood up. He felt shaken and furious and he realized it would give him pleasure to slap the fat, aging, disagreeable face on the other side of the table. "I'm not going to listen to any more of that. You're behaving like a fool."

Pokorny stood up, too, sniffing wetly, wrapping the stained robe around his pudgy body. "I think maybe you better stop worrying about me, Mr. Archer," he said. "Never mind about being a witness. It wouldn't make any difference, anyway. On black and white, I committed a crime. Nothing anybody is ever going to say can change that. I will write you from Austria." Suddenly he broke. He turned clumsily and shambled over to the wall. He put his head against the wall and Archer could tell he was crying. "How can I go back? he sobbed. "How can I go back there?"

There was the noise of a door opening in the hall and a moment later Mrs. Pokorny came in. She was at least six feet tall, square set, with a heavy, angry head, surmounted by a closely cut mop of iron-gray hair. She stood at the doorway, her large hands opening and closing at her sides, staring first at her husband, tragically bent against the wall, and then at Archer.

"Who are you?" she demanded. Her voice was booming and harsh. "What did you do to him?"

"I'm Clement Archer," said Archer, feeling that it was ludicrous to introduce himself so formally at a time like this. "He's all right . . ." Archer gestured vaguely at Pokorny. "He worked himself up a bit and . . ."

"Manfred!" Mrs. Pokorny shouted. "Stop that!" Her face grew very red. She strode across the room and put her hands on Pokorny's shoulders and turned him brusquely around. Pokorny barely came up to her shoulder. His face was wet and he took the end of the towel that was around his neck and wiped his cheeks. He was trying to control himself, but he couldn't raise his eyes to look either at Archer or his wife.

What a scene, Archer thought, feeling an almost uncontrollable impulse to flee the room, the house, the man, the problem. What a ridiculous scene. How did I ever get mixed up in something like this?

"Diana," Pokorny murmured. He patted the large, flat hand on his shoulder. "I'm sorry." He half-looked at Archer. "I apologize, Mr. Archer," he said, "for the embarrassment."

"Sit down," the woman said to Pokorny. Roughly, before releasing him, she pulled the towel close around his throat and yanked the robe tighter around his chest. "Sit down and behave yourself."

Obediently, releasing a last few sniffles, Pokorny padded over to an armchair and sat down in it, keeping his head bent and staring at the carpet.

"What did you do to him?" Mrs. Pokorny turned on Archer.

"He didn't do anything," Pokorny said hurriedly. "He's a good friend. He took the trouble of coming up here to explain to me . . ."

"What did he explain?" Mrs. Pokorny made no attempt to hide the doubt and suspicion in her voice. She stood, enormous, square, ugly, at the other end of the room, looking oversized and out of place among the flimsy furniture and the Tyrolean ornaments on the walls. She had a thick, long nose, with flaring, angry nostrils, and her mouth was wide and thin, cruel as a police sergeant's.

"Mrs. Pokorny," Archer began gently, "I came to try to help Manfred if I could . . ."

"How? By firing him?" Mrs. Pokorny laughed flatly. "Is that how you help people these days?"

"It isn't his fault," Pokorny said hurriedly. "He has to do what he is told. He is my friend."

The word friend, Archer realized, was a talisman for Pokorny, and he clutched it to him like an infant holding a fuzzy toy animal at bedtime.

"If he's such a friend," Mrs. Pokorny said, "why

doesn't he keep you on the program? Did he explain that?"

"It's out of his hands," Pokorny said, looking up finally. "It's the old Immigration business again. He was good enough to warn me."

"Oh," Mrs. Pokorny said, her large thick face frozen in a grimace of scorn, "they got you to do the dirty work. The tool."

"Now, Diana," Pokorny said mildly, "don't talk like that to Mr. Archer."

Mrs. Pokorny strode toward Archer, ignoring her husband. "It never occurred to your friend to fight for you, though, did it? His friendship doesn't go that far, does it? He doesn't raise a finger to keep you from being sent back to a country where all your people have been murdered."

"He's been very good to me, Diana," Pokorny murmured brokenly. "He's a very good man, very honest and upright."

"I'll believe that," Mrs. Pokorny said, standing close to Archer, glaring at him, "when I see him do something for you."

"I don't know what I can do," Archer said mildly. He felt curiously removed from the scene and untouched. Mrs. Pokorny, he saw, had a talent for removing any element of sympathy and gentleness from a situation. "It's very complicated."

"Complicated!" Mrs. Pokorny sneered. "If it's not one excuse it's another with people like you. I know your type, Mr. Archer. Pretending to help, being so honorable and polite all the time, then always finding a convenient way out when it begins to look as though you might be hurt. I know all about you. Weak, useless, ready to let the bosses use you, giving full value for your salaries, licking their boots, lying down and letting them walk all over you when it suits them. Now they want to drive the artists from the country, they want to shut up the ones they can't send away, and who is

the first one they pick on to do their dirty work . . ."
She turned oratorically to Pokorny and made a stiff,
heavy, pointing gesture in Archer's direction. "Your
good friend, Mr. Archer."

"Mrs. Pokorny," Archer said quietly, untouched, "if
you will come down off the editorial page of the *Daily
Worker* for a moment, perhaps we can talk about this
reasonably."

"Please, Diana . . ." Pokorny got up and put his
hand appealingly on his wife's arm as she turned
broadside on Archer. She shrugged off her husband's
hand savagely.

"That's right," she said loudly. "That's the line. I
expected it, but it came sooner than I thought. One
word of truth and you retreat to your standard argument—Red! Red!"

"Not so loud, please," Pokorny whispered troubledly,
looking around him as though he half expected to see
secret agents spring from the walls. "Please, isn't it
possible to talk in a lower tone of voice . . ."

"Hopeless," Mrs. Pokorny said, louder than ever.
"Every once in awhile I let myself be fooled—I think
that finally people like you can be educated, that you
can be made into useful citizens. Then something like
this comes up and I know I've been fooling myself.
You're useless. You're a drag on the future. Finally,
you're always on the wrong side. In the end you and
your whole class have to be wiped out."

"Diana . . ." Pokorny murmured unhappily.

"Wiped out!" she shouted. "Surgery!"

"Diana," Pokorny grabbed her arm and shook it like
a puppy. "You don't know what you're talking about.
You mustn't say things like that. It isn't right. It's . . ."

"You." Mrs. Pokorny wheeled and stared down at
her husband, her face contorted with loathing. "You
go to bed. You're a sick man. You don't know enough
to blow your nose by yourself. If I let you, you'd kiss
his boots after he kicked you. You always disappoint

me. I listen to your music and I think you're a great man. Then I listen to you talk and I wonder where the music comes from. You're not a man. You're a worm. And worst of all, you *want* to be a worm."

"Diana, darling," Pokorny said reproachfully, backing off.

"I'm going inside." Mrs. Pokorny strode toward the door. "And tell that man I don't want to see him in my house again."

She slammed the bedroom door behind her.

There was silence in the room for a moment. Embarrassedly, Pokorny fiddled with the towel around his throat. Archer ran his hand wearily over his head. Poor Pokorny, he thought, caught at home and abroad. In the line of fire of all batteries of all armies. Every gun zeroed in on the position he has no interest in holding.

"Well, Manfred." Archer went over to him and patted his shoulder. Pokorny smelled of sweat and onions and Archer felt his fingertips uneasy on the soiled rayon of the robe. "I guess I'd better be off."

"Yes." Pokorny looked up at him shyly and painfully. "I'm sorry about Diana."

"Forget it." Archer started toward the front door. Pokorny followed him with nervous little steps.

"I told you about her," Pokorny said. "She's fanatic. She's a very strong person and she has convictions."

Archer couldn't help grinning. He hid the smile with his hands.

"But there are other sides to her," Pokorny said earnestly. "She loves me. No woman has ever been tender to me like Diana . . ."

Helplessly, the vision of the Pokornys in bed together crossed Archer's mind. The pudgy, shabby man and the dreadnought-shaped, ham-handed woman . . . Impossible, Archer thought, you must never think of things like that.

"She's loyal," Pokorny went on, gathering strength. "She has a deep feeling for art. She gave me back my self-respect."

Amazing, Archer thought, the words people use to describe what has happened to them.

Pokorny bustled around Archer, helping him on with his coat. "Mr. Archer," he said, "I want to thank you. For taking the trouble. For coming to see me. For telling me the truth. No matter what happens—I will remember this."

Archer sighed. "Honestly, Manfred," he said, facing the composer, "I don't know what I can do. If anything comes up, I'll get in touch with you."

"Don't trouble yourself with me. Please." Pokorny ducked, reaching into a cupboard. He came up with a package. "I wonder if I can give you a gift, Mr. Archer," he said shyly, offering the package. "It's a quartet of mine. Records. It was just done two weeks ago. It's the only piece of mine that's been recorded in this country. Some time—when you have nothing else to do—you might listen to it."

"Thanks, Manfred. It's very nice of you . . ."

Pokorny waved deprecatingly. "It's just a small piece. Unimportant." He opened the door. "It will give me pleasure to think of you sitting in your nice study in New York, listening to it. Play it in the evening. When it begins to get dark. It's nice music for that time of day."

They shook hands and Archer went out. As he descended the steps he looked up and saw Pokorny standing at the opened door, his faded, long thin hair catching the dim light of the hall lamp.

Outside, Archer looked at his watch. It's not too late, he thought, maybe there's still time to take Kitty to the movies. For the late show.

13

The rehearsal had gone badly all day. The script was drab and lifeless and Barbante, who usually could be depended upon to make helpful last-minute changes, seemed languid and disinterested, yawning widely again and again, as though he had been up all night. The lines he suggested seemed to Archer consistently worse than the ones that had to be replaced. The girl who had been chosen to play the part which Frances Motherwell ordinarily would have done turned out to have a cooing ingénue's voice, cloying and calculatedly sweet, and Archer made a mental note that he was never going to use her again. Alice Weller was nervous and came in late on cues. In the final rehearsal she skipped a whole page and forced Archer to start the show all over again. Atlas was slow and outrageously broad and kept looking up at Archer sardonically after each offense, as though daring him to object. Only Vic Herres seemed immune from the general jitters. He looked very tired, but he played as usual, calmly, with quick intelligence, making the scenes he was in seem vigorous and truthful. He had come in late in the afternoon, directly from the airport, and Archer had only been able to speak to him for a few moments. His mother had passed the crisis and seemed on the road to partial recovery.

Ironically, Pokorny's score had been one of his best, very clever and useful, bridging gaps in the script with nimble arrangements, making flat scenes seem dramatic and tense. Pokorny wasn't in the studio. Archer had called to invite him to the rehearsal, but Mrs. Pokorny, who had answered the phone, had said, coldly, "He can't come. He's sick. He can't get out of bed."

Archer had hired a new composer, a man called Shapiro, who sat uneasily at Archer's shoulder, tapping nervously with his fingers on a stiff notebook all day. Shapiro was a pale young man with lank hair and he did not look promising. As Shapiro listened, Archer could sense the man's spirits almost visibly sinking. Shapiro, it was obvious, knew his talents well enough to realize that he could never do as well as Pokorny. Without saying a word to each other, both Archer and Shapiro knew that there were going to be bad moments ahead in the musical department.

O'Neill came in late, red-faced, moving with elaborate solidity, and smelling of liquor. It was the first time Archer had ever caught O'Neill drinking on the day of a program, so he knew that O'Neill was feeling the strain, too. O'Neill was not wearing his mink-lined coat. He only wore it when he was feeling humorous and satisfied with himself. There's nothing humorous about him today, Archer thought, watching O'Neill sit very straight, bulky in a small chair, keeping his eyes exaggeratedly wide open and making an obvious business of listening to everything that was going on and reacting too often and too energetically. Maybe it has nothing to do with the program, Archer thought, looking for comfort. Maybe he's having trouble with his wife. That'll keep a mink coat in the closet and make three Martinis before five o'clock seem like a necessity for survival.

Hutt had not appeared all day and there was no sign of the sponsor.

Uptown and downtown, it had been a bad week. Thursday, Archer thought, is a day that one should occasionally be allowed to drop from the calendar. All his life, he remembered, Thursday had been a special day. Somehow, his mother always seemed to take him to the dentist on Thursday. And for the two years that she had forced him to take lessons on the piano, the teacher, a sharp, unpleasant woman with pockmarks, had come on Thursday. And examinations in high school in geometry and algebra, subjects which had baffled him, seemed inevitably to come on Thursday. And the worst fight he had ever been in, which had cost him two teeth, had been on a Thursday afternoon, after a piano lesson. Probably, Archer thought, the day I am killed will turn out to be a Thursday.

Archer gave the cast a break a half-hour before the program was scheduled to go on. Most of them left the studio. O'Neill stood up and went out heavily, without talking to Archer. Shapiro left, saying almost apologetically, as though he were not quite sure that he deserved it, "I think I'll get a cup of coffee. Can I bring you anything?"

"No, thanks," Archer said. He sat at the control desk, feeling inelastic and slow, staring through the window at Herres, who was talking desultorily to the sound man.

"Mother," said Brewer, the engineer, who was sitting next to Archer, "we are carrying a full load of gremlins tonight. Look for headwinds and foreign matter in the air. What's the matter with everybody?"

"The approach of spring," Archer said shortly, worried that the engineer had noticed it, too, and wishing that the program was already behind him.

"Something's approaching. That's a cinch." Brewer got up and stretched enormously. "I'm going to go into the hall and get a smoke for my aching nerves. Call me if the wires begin to smoulder." He grinned and patted Archer comfortingly on the back. He started to go, then stopped. "Say, Clement," he said, in a low voice, "what's with this fellow, Shapiro?"

"What about him?" Archer asked defensively.

"You going to use him from now on?"

"Yes." Archer pretended he was busy looking at the script, hoping that Brewer would leave.

"What's the matter with Pokorny?"

"We're trying a change," Archer said. He made a busy, meaningless mark on the page in front of him.

"I'm just the big stupid engineer," Brewer said, "and all my brains are in my fists, but I think Pokorny's job tonight is one of the nicest little things I've heard."

"It's not bad," said Archer. He turned a page ostentatiously.

Brewer looked at him puzzledly. He shrugged. "Sure," he said. He went out, rolling his sleeves down over his huge arms.

Left alone, Archer took off his glasses, closed his eyes and rubbed them gently with his fingertips. I'll have to explain to Brewer, too, he thought wearily. He's too decent a man to be lied to. A vista of explanations loomed before him. To Brewer, to Barbante, to Herres, to friends, to enemies, to people who would approve and to others who would disapprove, all of them curious, all of them with a right to know why he was doing what he did. All my life, Archer thought gloomily, I will probably find myself explaining away these two weeks.

He heard the door click and opened his eyes resentfully.

"Amigo . . ." It was Barbante. Archer swung slowly in his chair and nodded to the writer. The control room filled with the scent of his toilet water as he sat down in an armchair, his legs sprawled luxuriously in front of him. "I saw you sitting here lonely and deserted," Barbante said, yawning, "and I came in to cheer you up."

"Consider me cheered," Archer said.

"God," Barbante said, yawning again, "I'm sleepy."

"I know," said Archer grimly. "That's been plain enough."

Barbante grinned. "I wasn't my usual glittering self today, was I, amigo?"

"You certainly weren't."

"Clement Archer," Barbante said, still smiling comfortably, "the master of the soft answer. Candid Clem, with the cast-iron conscience."

"This script is dead on its feet tonight. And you might just as well have stayed home in bed for all the good you did today."

"You can't win them all, amigo," Barbante said carelessly. "Don't give it another thought. Next Thursday's another week."

"Would it be ungentlemanly on my part," Archer said, "to suggest that you get to bed before three o'clock in the morning next week?"

"OK, Coach," Barbante said, "I'll eat at the training table, too, and I'll do pushups every morning. Say— what're you doing Saturday night?"

"Why?" Archer asked suspiciously.

"I'm giving a little party. Vic's coming. O'Neill. A few other people."

"Thanks," Archer said, a little surprised at the invitation. Barbante had never invited him before. "I'll check with Kitty and see if we're free."

"Oh . . ." Barbante said offhandedly. "Jane's coming, too." He took out his cigarette case and offered it to Archer. Archer looked down at the heavy gold box. There was an inscription on the inside cover. He couldn't read the words, but he saw a signature engraved there, in a woman's flowing handwriting. Probably, he thought, he has a whole collection of gold objects at home, suitably inscribed from satisfied ladies. He must have to search his memory carefully before he goes out each night, to make sure he matches the correct trophy for the particular date.

"No, thanks," Archer said. He watched Barbante put

a cigarette into his mouth and flick a gold lighter, no doubt also inscribed.

"When did you talk to Jane?" Archer asked, carefully keeping his voice flat.

"Last night." Barbante put the lighter away. "On the phone."

Why did he say that? Archer thought. Am I supposed to believe him? Is he making fun of me?

"I told her to bring that nice boy, too . . ." Barbante wrinkled his forehead. "What's his name? Bruce. I remember when I was a kid, I'd have given anything to get invited to a party like this. Actresses, figures in the literary world . . ." His voice was mocking, making little of his guests two nights in advance. "Debutantes with the bloom rubbed off. Divorcées in Dior dresses, equipped with fashionable alimony. Give him something to think about in the physics laboratory."

"Dom," Archer said slowly, "why don't you leave Jane alone?"

"What?" Barbante sounded incredulous, but the look of secret amusement on his face was still there.

"She's only eighteen years old."

"Some of my best friends," Barbante said, "are only eighteen years old."

"She's only a child."

"Why can't we use that line in the script, amigo?" Barbante's tone was not playful and he was staring coldly at Archer, his eyes half-closed, the thick black lashes almost hiding the pupils. "That's a dandy little old line and the script tonight could use something interesting and original like that. All poppas always think their daughters're only children. I once went out with a woman of forty whose father had bedcheck at eleven-thirty every night. And the lady was a nymphomaniac. She'd worked her way through the entire list of the Dramatists' Guild and the New York Philharmonic Orchestra by the time I caught up with her."

"I think it would be more friendly if you left Jane

alone, Dom," Archer said stubbornly, feeling that he was in the wrong, sorry that he had begun this conversation, and hoping that Jane would never hear of it.

"I'm begginning to worry about you, Clem," Barbante said. "The last week or so you've been acting very un-Clem-like. I find you slipping in my estimation, amigo, and I hate to see it happen. You're beginning to behave like all the rest of the frightened little people I know—and I'm surprised and disappointed. I'm not kidding now. Anyway—what're you worried about? You and Kitty're going to be there Saturday night and I told Jane to have Bruce escort her to the party. How much harm do you think I could possibly be planning?"

"OK," Archer said. He stood up. "Forget it." He went out of the control room and into the nearly empty studio. The sound man was crushing cellophane in his hands, making a noise that might be ice breaking or ladies opening candy-boxes at a matinee. Herres had drifted over to the piano and was desultorily picking out "We're Off to See the Wizard, the Wonderful Wizard of Oz," with two fingers, hitting the white keys only.

"Hi," Herres said as Archer approached him. "I saw you conversing with that talented literary chap, Barbante. Did you give him the word on tonight's little gem of wit and poetry?"

"It isn't one of the best, is it?" Archer leaned wearily against the piano.

"You could bottle it and sell it to cure insomnia." Herres used a third finger in a triumphant arrangement. "Put the pheno-barbital people on the rocks in two months."

"I was acting like a father," Archer said. "He's been taking Jane out and I filed a protest. I've never felt sillier." Herres pursed his mouth. He concentrated on the left hand for a moment. "Barbante," he said, "not only vicious himself, but the cause of vice in others."

"I wish Jane was thirty-five years old," Archer said.

"Soon enough. Soon enough," Herres said. "I really wouldn't worry, Clement. She's a solid girl."

"I suppose so." Archer sighed. "The trouble is, Barbante got insulted when I told him to quit, and I couldn't help feeling he was right."

Herres chuckled. "The dilemma of the modern man," he said. "He sees all sides of every question." He stopped playing. He sat and stared for a moment at the keyboard, his head bent, his thick, slightly disarranged blond hair very bright against the mahogany.

"What're you doing tonight," Archer asked, "after the show?"

"Going home," said Herres, "and sleeping for twelve hours. I haven't seen Nancy or the kids yet. And I've had a rugged week, and there was an old lady who puked all the way home from Detroit sitting right next to me in the plane. I'm a tired man."

Archer nodded. "How about tomorrow?" he asked. "I'd like to talk to you for an hour or so."

"I've got an hour show tomorrow night," Vic said. "We start rehearsal at ten in the morning and that maniac Lewis is directing it. By the time I get through I won't be fit to talk to anybody." He glanced curiously at Archer. "Can't it wait?"

"Not too long," said Archer.

"There's something funny going on," Vic said. "Nobody around here seems happy with nobody. What's been happening?"

"I'll tell you when we're alone," said Archer.

"How about Saturday? Why don't you come up to my place around one in the afternoon? I'll give you a drink and we'll launch the week-end."

Archer nodded. "Saturday. At one," he said.

Vic hit two notes on the piano. "You look bushed, kid," he said. "What's wrong?"

"I'll tell you Saturday," Archer said.

The door to the studio opened and Levy, the musical director, came in. He nodded to Vic and said, "Clem, I wonder if I could have a word with you."

"Go ahead," Vic said, beginning to play again. "I have to practice. I only have twelve more years before my debut at Carnegie Hall."

Archer followed Levy over to a corner of the studio. Levy was a tall, intense-looking young man, with a nervous, handsome face. Archer had worked with him ever since his first days in radio and they had hit it off well from the beginning. There was no nonsense about Levy. He was intelligent and without vanity and there never was any need to pamper him or waste your energies being tactful when you were working with him.

"Listen, Clem," Levy said in a low voice, standing close to Archer in the corner, "I'd like to know what's going on with Pokorny."

Archer sighed. Another man who deserved an explanation. "He's out, Jack," Archer said. "For the time being."

Levy shook his head gravely. "I guess you know what you're doing," he said, "but you can't get anyone better. He's a pest and I'm in one of my periods with him. I've forbidden him to talk to me. But I've got to admit—week in and week out, he does an awfully fine job."

Archer smiled wanly. It was a recurring drama between Pokorny and the musical director. Each year there would be a period of three of four weeks when Pokorny was reduced to sending notes into the music room by emissaries. Nobody but Pokorny ever took the situation seriously and each time there would be an emotional reconciliation, with Pokorny throwing his arms around Levy, and shouting, "I forgive you, my son. I forgive everything you have done to me."

"I know," Archer said. "He was prostrated by the trumpets last week."

"Why is he out, Clem?" Levy asked.

Archer hesitated. There had always been a brisk, time-saving candor in his relations with the music director. It would have been a relief to be able to tell him the truth now. "I can't say," Archer said softly. "Not tonight. I'm sorry."

Levy looked puzzled and Archer could tell that he was hurt. "You know, Clem," he said, "the music's supposed to be my department."

"I know. This has nothing to do with music. I can tell you that much."

"Oh." Levy scratched his head. "A composer gets fired, but it has nothing to do with music."

"Yes."

"Complicated, isn't it?"

"A little," Archer agreed. "Listen, Jack, will you go along with me for a while. On faith?"

"Of course," Levy said quickly.

"I'll tell you the whole story. But not now. In a week. Two weeks. I promise. Fair enough?"

"Fair enough." Levy nodded, although Archer could tell he was not quite satisfied.

"Thanks, Jack," Archer said.

"Now," said Levy, "about the new one . . ."

"What about him?" Archer realized uncomfortably that his voice sounded defensive and pugnacious.

"What's the matter, Clem?" Levy asked softly. "What's happening?"

"Nothing's happening. What about the new one?"

"O'Neill called me on Monday," Levy said, "and told me Pokorny was through and asked me to suggest another composer."

O'Neill and his Monday-morning telephone calls, passing trouble all around the city electrically. Momentarily, Archer felt a surge of sympathy for the agency man. Poor O'Neill, Archer thought, he certainly earns his money.

"For this kind of work, you can't get anybody who can touch Pokorny," Levy said, "and I told O'Neill that."

"Yes," Archer said impatiently. "Let's not go into that again."

"There's only one man I know," Levy said, restraining his temper, "who's in the same class and available and I gave his name to O'Neill. Freddie McCormick. When O'Neill hung up I was under the impression he was going to get McCormick. Then when I came into the studio this morning I saw that drip, Shapiro."

"I talked to O'Neill," Archer said, "and I said I wanted Shapiro."

"Why?" Levy made an eloquent, disapproving face. "You're going to get the dreariest collection of sounds you ever heard out of that fellow. I wouldn't hire him to make the arrangements for a three-piece band for the annual dance of a deaf-and-dumb walking society."

"I've heard some of his stuff," Archer said falsely, "and I don't think it's so bad."

"Clem . . ." Levy said reproachfully. "Don't kid your old friends in the business."

"I'm not going to argue with you," Archer said loudly. "Shapiro is hired."

"Why?" Levy persisted.

Why? Archer thought, feeling cornered. Because his name is Shapiro and because McCormick's name is McCormick. Because Archer had to prove to Manfred Pokorny that he was not being persecuted because he was a Jew. And how could you tell that to a man named Levy? Because Archer was ashamed of being moved by motives like that, ashamed of being caught in Pokorny's sickness, ashamed of behaving in a manner that was essentially dishonest and false, ashamed that here, in yet another department of his life, in his relations with a man who had proved himself a good workman and a good friend, candor had been replaced by subterfuge.

"I think Shapiro is going to be fine," Archer said. "That's all."

Levy bit his lip. Archer could tell that he was keeping himself from saying something ugly. "You want me to shut up, don't you, Clem?"

"Yes," Archer said. "I'd like you to shut up."

Levy turned suddenly and walked away. Archer watched the long, energetic figure crossing the bare floor, resentment and disappointment in every line of the body. As he reached the door, it opened and Shapiro came in, looking pale and unrefreshed. Shapiro held the door open and smiled tentatively at Levy. Levy didn't look at him, but strode past swiftly. Shapiro glanced unhappily around the room, deflated and embarrassed, hoping that no one had noticed the snub. His eye caught Archer's and he dropped his head as he realized that Archer had been watching. He let the door swing shut and shambled uncertainly past the piano toward the control room. If he ever had a chance, Archer thought, gloomily watching Shapiro, it's gone now. He was sorry for the man and annoyed at him for not being more talented.

Thursday, Archer thought. He went into the control room and sat down next to Barbante and waited for the program to begin.

Thursday.

14

The Herreses lived in an austere, old-fashioned building, from which you expected to see dowagers with pearl chokers emerge to get into 1912 Rolls-Royce limousines, and portly stockbrokers carrying newspapers that had ceased publication long ago, the pages neatly turned back to the financial section and the quotations for stocks that had long since vanished from the market. The doorman was a large, fierce-looking old man with a starched collar who always greeted Archer with quiet approval, probably because Archer was well over forty and wore a good hat. The hall had a hushed, marble atmosphere, as though kings were buried near the elevator shaft. The air in it seemed somehow to have remained intact from the day it was built, and when you breathed you got the odor of another century. If Herres is plotting revolution, Archer thought, as the elevator carried him upwards, he is putting up a clever disguise.

Herres opened the door himself. He wasn't wearing a jacket and his sleeves were rolled up and he looked very wide and young as he shook Archer's hand and helped him off with his coat.

"O excellent man," Herres said, "O sturdy friend. Enter and drink."

"I have something for the kid," Archer said, displaying the package. He had stopped at a toy store on the way uptown and bought a stereopticon viewer with colored slides of foreign scenes.

"If it makes a noise," said Herres, "throw it out of the window."

"I was thinking of getting a drum," Archer said as they went down the hall to the child's room, "but wiser heads prevailed."

"Oh." Herres put out his arm to stop Archer at the doorway. "How are you on the subject of impotence?"

"Never use the stuff," Archer said. "Why?"

"Nancy." Herres grinned. "Ever since the measles entered our life, she's become ferocious about it. She's a primitive woman. She goes to concerts and talks learnedly about foreign affairs, but when it comes to the sticking point, her interest is faithfully focused below the belt."

"Don't be vulgar about your wife."

"Consider yourself warned," Herres said. "The management cannot assume responsibility for any losses incurred on the premises."

"I am warned." Archer went through the doorway into the nursery. Young Clement was standing at the corner of his crib, methodically throwing toys from a diminishing pile in the crib against the opposite wall. He threw a fire engine and a wooden dog on wheels with a strong overhand motion, listening critically to the noise they made against the plaster.

"Hello, Clem," Archer said, going to the crib. There were some red blotches on the boy's cheeks, but he looked robust and immortal.

"Uncle Clement," the boy said, smiling at him. "Nobody is allowed to kiss me or they'll catch the spots. I shake hands now."

They shook hands. The boy looked craftily at the package Archer was carrying. "Did you bring me a surprise?" he asked.

"Don't be a gold-digger," Herres said.

"What's a gold-digger?" the boy said, keeping his eyes on the package as Archer unwrapped it.

" A gold-digger," Herres said, "is somebody with the measles who keeps asking people for surprises."

"I like surprises," the boy said. "When I grow up I'm going to have a surprise every day."

"I bet you will," Herres said. "Can I get you a surprise?" he asked Archer. "Say a Martini?"

"That would be most surprising," Archer said. "Thanks." He handed the bakelite viewer to the boy, after putting a cardboard circle of Aztec photographs into the slot. "Now, Clem," he said, as Herres went out to mix the drinks, "this takes a steady hand. Have you got a steady hand?"

"Yes." The boy peered suspiciously at the instrument. "Is this a gun?"

"No, Clem."

"I like surprises that are guns." The boy whirled in his crib, crouching over, shaking the viewer like a weapon, making a noise like a machine gun. "This is a shootgun," he said. "I shoot your mouth off with it."

"Let me have it for a second please, Clem," Archer said, thinking, I'd better remember how to handle kids again, I'll be going through this all over again soon. "I'll show you how to work it."

The boy gave Archer the viewer. "You see," Archer said, "you put it up to your eyes like this, facing the light, and you look through it. And then, when you want to see another picture, you press this button and the picture changes."

"It makes a noise," the boy said as the machine clicked. "That's good."

"Now you try it." Archer gave him the viewer and watched as the boy uncertainly put it to his face. "You have to look through both holes at once, Clem," Archer explained, "and face the light."

"I see a man!" the boy crowed. "I see a dead man."

"What?" Archer said. "You'd better let me take a

look." He retrieved the machine and held it to the light. A golden stone image peered blindly back at him, wreathed in jungle creepers, dumbly reminding him of blood sacrifices and a sinister civilization before the coming of the Spaniards. "No, Clem," Archer said, "it's not a dead man. It's a statue. The statue of a god."

"Oh," the boy said. "What's a statue?"

"A statue," Archer said, grateful that he hadn't asked, "What's a god?", "is carved out of stone. Sometimes it looks like a man, sometimes it looks like an animal. Sometimes it looks like something people make up in their heads."

"I would like a statue of Mr. Curran," the boy said. Mr. Curran was the doorman.

"Why?"

"I would throw him out the window," the boy said briskly. "On his head."

Mr. Curran was an old-fashioned believer in discipline in lobbies and elevators and was not popular with the younger set.

Archer nodded gravely. "Sometimes," he said, "people used to make statues for just that reason. They would make wax figures of their enemies and stick pins into them to punish them."

"Have I got enemies?" the boy asked, peering into the viewer again and moving the card around swiftly.

"No, Clem."

"Have you got enemies?"

Archer considered this. "I'm not sure."

"Will I have enemies when I grow up?"

Well, Archer thought, he might as well know now as any other time. "Yes," he said, "you probably will."

"Why?"

"Because you'll be rich and handsome and lucky," Archer said, feeling that this would very likely turn out to be true, "and there will be people who will be jealous of you. Do you know what jealous means?"

"Yes," the boy said, putting in another card. "Momma told me. Jealous is when I want Johnny's bicycle."

"That's it, Clem."

"I see a man with a gun," the boy said. "Am I Johnny's enemy?"

That remains to be seen, Archer thought. "No, Clem," he said. "Of course not."

"Could I be his enemy if I practiced?" the boy insisted.

"No, Clem, you can't be the enemy of your brother."

"He hits me. He hits me on the head when Momma isn't looking."

"Hit him back."

"He's too big," young Clement said practically. "He's four years older than me."

Herres came into the room carefully holding a tray with three cocktail glasses. "This will take away some of the pain," he said as he gave one of the glasses to Archer. Archer looked at the Martini. It was almost colorless. Herres' recipe for Martinis was one bottle of Vermouth to a case of gin and you had to be very careful about the way you approached them. He was proud of his ability as a bartender and his knowledge of wines and liquor and Archer always liked to have dinner at the Herreses' table because you drank so well there. "Gin and Burgundy," Herres would say, "carefully applied, are the answers to almost all the problems of modern living."

Herres went over to a small table and ceremonially poured some pineapple juice out of a pitcher into the third glass. He gave the glass to young Clement. "Will you join us?" he asked the boy formally.

Young Clement's eyes grew very grave and he watched his father closely, holding the glass in both hands.

"Cheers," Herres said.

"Chizz," said the boy, lifting his glass. They drank.

"Good drink?" Herres asked his son.

"Good drink," said the boy, mimicking his father's tone.

"How do you like Uncle Clement's surprise?" Herres asked.

"I said thank you," the boy lied quickly, suspecting a lesson in manners.

"That's good," Herres said.

"It's got a statue in it. A statue of Mr. Curran," said young Clement, deftly blending fact, fancy, conjecture and desire in one sentence. "He looks angry."

"Let me see," Herres said. He smiled at Archer and drained his drink as he waited for his son to find the slide and insert it into the machine.

"There." The boy handed the toy to Herres.

Herres peered into it critically. "Mr. Curran," he said. "To the life." He put the toy into the crib. "Clement," he said to Archer, "I wonder if you'd mind letting the young man entertain you for a few minutes. I have to go down to the drugstore to pick up a prescription. Nancy's out with Johnny. The nurse is off today. I'll be right back and you can mix yourself another drink when the well runs dry."

"Sure," Archer said. "Go ahead. We have a lot of things to talk about here."

"Tell Uncle Clement a story," Herres said to his son. "Grownups like to hear stories, too, you know."

"OK," young Clement said. "I'll tell him about the baby elephant."

"I'll just be a minute," Herres said, and went out of the room, buttoning his collar.

"Once upon a time," young Clement began promptly, "there was a baby elephant and a mother elephant in the jungle. That's woods," he explained helpfully, "in the country."

"Yes," Clement said, seating himself on the chair next to the crib and keeping his face grave. "I thought so."

"They ate grass and they drank rivers," the boy went on, squinting and fixing the picture firmly in his mind, the jungle in the country and the two animals leading a domestic existence well supplied with the necessities of life. "They slept in the trees at night and they talked to the monkeys when they weren't at the office. When they didn't like anybody they stepped on him. They sang through their trunks—like this . . ." He made a low, wailing sound and looked anxiously at Archer to see if the music was convincing.

Archer nodded helpfully.

"Sometimes they ate celery and mashed potatoes," the boy went on, "and when they went to a restaurant they looked at the menu. For dessert they had rhubarb and they always paid the check. They had ice cream for dessert, too, and chocolate cake. He had no brothers or sisters," young Clement said, getting rid of that problem early in the game, "and he played in the park in the afternoon and pushed people. When the mother elephant didn't want him to know what she was saying she spelled out the words. C-A-N-D-Y. But he knew what she was saying but he didn't tell her." Young Clement chuckled at this delicious turn of events. "One day he got angry with his mother and he stopped eating. Once in awhile he ate a little plate of ice cream, but that's all. And only chocolate. Do you like this story?" he asked anxiously.

"I love it," Archer said.

"His mother got real angry," the boy went on, re-assured. " 'Something bad is going to happen if you don't eat your grass,' the mother said. He said, 'I don't care,' because he wanted to show her. He kept on not eating for three Sundays. Then something bad began to happen. He began to grow downer and downer and downer. He got to be real close to the ground. Then one day his mother came and looked at him and his mother said, 'I told you to eat your grass. Look how little you are. Why, your trunk is so small it's like a necktie.' Then she took his trunk off and threw it into the closet and locked the door and he had no trunk. That's the story," young Clement said, in a final rush. He beamed at Archer, waiting for approval.

"That's a fine story," Archer said. "When I have a little boy I'm going to tell it to him."

There was a knock at the door and Clara, the maid, came in. She was a large Negro girl and Archer could tell from the expression around her mouth that she felt she was being overworked today. "Afternoon, Mr. Archer," she said. "I got to interrupt."

"Hello, Clara," said Archer.

"Clem . . ." Clara went over to the crib. "Don't you want to go to the bathroom?"

Young Clement lay down and put his feet up in the air and stared at the ceiling, pondering the question. "Maybe," he said, leaving lines of retreat open in all directions.

"It's time you went to the bathroom," Clara said, letting down the side of the crib. "Come on. I ain't got all day."

Young Clement bounded up, jumping on the mattress as Archer rose from his chair and moved off tactfully. "I have bathroom privileges, Dr. Lane said," the boy announced as he climbed out of the crib. "Do you want to watch me?"

Archer examined the expression on Clara's face. "Not this time," he said. "Another day."

"Don't you have to go to the bathroom?" young Clement asked, playing the host, as Clara laboriously put on his slippers.

"Not at the moment, Clem," Archer said, going to the door. "I have to make myself another drink."

"Chizz," the boy said, as Clara led him away.

Archer smiled, watching the small compact figure contentedly being escorted out of the room by Clara. It would be pleasant to have a son, he thought, and have him turn out as well as that. Then he went down the hall, holding his glass, to the small library off the living room where Herres kept a folding bar set up in a corner.

There was an air of luxury about the Herreses' apartment. The rooms were spacious, with old-fashioned high ceilings, and Nancy had used daring colors, bright vermilion draperies shining against dark walls, and severe and elegant furniture. Both she and Vic spent a considerable part of their time in galleries and at auctions and they bought carefully and with taste. "Live gracefully, friends," Herres had said, grinning, "for tomorrow the sponsor may die." He said it as a joke, but he privately took it quite seriously and used his ample income to make certain that he had a good address, that his wife was dressed by the best couturiers in town, as he was clothed by the best tailors, that his dinners were perfect, his home impressive, his servants orderly and well-trained. Especially since he had come home from the Army he had indulged his taste for luxury. "My motto," he had once said carelessly when Archer had warned him about his extravagance, "is— 'Nothing left each year after taxes.' It makes the bookkeeping easier and keeps a man from being tempted by bad investments."

Archer mixed his drink, enjoying the sound of the ice and the oily way the liquid looked in the lamplight. He poured it into his glass, sipped a little off the top, and looked around him at his friend's room. There were high bookshelves built in against the walls and a large desk near the window, with a leather letterpress and pictures of young Clement, Johnny and Nancy on it. Archer turned and looked idly at the bookshelves. *The Complete Greek Drama*, in two volumes. *The Plays of Ibsen. Plays Pleasant and Unpleasant*, by George Bernard Shaw. Archer moved away from the dramatic section. Beard's *The Rise of American Civilization*, Trotsky's *The Russian Revolution*, Reed's *Ten Days That Shook the World, Das Kapital, Mein Kampf*, by Adolf Hitler. Archer stared at the shelf. Was a man the sum of the books he read? Could it be said that *Mein Kampf* canceled out *Das Kapital*? And how did *The Complete Greek Drama* calibrate with Trotsky?

Archer had heard that investigators for the Government asked people what books their friends read, stitching disloyalty out of the threads of titles. What verdict would a bright young man from the FBI find on Herres' shelves? Perhaps, as a friend, he, Archer, should warn Herres to be more discreet in the reading matter he displayed. You never knew who came into your house these days. A vindictive servant, a rejected girl, an over-excitable patriot might make up a damaging list for the dossier of Victor Herres. Leaving out *The Complete Greek Drama* and *The Plays of Ibsen*, of course.

Archer looked at the desk. The top of the letter-press was awry and he saw a pile of mail haphazardly thrown into the box. He stared at the handsome leather box. The answer might be right there, exposed, final. You can judge a man almost as well by the letters he receives as those he sends. There might be a communication from some committee, a receipt for hidden dues, a threat, a warning, a message of congratulations from some clearly identifiable figure.

Archer took a step nearer to the desk, then stopped, ashamed. I'm getting as bad as everybody else, he thought, angrily, and left the library and went into the living room and turned on the radio. He sat there, listening to two people singing, "Oh, Baby, it's cold outside," finishing his drink and trying to forget that he had nearly gone through his friend's papers. How easy it is to be a spy, he thought, how quickly the technique comes to us! In a man's house, drinking his liquor, using the excuse that we have brought a gift to his sick child. And that's without practice or experience—imagine how expert you could get with two or three missions behind you.

"Oh, Baby, it's cold outside," the male voice sang, pleading.

"Hey, Clement . . ." It was Herres who had come in without being noticed by Archer, "I got a great idea." He turned the radio off and sprawled out on the couch.

"Listen carefully and don't fall over backwards when you hear. Ready?"

"Ready," said Archer.

"You haven't made any plans for the summer yet, have you?"

"No."

"The Mediterranean," Herres announced. "The blue Mediterranean. Do your eyes light up?"

"Partially," Archer said.

"Take another sip of your Martini," said Herres. "That reminds me." He jumped up and strode off toward the bar in the next room. "My hand is naked."

Archer followed him into the library. Herres poured the gin without measuring and added a few drops of vermouth. He mixed vigorously, looking at the shaker critically, as though he expected it to betray him. "America is beginning to pall on me," Herres said. Helplessly, Archer registered this and wondered if he ought to warn Herres not to say things like that in public.

"I long for foreign shores." Herres pushed the mixing spoon violently up and down, rattling the ice. "I would like to talk for a couple of months to people whose language I can't understand. That's the intolerable thing about America these days. I can understand every word everybody says." He poured his drink and held it up to the light to make sure it was properly pale. He glanced at Archer. "You don't look ecstatic," he said. "Have you got other plans?"

"No," Archer said. Now, he thought. Unconsciously he took a deep breath. "Vic," he said, "let's wait about the summer. Maybe after you hear what I have to say, you won't want to go anyplace."

Herres sat down. He sipped at his drink, looking gravely at Archer.

"I hope," Archer said, "you won't be offended at anything I say."

"Have I ever been offended before this?"

"No."

"OK," Vic said.

"Archer said, "I'm going to ask you a question. Don't feel you have to answer it. I don't really think I have the right to ask it. And no matter what you answer, yes, no, or it's none of your business—it won't make any difference between you and me . . ." He hesitated. "Vic," he said slowly, "are you a Communist?"

There was silence.

"What was that?" Vic said at last. "What did you say?"

"Are you a Communist?"

Again there was the long moment of silence. "Can I ask," Vic said, "why you want to know?"

"Of course," said Archer. "A week ago O'Neill told me that Hutt had ordered him to have me fire you from the program because you were a Communist or a fellow-traveler. You and four others."

"Who are the others?"

"Motherwell, Atlas, Weller and Pokorny."

Vic chuckled. "What company I'm in!" he said. "What sinister figures!"

"We have another week," Archer said, "to do something about it. I got that much from Hutt."

"Have you spoken to the others?"

"Yes," Archer said.

"You must have had a great week," Vic said, chuckling again. "No wonder you looked puce-green Thursday night. What did they say?"

"Motherwell admitted she was one."

"Joan of Arc," Vic said. "Mounted on a red mink." His voice sounded sharp and almost angry. "How about the others?"

"Pokorny says he was a Communist for two weeks," Archer said. "In Vienna. In 1922."

"Oh, God," Vic said.

"They're going to deport him, I think. He lied on his application for entrance into the country."

"My country 'tis of thee," Vic said. "Sweet land of the deportee."

"Atlas wouldn't tell me anything. And the only thing that Alice Weller could think of was a peace meeting she was supposed to make a speech at."

"You must have had a rugged half-hour with her," Vic said quietly. He lit a cigarette.

"It wasn't pleasant."

"If I told you I was a Communist, Clement," Vic said softly, "what would you do?"

"I don't know," Archer said. "I keep changing my mind every day. One day I tell myself I'd fight for your jobs, although I don't know just what I could do. The next day, I tell myself I'll quit. . . ."

Vic grunted. The smoke from his cigarette floated past Archer's head, drawn to the window. It smelled thin and bitter. "Clement," Vic said, "you've known me a long time. What do you think?"

"I don't think you're a Communist."

"Why not?"

"Well . . ." Archer smiled a little, "for one thing you don't have the vocabulary. You don't call Republican senators bestial, Fascist war-mongers and I never heard you suggest that Joe Stalin ought to be fitted out with a halo. And you're not neurotic or persecuted or sick or poor and I never saw any signs that you thought you were any of those things. And the FBI must have checked on you a little bit before they commissioned you in the Army. And during the last election campaign you told me you couldn't make up your mind whom you were going to vote for, and I never met a Communist yet who said anything like that. And, finally, especially since you came back from the war, you seem—" Archer searched for the word "—frivolous."

Herres grinned. "I must ask you for a reference," he said, "next time I look for a job." Then he grew serious. He doused his cigarette and stood up. He went to the window and stared out at the street. "Clement," he said softly, "you don't have to quit your job on my account. For whatever it's worth—I'm not a Communist."

Archer felt his hands begin to shake. He put them in his pockets. "Thanks," he said.

Herres turned and faced him. "Any other questions, Professor?"

"No."

"Clement, can an ex-student give some advice to an ex-professor?"

"Listening," Archer said.

"In football," Vic said, "there's a play known as a fair catch. Ever hear of it?"

"Yes," Archer said, puzzled.

"When the safety man is catching a punt and he sees the ends coming down on him ready to knock him down as soon as he gets his hands on the ball, he puts up his hand to announce to them that he won't try to run with the ball after he gets it. Then they're not allowed to tackle him and the ball is grounded where it was caught."

"Yes," Archer said, wondering what Vic was driving at.

"It's a kind of surrender," Vic said slowly, "brought on by the realization that for the moment you are in an impossible position. I think you ought to signal for a fair catch."

"What do you mean?" Archer asked, although he was beginning to understand.

"Don't try to run with this particular ball, Clement," Vic said. "They're too God-damn close to you. You'll get hurt. And I wouldn't want to see that. Maintain a delicate neutrality." Vic smiled. "Pretend it all happened a hundred years ago and develop a cool detachment on the subject. Sympathize gently with all sides and cultivate your garden with discretion. If you hear shots being fired in the street, tell yourself it must be a truck tire blowing out. And if you hear burglar alarms

going off at night, tell yourself somebody must have
left his alarm clock on. . . ."

"Do you think I could do that?" Archer asked,
feeling himself grow angry at this estimate of himself.

"I don't know," Vic said. "But if I were you I'd
try. You weren't mixed up in it when there were no
penalties involved. Why dive in so late in the game
when they'll pile all over you if they catch you looking
cross-eyed at a photograph of Herbert Hoover?"

"How about you?" Archer asked.

"The question doesn't arise for me," Vic said, his
voice low. "They're after me and I've got to fight for my
life." He grinned. "Actually, I don't mind so much. A
little fight now and then does wonders for a sedentary
liver. Life on Park Avenue has been pretty placid for
the last four or five years. This'll put a new sparkle into
the eye."

"It won't be easy," Archer said.

"No," Vic agreed. "I suppose they've got a case
against me or what passes for a case these days and
they'll push it for all it's worth. In my time I guess I
belonged to a few organizations that had Communists
in them. Maybe I still do. I'm not going to kid anybody.
I wouldn't hide it if I could. I hate the people who
pretend they never met a real live Communist in their
whole lives," Vic said, "and that they wouldn't know
one if he came up and hit them over the head with a
plaster bust of Karl Marx. For a long time the comrades
were real valuable citizens and we were all delighted to
give them a buck when they went off to get themselves
killed in Spain and when they smuggled refugees out
of Germany and kissed the Germans off at Stalingrad.
And if they're for low-cost housing and free milk for
babies and giving Negroes a high-school education, I'm
not going to spit in their faces now, either. I'm afraid
of what's happening, Clement. People feel that the best
way to prove how loyal they are is to be as nasty and
backward as they know how, and I'm not buying any of

that, either, no matter what Mr. Hutt says. I'm no great shakes as a politician, and I figured out that maybe the reason I gave a couple of dollars here and there and a little of my time is because I felt guilty. I've been lucky all my life. I've had dough and people have been clubbing each other over the head for the privilege of giving me things on a platter ever since I was two months old and it's made me feel a little better to pay up from time to time. If that's treachery, then everybody who endows a new wing on a hospital ought to be sent to Leavenworth. And I saw the Communists in Europe, in the underground, and they did a first-class job and they didn't have the USO and the Red Cross around to entertain them either. They were wrong a lot of the time, but they've done some very sticky jobs in the line of duty, too, and I want to reserve the privilege to cheer for them when they're on my side, and kick them in the ass when they're not. And if any two-bit patriot tries to make me kick them in the ass automatically and on sight, whether they're stealing atom secrets or trying to get doctors to cure hill-billies of pellagra, he's going to have a battle on his hands from me. The bugle will now blow assembly, after which we shall advance slightly north by left. Spectators are advised to buy their tickets early and to stay off the playing field at all times. . . ."

"Thanks for the hint," Archer said, "but it comes a little late."

"Why?"

"I'm in," Archer said. "I told Alice Weller I'd guarantee her job."

Vic pursed his mouth thoughtfully. He picked up his glass, but didn't drink. "Gallantry," he said. "Admirable, old-fashioned, characteristic and dangerous, not necessarily in that order."

"Also," Archer said, "I'm doing the same thing for you. Right now. When I leave here I'm going right up to Hutt's office and put it on the line."

Vic glanced across at Archer, his eyes measuring and troubled. "Archer," he said, "go to the locker room and get yourself a new uniform. The team colors are black and blue. I hope they're becoming to bald men."

"Mr. Hutt isn't here," Miss Walsh was saying. "He's in Florida. He left Wednesday night." Miss Walsh was putting on her hat, preparing for the week-end. The hat was very involved, with brightly colored artificial flowers on it and a dotted veil. But even the veil didn't help her. Miss Walsh was the one plain secretary on the entire floor. Long years of loyal sitting at the desk outside Hutt's office had spread her behind and made her skin the color of an old lampshade and her voice with everyone but Hutt was snappish and suspicious, as though defending his privacy against all comers had cost her whatever charm she might have had in her distant youth. If Miss Walsh ever thought about it, you knew she would have gladly accepted the sacrifice as a small price to be paid for the pleasure of guarding her master. "He went fishing," Miss Walsh said. "A friend of his has a boat at Key West. He needed it, he needed a vacation very badly," she said accusingly through her veil, as though it was because of the inconsiderateness of Archer and others like him that Mr. Hutt sometimes felt fatigue. "He's a very tired man."

"When is he getting back?" Archer asked, looking away from Miss Walsh. He always avoided looking at her when he was in the office, fearful that she would see the distaste in his eyes.

"I don't know," Miss Walsh said, whining. "I told him to stay away a long time. He was looking perfectly awful. Exhausted. I said to him, 'Let the others do some work for once,' I said, 'You can't carry the whole world on your own shoulders all the time,' I said."

"Yes," said Archer, patient and sourly polite, "but when did he say he'd come back?"

"He didn't say. When he's thoroughly rested, I hope."
She tied the veil behind her hat with thick fingers. A
thin smell of armpit came from Miss Walsh when she
lifted her arms. Loyalty, Archer thought, sometimes
comes rather high in a warm office building. She must
be sensationally efficient.

"He left word that Mr. O'Neill would handle whatever came up," Miss Walsh said. By her tone Archer
understood that she had little hope that Mr. O'Neill
could handle anything at all.

"Thanks," Archer said. He left Miss Walsh to her
artificial flowers, her week-end, her veil and her armpits. He walked through the empty office, past the
cleared desks and the antique furnishings to O'Neill's
office. O'Neill's secretary was gone and the door was
open. O'Neill was sitting at his kidney-shaped desk,
bulking over it, his eyes closed, sleeping, sitting erect.
Great, Archer thought, watching O'Neill, one fishing
and one asleep. He felt a surge of strong, unreasonable
anger at Hutt for going off at a time like this. The least
he might do, Archer thought, is hang around this week.
And O'Neill might have the grace to keep his eyes open.

"Emmet," he said loudly, "wake up. The building's
on fire."

O'Neill blinked. He looked up soddenly at Archer.
"What's the matter?" he asked thickly. "What'd you
say?" He shook his head, recovering from sleep. "Oh.
Clem. Forgive me. Saturday afternoon—nap-time.
What's new?"

"I want to talk to Hutt," Archer said.

O'Neill yawned. He had very white teeth and when
he yawned Archer could see that there were no fillings
in them. "Excuse me," O'Neill said. "Some day I'm
going to take a vacation. Sleep for two months." He
shook himself vigorously and stood up, rubbing his
hands briskly through his hair. "Hutt's in Florida."

"I know," Archer said. "I spoke to the exquisite
Miss Walsh."

"On a boat. Sailfishing."

"How do I get in touch with him?"

O'Neill shrugged. "Beats me. Put a note in a bottle."

"Will he be back this week?"

"Ask Miss Walsh."

"I did."

"What'd she say?"

"He's exhausted, she said. He'll be back when he stops being exhausted."

"That's what he told me," O'Neill said. "He called me two o'clock Thursday morning from Palm Beach. The reins're in my hands, he said, until further notice." O'Neill extended his hands and gazed at his palms soberly. He flexed his fingers.

"Just this week," Archer said. "The bastard."

"President of the concern," O'Neill said complacently. "One of the biggest men in the business."

"The reins are in your hands," Archer said. "What did he mean by that?"

"Depends," O'Neill said. Archer could see that he intended to be cautious. "I don't imagine I can sign checks for more than ninety thousand dollars or hire Lana Turner for a year or anything like that. In a moderate way, I guess you could say the reins are in my hands."

"What about Herres and Atlas, etcetera?"

O'Neill yawned again. It was a nervous yawn this time. Deep wrinkles appeared around O'Neill's eyes, making him look less youthful. "Sit down, pal," O'Neill said. "Times're tough enough as it is."

Archer sat down on the edge of the desk. "All right," he said.

"Want a drink?" O'Neill asked, pulling open a drawer in the desk to reveal a bottle. "To celebrate Saturday afternoon?"

"No."

O'Neill closed the drawer, sighing. "Always feel sad on Saturday afternoon," he said, rubbing his eyes. "Gray weather . . . gray weather. . . ."

"Waiting," Archer said.

"Clement," O'Neill said gently, looking up, "I'm afraid they've had it. All of them."

"Hutt said he'd give me two weeks," Archer said, trying to keep from speaking too fast. "I've dug up a lot of information. . . ."

"Hutt's been digging up information, too, he says," O'Neill said, neutrally. "When he called me from Palm Beach, he told me to tell you that as far as he's concerned, his position stands."

"You knew that Thursday," Archer said, standing up. "Why did you keep me on the string?"

"Orders from the man I work for," O'Neill said quietly. "I'm sorry, Clem. He told me not to bring it up until you did. Mine not to reason why, mine but . . . oh, hell." He stood up, too. "Let's go out and have lunch."

"That was a cheap thing for Hutt to do," Archer said. "Run out at a time like this, leaving you with the dirty work."

"I'll pass on your feelings in the matter," O'Neill said formally. "I'm sure Mr. Hutt is always open to constructive criticism."

"Exactly what did he mean by saying that his position stands?"

"No one of the five works next week or thereafter, to infinity," O'Neill said. "Exactly."

"I threatened I'd quit," Archer said, "when I talked to him. What's the word on that?"

"Lunch," O'Neill said, "I'm dying for a large, wet lunch."

"Come on, Emmet," Archer said. "Let's have it."

O'Neill walked slowly toward the window, then turned and faced Archer. There was a look of troubled pleading in his eyes. "He said that if you wanted to quit, Clem, I was empowered to accept your resignation."

There was silence for a moment. In the quiet building, Archer could hear the faint sound of an elevator dropping hollowly in its shaft. Archer got off the desk. He rubbed his head thoughtfully. Here it is, he thought, here's the moment again. Once more around the track and in front of the judges' stand still one more time.

"Clem," O'Neill said. "That's all for me. That's as far as I go. My duties to the firm of Hutt and Bookstaver are discharged for the week. I won't say another word. Let's go and have lunch."

Archer hesitated. "Sure," he said, after a pause. "Might as well eat."

He watched as O'Neill put on his hat and coat. "I have to meet my wife for lunch, too," O'Neill said. "You don't mind, do you?"

"Delighted," Archer said absently, feeling blank.

"We've been quarreling," O'Neill said, as they got to the door of his office. "I've discovered a natural truth about marriage. The prettier they are, the more they fight. You can act as a buffer state."

Archer stopped before O'Neill could close the door. "What's the matter?" O'Neill asked nervously.

"Emmet," Archer said slowly, "I have a call to make. Do you mind if I use your telephone?"

"Of course not." O'Neill waved toward his desk. "I'll wait for you."

"I don't think you'd better hear this call," said Archer.

"Sure," O'Neill said. "I'll wait for you at the elevator."

"I'm going to call the sponsor," Archer said. "I want to go to him and put the whole thing up to him."

O'Neill blinked. He looked uneasily up and down the empty outer office, at the neat, vacant desks and the covered typewriters. "The rule is, of course," he said flatly, "that nobody but Hutt talks to the sponsor."

"I know all about the rule."

"It's Saturday afternoon," O'Neill said. "He won't be in his office."

"I'll call him at his home."

"He lives in Paoli," O'Neill said. "He has an unlisted phone. You won't be able to get him."

"You have his number," Archer said. "I know that. You've called Hutt there when Hutt went down for week-ends."

"The last man who went over Hutt's head and talked to a sponsor was fired the next week," O'Neill said.

"I know."

"Just wanted to keep you *au courant* with the local customs."

"What's the number, Emmet?"

They stood facing each other, very close. O'Neill's face was serious and tight. Then it relaxed. He grinned, his face looking boyish and mischievous. "Sometimes, Clem," O'Neill said, "I wish I was back in the old carefree United States Marines. I'm going down to meet my pretty wife, because I'm late already, and our marriage is tottering as it is. On my desk, there's an address book. In it, it's just barely possible you might find an unlisted number or two. Under S. Don't tell me about it. I'll be waiting for you at the bar, with a Martini in reserve."

He patted Archer's arm with a swift gesture, and swung on his heel and walked sturdily toward the elevators, a man having trouble hanging on to his eighteen thousand dollars a year.

Archer watched him march past the empty desks, then went into the office. The address book was of heavy green tooled leather and was standing against a leather-framed photograph of O'Neill's wife. O'Neill's wife had long, blond hair and she regarded the transactions on her husband's desk with a pure, delicious, sidelong air. Under S, Archer found the name, Robert Sandler, with a Paoli number. Archer sat down at O'Neill's desk and, staring at the pretty, framed face, dialed the operator.

Fifteen minutes later, when he joined O'Neill and his wife at the bar downstairs, he casually dropped the information that he had to get a morning train on Monday for Philadelphia.

15

Nobody should approach Philadelphia, Archer thought, as the train sped through the outskirts of the city. It is too depressing. It was a gray morning and the clouds hung low over the stucco wastes of the suburbs. All our cities, Archer thought, peering through the flecked window, are surrounded by belts of apathy. Low-priced regions for the discouraged, flimsy walls behind which people moved wearily, worrying about the rent. Even the trees looked desolate, thin and without vitality, as though they would never reach a season in which they would put forth leaves or provide a nesting place for birds, never grow large enough for a boy to want to carve his initials in their trunks.

Archer closed his eyes, displeased with the way his thoughts were running. He wanted to be jovial and self-confident for the morning's work. Hearty, he decided, robustly Rotarian, that's the way to be when talking on the subject of treason to a man who runs a ten-million-dollar business. Mr. Sandler had been pleasant on the phone when they had spoken on Saturday. Clipped, but pleasant. There had been a moment's hesitation and then Mr. Sandler had said, "Be at my office at twelve-thirty Monday." He hadn't asked what

Archer wanted to see him about and hadn't said a word about Lloyd Hutt or proper channels of communication. Somehow, after the call, Archer had felt encouraged. Mr. Sandler had sounded like a reasonable man.

He took a cab from the station. The factory was on the outskirts of the city. Archer had never seen it before and he was favorably impressed with the large, trim building, set behind lawns, with the name of the company on a white sign along the road. It was a drug company which made a wide variety of patent medicines, skin preparations and pharmaceutical products, and the architect had cleverly made the building and its grounds suggest an austere and well-run hospital. Driving through the gates along a graveled road, Archer had a feeling of being involved in a dignified and public-spirited enterprise. The sponsor's office was on the ground floor, and from the large ante-room you looked out through curtained windows at the sweeping lawn and the shrub borders. The room itself was comfortably furnished, with low chairs and sofas, and magazines on small tables. At a desk at one end sat a mulatto girl, behind a telephone. The girl was pretty, with golden skin and soft, wavy dark hair. She wore a trim blue dress with a white collar and her voice was shy and soft when she spoke to Archer. She called in immediately when Archer gave her his name.

"Mr. Sandler says for you to go right in, please," she said, after speaking briefly on the phone. She smiled at him and pressed a buzzer. Not a hospital, really, Archer thought, as he went through the door. More like a sanitarium for rich patients with mild and fashionable diseases.

Mr. Sandler was a short, plump man with thinning hair. He had a rosy complexion and a large pink nose. His face looked soft and pliant and only his eyes, which were cold pale blue and almost opaque gave a hint of strength and stubbornness. Just now there was a polite, welcoming smile on his face as he stood up and came

around from behind his desk to shake hands with
Archer. There was another man in the room, large,
stocky and about fifty, with a leathery and wrinkled
face, like an old catcher's mitt. He stood up, too, and
smiled agreeably when Mr. Sandler introduced them.
His name was Ferris and when he shook Archer's hand,
his palm was hard and callused, like a farmer's.

"I'm going, now," Ferris said. "I'll take a last swing
around the plant and I'll look in this afternoon, Bob."

"I hope it rains in Florida for the next two weeks,"
Mr. Sandler said. "Hard."

Ferris laughed. "Thanks," he said. "That's generous
of you."

"Ferris is taking a two-week vacation," Mr. Sandler
explained to Archer. "He's a golfer, when he isn't busy
being a vice-president. I always hate people to go off
on vacation when I can't go. Ever since I was a kid.
My mother used to tell me it was a bad character trait.
I guess she was right. Still haven't gotten over it,
though." He grinned at Ferris, who was at the door by
now. "Don't tell me if you break eighty, Mike," he
said. "I don't want to hear about it."

Ferris laughed, opening the door. "Good-bye, Mr.
Archer," he said. "Glad to have met you, after all these
years." He had a strange way of looking directly and
unblinkingly at you, Archer thought, as though he were
making a report to himself on your strength and weaknesses. Big business, Archer realized, as he smiled
good-bye at Ferris, I am always uncomfortable in its
presence.

The door closed behind a final wave of the big,
leathery man, and Mr. Sandler indicated an easy-chair
near the desk for Archer. "Sit down, Mr. Archer," he
said. His voice was swift, but soft and breathy. He
waited for Archer to seat himself, then went around
behind his desk and lowered himself neatly into his
own high-backed swivel chair. His whitish hair and pink
scalp against the brown leather looked like an academic

painting of a judge of a minor court. "Mike deserves this vacation," Mr. Sandler said. "No matter what I say. He keeps this plant going as though it was running in oil. Been with me twenty years. Started in the shipping department." He looked at Archer as though he expected Archer to say something appropriate.

"Oh," Archer said, baffled by this industrial loyalty. "That's a long time." There was a flicker of the pale eyes and Archer felt that Mr. Sandler had expected something more original.

"Some day," Sandler said, "you ought to let us take you around the plant. See where we make the stuff you sell."

"I'd be delighted," Archer said formally, not pleased at being included on the sales force of the organization, although technically it was accurate enough. Factories left him confused anyhow. No matter how closely he listened to the explanations, the machinery always seemed hopelessly intricate.

"How's Hutt?" Mr. Sandler asked.

"Very well, I think. He's in Florida, too."

Mr. Sandler smiled. "Everybody gets to Florida but me. I'm in the wrong end of the business, I guess. That Hutt's a good man, though. A steel-trap intelligence."

"Yes," Archer said, feeling that Mr. Sandler perhaps read the business sections of the newspapers too carefully. "A very good man indeed."

"That program you do," Mr. Sandler said. "Like it." He nodded sturdily. "Listen every Thursday. It's artistic, but it sells drugs, too. I keep my finger on the pulse. I asked Hutt who was responsible—and he said, Clement Archer's the man."

"That's very generous of Mr. Hutt," Archer said warily.

"Sign of a good executive," Mr. Sandler said. "Knows when to give other people credit. Always mistrust a man who says he does everything himself. Know he's lying. Small man in a big job. Finally disastrous. So when you called, I said, come on down." He peered sharply at Archer. "I understand it isn't customary," he said, showing Archer that he knew this was an extraordinary occasion, "but, what the hell, you're a big grown man, you didn't travel to Philadelphia just to waste my time."

"Thank you," Archer said, trying to wind himself up for what was to follow. "I appreciate it. The reason . . ."

"Like oysters?" Sandler asked abruptly. "Fried oysters?"

"Why . . . why, yes."

"You didn't have lunch yet, did you?"

"No. I came right from the train."

"Good." Sandler jumped up from behind his desk. "We'll go to my club. Best fried oysters in Philadelphia." He was rapidly putting his coat on. He moved with bustling youthful movements, his pink hands flashing into sleeves. "Of course," he said, picking up his hat, "you don't have to have oysters if you don't want to. Don't believe in dictating a man's diet. You might have ulcers, high blood pressure. Who knows?"

Archer laughed as he put on his coat. "I don't have an ulcer to my name."

"Good." Sandler led him to the door, his hand on Archer's elbow. "Mistrust people with ulcers. Unreasonable prejudice. My wife gets furious when she hears me say it. Her two brothers have ulcers as big as garden baskets, but I can't help saying it. Ulcers're the result of a sour constitution, and a sour man is bound to behave in an undependable manner. Stands to reason."

They were passing the mulatto girl at the desk by this time. "Back in an hour and a half, Miss Watkins," Mr. Sandler said. "Have to have my lunch."

"Yessir," the mulatto girl said softly, smiling goldenly.

"Prettiest girl north of Washington," Mr. Sandler said in a hoarse whisper. "Wish I was twenty years younger." He laughed heartily. "Disadvantage of acquired wealth. It comes when the muscle tone is gone.

Got scientists working on hormones this minute in there . . ." He waved vaguely at doors behind him in the corridor. "Rejuvenate the dying cell. Race against time, I tell them when I talk to them. I'm going to be sixty-one next month." He roared again, plump, bouncy, pink, dapper in his gray coat and soft brown felt hat.

They went out of the severe main doors, Mr. Sandler nodding briskly to the uniformed guard behind a glass grating. Mr. Sandler stopped for a moment at the top of the stairs and surveyed the lawn. Archer had the feeling that each time Mr. Sandler came out of his office, he stopped in the same place and gazed around him with the same expression of affection and criticism. "Ought to see this place in the summertime," he said. "An ancestral garden. Phlox, peonies, hyacinth, daisy borders. Three men just to take care of the lawn. Restful to the tired eye. Grass and a few trees. Turn back to your work refreshed. Interior entirely air-conditioned, too. Can't stand weary summertime factory faces all around me. If I had my way we'd close down May first and send everybody fishing until October. Like to do it, but the competition would murder us." He grinned and trotted down the steps to a shiny green Ford convertible which was parked just in front of the door. "Here it is," he said. "My car. Hop in." He opened the door for Archer and bounced around to the other side. Archer got in and Mr. Sandler hurled himself in under the wheel. They started with a spurt, the gravel spinning loudly behind them. "Like little cars," Sandler said, driving too fast through the gates. "Like to drive myself. Don't like the big ocean-liner type of automobile. Feel as though you're driving an institution. In the summertime I keep the top down all weathers. Get as red as an Indian. Hair bleaches out. Gives me a unique appearance." He grinned at the wheel. "Surprising, the number of girls who wave at me on the road. Very useful at board meetings, too. I look so energetic I discourage all the vice-presidents and representatives of stockholders who think they want to argue with me. If I drive too fast, tell me. Only man I know who drives faster is my son. He'll kill himself some day. He was in the Air Force during the war and he's still trying to cruise at three hundred miles an hour. Ever meet him?"

"No," Archer said, watching the road ahead of him worriedly.

"In New York half the time. Night-club type. Always seems to be going around with singers who don't get through work till four A.M. Not much good for anything else. His mother said he was ruined by the Air Force. Not true." Mr. Sandler grinned. "He was ruined at the age of eight. Amusing boy. Big feller, always getting into trouble. Not worth a damn anyplace but in a B-17." Mr. Sandler paid attention to his driving for a moment, debonairly. "You've got some trouble to lay in my lap, haven't you, Mr. Archer?"

"Yes," Archer said. "I'm afraid so."

"Lunch will help us bear it. Lunch has a civilizing influence on trouble," Mr. Sandler said. "But you can start now. Let's have it."

"It's about those five people connected with the program," Archer said carefully. "Hutt said you knew about them."

"Yes." Mr. Sandler was looking straight ahead through the windshield. "I got that piece from the magazine."

"Hutt gave me two weeks to investigate them," Archer said. "Or try to. As much as one man can in that short space of time."

"I know," Mr. Sandler said. "Hutt said an assistant promised you the two weeks and he had to back the man up. Approve of that. No sense having assistants unless you give them some responsibilities."

"The two weeks're up Thursday," Archer said.

"I know." Imperceptibly, Archer noticed, Mr. Sandler was slowing down as they wove through traffic. There was no way of knowing what his attitude was at the moment. His tone was distant, noncommittal, neither friendly nor unfriendly.

"I've been talking to the people," Archer said. "I learned a few things about them. But when I tried to get in touch with Hutt, they told me he was down in Florida. They don't know when he's coming back. And he left word that his position had not changed." Archer consciously tried to keep a tone of injury or complaint out of his voice.

"Very important," Mr. Sandler said. "Vacations for executives. Believe in it. Keeps the brain fresh for decisions."

"I understand that," Archer said, too hastily. "It's just inconvenient that it came just at this time. That's why I was forced to come to you."

"No apologies necessary," Mr. Sandler said. "That's what I'm paid for. To deal with the uncomfortable situations. I can hire people to deal with the easy ones."

Archer didn't feel that he had made any apologies, but he didn't go into it. "Hutt left word," he said, choosing his words with care, "that my resignation would be accepted if I insisted on pushing the matter."

There was silence in the car as Mr. Sandler slowed down for a red light. "Is that a threat, Mr. Archer?" he asked flatly, staring straight ahead. "Are you trying to push me?"

"No," Archer said, surprised that Mr. Sandler felt he was important enough to be in a position to threaten anyone. "I just wanted you to have an absolutely clear view of the situation."

"I have a clear view of the situation," Mr. Sandler said. The light turned green and he started with a spurt. "I talked to Hutt and I told him that he could let you go if necessary. Clear enough?"

"Clear enough," Archer said. He hesitated. "Maybe you don't want me to go on. Maybe I'm just wasting your time."

"If you were wasting my time you wouldn't be here," Mr. Sandler said, without emphasis. "You've worked for me a long time. You've sold my product. You've earned your money. You have a right to state your case."

"First of all," Archer said, "all five people have done their job well. Two or three of them have done it extremely well . . ."

"Understood," said Mr. Sandler. For the first time, there was a note of impatience in his voice, as though he felt Archer was bringing in irrelevant material.

"Whatever their political opinions may be," Archer said, "they've performed loyally for your company. As you put it in my case, they've earned their money."

"I said that was understood." Sandler stepped on the accelerator and the car lurched around a truck.

"Beyond that," Archer said, trying to organize everything neatly, "they have just been accused. They haven't been found guilty of anything. And the magazine that accused them has made some very queer charges in the past and has been forced to retract publicly when the people they've accused have been strong enough or wealthy enough to afford to fight. Also, the idea that any man who happens to run a two-by-four magazine can set himself up as a judge on a whole industry and prepare blacklists which force people out of work is an unpleasant one."

"Unpleasant," Mr. Sandler said. "Yes."

"Each case is different, too."

"It always is. Mr. Archer . . ." For the first time in the car, Mr. Sandler looked over at him. His face was grave and his eyes were cool. "For my own information, I'd like to know what your relationships to these five people are. To orient myself. Is that a fair question for me to ask?"

"Yes," Archer said. "I think so. They vary."

"Of course."

"First—the composer. Pokorny. Professionally—I admire his music. He's very good. You've heard his stuff . . ."

"Yes."

"Personally—" Archer almost smiled. "I find him somewhat trying. He's rather—emotional. Unstable. I pity him. He's a Jew . . ." Archer saw the lids go down for a half-second over Mr. Sandler's eyes. "He's had a hard time. His parents were killed by the Germans. He's terrified . . . He's married to an obnoxious woman."

"Member of the Communist Party," Mr. Sandler said. "Very active."

"Yes," Archer said, wondering how much Mr. Sandler knew about the others, too. "Then there's Frances Motherwell."

"She was off the program this week," Mr. Sandler said.

"Yes."

"I thought you said they were going to have two weeks."

"She quit," Archer said. "She got an offer for a play."

"I didn't like the girl you replaced her with," Mr. Sandler said. "When I was a young man I used to avoid girls with voices like that like the plague. Sex with marshmallows all over it. For the high-school trade."

Archer grinned. "On the target," he said. "She has cooed her last coo for University Town."

"Delighted to hear it," Mr. Sandler said. "What else about Frances Motherwell?"

"Professionally?"

"I know all about her professionally," Mr. Sandler said. "Top-grade. The real thing."

"Politically," Archer said slowly. "Politically . . ." He hesitated.

"Go ahead," said Mr. Sandler.

"Well, she's a Communist. She admitted it."

"The magazine was right about her, wasn't it?"

"Yes," Archer said. "She doesn't hide it. She's proud of it. She's very romantic. A man she knew who got killed in the war converted her. She'll meet someone else finally and she'll get converted to something else.

Anyway, she's out of the picture. She quit before she could be fired."

"She's pretty, isn't she?" Mr. Sandler asked.

"Yes."

"Damn fool." Sandler made a decisive move between two cars. "What do you feel about her?"

Archer thought for a moment. "She scares me."

Mr. Sandler looked surprised. "Why?"

"I'm a married man."

Mr. Sandler chortled once, briefly. "Know what you mean," he said. "We live in the damnedest world. Girls who look like that turning Red. Early marriage," he said firmly. "Only solution. What about the colored man? The funny man?"

"Atlas?" Archer waited, realizing that he wanted to say something unpleasant about the comedian, and annoyed with himself for the impulse. "What do you think about him?"

"He makes me laugh," Mr. Sandler said. "I'm going to miss him."

"You're not the only one," said Archer.

"Did you talk to him?"

"Yes."

"What did you get out of him?"

"Nothing. He just laughed at me. He's hipped on the color thing. If your skin's white you're his enemy. He says he's going to live in France."

"Business is getting too complicated," Mr. Sandler said. "Twenty years ago, your colored help didn't threaten to go live in France when you asked them a question."

"Twenty years ago they didn't make twenty thousand dollars every thirty-nine weeks, either," Archer said.

"I suppose not. You're not fond of Atlas, are you?"

"Not very," Archer admitted. "He's a lot of trouble. And he makes it perfectly clear that he despises me. He's not an engaging character."

"Actors," Mr. Sandler said. "Baffling. Too much for

a drug manufacturer, really. He sounds so pleasant on the radio, you want to wrap him up and take him home with you."

"Talent," Archer said, "is the best disguise in the world."

"What would you want to do with him?" Mr. Sandler asked sharply.

"I'd like to keep him," Archer said. "He's awfully important. And I have a feeling he's not a Communist. He's not anything. He's out for himself and that's all."

"In the last presidential election he spoke for that feller Wallace," Mr. Sandler said, "and he's signed some very lively petitions of one kind and another."

"Anything," Archer said, wondering how Mr. Sandler had discovered these facts, "that means trouble for the white folks. That's his motto. But I don't think it's even political with him. It's a reflex action."

"Can you replace the sonofabitch?"

"No."

Mr. Sandler grunted, over the wheel of the car, and Archer for the first time had the feeling that he was getting somewhere.

"How about the others?" Sandler asked. "The Weller woman?"

"If she were on the stage," Archer said slowly, "she would be what the critics would call adequate."

"What does that mean?"

"Not especially good," Archer said. "Not especially bad."

"She's replaceable, then?"

Archer hesitated. There's no sense in this conversation, he thought, unless I'm absolutely candid with the man. "She's replaceable," he said, "but I don't want to replace her."

"Nice lady?" Mr. Sandler hooted his horn impatiently at a woman driver ahead of him. Waveringly, the woman swung over to the side and Mr. Sandler sent the Ford past her.

"Very nice lady," Archer said. "The one thing against her that I've been able to find out is that she lent her name to a peace conference that was sponsored by the Communists."

"That the only thing?"

Archer had a troubled feeling that perhaps Mr. Sandler knew some more damaging evidence against Alice, since his information seemed to be so complete about the others. "As far as I know," he said.

"You wouldn't hide anything from me about the lady, would you, Archer?" Mr. Sandler leaned forward, his hands manicured, plump and pink on the wheel.

"I'd be tempted to." Archer smiled a little. "But I don't think I would."

"Uh," Mr. Sandler said. "Why?"

"She's a widow. She's not getting any younger. She supports a fourteen-year-old son." Archer spoke rapidly. "Her husband was a good friend of mine and I feel responsible for her."

"Uhuh," Mr. Sandler said. He turned and glanced at Archer. He looked serious, but approving, as though pleased with Archer's honesty. "You still feel responsible for her?"

"I feel sorry for her," Archer said, remembering the sagging face, the clumsy clothes, the sandy skin.

"What about the other feller," Mr. Sandler asked, "Herres?"

"He's a very good actor," Archer said, feeling nervous for the first time since they had started in the car. "They don't come any better."

"That's what my wife says. She listens every week. Religiously. She's a good judge, too. She goes to New York and sees all the shows. Very smart woman. She thinks he's a very handsome feller, too. Met him at a party somewhere last year. She's social."

Maybe, Archer thought, Victor Herres is going to be spared because of the effect he had over a drink on an aging Philadelphia housewife who came to New York to see all the shows. The close blond hair, the easy, white-toothed smile, the automatic good manners with ladies would pay off now. . . .

"What else do you know about Herres?" Mr. Sandler asked.

"He was in the Army," Archer said. "He was discharged as a captain. He was wounded and he won the Silver Star in Sicily."

Mr. Sandler frowned over the wheel. "Silver Star, eh?" He drove in silence. Archer could see that this was news to the old man. "My youngest son was killed in the war," he said. Archer had the feeling, listening to him, that Mr. Sandler gave that bit of information automatically as soon as any mention was made of the war. "Tunisia. I got a very nice letter from his captain. Said Arnold—that was his name, Arnold—was very well liked, very popular in the company. He was up to corporal by the time he died. Stepped on a mine, the captain wrote. Just walking along and stepped on a mine. I wrote to the captain to thank him for his letter, but by the time it got there, the captain was dead, too. Taft, the captain's name was. Same as the senator's. My wife blames me because the boy is dead." Mr. Sandler was talking to himself now, staring out through the windshield, mumbling, going over this old loss and this continuing intimate injustice. "She said I forced him to join up. His draft number was high and he could have hung back a long time. But I couldn't stand seeing him staying at home, sleeping till noon every day, with the war on. Make it or carry it, I said. Get a job in a war plant or pick up a gun. Never worked a day in his life, so he enlisted. My wife insisted on having his body brought home after the war. Goddamn fool sentimental thing to do, I told her, no wonder the income tax is up to eighty-six percent, disturbing the bones of the dead. But she wouldn't listen for a minute. Nothing for it but a great big funeral, with relatives weeping by the dozen, all over again. Women get their satisfaction out of the God-damnedest things."

Mr. Sandler lapsed into silence, his face aggrieved as he thought of elderly, bereaved, unreasonable women and dead, twice-buried sons. He seemed to have forgotten that Archer was sitting beside him and what they were talking about. But, a moment later, he said, "What else about Herres? You know him a long time?"

"Yes," Archer said. "Fifteen years. He was a student of mine in college."

"You taught in a college?" Mr. Sandler asked.

"History."

"I know a couple of professors," Mr. Sandler said. "That's the life. They all live to the age of eighty."

Archer laughed. "I guess I'm not interested in living to eighty."

"You won't in radio," Mr. Sandler said. "That's a cinch. Neither will I." He snorted. "My whole family dies at the age of sixty-five. Mother, father, grandfathers. On schedule. I got four more years. I ought to do something enormous with the next four years, I suppose. Only, I don't know anything else but running a drug business." He drove thoughtfully, reflecting on the next four years. "What about Herres?" he asked abruptly. "Is he a Communist?"

"No," said Archer.

"How do you know?"

"I asked him and he told me."

"Do you believe him?"

"He's my best friend," Archer said slowly.

"Oh." Mr. Sandler considered this. "A little complicated for you, isn't it?"

"No," Archer said.

Mr. Sandler glanced curiously at him, his pale eyes puzzled. Then he jerked his head around and watched the traffic. "Now," he said, "we get to you. You want to answer some questions about yourself?"

"Of course."

"What are your politics?"

"I voted for Truman in the last election."

"That was a God-damn fool thing to do," Mr. Sandler said, the fires of previous Novembers flaring briefly within him. "Look where we are now. No . . . skip it, skip it. I'm not particularly proud of the Republicans either, although I've voted Republican all my life, except the first time Roosevelt ran. Thirty-two. Scared then. First deficit in the history of the concern. Ran for cover with the rest of the damn fools. I've paid for it, though," he said darkly, thinking, Archer was sure, about his income-tax returns. "You had anything to do with the Communists?" he asked sharply.

"Let me think about that for a minute," Archer said.

"Why?" Mr. Sandler looked at him suspiciously.

"Because I would like to figure out once and for all just what I *have* had to do with them," Archer said.

"You just getting around to that now, Archer?" Mr. Sandler asked.

"In the last week or so. Until now I guess I haven't had to. I suppose I was lazy. A little afraid. Ashamed, perhaps," Archer said. "Unwilling to be engaged."

"Well," Mr. Sandler asked, his voice harsh for the first time, "what did you find out?"

"In the thirties," Archer said slowly, "I guess I was mixed up with them a bit. In a college in those days, a great many people were. Especially the younger ones. A chapter of a teachers' union was being started on the campus and I joined, and I imagine three or four of the leading spirits were comrades . . ."

"You imagine." There was flat sarcasm in the old man's voice now.

"I knew, I suppose," Archer said. "I didn't inquire too closely. They worked hard and the things they were asking for seemed reasonable enough. More money. Tenure. There didn't seem to be anything sinister about that." He half-closed his eyes, trying to remember what it was like in that distant time, twelve or thirteen years ago. "It seemed fairly respectable, then, remember."

"Not to me it didn't," Mr. Sandler said.

"Well, it did to a lot of people," Archer said mildly.

"Perfectly decent Americans. There was no talk of revolution, then, remember. And there was something called the Popular Front in France. And they talked so loudly about democratic methods, collaboration against Fascism, all those old phrases. And then, during the war, everybody loved everybody else. Senators getting up in Madison Square Garden at Aid-to-Russia meetings. In the radio industry, on all those war-boards, the Communists seemed to work harder than anyone else to help, and I guess I didn't see anything very wrong with them then, either. And after the war, everybody was so friendly with everybody else. All that talk about World Peace, One World . . ."

As he said the words, the phrases seemed remote, without meaning, their only flavor a residue of mockery and ignorance. They sound, Archer thought, going back to his history classes, like the speeches that were made by orators in the legislature of Southern states before Secession. Just that orotund, exactly that dead. Four, five years ago, in the lost, defeated past.

"And the people who were yelling loudest about the Communist menace were so outlandish," he went on, picking his way troubledly through the maze of argument. "They called Roosevelt a Red, remember, and they said Truman was out to set up Communism in America. And anybody who thought that the miners ought to get five cents more an hour or that Franco wasn't a perfect gentleman they called a traitor . . . And that magazine—*Blueprint*—is a bit on that side, too— they've attacked the mildest kind of liberals as subversive and they're perfectly willing to ruin people without the semblance of a trial or any kind of reasonable investigation. You can't help but feel that there's something sinister about them . . . And now, recently, on the other side, you find out that Americans have been passing on military secrets to the Russians . . . Frankly, I was surprised. I guess I was naive. I still don't think that any of the Communists I've known would do anything like that. Maybe Mrs. Pokorny . . ." Archer added as an afterthought. "But I don't really know. I only saw her for ten minutes. I guess I feel that there are two kinds of Communists . . . The conscious conspirators and the ones who've been misled into believing it's a kind of noble reform movement. And the conspirators can be handled just like anyone else who breaks the law. The others . . ." He shrugged. "I guess we have to bear with them. As long as they don't break the law we have to regard them as innocent, with full rights to speak, to earn a living . . ."

Mr. Sandler made a grunting noise. It was impossible to interpret. He was searching for a place to park on the crowded street and he hardly seemed to be paying attention to Archer. Archer sat back, feeling that what he had said was lame, unconvincing, but feeling, too, that as clumsy as it was he had clarified his position for himself for the first time. The chaotic impressions, the welter of conflicting forces, the complex claims of affection and dislike were for once organized and compartmentalized, however rudely. At least, he thought, I've come to a working basis on this. Whatever Hutt thinks or Sandler does, I can locate my own position on the emotional map.

Mr. Sandler found an open space and backed his car in skillfully, grunting loudly as he spun the wheel. "Too many cars on the streets these days," he complained. "No reason for it. Just restlessness. Women," he said. "Haven't got anything to do at home. Get in the car and roam around the block up the streets." He took the ignition key out of the lock and got out. Archer got out on his side and waited for Sandler to come around and join him.

"Club's only a block away," Sandler said, as they started walking. "That's par for the course. One day I had to park nine blocks away."

He bounced swiftly along the sidewalk and Archer had to stretch his legs to keep up with him. Almost impersonally, Archer wondered what was going through his companion's mind. Obviously, Mr. Sandler was interested in finding out about the people on the program and about Archer himself, information that went beyond what Hutt had given him. That alone was hopeful. The old man must still have doubts or be prepared to compromise in some way, Archer thought, or he'd have closed me off long before this.

A colored man took their coats at the entrance and there was the clink of ice from a small bar off the lobby. Archer's mouth felt dry and he wanted a drink, but Mr. Sandler merely poked his head through the door of the bar, muttering, "Want to see who's there." He looked in for a moment, then bobbed out. "God be praised," he said, "for once my son isn't holding up the bar at this hour." Then he took Archer's elbow and guided him toward the dining room. He indicated a staircase rising to the next floor, saying, "Used to be some of the biggest poker games in the state of Pennsylvania went on up there. In the old days. No more. None of the old spirit left. Now they come here with their wives," he said darkly, indicating with a gesture of his head a man and a woman going through the dining-room door ahead of them.

The dining room wasn't crowded and Mr. Sandler guided Archer over to a small table in a corner, away from any of the other diners. As they passed the other tables, Mr. Sandler nodded brusquely, and grunted greetings. The men who said hello to him were mostly middle-aged, substantial-looking, with that look of being a little behind schedule that businessmen have at lunch.

"Hello, Charlie," Mr. Sandler said to the headwaiter, who had come over to their table. "Got any oysters today?"

"Yes, sir, Mr. Sandler," the headwaiter said.

"I praised them to Mr. Archer. Fried. Make sure they're nice. Mr. Archer's from New York and he's critical. He eats in the best restaurants. Or he ought to, the money he's making." Mr. Sandler grinned. "I'll have them, too. What're you drinking, Archer?"

"Bourbon old-fashioned, please," Archer said.

"Two, Charlie," said Mr. Sandler. "And don't seat anyone near us, will you? We're talking business."

"Of course, Mr. Sandler," the waiter said. He went off toward the bar.

"Didn't drink until I was fifty," Mr. Sandler said. "Then I heard a hotel owner at a summer resort say he didn't like Jews to come to his place because they didn't drink, and all his profit came from the bar. Thought that was a reasonable enough attitude. Promptly went at the bottle. Haven't stopped since." He smiled briefly. "Pleasantest way of combating anti-Semitism yet devised. You knew I was Jewish, didn't you?"

"Yes," Archer said, feeling uncomfortable.

"The nose." Mr. Sandler tapped his nose vigorously. "Gets longer every year. Never stops growing. Hell of an imposition on the chosen people. Ever see Napoleon's death mask?"

"No, I don't believe I have," Archer said wonderingly, feeling that Mr. Sandler jumped around unfairly.

"Nose nearly down to his chin. With all his other troubles. Tough on a vain man. Often wondered what Napoleon thought when he looked in the mirror in the morning on St. Helena. Now," he said, "I suppose you're waiting to hear from me."

"Well, yes," Archer said. "Naturally."

"What would you like to hear me say?" Mr. Sandler leaned forward over the table and peered shrewdly at Archer.

"I suppose I'd like you to say I can go back to the old system of putting on the show," Archer said. "Hire anyone who's good for the show and fire anyone who's bad for the show."

"Uhuh." Mr. Sandler nodded. "Thought you'd say that. Won't do it, though. Can't do it. If you're going to stick to that, I guess I'll just have to shake your hand, wish you good luck and say good-bye. After lunch, of course. Do you still want to listen to me?"

"Yes," Archer said.

"Good. Glad to see you're a reasonable man. Thanks, Charlie," Mr. Sandler said to the waiter, who was placing their drinks in front of them. He lifted his glass. "Health," he said.

They drank. The old-fashioned was very good, almost straight Bourbon, with just a twist of lemon-peel to point up its flavor.

"I hate to have to say what I just did," Mr. Sandler said. "For thirty years I've run my business on one basis and one basis only. Does a man produce or doesn't he? If he produces he goes up. If he doesn't —out. That receptionist in my office—that colored girl. Some of the people around me raised hell when I brought her up from bookkeeping. Thought it would antagonize some of our contacts, seeing her sitting there in the front office like that. But she's smart—she's pretty—she's got a nice, soft voice on the telephone, I like to hear it—and she knows how to let the right people in without falling all over them and keep the wrong people out without making them feel as though they had leprosy. Best girl for the job I've ever had. And she's worked out fine. Nobody's complained. Just the opposite. People wait for hours, with pleasure, feasting their eyes. And Ferris. My general manager. An Irishman. Big, rough Mick, and when he first came up he was as crude as a stone club. But I gave him a big share of stock in 1940 and when I die, he's getting enough to give him a controlling interest in the business. My wife's been after me to put my boy in. Not a chance. Boy's useless. I'm very fond of him, but he'd run the business into the ground in three years. I didn't work all my life for that. I'd spin in my grave like a rotisserie. Affection is for the home. Domestic consumption only." Mr. Sandler looked up as the waiter put the plates of fried oysters on the table. "Taste them," he commanded. "If you don't like 'em, send 'em back."

"Delicious," Archer said. The oysters were tender and nut-like, with a crumbly brown crust. Mr. Sandler ate with evident pleasure, using his knife and fork neatly and methodically.

Mr. Sandler waited until the waiter left the table. "Now," he said, "I have to change the pattern. The old days're over. The free and easy days're gone. I don't pretend I like it. I won't say it wasn't better when you hired and fired as you damn well pleased and could tell anyone who poked his nose into your business to get the hell out of your office. These days everyone and his brother is strolling in as though he had seventy-five percent of the stock and telling you, Do this, you can't do this, pay so much, withhold, deduct, add, get permission, open your books. The labor unions, the Government, the God-damn Treasury Department. Do over ten thousand dollars a year and you're a bloody public institution. And I didn't bring it about." Mr. Sandler waved his fork for emphasis. "Your sainted Mr. Roosevelt and his holy heirs and assigns. This is the age of the meddler, and you and your fellow Democrats started it, so don't be surprised if people you don't like very much also get the notion into their head to do a little meddling on their own account. You strapped business onto the operating table, and there's no way of our stopping it if some butcher gets into the operating room with a knife in his hand. Well, the meddlers're now telling me I can't advertise my product in a certain way. If I fight 'em, what happens? They boycott me, they get columnists to denounce me, they threaten my customers. I spend a million dollars a year for advertising. The function of advertising is to sell your product. What sort of businessman would I be if every dollar I spent for advertising lost me two dollars in trade? You're worried about five people. I'm trying to protect five thousand. And about the Communists. You have a fine, lofty notion about them, about protecting their rights. You haven't ever had to deal with the bastards. I'm a businessman. I have a big plant. I own land. I have stocks and bonds. What the hell do you think they'd do to me if they could? I'd disappear. Like that." Mr. Sandler snapped his fingers. His face was flushed now and he was speaking in a grumbling, driving tone, as though long years of grievances and fears had piled up in him and were all being expressed now. "They wouldn't even waste a bullet on an old cock like me. A club to the back of the head and they'd drop me into the nearest ditch. And this isn't fancy. It isn't poetry. It isn't theory. It's fact. Read anything the bastards have ever written, where they've been honest for more than a minute at a time, and you can see it. Liquidation of the bourgeoisie they call it. What do you think that means? Well, I'm the bourgeoisie and I'm not ready to be liquidated and I'll fight them till one of us drops. I know them. They've been sucking around this plant since 1930—and the God-damn New Deal pampered them and blew them up with their own importance and put them where they really could do you harm. There hasn't been a year since then that they haven't started trouble in this plant. And if you think that all they wanted was more money for the help and better working conditions, you're out of your mind. In 1940, I was making a lot of stuff for lend-lease to France and England and they tried to strike me. I don't mind a union coming up and asking for ten cents an hour more if they think they've earned it, but I'll see them in hell first before I sit down with them and give in to them just because their pals in Moscow have a dirty deal on for the time being with the Germans. I had the FBI in here and I fired every last one of them we uncovered. For a couple of days it looked as though we'd have to close down, and we've never closed down for a day in thirty years now. But I'd shut up tomorrow rather than give in to them. I know the bastards and I won't have one of them near enough to piss on. I kicked my own nephew out of the house because he came home from college telling me about the glories of Lenin and the inevitability of revolution. God-damn little fool. If there's any kind of crisis, I'll turn his name in to the Government and have him locked up, so help me God."

Mr. Sandler had long ago forgotten about eating. He sat with both fists clenched on the table, his face flushed, his eyes pale and angry. Archer listened helplessly, pretending to eat, wondering if there was any sense in staying on.

"And I told his mother that," Mr. Sandler said. "Right to her face. My own sister. The tears rained down like a waterfall. A disgraceful thing for a Jewish boy. All those Jewish names you see on the Communist lists. Ammunition for the enemy. And they're senseless. Back in '39 and '40, they were all for helping the Nazis, just because Stalin had signed a paper with them. What sort of people are they? A dumb animal in the field has more sense of self-preservation. And I've heard all the arguments. They feel rejected, they can't get into some colleges, clubs, hotels, professions. They're suffering from a wound and they rebel. Crap. There're a lot of hotels I can't get into. I can't even play golf with Mike Ferris at his club. So what? What wound am I suffering from? I graduated from the University of Pennsylvania. I started a business. I got rich. I sent my two boys to college, and my oldest son was a captain in the Air Force. If I was wounded, I just worked harder because of it. There's a joke about it. A typical Jewish joke. Cohen is angry. He can't get into a hotel. He tells Levy, 'You know what we are—we're second-class citizens in this country.' Levy thinks for a minute and he looks up to Heaven. 'God forbid,' he says, 'it should ever change.'"

Mr. Sandler looked fiercely at Archer. Archer didn't laugh. He was sorry he had heard the joke. Its bitter lilt, he knew, would echo and re-echo in his brain whenever he talked to a Jew from now on. There was nothing to be said, he felt. This was intra-mural information, not to be commented on by strangers. Mr. Sandler sighed, surprisingly. He resumed eating, moving the food neatly on his plate. The flush receded from his face, and his old man's grouchy anger seemed for the moment to be spent. "And what do they think would happen to them if there was Communism here?" Mr. Sandler asked mildly, his voice adapted to theory. "What's happening in Russia? The Jews're being wiped out. First the religion—then the community—then the individual. It's in the papers every day and even so they won't believe it. There's no room for a minority. Everybody's got to be the same. They wiped out millions of their own people. Why do you think they'll stop at the Jews? And it's in the papers every day. All you have to do is read. Aaah—sometimes I wake up in the morning and I say, 'Thank God I'm an old man and I'm going to die in four years.'" He stared down thoughtfully at his plate. "I was the one," he said softly, "who told Hutt Pokorny had to be fired immediately. I hate Pokorny—personally—even though I've never met him."

"I don't think you're being quite fair," Archer said. "Pokorny hasn't said a political word since 1925."

"Maybe not," Mr. Sandler said. "But he lied to get in here. And he's married to a Communist. If you live with a woman you're responsible for her."

Archer thought of the enormous and furious woman and the meek, slipshod little round man. He grinned at the possibility of anyone's being responsible for Mrs. Pokorny. "You ought to see the lady," he said.

"I'm not interested," Mr. Sandler said curtly. "And the sooner the sonofabitch is out of the country the better I'll like it."

Archer looked across at the old man picking gingerly at his food. The face was set, implacable, sixty years of stubbornness freezing the long, thin mouth. Pokorny, Archer thought, doomed in Vienna, Mexico, Philadelphia, unacceptable to Gentile or Jew.

"I think," Archer said gently, more for his own sake than from any hope of saving the musician, "that you might at least give him fifteen minutes and talk to him . . ."

"I don't want to hear anything more about him," Mr. Sandler said flatly. "Not a word." He put down his knife and fork with a gesture of finality. "It's getting late," he said, looking at his watch. "I have to get back to the plant. I'm going to offer you a proposition. I'm not going to bargain with you, Archer. Take it or leave it as I give it to you. Pokorny is out. Motherwell is out. Permanently. Atlas is out. If he won't lift a finger to defend himself, I can't be bothered with him."

Archer stared at the old man. He was speaking in a clipped, decisive voice, giving orders as he had been giving orders for forty years. His teeth clicked as he talked. They were his own teeth, Archer decided. How many thousands of dollars, Archer speculated, listening, have gone to dentists to preserve those old, cleansed bones.

"Weller . . ." For the first time, Mr. Sandler hesitated. "We'll see about her. Keep her off for awhile, three weeks, a month. Then maybe you can slip her back once or twice and see what happens. As for Herres . . ." He stopped.

Archer felt himself growing rigid in his chair. The fork in his hand trembled a little and he put it down carefully on the plate in front of him.

"You guarantee," Mr. Sandler said softly, "that Herres is not a Communist."

"Yes," said Archer, after a moment.

"You've known him a long time," Mr. Sandler said. "I trust you." The words were intended to be kind, Archer realized, but the tone was cold and threatening. "I've decided you're an honest man and I'm taking your word on Herres. And it's hard to fire a man who was wounded and won the Silver Star. But, remember —I'm doing this on your responsibility. No one else's. I hold you personally accountable for Herres. Is that understood?"

"Understood."

"Now—" Mr. Sandler said. "That's the deal. If you want it, I'll call Hutt this afternoon and tell him who's staying and who's going. If you don't want it—I'll accept your resignation right now."

Mr. Sandler peered at Archer, his eyes narrow and searching. Archer looked down at his plate. Three sacrificed, he thought, three saved. Counting himself. Actually, including Motherwell, it was only two sacrificed. And Pokorny was hopeless, in any event. Outlawed, rejected, caught in clumsy, long-ago errors beyond anyone's power to rectify. Fighting for him was hopeless, romantic, meaningless destruction. And Atlas . . . Money in the bank, rents from two buildings, with a passage to France in his pocket . . . You might feel, perhaps, that it was unjust, but pity was not demanded.

"All right," Archer said, "I want it."

Mr. Sandler nodded. He looked down at his watch again. "If you skip coffee," he said, "you can make the two-o'clock train."

Archer stood up. "I'll get my coffee in the diner," he said. "Thanks for the lunch."

Mr. Sandler sat in his place, looking up at Archer, his forehead wrinkled, as though there was one last doubt he was pondering. Then he shook his head and stood up. He put out his hand and Archer shook it.

"Come down again, some time," Mr. Sandler said. "I'll take you through the plant."

"Thank you," said Archer. "I'll try to make it."

"I think I'll just sit here for a moment," Mr. Sandler said, sliding back into his chair. "If you don't mind. Have my coffee quietly." He was almost mumbling now. Suddenly he seemed like a tired old man, wrinkled, low in energy, full of doubts and premonitions, testy, wanting to be left alone with his old-man's reflections.

"Of course," Archer said. "Good-bye." He walked past the other tables. Somebody had just told a joke and the four men at one table were laughing loudly.

By the time the train reached Trenton, Archer felt that he had engineered a triumph that noon in Philadelphia.

16

"You can go in now," Miss Walsh said. "Mr. Hutt is ready for you now." There was a frost on Miss Walsh this morning. Like a sensitive pet, she reflected the mood of her master. As Archer went toward Hutt's door, he noticed the slight glitter of perspiration all over Miss Walsh's face. Maybe, he thought cruelly, I'll put one of those advertisements for the new deodorants in an envelope and send it to her through the mails, anonymously. The Chlorophyl tablet, to be taken by mouth, and guaranteed to neutralize all body odors, all vapors of sweat and metabolic processes, for twenty-four hours at a time. Neutrality in Miss Walsh was much to be desired.

Hutt was behind his desk, his face sunburned and peeling over his neat gray flannel suit. O'Neill was sitting, very straight, near the window. The night before, at midnight, Hutt had called Archer from the airport in Florida and had told him to be in the office at three o'clock. Over the long wire, Hutt's voice had been remote and without passion. "I'll be in by then," he had said, without any preliminaries. "I want to talk to you."

Whatever O'Neill or Miss Walsh had said to the

contrary, Hutt had not been out of reach of the telephone. Momentarily, Archer wondered what the conversation between Mr. Sandler and Hutt, sunburned, in a gay shirt, on a warm beach, had been like the day before.

"Sit down," Hutt said, in his soft voice. O'Neill said nothing. He stared at Archer, his face grave, sober, waiting.

Archer seated himself on a hard chair. He tried to arrange his legs so that he looked at ease.

"You've been very clever, Archer," Hutt said flatly, almost whispering. The bright wedge of his vacation-stained face was calm and expressed nothing. "You've won what might be called a temporary success." He waited, as if to hear what Archer had to say to this. But Archer remained silent.

"I don't know what you said to Mr. Sandler," Hutt went on. "But you must have been very convincing." There was almost a tone of flattery in his voice. "The old man is not ordinarily easy to convince. You also managed to get me on a plane and interrupt a very pleasant vacation." Still, there was no complaint or censure in his voice. Even now, he sounded as though he was surprised and impressed by the far-reaching ingenuity of a man whom he had not regarded particularly highly before this. "Prior to your little journey to Philadelphia," Hutt went on, "you knew, of course, about our rule about approaching any of our sponsors?"

"Yes," Archer said. "I did."

Hutt nodded pleasantly. "I thought as much. So it wasn't ignorance that led you to violate one of the oldest customs of this organization."

"No," Archer said. "It was quite deliberate." He saw that Hutt was waiting for him to continue, but he kept silent, resolved not to defend himself.

"It may interest you to know," Hutt said, "that before you came in here O'Neill and I were discussing the advisability of dropping the Sandler account altogether." He waited again, but Archer merely peered blandly at him, refusing to be drawn out.

"We decided not to drop it," Hutt said, "for the time being. We will go on with it—under the—ah—new conditions imposed by you and Mr. Sandler. Looking at the question in the round, we agreed that it was inadvisable to force this particular issue at the moment. Didn't we, Emmet?"

"Yes," said Emmet, staring stonily ahead of him.

"From now on, Archer," Hutt whispered, his freckled hands flat out on the desk in front of him, "we will institute a change in system. Emmet will do all the hiring for University Town. You can, of course, submit a list of people to him, but the final choice will be with him. Is that clear?"

Archer hesitated. When he had signed the contract for the program, he had fought hard for the right to choose his own people. Without it, a director could hardly be responsible for the quality of what went over the air. Still, he thought wearily, I've made so many compromises—one more or less is of small importance. And O'Neill was a reasonable man. "OK," he said. "If that's the way you want it."

"Exactly." Hutt smiled gently. "We've decided that University Town is in need of more direct supervision than heretofore."

Heretofore, Archer thought, I don't know another man who would use "heretofore" in conversation.

"I don't know," Hutt went on, "whether you've informed Mr. Herres and Mrs. Weller of their new—ah —status. . . ."

"No," Archer said, "I haven't. I was waiting to talk to you and O'Neill."

"Ah," Hutt said softly, "were you? Technically, which would you prefer? Would you like Emmet to speak to them or would you prefer to do it in person and savor the full taste of victory yourself?" Hutt smiled obliquely and softly at him from behind the desk.

"I'll call them," Archer said.

Hutt shrugged. "Whatever you say." He looked down at his desk reflectively, incongruously and humorously sunburned, with his nose peeling and the tips of his ears very red. "I think that about clears it up. Except for one thing. I'm sorry you didn't decide to heed my warning the last time you were in this office. If you recall, I told you that it was dangerous in these times to find yourself defending unpopular causes. . . ."

"I'm not defending any cause," Archer said. "I'm defending two people who deserve it. That's all."

Hutt waved his hand deprecatingly and smiled again. "Unpopular people, then," he said gently. "I don't know exactly what your reasons are but I no doubt shall discover them in good time." The threat was there and Archer noted it. "Meanwhile," Hutt went on, his voice barely audible on the other side of the desk, "I'm afraid I have to tell you that you've destroyed any value you might have had in the future to our organization. . . ."

Our organization, Archer thought. He says it in the same way he might say our church, our regiment, our flag, our country. He never uses the word company or corporation or business.

"Somehow," Hutt said with a thin smile, "you seem to have mesmerized poor, foolish old Mr. Sandler, and I must keep you on for the time being for his sake. . . ."

Archer stood up. "I got him full of gin," he said, "and promised him two blondes the next time he came to New York, if you want to know how I worked it. I'll be going now. I have some work to do." He felt himself trembling and knew that a dozen rash and hateful and hurting things were forcing themselves to his tongue and he knew he shouldn't say them. He made himself walk slowly to the door.

"One final word, Mr. Archer," Hutt said, still seated

at his desk, looking down reflectively at his hands, flat on the desk, with the mark of the Southern holiday sun on them, "before you leave. Let me advise you to be discreet. After University Town is finished—and perhaps sooner—you will find yourself no longer working for us. I would be less than candid if I didn't tell you that it is entirely possible that you will find yourself working for no one at all." He looked up then, staring at Archer, thin-faced, urbane, baleful, pleased to let Archer know that he was his enemy and that he was powerful.

Amazing, Archer thought, even when he threatens a man, he does it in paragraphs. Archer looked at the slender man behind the desk, feeling that all means of communication were down between them. There was nothing to say. Archer turned on his heel and went out. Miss Walsh looked at him damply as he passed her.

Standing in the telephone booth downstairs, Archer listened to the buzzing in the receiver and watched the traffic in the lobby. Portly middle-aged men in overcoats trotted by, stenographers with glasses, office-boys carrying bags in which the mid-afternoon coffee was put up in containers. All of them with hurried business faces, discontented, wishing it was five-thirty. Watching them, Archer decided that he would be more careful from now on about the expression on his face. The mouth, he decided, is the crucial feature. The women, he thought, are the worst. Woman after woman who would otherwise have been quite pretty passed the booth window, unconscious of being watched, their youth and their good looks canceled by the down-pulling lines of petulance, self-pity, disappointment, hunger. Has it always been like this, Archer wondered, or is this a special stigma of the time and place, of New York and 1950?

He heard the click at the other end of the wire, and then Vic's voice.

"Vic," Archer said, "this is Clement."

"I remember the name," Vic said.

Archer smiled. "How are things at home?"

"The measles," Vic said, "have been contained. I'm spending a quiet afternoon trying to decide whether to take a nap, pay last month's bills, or go out and get the evening papers. What's doing in your sector?"

"You're still in business," Archer said lightly. "The American public is not going to be deprived of the sweet sound of your voice after all."

"Oh," Vic said. There was a pause on the wire. "Many thanks," he said offhandedly. "How did you do it?"

"I went down to Philadelphia and talked to the sponsor."

"You must have made quite a speech," Vic said. He sounded embarrassed. "I'm sorry I wasn't there to hear the golden flood of oratory."

"I hardly said anything," Archer said. "He talked most of the time. But his wife met you at a cocktail party. . . ."

"I remember her," Vic said. "Weight one-ninety, growing bald on top."

"Don't say anything mean about her. She dropped to the floor senseless with your charm."

"Delightful lady," Vic said. "I wouldn't have her a pound lighter. Still, you don't mean to say the old man really let that change him."

"Not exactly," Archer said. He hesitated, sorry that he was conducting this conversation over the phone. "I told him about the Silver Star and the wound."

"Oh," Vic said, "did the patriot weep?"

"He had a kid killed in Tunisia," Archer said, displeased at Vic's light tone.

"I will appear at the next broadcast," Vic said, "in full regimentals, with fourragère, carrying a well-worn carbine."

"It wasn't only that, Vic," Archer said seriously. "I told him what you'd said to me."

"You mean you vouched for me?"

"I suppose you could call it that," Archer said.

"I get all kinds of service out of you, don't I?" Vic's tone was still light, but Archer could detect the note of tenderness behind it.

"Forget it," Archer said brusquely, anxious suddenly to hang up the phone.

"How about Hutt?" Vic asked. "Is he being sporting?"

"Not very. He had to cut his vacation in Florida short."

Vic chuckled. "Sad," he said. "Oh, that's very sad." Then he became serious. "How about the others?"

"I'll tell you about it when I see you."

"Not good, eh?"

"Not too good," Archer admitted.

"From now on," Vic said, "have more foresight. Hire character actresses who have the Purple Heart."

Archer disregarded the sour joke. "When do we see you?" he asked.

"Tonight at five-thirty," Vic said. "Nancy and I're going with you to see Jane's play. Nancy arranged it with Kitty. We're going in my car. We can eat on the road."

"Don't expect too much from the play," Archer said, protecting Jane in advance. "I heard her reading over her lines on Sunday. She's not the most accomplished young actress in the world."

Vic laughed. "Don't worry, Papa," he said. "I'll take into account age, weight and the playing conditions of the field. See you later. And thanks again for Philadelphia."

"Sure," Archer said hurriedly. "I'll let you pay half the fare."

Vic was chuckling as he hung up. Archer held the receiver down with one hand, while he dug in his pocket with the other hand for some nickels. That was the easy one, he thought, as he put the nickel in the slot and dialed Atlas's number. Now it gets tougher.

There was no answer at the other end of the wire.

Archer waited for five rings, then hung up and took back his nickel with a sense of relief. Atlas, he decided, could wait till rehearsal on Thursday. It was a pleasure that could bear postponement, Archer thought grimly. He put the nickel back in the box and dialed Alice Weller's number.

"Well," Alice said worriedly, when Archer asked her if he could see her immediately, "I promised Ralph I'd take him ice-skating this afternoon and we were just going out the door when the phone rang. . . ."

"Where does he skate?" Archer asked. He wanted to get it straight with Alice as soon as possible.

"Rockefeller Center," said Alice. "And he likes me to watch him and I . . ."

"I'm down near there now," Archer said. "He won't mind if his mother talks to an old friend while he's doing his figure eights, will he?"

"Now, Clement," Alice laughed uncomfortably, "now you're making fun of me. It's just that I've sort of gotten into the habit of going with him on Tuesday afternoons . . ."

"Do you skate, too?"

"Sometimes." She giggled. "Do you think it's silly?"

"Of course not. Bring your skates today, too," Archer said. "I can say everything I have to say in fifteen minutes." He looked at his watch. "It's three-thirty now. Will you be here by four o'clock?"

"I don't like to inconvenience you, Clement," Alice said worriedly. "If you'd prefer coming up here, I'm sure Ralph would understand. . . ."

There was a murmur on the other end of the wire and Archer was sure Ralph was in the room, listening, and showing signs that he wouldn't understand at all. "Now, Ralph," he heard Alice say firmly, away from the phone, "I'm talking to Mr. Archer. . . ."

"Four o'clock," Archer said loudly, annoyed with Alice's self-sacrificing politeness. "At the entrance." He hung up before Alice could say anything else.

With a half-hour to waste, Archer strolled idly down Fifth Avenue, looking in the shop windows, trying consciously not to think of the interview with Hutt and its implications for the future. He passed the window of a men's wear shop and remembered that Kitty had told him last week that his tailor had called and asked him to come up for a fitting of a new suit that he was having made. The tailor's shop was only a couple of blocks away and he turned in that direction.

Teague Brothers was a dark establishment one flight up on a side street. Mr. Teague was a tall, gloomy-looking gentleman who wore a high starched collar and a piped vest. He often worked over the cloth himself, his jacket off, the piping on his vest immaculate, his cuffs impeccably starched. Kitty, who liked more dashing clothes than Archer, complained that Teague Brothers made all their customers look like retired police captains and it was true that most of the people Archer had seen in the course of years in the shop were bulky men with grave, official faces. They all had wide middles that Mr. Teague took a gloomy satisfaction in covering in fine, loose, dark cloth. Mr. Teague always made the waistband of Archer's trousers an inch too large, as though it was inconceivable to him that any man who could afford his suits would not eat too much in the years ahead. Archer liked the slow, dark atmosphere of the shop and its hushed air of belonging to an older and more substantial time.

Ministerially, Mr. Teague made marks with his tailor's chalk on the soft tweed of the new jacket, as though he were conducting a baptism. The jacket felt free and light on Archer's shoulders, and as he regarded himself in the three-way-mirror he looked forward with pleasure to wearing the suit. Mr. Teague disapproved of padding in the shoulders and stiff reinforcements under the cloth. "I send men out of my shop," he was accustomed to say, "ready to go to board meetings and appear in proper restaurants, not to play in the line for the New York Giants." Many of his customers had found the suits appropriate to be buried in, too, but Mr. Teague, whatever private satisfaction he might have taken in this fact, did not refer to it in his conversation.

"Mr. Spinelli," Mr. Teague called into the back room, where the cutting was done, "Mr. Spinelli, will you come in here, please?" He turned back to Archer and said, "Mr. Spinelli is our new head fitter, Mr. Archer. He has one or two bad mannerisms; he worked for a department store on Fifth Avenue which will be nameless . . ." The soul of discretion and disapproval, Mr. Teague lowered his voice as he said this. "But we are working on him."

"What happened to Schwartz?" Archer asked, looking over his shoulder at the reflection of his back in the mirror. Schwartz, a pale little man with bifocal glasses and a silent, swift, loving manner of touching cloth, had been with Teague Brothers for more than thirty years. He had made perhaps ten suits for Archer without speaking more than a hundred words to him.

"We buried Schwartz last week," Mr. Teague said, sighing. "He had cancer of the lungs for two years. Worked until the end. We closed the shop for the morning and all went to the funeral. Have you ever been to a Jewish funeral?"

"No," Archer said.

"Barbaric," Mr. Teague said. "They all keep their hats on. And the women scream like banshees. He was a good tailor, Schwartz. Irreplaceable. Ah, Mr. Spinelli," Teague said to a tall dark-faced man with white hair who came in from the back room. "This is Mr. Archer. I'd like you to take a look at the jacket, if you will."

Mr. Spinelli walked consideringly around Archer, as though he was contemplating buying him. "The shoulders," he said finally, "perhaps a little low. . . ."

"Mr. Archer likes the shoulders low," Mr. Teague said rebukingly.

"In that case," Mr. Spinelli said, retreating, "the garment is just about right." Archer felt a momentary touch of pity for the new master tailor, competing with the perfect ghost of the silent Schwartz. Mr. Spinelli, with a little bow, went back to the bench in the rear of the shop.

"You see what I mean," Mr. Teague said. "And it will get worse. The suits will get uglier and more expensive every year." He sighed. "Everything goes up but quality. In ten years we'll be lucky to be able to make a suit to order. The custom trade is dying. People are reconciling themselves to be dressed by machines. In your lifetime, Mr. Archer, I am afraid you will see every man on the street looking as though he has been manufactured by the same company. And it is impossible to find tailors any more. Only old men, who are dying off. And there are no new ones coming up. All the Polish Jews who knew how to sew and who used to immigrate here have been killed off by the Germans. The English . . ." Mr. Teague stared unhappily up at the ceiling, thinking about the English. "They do not immigrate—and at home—a Socialist government. What does a Socialist care about a fine seam or a good piece of cloth? And young Americans . . ." Mr. Teague sighed, reflecting upon his youthful compatriots. "They scorn the trade. They'd rather work in a garage or in a factory for less money than sit down and learn tailoring. They turn their backs on the opportunity. They think there's something degrading about sitting in a nice, warm, comfortable shop sewing on a gentleman's garment. Sometimes, Mr. Archer," Mr. Teague said soberly, "I must confess I am tempted to retire once and for all. The suit will be ready next week. I'll send it down." He smiled bleakly at Archer and turned toward the front of the shop, where a retired Regular Army colonel was waiting, staring patiently at English magazines from 1925 that were carefully placed each morning on a big oak table.

Archer went into a cubbyhole and dressed slowly, thinking of the silent Mr. Schwartz, only slightly more still now than in life, and of massacred tailors, of stubborn young Americans in workman's overalls, and of the gloomy, ill-clothed future of the world. I'd better be careful with this suit, Archer thought, taking a last look at the jacket hanging on its hook. Who knows when I'll be able to afford another one?

It was getting late now, and he hurried over to the skating rink at Rockefeller Center, where Alice Weller was waiting for him.

She had arranged the usual disaster with her clothes. A bright red skirt that was too short for her long, thick legs made her seem very wide and it was topped by a bulky jacket of nondescript fur. She had put on red wool socks over her stockings to keep her feet warm, and they made her look like a sorrowful parody of a bobby-soxer. Squarish and sagging, she suffered in contrast to the swift and charmingly dressed girls swooping around the ice with quick swirls of their short skirts. As usual, Archer felt a pang of guilt for noticing these things. She was standing at the railing, peering out at her son Ralph, who was slowly and clumsily making his way around the rink. Ralph was a gangling and serious-faced boy, very pale, and with one look at him you knew that the easy and instinctive movements of an athlete would be forever beyond him. The loud-speaker was blaring a waltz and Alice didn't hear Archer come up behind her. Archer watched her for a moment, the loving, aging, proud, anxious face below the massive flying gold figure of Prometheus in his ring across the rink. Whatever happens, Archer thought, before touching her shoulder, it is necessary to protect this decent and wavering woman and her awkward, serious child.

"Alice," Archer said. "I hope I didn't keep you waiting too long."

"Oh, no." She turned, smiling her soft, uncertain

smile. "I love to watch Ralph anyway. Wave to him."

Archer waved to him. With a great look of concentration, Ralph waved back, once, almost upsetting himself with the movement.

"He's getting much better," Alice said, looking fondly at her son. "He'll be a wonderful skater by the time he grows up."

"I'm sure," Archer said.

"He has weak ankles," Alice said. "The doctor said this would be very good for him."

"Alice," said Archer, "let's go in and get a drink there. We can sit at the window and watch just as well. It's cold standing down here."

Alice looked worried, as though even putting just a pane of glass between her and Ralph was a problem. "Ralph," she called, as the boy scraped slowly toward them, "we're going in for a minute. We'll be right at the window, so we can see you."

"All right, Mother," Ralph said. "Hello, Mr. Archer," he said, holding onto the railing.

"Hello, Ralph," Archer said. "Your mother says you're improving wonderfully."

"I have weak ankles," Ralph said.

"Be careful now, darling," Alice said. "Don't try anything too hard."

Archer watched the boy push cautiously away from the railing. No, Archer thought as he and Alice walked toward the entrance to the café that lined one side of the rink, there's a boy you can depend upon will not try anything too hard. If our new child is a boy, Archer thought unreasonably, I will brain him if he has weak ankles.

They found a table at the large plate-glass window and Archer helped Alice off with her fur jacket before taking off his own coat. They both sat facing the rink. The skaters sailed silently up to the glass, brightly colored figures in a fluid winter mural, making a charming quarter acre of holiday in the heart of the city, young, playful, and oblivious of the world's work being conducted in the gray buildings which surrounded them. Archer ordered tea for Alice and a whiskey for himself.

"I love this spot," Alice said. "It's so—faraway."

Archer nodded at the strange word. "I know what you mean."

"It's extravagant for us to come here twice a week," Alice said, "but I can't resist it." She turned her eyes away from the figure of her son on the ice and looked at Archer worriedly. "Clement," she said, "have you any news for me?"

"Yes."

"Good or bad?"

Archer hesitated. "Good," he said. "Pretty good."

"What does that mean?" Her voice was immediately fearful, the voice of a woman for whom all modification of the word good had inevitably been disastrous.

"I got a promise out of the sponsor," Archer said. "Or at least a half promise. After awhile you can work again. . . ."

"After awhile?" Alice's voice sank. "How long?"

"Three, four weeks."

"Is that definite?"

Archer looked out the window. A girl in a flying pale-blue wool skirt was doing intricate figures on the center of the ice, exultant, effortless, beyond the fear of gravity or failure. "It's almost definite, Alice," Archer said gently, still watching the girl, who was down on the point of one skate now, in a tight, whirling dance. In the foreground, just in front of the window, Ralph plodded past. He waved soberly at his mother. Alice made herself smile and waved back at her son.

The waiter came over with Alice's tea and the whiskey. Archer measured the soda into his glass, glad to have something to occupy his hands.

"What does it depend on?" Alice asked. "Can I do something to help myself?"

"I'm afraid not, Alice. I think the sponsor wants to wait and see how much of a fuss is kicked up in the next couple of weeks."

"It's not fair," Alice said. She was nearly sobbing, and her lined, tragic face was incongruous over the gay skating sweater that she had worn under her fur jacket. "I ought to be allowed to do something, say something . . . They don't understand. They don't care. Nobody cares."

Archer put his hand over hers in sympathy, hoping to keep her from crying. "I care, Alice," he said lamely. "I'm doing my best. We live in queer times. We just have to hope we can weather them. Honestly, I think you'll be back at work within a month and this whole thing will have blown over."

"A month," Alice said, trying to control herself. "How am I going to live for a month without working? Why couldn't they have told me about this three weeks ago when I was offered that job on the road? Why did they have to wait like this? Why is everybody so mean?"

"Look, Alice," Archer said, "I'll help you. Do you need money?"

"I can't take money from you," Alice said brokenly. "What right have I to take money from you?"

"Don't talk like that. How much do you need?"

"I have a hundred and sixty-five dollars," Alice said, "and the rent hasn't been paid yet this month and. . . ."

"Is that all you have?" Archer asked incredulously, sickened at the thinness of the shield between Alice and extinction.

"What did you think?" Alice asked with a flat attempt at irony. "Did you think I had a million dollars hidden away in bonds?"

"I'm sorry." Archer reached into his pocket and took out his check book and pen. He wrote out a check for a hundred dollars. "Here." He put it in her hand. "This'll help for awhile." Alice looked down dazedly at the check in her hand, as though she couldn't quite make out the handwriting. "It's not much," Archer said, quickly, anxious to forestall thanks, "but it may tide you over. And if you need more, call me."

"Oh, Clement . . ." There was no stopping the tears now, and people at other tables looked over curiously at the large, gaily dressed woman, weeping and clutching a check among the tea things. "I don't know how I can do it. And I have to do it. I have to . . . I'm so afraid. I haven't been able to go to sleep since you came up to my house last week. There's no one I can turn to. You're the only one. No one is interested. Except Ralph. And I have to pretend to him that everything is fine. It's so lonesome . . . lonesome . . ." She choked up and bowed her head. Her hands, with their inaccurate polish on the uneven nails, worked convulsively, crushing the check. Sniffing, she spread the check out on the table, smoothing it. Then she folded it neatly and put it in her bag.

The girl in the pale wool skirt swept past the window. She had short black hair and blue eyes and her face was young, empty, almost bored with her proficiency.

"You don't have to sit here with me," Alice said after awhile. "I'm sure you're busy." She was embarrassed now and didn't look at Archer. She stared at the girl making her lazy perfect circle of the rink. "When I was young," she said, "I had legs like that. Go ahead, Clement." There was sudden pleading in her voice. "Please go."

"You'll call me if you need me, now," Archer said.

"Yes."

"Promise?"

"I promise."

Archer put down some money for the drinks and stood up. "And I'll call you and let you know what's happening, Alice," he said. "Don't worry," he said, knowing that it sounded inane, but not having any other comfort to offer. He patted her shoulder and went out, leaving Alice at the window, watching her awkward son among the lilting figures of the swift, brightly colored girls.

17

"Come on, girls," Archer called upstairs. "Let's try to get there before the beginning of the third act."

Kitty was still getting dressed, with Nancy assisting. There was a giggle from above and then Nancy came to the head of the stairs. "Don't be a tyrant," she said. "Your poor pregnant wife is struggling with a stuck zipper." She smiled down at him. She was dressed in a plain black dress that Archer had seen on her before and thought very becoming. But tonight it somehow seemed too severe. Nancy looked tired and her hair, which was usually fluffed out and full of life, looked stringy and dull. Never a plump woman, she seemed to have lost weight in the last few weeks, too, and her face, under the clever makeup, looked drawn. Archer stared up at her, as she stood at the head of the short stairwell, leaning on the newel post. Something of what he was feeling must have shown in his face, because Nancy stopped smiling and said, "What's the matter, Clement? Is anything wrong?"

Archer shook his head. "No. Nothing." He was old enough to know that you never told a woman, no matter how friendly you were with her, that she was not looking her best. "I just don't want to be late. Jog my wife a little, like a good girl."

"Don't be mean to her," Nancy said. "You've got to pamper a lady at a time like this." She went into the bedroom.

We're getting old, Archer thought, remembering what Nancy had looked like when he had first seen her in the Indian summer classroom so many years ago. Old.

He went slowly into his study, where Vic was lounging in the easy chair.

"Don't worry, Clement," Vic said, "we've got plenty of time." He stood up. "Do you mind if I make a call? I promised young Clem I'd call him after he had his supper."

"Go ahead." Archer sat down wearily.

Vic went over to the telephone at the desk. He picked it up and dialed swiftly and carelessly. In the middle of the process, a strange expression came over Vic's face. He listened intently, holding the instrument close to his ear, his eyes downcast and serious. Briefly he glanced at Archer and opened his mouth, as though he wanted to say something. But the phone was answered before the words came out.

"Hello," Vic said into the phone. "Clem? How're things?" He held the phone a little away from his ear and Archer could hear the high, shrill, excited voice of the child at the other end of the line. "That's good," Vic said. "How was the lamb chop? Nice and rare? That's it. Never let them get away with it. The world is full of people who'll try to cook a man's lamb chop to death if you're not careful. Applesauce, too. Oh, that sounds delicious. That's just what I'm going to have for dinner, myself. Have you been nice to Johnny and Miss Tully? Remember, I'm depending on you, Clem." Vic smiled gravely into the phone at the boy's answer. "OK, son. I'll tell her. Good night. I'll be home early. No, not that early. I'll read to you tomorrow night. Tell Johnny I said to behave himself. Cheers." He put the phone down slowly, staring at it. "Ever since Saturday afternoon," Vic said to Archer, "he insists that everybody say 'Cheers' to him at least once every fifteen minutes." Vic didn't move away from the desk. "Clement," he said, "did you know your phone was tapped?"

Archer was staring at the evening paper on his lap. He looked up. "What was that?"

"Your phone is tapped," Vic said. "Did you know it?"

"What?" Archer said dazedly.

"Your phone is . . ."

"Yes. Yes. I heard you." Archer stood up and went over to the desk. He looked down stupidly at the black plastic instrument with the white divided dial. 1, ABC 2, DEF 3, 0, at the end, all by itself, to call the Operator. "No, I didn't know. How do you know?" He looked sharply at Vic to see if he was joking.

Vic wasn't joking. "During the war," he said, "I had a friend in the OSS. They showed him how to recognize it by the tone. He let me listen in on a telephone booth in Washington that was tapped. In a restaurant frequented by certain gentlemen from governments in exile."

Archer looked down incredulously at the innocent-seeming piece of machinery, no different from ten million others all over the country. He picked it up and listened. It sounded like every other telephone he had ever put to his ear.

"Dial a few numbers," Vic said in a low voice. "You'll hear a kind of echo after each click."

Archer hesitated a moment. Then he dialed four times, at random. The echo was there. He put the phone down. His first emotion was anger. "God damn it," he said. "God damn it."

"Don't worry about it," Vic said carelessly. "There're probably fifty thousand taps on at this minute in this country. Maybe a million. You've got a lot of company. Tribal custom of the people."

"Who does it?" Archer asked. He was surprised at the thickness of his voice and the difficulty with which he formed the words. "Who the hell does it?"

Vic shrugged. "The FBI, most likely. They're busy little boys."

"You mean to say they have a man sitting somewhere all day and all night just listening to my phone?" Ludicrously, as he said it, he thought of the money it would cost the Government, three shifts a day, three men, with a fourth one for relief. How much did an FBI agent get? Four thousand, five thousand a year? Multiplied by four.

"No," Vic said. "I don't imagine so. They have recording sets. It all goes onto wax and somebody collects them and listens at his leisure."

Helplessly, Archer thought of a hard-faced young man in a slouch hat, like the ones you see in the movies, sitting alertly in an official-looking room, listening to Kitty ordering roast beef and lettuce from the market; to Gloria, in the slack part of the day, calling her niece in Harlem, complaining about finding Mr. Archer's pipe ashes all over the tables; to Jane agreeing to attend a football game with Bruce and going over the date the next day with her best friend, giggling icily and heartlessly about the transparency of the male sex; to Archer talking to O'Neill, asking him if he had a hangover, too, after the last night's drinks at Louis' bar. And to what other invitations, purchases, secrets, expressions of hope, of weariness, weakness, intimacies?

"Why do they do it?" Archer asked stupidly. "What's it for?"

"I couldn't tell you," Vic said soberly. "You'd have to tell me."

Archer stared at his friend. Is he suspicious, too, he wondered. "How about your phone?" he demanded. "Is that tapped, too?"

Vic rubbed the edge of his jaw. "No," he said.

"What does a man do about it?"

"Nothing," Vic said gently. "Absolutely nothing." He looked across at Archer, smiling. It was a strange, rather unpleasant smile.

"Is there something to be done? Isn't there someone to see? To explain . . . ?"

"Write a letter to the New York *Times*." Vic grinned crookedly. "Establish radio silence. Move to an island . . ."

There was the sound of footsteps descending the stairs, and the mingled voices of Nancy and Kitty. Archer jerked his head around toward the door. Then he swung back, just before the women entered the room. He shook his head warningly. Vic nodded, and Archer knew he wouldn't say anything about the phone in front of Kitty.

"Both you boys dead drunk by this time?" Nancy asked.

"Just about," Vic said. "Kitty, you look glorious."

"I'm glad to see you like fat girls," Kitty said. She did look beautiful. Her skin was plumped out by her pregnancy, silky and unlined, and her throat looked full and warm as it swept down into the low V of her silk jacket. Her eyes were bright and unshadowed and Archer could tell that she was prepared for joy and triumph as she sat in the audience watching her pretty and talented daughter add glory to the honor of the family that night.

"Vic," Nancy said, "I think we'll have to have another baby. Purely as a cosmetic measure. I want to look like that, too."

"Sure," Vic said. "I'll ask the boss for a raise for breeding purposes."

It all seemed unreal and distant to Archer. Was there a dictaphone hidden in the room, too, he wondered, along with the betrayed telephone? Why not? What would an FBI agent deduce from this conversation? That they were vulgar people, irreverent in the face of Motherhood, and by inference equally unreliable in their attitude toward other capitalized words? Patriotism, Loyalty, the Constitution? He shook his head. Kitty was saying something, and he hadn't heard.

"What's the matter, Clement?" she repeated, staring at him. "You're miles away. Are you worried about something?"

"He's a dreamer of dreams," Vic said. "He is seeing beauties that are not of this world."

"I am dreaming of dinner," Archer said. "I had a light lunch." He shook himself slightly and said, "Let's go," and they went out in a bustle of fur coats and scarves.

The auditorium was full and the audience, composed of parents and friends, was indulgent and friendly, laughing heartily at the familiar humor of the play, the loud ex-football hero, the young campus intellectual, the abstracted but upright English professor, the belated flirtatiousness of the professor's wife confronted with her ex-beau, the meek wisdom of the dean attempting to steer a humorous and respectable course between the roaring demands of the trustees and the principles of academic freedom. The play was all about the trouble the unpolitical English professor gets into by announcing that he is going to read as a model of English composition the last letter of Bartolomeo Vanzetti, written before his execution. It was a curious device to use as a basis for a farce, but, watching it from his seat next to Nancy, Archer realized how cleverly the authors had done it, avoiding tragedy yet not vulgarizing the document itself or the principles involved, comfortably assuring the audience by little deft strokes that all would in the end turn out well, that the ex-football player for all his bluster was a thoroughly good sort, that the Dean, when forced to a decision, would behave admirably, however much he might sigh over his dilemma, that the trustee would see the light, that no one would be expelled, no one fired, that the wife would return to her husband and the young girl settle with the bright if somewhat radical young man, that all men were decent and susceptible to reason because the play-

wrights themselves were transparently decent and reasonable men. No wires were tapped and the Federal
Bureau of Investigation was not mentioned at any point
during the evening.

Listening to the amusing lines that came across the
footlights, laughing with the rest of the audience, Archer felt a nostalgia come over him for the lost, rueful
academic world of the play, in which loud-mouthed
trustee hundred-percent Americans and callow radical
intellectuals could all be treated with the same gentle
humor, with forgiveness and delight. When had the
play been written? 1938? 1939? Where had that world
gone? What would happen if the play had been written
this year? Would it be stormed, denounced, investigated,
picketed? And who would be right this year . . . the
gentle and witty playwrights or the bitter picketers and
investigators? Archer knew that as recently as two
weeks ago he would have answered that question automatically.

Now . . . seated among five hundred smiling, agree-
able-faced people, charmed by the reflection of their
own humanity and modest idealism which came from
the stage, comfortable and seemingly oblivious to the
threats that were hanging over them—now, Archer
didn't know. This is a play, he thought, to be regarded
as a historical costume piece, in which the characters
are dressed in quaint and admirable moral clothing
which no longer is in fashion today. The hand-made
moral garment, fashioned to fit the individual man and
sewn with a patient fine seam, Archer thought, remembering Teague, is being pushed off the market by mas-
sacre and improved machinery, to be replaced by the
standard garment, stiff and padded to cover, with an
anonymous, uniform, mass-produced garment, all personal flaws and beauties. He wondered what the people
around him would say if they knew that the father of
the pretty young girl assiduously attempting to appear
thirty years old on the stage was suspected of treason

by the Government and that if any member of the audience called him on the telephone to invite him to dinner the invitation would be overheard, checked and filed against the possibility of future disorders by the police power of the State.

Archer shook his head, unwilling to wander off once more into these reflections, which had made him suspiciously silent on the ride up to the college and at the dinner table. He made himself pay attention to the stage and regard his daughter critically, so that he could speak intelligently about her performance later on.

Jane was surprisingly good. Listening to her go over her lines in the living room on Sunday he had felt indulgently that she was gauche and coltishly amateurish. But here, prettily made up, enjoying herself under the lights, warmed by the laughter which greeted her, and surrounded by people of her own age who, if anything, had considerably less talent than she, Jane was attractive and convincing. Even if I weren't her father, he thought defensively, I'd be impressed. And there's no doubt about it, by the most stringent objective standards, she's awfully pretty. She had put her hair up to give her age, and the high heels she wore made her legs seem more slender and someone had had the good sense to pick out a dress for her that lent her robust young figure a graceful maturity for the evening.

Archer glanced at Nancy, seated beside him. She was sitting back in her chair, her face, in the light reflected from the stage, curiously hungry and intent. She was not smiling as were the other members of the audience and her attention was so directed to the stage that she didn't notice Archer's long stare of inspection. What is it in her face? Archer wondered. Disappointment, regret, sorrow for opportunities that have long ago vanished? Does she see herself in Jane, very young, very serious, acclaimed, full of limitless hopes for the future? Does she remember the excitement of the nights when she, too, performed to applause and laughter, and told a young man that she wouldn't marry him, wouldn't even become engaged to him because she had a career to make in the theatre in New York? Is she going over in her head, Archer wondered, the claims of love, the blunting of ambition, the arrival of children, the slow submersion of herself in the career of the handsome man two seats away from her, the man who, fifteen years before, had picked his life work with confident haste, merely to be close to her? Was that hungry, drawn face hiding uneasy speculations on the tricks of life, on the subtle work of accident, on the sickening passage of time, on the penalties of love which come disguised as gifts and pleasures? As Nancy watched her friends' daughter delightedly sweep through the amber lights, was she saying torturedly to herself, "What did I do? What happened to me?"

Finally, Nancy realized that Archer was staring at her and had been for some time. She turned her head slowly from the stage, as though she hated to miss a single movement there. There were tears in her eyes, trembling and unshed. She put out her hand and Archer held it on the arm of the chair between them. She gripped his hand hard before she turned her eyes back to the stage.

Archer felt that he had known her forever, that he understood her completely. He would have liked to kiss her to show her that he pitied her and loved her.

When the play was over they all went back to Jane's dressing room to congratulate her. There were flowers and several telegrams, stuck professionally on the side of the mirror, and Jane was dabbing happily at her makeup with cold-cream, trying not to smile too widely when her parents and Vic and Nancy came into the room.

"Don't kiss me," she said, as Kitty embraced her, "you'll get all smeary."

"This evening," Vic said solemnly, "it is the pleasure of your reporter to tell you that he was present at that rarest of theatrical experiences—the revelation of a new tragic genius . . ."

"Oh, Vic," Jane said, giggling, "don't be insufferable."

"With all the mature passion of a great artist of thirty," Vic recited, "Miss Archer dominated the stage at every turn. Beautiful, with a wide, serene brow which reflects an ageless and noble melancholy of spirit, Miss Archer held a fashionable and critical audience in the palm of her long, white hands. To our utter amazement, we learned in the dressing room, where we went to pay homage after the performance, that the dazzling woman who had won every heart that night was only eleven years old."

"Daddy," Jane said, giggling again, "you must make him stop."

"You were wonderful, baby," Archer said. "Really."

"I was foul," Jane said complacently. "I was falling all over myself."

"It was so queer, seeing you up there," Kitty said. "You made me feel so *old*."

Nancy didn't say anything. Her eyes were still shining in the same strange, hungry way that Archer had noticed in the theatre. She went up to Jane and put her arms around her and held her, hard. For a moment everyone in the room was silent. Then three girls came bursting into the room, full of high, excited compliments, and Jane sat down in front of the mirror and made a pleasant little show of scrubbing her makeup off, while everyone grouped around her, consciously collaborating with Jane and one another to make this moment as high and memorable as possible. Archer looked at the flowers in their boxes. There was his corsage, a pleasant spray of tea roses, and a big bunch of gladioli from the Herreses and an impressive cellophane box with two perfect green orchids in it that was ostentatiously displayed in front of the others. Archer picked up the card. "Be delightful," the card read. It was signed Dom. Archer put the card down, conscious of a twinge of annoyance, feeling resentfully that Barbante had probably sent the same flowers and the identical message to a dozen other dressing rooms over the course of the years. The orchids looked cold, extravagant, too showy for an eighteen-year-old schoolgirl unpinning her hair in front of her parents after an amateur production. A moment later Barbante came in, followed by Bruce. Archer hadn't seen the writer while the play was on and no one had told him Barbante would be present. Bruce looked shy and unhappy.

"Jane . . ." Barbante went over and kissed the top of her head, after smiling his greeting at Archer and the others. "Jane, you were charming."

"Dom . . ." Jane switched around in her chair and looked up at him. "Don't lie. I was unutterable. And the orchids . . ." Jane waved at the cellophane box. "Everybody look at the orchids. Aren't they *slinky*?"

"Jane," Bruce said, moving truculently in her direction but not daring to touch her, "you were great. I didn't think you had it in you."

Archer saw Vic grin slightly.

"Thanks, Bruce," Jane said, turning back to her mirror. "It was nice of you to come."

"I managed to get away," Bruce said heavily, suffering. He was a large boy with an infant's pink complexion. Carefully dressed and shaven, he looked as though he had been boiled briskly and set out to cool before going out for the evening. He looked around him at the flowers. "I didn't know people were supposed to send flowers," he said miserably.

"Don't make it sound like a funeral, Bruce, darling," Jane said, winding a towel around her head. Vic grinned more widely and Archer wished there was some way he could, in one moment, put compassion for her contemporaries into his daughter's heart. Bruce took a step backward and leaned against the wall, anguished and stoical.

"Now, really, everybody," Jane said, firmly in the center of the stage, "I do have to change. Why don't you wait outside and think up some more compliments for me and I'll be out in a shake."

"Isn't there a bar somewhere near here?" Vic asked. "We can go and toast the prima donna in lemonade."

"I have an even better idea," Barbante said. Archer watched him suspiciously. "Why don't we all go downtown and celebrate at Sardi's? That's what everybody does after an opening night. We'll sit in the center of the room and let the people admire Jane."

Jane swung around, smiling delightedly at Barbante. "Oh, delicious," she said. "I'll pretend I'm waiting up for the reviews."

"Don't you have classes tomorrow, young lady?" Archer asked, feeling solemn.

"I'll cut them," Jane said swiftly. "The Dean'll understand. She has a lovely reputation for being flexible."

"I think it's a fine idea," Kitty said, as anxious as her daughter to prolong the excitement of the evening. "It's early yet, anyway, and anyplace we'd go around here'd be so dreary."

"Kitty, are you sure you feel strong enough to stay up so late?" Archer asked, in a forlorn last effort. "Don't you think you ought to be getting to bed?"

"I feel fine," Kitty said. She touched Archer's hand. "Don't be stuffy."

"The Sardis have it," Vic said, "Papa dissenting."

"I'm not dissenting," Archer said, displeased at seeming to be opposed to his daughter's pleasure on this night of triumph for her. "I just wanted to make sure everybody was willing."

"I have my car here," said Barbante. "I'll wait for Miss Duse and bring her and Bruce down and meet the rest of you there."

"Will you put the top down?" Jane asked, bending down and kicking off the high-heeled shoes and beginning to peel off a stocking.

"Jane," Archer said, "it's winter."

"It's a beautiful night," Jane said. "I want to see the stars tonight."

"The top is down," Barbante said, "because until midnight no request can be denied you."

God, Archer thought, I don't have to stand here and listen to this. "All right," he said curtly, "see you in Sardi's. Come on, folks."

"Bundle up, dear," Kitty said, as she prepared to leave.

"Don't worry, Mrs. Archer," Barbante said. "I have a fur robe."

The sonofabitch, Archer thought, prepared for everything. Following Nancy and Kitty out of the door, he passed Bruce. Bruce stood rigidly against the wall, his face frozen and hurt. The fool, Archer thought, annoyed with Bruce, too. He might have had the sense to invest a couple of dollars at a florist's.

"Come on, Bruce," Barbante took the boy's arm. "Let's go out and have a smoke while the lady rearranges herself for civilian life."

"I don't smoke," Bruce said, allowing himself to be guided out of the room.

"Lucky man," Barbante said. "It's a dirty habit."

Vic chuckled as they went down the corridor.

Vic ordered two bottles of champagne and they were standing in their frosted buckets when Jane came in. Everyone, thought Archer, your wife, your friend, conspires to rush your daughter away from you into maturity. He tried to be sensible and not jealous at the inevitable process, but he knew that he was hurt and disappointed as he thought of Jane wrapped in the fur robe, speeding down the highway, in the open car under the stars, having chosen to make the trip down from the college not with her father, but with another man. He noted, coldly, that Jane was wearing Barbante's green orchids as she came in. His own plain little tea roses were nowhere to be seen. Probably carelessly discarded on the dressing-room table, he thought painfully, with the cold-cream pots and the box of cleansing tissue.

Jane made a showy entrance, very pretty and young and on top of the world, coming into the famous restaurant flanked by two men, warmly conscious that many eyes were on her as she made her way among the tables. Her cheeks were flushed from the cold and her hair was in the windy, fluffed disarray that no woman over twenty-five would dare to exhibit in a public place.

Vic stood up ceremoniously to greet her and Archer found himself on his feet, too. The first time, he realized, that I have stood up in deference to my daughter. Staring at her, approaching the table, her face flavored by youth and the touch of winter, he thought, Please, not so fast. Don't rush. Please don't rush.

"Oh," Jane said, sitting down in the middle of the three chairs that had been left vacant for her and the two men, "it was lovely. The stars were just cold little bubbles sitting on top of Radio City . . ."

Literary, Archer thought glumly. For Barbante's benefit.

Jane touched one of the champagne bottles. "And here's some more bubbles. I don't think I can bear going to sleep until the Fourth of July."

"We ordered milk for you," Vic said gravely. "The champagne is for grownups."

"Vic," Jane said, laughing, "don't be a traitorous old poof."

"Come to think of it," Vic said, "I am a little poof-like."

Jane leaned over and touched his hand in a forgiving, womanly, coquettish gesture. "Not really," she said. "You should have heard what the girls were saying about you when you left."

Vic leaned forward, playing the game, holding Jane's

hand in both his. "Tell me," he said. "Repeat every word accurately."

"I will not," Jane said. "Nancy'd never forgive me. But they were absolutely prostrated when they heard you were married."

Sexual play, Archer thought heavily, that's what they call it in all those heavy books they sell on Sixth Avenue.

The waiter opened the first bottle and they all toasted Jane and she blushed and for a moment looked childish and flustered. But the first few sips of the wine made her eyes glitter and her cheeks flush redder than ever. Everyone talked animatedly, going over the evening, keeping Jane's triumph alive for another hour. Archer made a conscientious effort to like everybody at the table and joined in the conversation, trying not to be censorious as he noticed Jane ignoring Bruce more and more for Barbante. Bruce gulped his wine gloomily and swiftly, suffering under the burden of his youth and his unprivileged position. His eyes soon became glazed and he laughed stiffly and mechanically at moments when he remembered that he intended to look as though he was a debonair gentleman accustomed to good restaurants, fine wines and frivolous women.

No help there, Archer thought, staring coldly at the boy. Not for another ten years.

"It's a nice little play, *The Male Animal*," Archer heard Barbante saying, his rich, low, condescending voice carrying through the little conversations around him at the table. "But it's a lie."

The word made the others stop talking and they all looked at the writer. Barbante was leaning nonchalantly back in his chair, his deft, dark hands playing with the swizzle stick on the cloth in front of him. He smiled, using his eyelashes, conscious that the audience was now his.

"All comedy is a lie," Barbante went on easily. "For one good reason. What's the definition of a comedy? A play with a happy ending. The hero prospers. He marries the girl of his choice. Virtue triumphs. The audience goes out of the theatre with a false, utopian sense that the world is better than it really is. In a completely moral society, where the promulgation of truth was mandatory, comedies would be barred from the stage. The authors would be accused of spreading false doctrine and be locked away in jail or beheaded, depending upon the degree of enthusiasm with which the society attempted to keep itself pure. In life, where do we find the happy ending? Who gets the girl of his choice? And having gotten her, how does it turn out? Which one of us sitting at this table believes that the world is arranged for the triumph of virtue? Comedy depends upon the assumption that most human beings are good at heart. Well, who can look around him today and say, with a straight face, that he believes in that now? Everywhere we see predatory animals, leaping upon each other, tearing each other, dabbling in blood. And, what's more important—*enjoying* it. Death is our most profound amusement. The hunt is the one true symbol of existence—the despair of the victim is the necessary titillation to the joy of the victor. Pity is a pious afterthought to carnage."

Archer looked around him uneasily, wondering if any of the chattering people at the nearby tables were listening. Was it wise, he thought, for a man whose phone was tapped by the Government to be observed listening to doctrine like this?

"Where is the place for comedy among these ferocious truths?" Barbante demanded. "We put happy endings on the fairy tales we tell children to prepare them for bed, but both we and the children know that we are engaged in fantasy for a sedative purpose. As an adult, I reject that as a function of art. Even if I wanted to accept it, the evidence all around me would prevent it. That play tonight, for example . . ." He smiled at Jane. "So persuasively performed. What do you think really would happen if a professor lined himself up so boldly against the established powers? The trustees would demand his scalp, the newspapers would crucify him, his superiors would defend him halfheartedly, then give in to the practical considerations of their own survival. He would be hounded out of his profession, and wind up his life broken and povertystricken."

"Oh, Dominic," Vic said lightly, "what a grim fellow you are!"

"Not at all," Barbante said. "I laugh a good deal of the time. That's one of the reasons I never try to write anything more permanent than radio scripts. I'm not properly equipped. I'm too frivolous. I am not in despair, and the only writing that's worth anything must come from the most profound despair. From pain, sickness, hatred, violence, suspicion, loss of hope. It is only the victim who can report the hunt truthfully and I'm too modest to put myself in that enormous role."

"As a father," Archer said, trying to keep his tone light and conversational, "I can't sit at the table and permit my daughter to be exposed to this black religion without saying a word or two on the other side." Jane slowly turned in his direction and watched him, soberly. Neither Nancy nor Kitty, he could tell, were taking the discussion very seriously, merely regarding it as just one more example of the wandering and casuistic theorizing with which men unaccountably amuse themselves late at night after drink. "The idea of comedy," he said, "comes from something that's just as real as despair—the conception that men are fundamentally good—or at least that some men are fundamentally good—that they wish to do good to their neighbors, that over the years they can advance from the jungle philosophy of the victor and the victim—that, in fact, they *have* advanced . . ."

Barbante nodded genially. "I knew you could be depended upon to say something like that, Clem," he said pleasantly. "It does credit to your heart even if it does less credit to your intelligence and powers of observation. Look around you today, Clem . . . Can you honestly say that you feel we've advanced, say, from the period of the Pharaohs or the tribal times before that?"

"Yes," Archer said.

"When we send a thousand planes over a city to drop bombs on women and children," Barbante asked, "are we better than the warrior who raided the next village for a wife? When we let loose an atomic bomb and kill a hundred thousand people in a moment, are we better, say, then the Aztec priests who ceremonially slit the throats of human victims on their altars and tore open the breasts of the victims to rip out the still-pumping hearts and offer them up as sacrifices to their gods? Are those highly civilized people, the Germans, who cremated millions of human beings in their furnaces, better than their ancestors who wore horns on their helmets and ambushed each other along the trails of the Black Forest? Would you say that the Russians, with their torture chambers and Siberian concentration camps and their state labor forces, are better than the Arab slave dealers supplying eleven-year-old eunuchs to the markets of Constantinople? Where are the fundamentally good people you spoke of? On what continent do they operate? Or do you see some obscure intention to do good to your neighbor in dropping a bomb on him or putting him in a furnace? Or is goodness a quality that exists by itself, in a pure state, with no necessity to be reflected in action? Or are we better than the jungle merely because we kill at a distance, impersonally, from thirty thousand feet, or with a state regulation, rather than with our own teeth and claws? Are we less bloodthirsty because we kill more expertly and we are too far away from our victims in their last moments to hear their cries? Are we more holy because we offer up our living sacrifices not to a stone god, but to the State? Do we pretend that we do not feel the hunter's pleasure when we read in our newspapers that our forces have destroyed another ten thousand of the enemy the day before? No," Barbante said, smiling curiously, speaking so smoothly that Archer was confident he had worked out this argument many times before and had claimed the attention of many gatherings again and again with its horrors, "no, I don't believe we're any worse. We're the same. We're human beings, just as they were, with all our airplanes and automobiles and vacuum tubes. We kill because we take pleasure in it. We're vindictive, crafty and violent, and we like the taste of blood, whether we wipe it off a stone knife or the front page of the latest edition of the New York *Daily News*. If I were asked to put down, in as few words as possible, my reaction to the human race, I'd merely write, 'Beware us.'"

"Beware. Beware." It was Bruce. He was struggling to his feet, his eyes thick, his face flushed. He had been drinking steadily and he teetered, holding onto the back of his chair. "Beware. He's right. I don't like him, but he's right." Bruce turned inaccurately toward Jane. "You're terrible," he said, as though Barbante's diatribe had given him new insight into the characters of the people around him. "You're a terrible girl."

Jane looked up at him puzzledly for a moment. Then she laughed. "You're a funny boy, Bruce," she said. "You'd better go home."

Bruce bowed, stiffly, a little to one side. "The victim and the victor," he said loudly and ambiguously. Then he bowed again to the company at large. "How was I supposed to know I was expected to send flowers?" he demanded. He shook his head slowly and sadly. "I'm a funny boy," he said. "I'd better go home. Thank you very much. Thank you one and all."

He walked out through the crowded restaurant, holding his head carefully straight on his shoulders, containing his anguish and his loneliness. Archer watched him, half amused, half pitying. Jane ought to go after him and say good night, he thought. He looked at his daughter. She wasn't even watching Bruce. Her eyes were on Barbante again and her face looked hard and excited and older than when she had come into the restaurant less than an hour before. Somehow, Archer realized, Barbante had captured her imagination with what he had said, perhaps because by saying it in front of her, and in fact directing it almost completely to her, she had been flattered and made to feel grownup. And perhaps she had felt that there was something wickedly passionate, lawlessly cruel and strong in his soft-voiced nihilism, something that awoke forces in her that her protected, easygoing schoolgirl life had never touched until now. Archer hated the expression on his daughter's face.

"Clement, darling," Kitty said, "I think Bruce had the right idea. I think it's about time we were all getting home. I'm awfully tired . . ."

"Yep," Vic said, "I'm going to go home and practice up on my despair and start writing *The Brothers Karamazov* tomorrow."

They all laughed and Jane finished her champagne while Barbante insisted upon taking the check and Archer helped Kitty on with her coat. Standing outside, on the windy street, with all the other lights extinguished and the taxis ranked along the curb, Jane looked up to the faint stars above the glow of the city in the sky. She stretched her arms and said, "I can't. I just can't go home and try to sleep tonight."

"Why try?" Barbante asked. He looked at his watch. "It's early yet. Everything's open but the museums. Why don't we all just keep going?"

"Not me," Vic said. "Thank you very much. My sons wake me at six-thirty every morning. Come on, Nancy." He took his wife's arm. "The old folks're going to retire and leave the new generation to their revels."

Archer waited for Kitty to say something, order Jane, as tactfully as possible, to come home with them. I've acted the policeman enough tonight, he thought resentfully, let her take on some of the responsibility now.

But Kitty, who was half asleep, standing up and leaning against his arm, merely tried to hide a yawn. "All right, darling. Have a nice time. Just don't come home too late . . ."

Archer set his face. Coldly, he said good night to Barbante and to his daughter. He could tell that Jane knew he was angry and he hoped that that realization would drive her home after a half hour or so in a night club or wherever Barbante was taking her.

He got into a cab with Kitty, leaving Barbante and Jane standing on the sidewalk, debating where they wanted to go. Kitty fell asleep immediately against his shoulder as the cab rattled downtown through the dark streets.

At home, Kitty went to bed like a sleepy infant, hardly conscious as Archer helped her undress and tucked her in. Drowsily, she reached up her arms and pulled his head down for a kiss. She smelt warm and soapy and her hair was tumbled around her because she had been too tired to put it up. "Wasn't it nice?" she murmured. "Champagne. Wasn't that boy silly?" She giggled drowsily. "Wasn't Jane beautiful?"

She dropped her arms and closed her eyes. Archer stood up and put out the lamp. He wasn't sleepy. He went downstairs and into his study. The evening papers were there, but they looked stale. All the news, he thought, happened a long time ago. Since then new editions have come out and everything is different.

The telephone reflected the light of the desk lamp blackly. He looked at it curiously. Somewhere, in a bright room, connected to the line, there was a wakeful instrument, ready to note down each inflection of his voice, each word, to be assayed and put in an obscure future balance. He felt a crazy desire to communicate with the man who finally would listen to what he said over the phone. The blank invading presence lurking behind the instrument should be addressed, questioned, exhorted. "This is the suspect speaking. This is Clement Archer. What am I suspected of? What do you expect me to say? What do you want me to do? What information can I give about myself? I'm forty-five years old and I'm tired. My life is complicated and I'm worried about age, love, money, work, the health of my wife, the virtue of my daughter, the end of the world. As far as I know, I have committed no crimes, but perhaps you have a secret list of actions which have not yet been revealed as crimes but which will be in good time. How do you avoid committing crimes of whose existence you are ignorant? How do you purge yourself of sins which could only exist in the future? I contemplate nothing. I contemplate merely living. From a loftier point of view that is perhaps the grossest sin of all, but I doubt you were linked to my phone to convict me of that. What are *your* sins? The man who listens to the intricate private conversations of another man necessarily sits in judgment. What standards do you judge by, where are the books of law you use, what is your rectitude, what judgment do you record? Will I ever be told? What are the penalties? Or is the only penalty the knowledge that every time I pick up the instrument to call a shop or tell my daughter I love her, I am overheard? What do you think of me, having heard me speak so often and so candidly, not knowing before this that you were listening? Do you think I am sinful? Do you believe I am guilty—and if so, of what? Have you been moved to pity? Have you chuckled from time to time over the easy jokes I've exchanged with my friends? Do you approve of my wit? Do you sometimes feel like warning me when you discover that I am going to be involved in a business venture that you feel will turn out badly or that I have accepted an invitation to a dinner that you are sure will be boring? Do you hate me? Do you have any feeling or is it requisite to your particular craft to divorce yourself absolutely from all feeling? Have you learned anything from me? Have you passed me in the street and said to yourself, 'Why, he looks surprisingly decent.' Is it possible that after listening for a certain length of time, to record after record of unconsidered conversation, you will finally report to your superiors, 'I find the suspect to be an admirable and charming man and fully intend to make his acquaintance and invite him to my home for a drink. He likes Martinis and beer on tap.' Or is it never possible to come to a benevolent conclusion in your field of work? We were talking about hunting this evening, unfortunately out of earshot from you, and one of the gentlemen at the table pointed out that the pleasure of the hunter is only fulfilled with the pain of the hunted. Now, certainly, you are hunting me. Can you only be fulfilled at the price of my pain? Or are you engaged in a particular and curious kind of hunting in which gratification can be gained from the escape of the prey through innocence? On the subject of innocence, what can I say? It is a subject which I have not studied exhaustively as yet, since I have only known that my innocence was at question since six o'clock last evening. As far as I know, as I have said, I am innocent, but I must confess that I am no good judge of the matter, since I am committed to using rules and standards that have been made public and are no doubt obsolete. You, sitting in your secret room, wherever it is, have modernized guilt and innocence and operate only under the most up-to-date regulations, which, of course, cannot be revealed. Naturally, my first reaction was one of anger when I discovered that you were observing me. I had two childish and complementary impulses. 'Well,' I thought, like an unfairly punished child who resolves to commit the deed after the punishment in a blind approximation

of justice, 'well, if that's what they think of me, I'll
show them. I'll give them something *really* to worry
about. If they believe I am disloyal, I *will* be disloyal.'
But, then, what could I do? Go out into the streets
and call for the overthrow of the Government? I do not
believe in the overthrow of the Government, regardless
of what the agents of the Government believe about
me. Caught in my own reasonableness, I am frozen
in inaction. My other impulse was to leave. Abdicate.
Go to another country, since my own country had
shown its mistrust of me. But, even overlooking the
hardships and impracticality of this self-exile, I had
to reject it. I am part of the nation. I have profited in
it; I have had my fair chance to influence its actions.
Feeling grandiloquent, I remember Socrates, who, when
he had the opportunity, refused to leave the prison in
which he was awaiting the poison, because of his at-
tachment to the state which had doomed him. The laws
are my laws—you, sitting in the room listening to
the circling wax on which my voice, unknown to me,
may already have convicted me—you, as the politicians
put it, are my servant, my employee, the extension
of my will. In other matters, I rely upon you implicitly.
I rely upon you to protect the peace of my home, to
defend me against kidnappers, counterfeiters, fraud
through the mails, corrupt business practices, domestic
riot and political murder, against the peddlers of narcot-
ics, the infringers of copyrights, the adulterers of foods
and drugs; a good part of my life is based on the
almost unexamined assumption that you are busy and
competent. Now when I find that in the course of
what I must consider your proper business I am under
your scrutiny, can I fairly say that you are my enemy
and that I reject you? If it were in my power to abolish
your office, could I, believing that I am an honest
man and a responsible citizen, could I properly bring
myself to force you to halt your activities?"

"To satisfy my curiosity, I would like to ask you

several other questions. How did you happen to decide
to tap my line? While listening secretly to another
phone, did you hear my number called or my name
mentioned? And whose phone would it be? Frances
Motherwell's, Mrs. Pokorny's, Hutt's, O'Neill's? And
how far have you gone in your supervision of my
activities? Are you content with the morsels you glean
over the wires or do you read my mail and have me
followed by the clever young man I see in the movies?
If I look behind me suddenly on the street tomorrow,
will I see a figure turning into a doorway or ostentatiously inspecting a window thirty paces away? Have
you had a skeleton key made for my front door and
have you deftly entered and quietly and expertly gone
through my papers some weekend, when the house was
empty? Have you read my old, unproduced plays,
neatly stacked on the shelf over there? What did you
make of the play about Napoleon III, with its study
of the tragedy of the weak man who believes he is
powerful because he is in a powerful position? Did
you think it was hopeless or did you think that with
a little polishing, as they say in the theatre, it would
run for a season? How complete is your surveillance
and how deeply have you gone into my past? Do
you remember that I belonged to organizations whose
names I have forgotten, which raised money or medical
supplies or pity for the defenders of Madrid? Do you
know for certain that I signed a petition to a Southern
governor to stay the execution of a Negro boy who
was convicted of rape? I remember vaguely that the
mimeographed sheet was on my desk a long time ago,
but whether I put my name to it or neglected it,
I'm not sure. If I write to you or to your superiors
in Washington, would you be good enough to send
me a résumé of my past, succinct, complete and more
accurate than my own aging and fading memory can
supply me? In the same letter, can you offer for my
study the contradictory statements that I have made

over the years on so many subjects? Or, to present a character that, in the field of the drama, would be called artistically consistent, do you conscientiously weed out the contradictions, so that the finished product is comprehensible and logical, a character who in Act III can be depended upon to do nothing that could not be predicted in Act I by any intelligent observer? Does your organization, as an agency of the Government, supply this information free of charge, as the Department of Agriculture supplies pamphlets on soil conservation and animal husbandry and as the Department of the Interior supplies charts of channels and sandbanks in inland waters to the owners of pleasure boats? I have seen posters inscribed 'Know Your Government' and when I was a schoolboy I sat through what seemed interminable lessons in a course called Civics, which were designed to teach me the mechanics of democratic rule. Legislative, Executive, Judiciary, the system of checks and balances, I still remember. I'm afraid I've been lax about my civics lessons in recent years, for I actually know very little about how your organization operates. I know, of course, from admiring newspaper and magazine articles, about the wonderful file of fingerprints in Washington, and the movies have demonstrated again and again how courageous and ingenious your colleagues are in tracking criminals and bringing them to justice, but in these other matters I must confess ignorance. If, as an interested citizen, I were to write a polite letter to the head of your Bureau, asking for clarification and enlightenment, would I get a civil and informative reply? Or, being suspected of treason and espionage, as I must be to warrant the attention you have already paid me, have I forfeited my rights to information about my Government?

"Finally, I must ask one more question. Are you serious? Do you honestly believe that a man can commit treason or perform the duties of a spy for a foreign government without being conscious of it himself? Is there a new philosophy, created for these confused times, which is based on the concept of unconscious crime? Is this interesting and probably defensible theory the foundation of your activities in my case? Or is your vigil at some midpoint between my study-desk and the telephones of my friends and associates the result of that proliferating process of a bureaucracy which blindly and almost biologically enlarges itself by a constant increase in function, however socially useless that increase may be? So, having noted that I was called two or three times on some telephone that you had already tapped, did you conclude that I must be watched and listened to? And, continuing the process, do you find yourself forced to apply clips to the wires of all the people you hear me calling more than once or twice? And, going on from there, do you repeat the process to the instruments of those people who are called by those friends of mine to whom my calls have led you? Where does it stop? What does this gigantic, overheard, secret conversation teach you? What truth have you extracted from this humming torrent of talk? Can you bear it? If you revealed it to us, could we bear it?"

The lamplight glittered on the telephone. Archer stared at the instrument, feeling almost hypnotized in the quiet, shadowed room by the reflection of light from the dial. He stood up wearily and switched off the lamp. He climbed the stairs slowly, looking at his watch. It was three-fifteen. Jane hadn't come in yet, but he was too tired at the moment to worry about that.

Kitty was sleeping soundly, breathing softly. Through the open window, in the distance, came the sound of a siren. An ambulance or a police car wailing on its errand of violence and pain along the dark streets of the city.

Archer undressed quietly and got into the bed which

was separated from that of his wife by a small table on which Kitty had piled a book, her glasses, a sewing basket. The siren sounded far off, anguish dissolving remotely in a sleeping world, as Archer closed his eyes.

18

There was a lull for the next three weeks. The program went along in much the same manner as it had before, the only noticeable difference coming in the parts that Atlas had usually played, which were now being performed by a white man O'Neill had found who was acceptable but ordinary. O'Neill was as polite and agreeable as possible when Archer submitted the lists of actors he wished to cast each week and apologized gently when he told Archer the next day which ones were not acceptable. There were only one or two of those, and not in important parts, and Archer silently and without protest took the substitutes whom O'Neill offered him. Hutt was never in evidence, and as far as Archer could tell the program neither gained nor lost in popularity because of the shuffling of talent that had taken place. When Archer submitted Alice Weller's name for the fourth week's show, O'Neill made no comment on the choice and passed it. Shapiro had turned out to be hopeless in the music department and Levy, the musical director, had asked no questions when Archer had fired Shapiro and hired McCormick, Levy's earlier choice. Barbante seemed to want to avoid Archer after the night of the play at Jane's college, but he turned in clever enough scripts and didn't seem inclined to press Pokorny's case, for which Archer was grateful.

For long periods of time, Archer even forgot that his telephone was tapped, and talked quite normally over it. Even when he remembered, he didn't censor his conversation. Neither Alice nor Pokorny called him during that time, and Archer felt that there was nothing that he might ever say, himself, that could incriminate him in the slightest. From time to time he told himself that he should be angry about the tap and perhaps take steps to have it removed, although just what steps a man could take he couldn't imagine—but finally, he found himself disregarding it, like a soldier in the army in wartime who ignores the fact that all his letters, even the most intimate ones, are being read by an anonymous lieutenant at base headquarters. The despair that had settled on him on the night of the play seemed to have vanished. The magazine that had threatened to expose the people on the program had not run the article, its editors probably placated by the disappearance of Motherwell, Atlas and Pokorny, plus whatever assurances Hutt must have given them. The alarms and disputations of the preceding month now seemed distant and almost unimportant. The question which was discussed most often at the dinner table was whether to go to Cape Cod or Long Island for the summer.

Then, one morning, while Archer was still in bed, Pokorny called. Archer reached over, noticing that Kitty was moving uneasily in her sleep, disturbed by the muted ringing. As he picked up the phone he saw that is was only eight o'clock. For a nickel, he thought angrily, any damn fool can annoy you at any time of the day or night.

"Hello," he whispered, trying to defend Kitty's rest. "Who's this?"

"Mr. Archer." Archer recognized the high, excited voice immediately. "This is Manfred Pokorny. I hope

I have not wakened you, but I wanted to be sure to get you before you went out. I, myself, have been up since five-thirty."

"Yes, Manfred," Archer whispered, annoyed at this customary excess of information. "What do you want?"

"I must see you, Mr. Archer. Right away." Pokorny's voice sounded shrill and urgent, but he sounded urgent about everything, even when merely asking the time of day, Archer remembered. "I would like to come over immediately. I am just around the corner. I could be there in five minutes."

"Manfred," Archer complained, "I'm still in bed."

"Oh. I am so sorry. A thousand apologies. I have been up since five-thirty and I. . . . Go back to sleep, Mr. Archer. I will call you later. I didn't mean to . . ."

"That's all right, Manfred," Archer said crossly. "It's time I got up anyway. What do you have to see me about?"

"I need some money," Pokorny said shrilly. "I am desperate for funds. Today. I have borrowed from everyone else. You are the last one I can turn to."

Archer hesitated before answering. He looked down at the phone, remembering that every word of the conversation was being recorded. Kitty turned over in bed and opened one eye, frowning.

"Tell him to call later," Kitty said, pressed into the pillow. "Whoever it is."

"Mr. Archer, Mr. Archer . . ." Pokorny was almost screaming into the phone. "Are you still there, Mr. Archer?"

"Manfred," Archer said, "it's eight o'clock now. Give me time to dress and have breakfast. Come here at nine o'clock."

"Oh, God," Kitty groaned into her pillow.

"I knew it," Pokorny said earnestly, "I knew there was one man I could depend on. Good appetite, Mr. Archer."

"What?" Archer asked, puzzled.

"Good appetite. For breakfast," Pokorny explained. "I will be there on the dot. Promptly." He hung up.

Archer put the phone down slowly and looked longingly at his bed. He had been up late the night before reading, and his eyes felt hollow. He stood up, sighing.

"Go to sleep," Kitty whispered, out of her doze. "You'll be dead all day."

Archer didn't answer her. He went into the bathroom and took a cold shower and for a little while he felt wide awake.

He ate his breakfast quickly. He didn't want to be at the table when Pokorny came and have to offer the musician any food or drink. He felt bad enough, Archer decided, without having to watch Pokorny eat so early in the morning.

He was reading the newspaper in his study when the front doorbell rang. The newspaper was no help. Spies were being arrested in Philadelphia and Hungarian officials were disappearing from Budapest, the usual Congressmen were calling the usual Cabinet officers Communists and traitors and the officers were making the usual replies. The jails were slowly filling with college graduates and people you had met at nice parties in the East 60's and 70's.

"I'll get it," Archer called in to Gloria as he stood up and went to the door. The bell was ringing wildly, as though Pokorny felt that he was being pursued and had to get into the house before his pursuers caught up with him.

Pokorny was wearing his pink raincoat and black velour hat. Behind him the day was cold and gray. It was windy and Pokorny was holding onto his hat as he stood outside the door.

"Come in, come in," Archer said. Pokorny took off his hat and trotted in, his face red from the cold, his hair long and uncombed, his eyes, behind the little glasses, nervous and searching. He was carrying his briefcase, and as usual it was bulging.

"Thank you, Mr. Archer," Pokorny said. "It is so good of you to . . ." He blew on his hand. "The warmth is welcome," he said. "It's going to snow."

Archer glanced out into the street. All the houses were shut tight under the weight of winter. An old man was walking slowly on the opposite side, blending into the dead colors of the old houses. Archer shivered a little and closed the door.

"Let me have your coat," he said.

"I don't wish to absorb your time," Pokorny said anxiously. "You are, of course, very busy, and what I have to say will only take a minute."

"Give me your coat, Manfred," Archer said irritably. "We can't stand here in the hall." He went behind Pokorny to help him. Pokorny put his hat and briefcase down carefully and wriggled fatly out of the trenchcoat. He took the briefcase with him when Archer led the way into the study. Pokorny stood in the middle of the room uncomfortably, looking out of place, like a man who knows he is not welcome in most of the rooms he enters.

"Sit down," Archer said, indicating a chair.

"After you," Pokorny said, bowing insanely.

Archer repressed a sigh and sat down behind the desk. Pokorny seated himself on the edge of a stiff wooden chair, keeping his knees together primly, his pudgy hands holding onto the scuffed briefcase on his lap.

"This nice room," Pokorny said, looking around him and nodding his head swiftly. "So warm, such evidence of culture . . . I always enjoy coming into this room."

"Manfred," Archer said firmly, to lead Pokorny away from his role of the effusive guest, "what were you talking about on the phone?"

"Yes. Of course. Once more I must apologize for the hour. I trust I didn't awaken Mrs. Archer . . ."

"That's all right," Archer said, trying to keep the note of impatience from his voice. "Don't worry about it. Now, let's have it . . ."

"First of all, Mr. Archer," Pokorny leaned forward, his short legs curving under him so that only his toes touched the floor, "I would like you to understand that it is not a loan. It is an investment. It might be a very good investment, you might look back on this morning and say, 'Thank you, Manfred Pokorny, for giving me this excellent commercial opportunity.' "

"What are you talking about?" Archer asked.

"It is true I need some money. I need two hundred dollars. This morning," Pokorny's voice began to rush and go into the upper registers again. "But not as a gift. No. Not as a loan. No. Value given for value received. You are my friend and I do not wish you to say in the future Manfred Pokorny is a man who imposes on friendship. I wish it to be strictly business, an up and up transaction."

"What do you need two hundred dollars for this morning?"

"The lawyers." Pokorny rocked on the edge of his chair and looked mournfully up at the ceiling. "Lawyers are a bottomless pit. Every paper they prepare is another fortune. Of course," he said hastily, placating all lawyers, "I know they have their expenses, the offices, the clerks, the research, the education, the cost of living. I do not begrudge it to them. But they have swept me clean."

"What're you paying lawyers for?" Archer demanded.

"My action," Pokorny said. "My investigation. The Immigration. Tomorrow morning at ten, I have to go there. The Government wishes to deport me. There are appeals to be filed, briefs, depositions from witnesses, character statements. There is a man in Chicago who knew me in the old days in Vienna and my lawyer says it would be useful if he could fly there today and get an affidavit from him. He knew me well, he knew I dropped out of the Communist Party in two months. He used to play the oboe, but he gave up the art. He is in the insurance business now, very respected. You and I together should have his bank account. My lawyer says his word will carry a lot of weight. For two hundred dollars, maybe, Mr. Archer . . ." Pokorny's eyes blinked nervously behind the thick glasses and his chubby hands pulled at the lock of the briefcase on his knees. "For two hundred dollars it is a good chance I stay in America . . ."

Pokorny sat up stiffly, facing exile at a cut-price. "I know," he said, "two hundred dollars is a great deal of money. A man has to work hard these days for two hundred dollars. And I know you are a man with responsibilities, a family man, with a beautiful home to support. You can't be expected to give two hundred dollars to every fellow who comes into the house. It would be unreasonable to suppose that . . ."

Two hundred dollars to him, Archer thought. Three hundred to Burke. One hundred, as of this date, to Alice Weller. The anti-Communist purge of non-Communists in the radio industry is going to break me finally.

"So," Pokorny was saying, "I wish to put it on a fair business basis. An investment basis. Not to take advantage. I have a certain property and in return for the two hundred dollars, I give you a share in it. A large share. Whatever you think is right, Mr. Archer . . ." Pokorny was pleading now and the sweat was rolling down his cheeks into the collar of his dark-blue shirt.

"What is the property you're talking about, Manfred?" Archer asked gravely.

Pokorny took out a key ring and fumbled with a small key. He put it into the lock of his briefcase and wrestled clumsily to open it. "It is not the usual thing, of course," he said, his head bent over the lock. "Naturally, I do not own large apartment houses or shares in an automobile company." He laughed nervously at this and Archer tried to smile in reply. "I am a composer and my property is music." Finally he got the briefcase open. He reached in and brought out a sheaf of music paper and some typewritten sheets. "Here . . ."

He waved the papers anxiously at Archer. "It is not quite finished, but you know how fast I can work when my mind is clear, when I am not troubled. In four weeks, two months, I guarantee it will be done, and Mr. Barbante has promised me he will be ready, too . . ."

"What is it?" Archer asked, puzzled. "What in the world have you got there?"

"A musical comedy. Mr. Barbante and I have been working for six months. About the West." Pokorny patted the papers lovingly.

"Oh, yes," Archer said. "Barbante told me."

"He has written such clever things, Mr. Barbante. Witty lyrics. Love songs that are tender yet modern. And the music . . . I don't wish to boast, Mr. Archer, but we have already played some of the songs to people, professional people, in the business, and they have been impressed. Hard, professional people, but they were crazy for it. They have told us it is very hopeful. That's the word that was used, you can ask Mr. Barbante— hopeful." Suddenly Pokorny sprang up and rushed over to the desk. He put the sheaf of papers in front of Archer. Archer could see that many of the sheets were stained, as though Pokorny made a practice of eating while he worked. "Here—look—" Pokorny said excitedly, standing very close to Archer's chair. "Pick any sheet at random. Read it, sing it over to yourself. Get a conception of the quality. Of course it is rough, it needs polishing, but even so—try it . . ."

"Manfred," Archer said, pushing his chair back a little. "I can't read music. I don't know the first thing about . . ."

"Musical comedies can make millions of dollars. Look at the things on the boards today. Twenty, thirty dollars a seat, and they run for three years. Men are millionaires today who didn't have the price of a cup of coffee at the Automat five years ago. A song can catch on and a man can retire for life. Juke boxes, radio, the movies . . ." Pokorny was almost incoherent now, rushing on through the wild dreams of grandeur and wealth he was conjuring up for himself. "As an investment—unequaled!" He was almost shouting by now, the sweat soaking his collar. "For two hundred dollars, I give you twenty-five percent of my share. Is that fair?" He peered anxiously into Archer's face. "Not enough? You feel I am not generous enough? Fifty percent. I write it down now. Black and white. We can go and have it notarized. Two copies for the files. Just read one song. Hum the melody." He searched frantically among the papers. "Just this one." He picked out three sheets of music paper, with words written under the notes. "The title," he said, "is, 'I Can't Tell You.' "

"I'm sure it's fine, Manfred," Archer said. "But I told you I can't read music. And anyway, I wouldn't want to take your . . ."

"Sit back," Pokorny said hurriedly, as though fearful to let Archer finish his sentence. "It is not necessary to read music. Merely sit back and listen. I'll sing it for you." He looked around him wildly. "Where's the piano? I will accompany myself."

"I'm afraid we don't have a piano," Archer said. "None of us knows how to play."

"No matter," Pokorny said. "Of no importance. I sing without the piano. You will get the idea, just the same. It is necessary to get the picture. It is a play about the West. You know that . . ."

"Yes," Archer said, hoping to prevent Pokorny from singing. "Barbante told me. But . . ."

"It is a scene in a dance hall," Pokorny went on. "The main character is a cowboy. He is bashful, and every Saturday night he comes into the dance hall, all dressed up, and he looks with moon eyes at one of the girls, a soprano. He is a big, rough man, but he is tongue-tied when he looks at Ellie. That's her name. He wants to say that he loves her, but the words won't come out."

Pokorny stepped back and adjusted his glasses, and

peered down at the music in his hand. He cleared his throat loudly.

"Manfred!" Archer began to feel a kind of panic. "There's really no necessity. I take your word for it. I have no ear for music and besides I wouldn't dream of taking a share from you for . . ."

Then Pokorny began to sing. He closed his eyes from time to time, to dig more deeply into his inward emotion. *"I can milk, I can ride,"* he sang, *"I can rope when I'm fried, But I can't tell you— I can preach or palaver, I can shave without lather, But I can't tell you — I can fight or frolic, Cure a calf with the colic, But I can't tell you, Can't Can't Can't tell you—"*

Archer watched the fat little man, standing in the middle of the floor, waving his arms in time to the music, sweating in his bright, unpressed tweed suit, singing on key and with feeling, his accent making the words of the song seem incongruous and funny, singing in desperation, singing against exile, putting into the flat, unoriginal little song all his hopes of rescue from forces that long ago had doomed him. As he listened to the song, Archer knew that he was going to give Pokorny the money he had asked for.

Pokorny finished and there was silence in the room for a moment. He looked shyly at Archer. "Well," he asked, almost in a whisper, "what did you think of it?"

"It sounds like a very nice song," Archer said.

"Thank you." Pokorny smiled briefly. "Of course, you understand, it should be sung by a young man, a tenor, a very handsome young man in front of scenery, and with a twenty-five-piece orchestra. There's a very important passage for the clarinet indicated, too . . ."

Archer got out his checkbook. "Look, Manfred," he said, "I'm going to give you the money. And I don't want any share of your music . . ." He started to write out the check.

"Oh, no, Mr. Archer," Pokorny said. "Please. I can't take it as a loan. I insist . . ."

"When you can," Archer said, finishing on the check

and noting it on the stub as he ripped the check out and waved it to dry it, "you pay me back. That's all."

"You're good," Pokorny said quietly, folding the music sheets. "You're too good."

Archer looked down at the check. Pay to the order of Manfred Pokorny, two hundred dollars, signed Clement Archer. He didn't hand it to the musician. Suddenly he tore it up. "Come on, Manfred," he said, standing up and throwing the small bits of paper into the wastebasket. "I'll give it to you in cash. I'll walk down to the bank with you. It's only around the corner. I'm sure the cash will be more useful to you." But even as he said it, Archer knew that he wasn't doing it for Pokorny's sake. A deep feeling of shame overcame him as he looked at the scraps of paper on the bottom of the basket. But he put on his coat and went out with Pokorny, knowing that he had been afraid to have a record in his checkbook of a loan to a friend who was on his way to exile.

They walked swiftly to the bank. Pokorny spoke very little and waited on the other side of the room while Archer cashed the check. Archer crossed over and gave the ten crisp new bills to Pokorny, who carefully put them into a tattered wallet. The musician looked very tired now, as though his performance had exhausted him. "Thank you, thank you," he said, in a low voice, avoiding looking at Archer. They shook hands outside the bank and Archer said, "I hope this does it for you, Manfred."

"Oh, yes," Pokorny said. "The lawyer was confident. Very confident." He looked up at the austere gray stone front of the bank and the large clock that was hanging there. It was nearly ten o'clock. "I suppose I have to hurry," he said. "The lawyer has to travel two thousand miles today." He laughed a little. "That's a queer profession," he said. "The law. How does anyone decide to enter it? He looked around him at the quiet street in the heavy winter light. "This is a nice neighborhood. A good place to live." Finally he met Archer's eyes. There was a strange, tremulous expression behind the thick glasses. "Ah, don't worry about me, Mr. Archer," Pokorny said. "It hasn't been so bad here. Many happy years. Even if they send me away . . ." He shrugged. "In Germany or Russia I would be dead a long time already . . ." He smiled, surprisingly. "The piece I gave you the other day," he said. "The recording. My quartet. Do you like it?"

Archer blinked. He had forgotten to play it. "Yes," he said. "I thought it was very good. I liked it a lot."

Pokorny nodded. "I'm glad," he said. "Of course— the recording is not first class—the second violin is weak—but . . ." He shrugged again. "I must go to my lawyer," he said. He turned and walked slowly away, an improbable pink figure topped by a lustrous black hat with the brim turned down all the way around.

Archer watched him for a moment, then went back to his house and tore the check stub out of his book. He ripped it into little pieces and dropped it into the bottom of the basket along with the other scraps of paper.

19

Pokorny called again that night, at seven-thirty, just as Archer and Kitty were sitting down to dinner. Gloria came into the dining room and said, "It's for you, Mr. Archer. It's a Mr. Pokorny."

Kitty made a face. "Tell him to call later, Gloria. Tell him we're at dinner."

Archer half stood up, then sat down again as Kitty waved her hand at him imperiously. "One hour out of the day," Kitty said, "they can leave you alone."

"OK, Gloria," Archer said. "Tell him to call in an hour."

Gloria went out of the room and Kitty said, "We have steak tonight. Steak can't wait. That Mr. Pokorny is getting to be a real pest, isn't he?"

"A little," Archer said absently, trying to listen to Gloria's voice on the phone in the hall. A moment later, Gloria came in, shaking her head.

"The man says he can't call you later, Mr. Archer," she said. "He told me please try you one more time."

Archer stood up. "I'll be right back," he said to Kitty.

"Steak costs a dollar a pound," Kitty said sourly. "Tell Mr. Pokorny that."

Archer smiled at her and went into the hall. "Yes, Manfred," he said into the phone.

"If it was possible to call you in an hour," Pokorny said, "I would do it. You believe that, Mr. Archer, don't you?"

"Yes," Archer said patiently. "Of course. What's happening now?"

"But it is not possible," Pokorny said. His voice was down to a strange whisper and seemed faraway, rising and falling in strength as though he was moving his head back and forth from the mouthpiece. "It will not be possible. I just wanted you to understand that."

"Manfred," Archer said. "Please speak more loudly. I can hardly hear you."

"Of course," Pokorny said. But his voice still was remote and he spoke very slowly. "I have some information. I thought you might be interested, but I shouldn't have called during dinner, but later on it would not be possible . . ."

"Are you all right, Manfred?" Archer demanded.

"I am fine. I have had a quiet, peaceful day. I have been all alone. I played the piano all afternoon and no one complained . . ."

"Manfred," Archer said, "you will have to speak more clearly."

"The telephone rang," Pokorny whispered. "Long distance. From Chicago. My lawyer. His flight was excellent, only three hours. Thank you again for the money. You are most generous. I wanted to tell you I thought you were most generous. I wanted to tell you, of all the people I have met in this country, you have treated me with the most consideration. Consideration . . ." His voice trailed off.

"Have you been drinking?" Archer asked impatiently.

"Drinking?" Pokorny's voice was a little stronger. "I never drink, Mr. Archer. The doctor forbids me. The high blood pressure and the excess weight. The warmest heart, Mr. Archer, I will always remember it, in this day and age . . ."

"Clement!" Kitty called from the dining room. "Everything's getting stone-cold."

"Manfred," Archer said, "I really do have to get back to dinner."

"Of course. Extend my apologies to your wife. I thought you might be curious what happened in Chicago. After all, you have a right to know, on your money . . ."

"What did happen?"

"The man, my old friend, the one who used to play the oboe . . . My lawyer went to him, but he changed his mind. He won't sign any affidavit about me. 'To be quite frank,' he told my lawyer—those were his words—'to be quite frank,' he had to consider his position in Chicago, in the insurance world, he could not risk having his name in the papers as a supporter of a man who was being deported as an undesirable alien. You understand, I am what is technically known as an undesirable alien. Especially in Chicago, he said, people are very sensitive these days. He doesn't know how it is in New York, he has to consider his family and his colleagues. He himself is a naturalized citizen, he does not wish to impose on the hospitality of the country, he said." Pokorny's voice trailed off.

"I can't hear you," Archer said. "Hold the phone closer to your mouth."

". . . two hundred dollars," Pokorny was saying when Archer heard him again. "A warm-hearted gift at a time like this. The lawyer flew back and forth. His plane is probably over Ohio this minute, the weather is clear. I apologize. Such waste, these days, when everything is so expensive. All my life I knew I should start a bank account. So much each week. Thrift, like the advertisements say for the banks. For a rainy day, when it is necessary to hire lawyers. Accept my apologies . . ." His voice drifted off again. Archer could hear a whispered, distant mumbling. Then there was a click as the phone was put down.

Archer shook his head and went back slowly to the dining room. Even in his best days, Archer thought, Pokorny talked in complicated circles. Now, battered and worn by his troubles as he was, it was almost impossible to make head or tail of his conversation.

Kitty was sitting accusingly at her place, ostentatiously waiting without eating, staring at the food on her plate. "From now on," she said, "we only have stew. Something you can heat for days without ruining it."

Archer kissed the top of her head before sitting down. "I'm sorry," he said. "I promise not to answer the telephone any more."

He tried to seem interested in Kitty's small talk about the house, about several new symptoms of her condition, about Jane, but it was difficult to concentrate and he found himself remembering Pokorny's strange, dwindling whispering on the phone, so unlike him, and picturing the musician alone in the shabby house, his wife probably off at a meeting somewhere, while he played aimlessly on the piano, thinking of the ex-oboe player who had failed him in the sensitive Mid-Western city, trying to get through the hours that still intervened before the next morning's trial.

In the middle of the meal Archer decided he had to go over and see Pokorny that night. He almost broke off eating to start at once, but he knew that Kitty would complain bitterly and ask a lot of questions he was in no mood to answer. He ate impatiently and was grateful when Kitty said she was going to go upstairs and do the bills.

"I'm going out for a walk," he said. "I need some air. I'll be back in a little while. Don't pay the telephone company twice."

There were continual small mixups in the bills and in in nearly twenty years of marriage he and Kitty had never quite arrived at a sensible system of filing paid

and unpaid accounts and it was one of Archer's gloomy
obsessions that he paid most bills at least twice.

"Go out and cool your head," Kitty said, "and come
back when you've learned to keep a civil tongue in
your mouth." But she smiled and kissed him before
she went upstairs, to show him she wasn't taking his
charges seriously.

The weather, as Pokorny had said, was clear, and
after a speculative glance at the cold stars above the
roofs of the city and a sniff of the crisp air, Archer
decided to walk rather than take a cab. He walked
briskly, taking deep gulps of air, feeling warm and comfortable under his soft coat, conscious that he had eaten
a good dinner and that the exercise was doing him
good. He didn't know exactly what he would do for
Pokorny, but he felt that even a fifteen-minute visit
with the musician might cheer him a little on this bad
night.

The light in the hall of the old brownstone house in
which the Pokornys lived was broken and in the darkness Archer couldn't find the bell. He tried the door.
It was open and Archer went up the dim steps, remembering from his earlier visit that the musician lived on
the third floor. The door to the Pokornys' apartment
was standing open. Archer knocked on the door frame
and waited. There was no sound from within, although
light was streaming out from the apartment onto the
shabby landing. Archer knocked again and then went
in.

In the living room, seated stiffly at the table, staring
down at her hands, Mrs. Pokorny was sitting. She had
her hat on, a rust-colored old felt with two curly pink
feathers clipped onto the side, absurdly frivolous over
the raw, uneven shock of her gray hair. From the way
Mrs. Pokorny was sitting, Archer knew that something

was terribly wrong. All the lights were up in the apartment and it looked glaring and uncomfortable.

"Mrs. Pokorny," Archer said gently, taking off his hat, and standing at the entrance to the room. The woman didn't move. "Mrs. Pokorny," Archer said again, coming in.

Mrs. Pokorny didn't say anything or look up at him. She raised one hand slowly and pointed behind her, her thick fingers steady and dangerous-looking. Archer went into the narrow hallway, past the enormous, silent woman.

It was in the bathroom. The tub was full. Pokorny was lying there, with his knees bent and his head under water. For a moment Archer stood there, staring down at the blurred face, magnified by the greenish water in the old-fashioned tub, curved and standing on ornate stubby legs on the tiled floor. Insanely, Pokorny was modestly covered in his orange dressing gown, the sash neatly and tightly tied in a bow over the bulging stomach. On a small stool next to the tub stood a small empty pill bottle and the telephone on a long wire that wound in along the hall from the living room.

As he looked down at the dead musician, Archer knew that he had expected this sight for a long time. Only not with the bathrobe on. Pokorny had even found a ludicrous way to die.

Archer felt dazed. The room was steamy from the water, which was still warm, and Archer felt hot in his coat. Automatically he took it off and threw it over a clothes hamper, never taking his eyes off the shining bright rayon and the pale globular head under the water. He noticed that Pokormny still had his glasses on, not trusting his naked, inaccurate, ruined eyes for an important event like suicide. Foolishly, Archer picked up the phone and put it to his ear. There was a businesslike, normal, uneventful hum. Archer wondered if Pokorny's phone was tapped, too, and if someone had been listening and understanding that the man was taking his life when Pokorny had called Archer earlier in the evening. What would the procedure be then, Archer speculated. Would the agent call the police, the Health Department, the Fire Department, to warn them and attempt to get them over quickly to save Pokorny's life? Or was his function at all times so strictly limited to listening and recording that no extraneous action like rescue could possibly even be imagined?

Archer bent over clumsily and put his hands into the water, grabbing the body under the armpits. He felt frightened. Pokorny, who in life had never had the power to frighten anyone, was adding this last achievement to his score now. Archer felt the water soak into his cuffs and sleeves and too late noticed that he still had on his wristwatch. The flesh under the armpit was fat and flabby and there was no feel of muscle there. Averting his eyes, Archer pulled. The effort seemed enormous and he heard himself panting. Pokorny slid up against the back of the tub, the water momentarily making his eyeglasses opaque before it ran off. His knees slid down, the robe rippling back over the pale chubby legs. Archer made himself look down as he held the musician's head and shoulders out of the water. The gray hair was plastered to the sides of the large, knobby head, and the eyes were open, frightened and searching, as though at the last moment Pokorny had been confronted with a terrifying puzzle. His mouth hung open, the little bow lips red and childish, but Pokorny's mouth usually had been open a good deal of the time, anyway, so he didn't look any different than when he sat in the control room behind Archer's chair, disapproving of what Levy was doing with the trumpets. Archer felt with one hand for Pokorny's heart, disregarding his wristwatch. There was no movement that Archer could detect under the womanish pale breast. He stood up, shaking his hands to get the water from them. Slowly, with seal-like grace, Pokorny slid under the water

again, like a man washing his hair. Archer bent to pick
the head up out of the water again, then stopped. I
could do this all night, he thought, and he'd slide back
every time I stepped away.

He dried his hands on a small guest towel. The towel
had a nude woman on it in yellow embroidery. He
stared down at the empty bottle and the telephone,
suddenly a baleful composition of symbols on the
chipped white stool, sleep and communication combined for the purposes of destruction. Almost automatically, he slipped the bottle into his pocket. He had
to bend down and pick up the bottle cap, which had
rolled into a corner under the basin. Then, carrying
his coat, he went into the living room, where Mrs.
Pokorny was sitting in her silent contemplation of her
folded, brutal hands.

"Well," Mrs. Pokorny said loudly, the sound shock-
ing in the bright room, coming from the monumental,
immobile figure, "are you satisfied now?"

Archer sighed. Christ, he thought, is that how she's
going to take it? "Manfred called me about an hour
ago," he said, keeping his voice gentle, "and he sounded
queer so I decided to come over. But I never imagined . . ."

"I bet he sounded queer," Mrs. Pokorny said. Her
voice was harsh and without inflections. "I bet he
sounded damned queer an hour ago."

"Have you called the doctor yet?"

"What's the doctor going to do?" Mrs. Pokorny
asked, talking down to her hands. "Put the breath of
life back into him? Give him a magic injection against
suicide?"

"Anyway," Archer said softly, feeling that he ought
to go over to the huge, square, fleshy woman and touch
her shoulder, attempting comfort, but flinching from the
act, "anyway, a doctor'll have to be called."

"You call him," Mrs. Pokorny said. She closed her

eyes, but still kept her head in the same rigid position on her thick neck. "I don't have to call anyone."

"The telephone's in there," Archer said irrelevantly, glancing down the hall.

"That's very convenient," Mrs. Pokorny said. "You can have the patient right in front of you and you can describe the symptoms from life when the doctor asks you."

Archer took a step toward the bathroom, then stopped. He went to the table and sat down opposite Mrs. Pokorny. Her large, gray face, under the foolish, curled pink feathers, looked blind, with the large, heavily pouched eyes closed and folded in under the thick lids. "Before the doctor comes," he said softly, "you and I can do something for Manfred."

Mrs. Pokorny opened her eyes and stared at Archer. "You've done enough for Manfred," she said. "You can go home now."

"He's got his robe on. In the bath," Archer said slowly and clearly, trying to penetrate behind the heavy staring eyes. "We could take that off. And . . ." He took the pill bottle and cap out of his pocket and placed them on the table in front of him. "I could throw this away."

"What're you driving at?" Archer could see the thick, coarse lines around her mouth setting stubbornly.

"If he was found naked," Archer said, "just as though he were taking a bath . . . If there was no sign of the pills. He had high blood pressure. A bad heart. It might very well be that he had an attack—that he died naturally."

"He didn't die naturally," Mrs. Pokorny said. "He killed himself."

"Perhaps," Archer said. "But if we could re-arrange things just a little bit . . . There would be some reason for doubt. The newspapers might be kind, the doctor . . . It would be better for his memory, for you . . ."

"Better for you, you mean," Mrs. Pokorny said flatly

and without heat or without expression of any kind. "So that people wouldn't be able to tell the truth—that you and your kind killed him."

"Forgive me for arguing at a time like this," Archer said, ignoring her hatred. "But if we do anything it has to be now, before anyone comes. I'm not going to try to defend myself. But don't be vindictive. Try to act calmly and sensibly. Don't think only of this minute. Try to think of what people are going to remember about your husband ten years from now . . ."

"I want people to remember that they killed an artist," Mrs. Pokorny said, closing her eyes again and speaking blindly and without inflection. "An artist who tried to give them a little music in their lives, a man who never harmed anyone, a man who didn't know how to take care of himself any more than a two-year-old child. I want them to remember that he was hounded to death by you and the other Fascists . . ."

Oh, God, Archer thought, even now, even with her husband only thirty minutes dead, doped and drowned fifteen feet down the hall, she still divides the world by slogans and catch-phrases. Looking at the blank, hating, thick woman who had somehow loved the ridiculous, frightened, finished man inside and who somehow (no one would ever understand exactly how any more) had engendered love in him, Archer knew that there was no hope of persuading her to help him. Pokorny dead was going to be sacrificed to her cause as he had been sacrificed, living, to others' causes.

Archer stood up. "What's the name of your doctor?" he asked wearily. "And how do I reach him?"

"His name is Gordon," Mrs. Pokorny said without opening her eyes. "You'll find his number in that address book on the table in the hall."

Archer went into the hall and got the address book. He found the number and entered the bathroom once more. He dialed the number and waited. While he listened to the long, steady ringing on the wire he looked down at Pokorny. The musician rested under water, the bow of his sash neatly and modestly tied, his eyeglasses shinning like divers' windows on the wavery, resting, escaped face.

Kitty was still awake when Archer got home two hours later. She was sitting up in bed, her glasses on, giving her a studious look in her lacy nightgown that would have struck Archer as humorous and charming at any other time. The bed was covered with bills and slips of paper and canceled checks and Kitty had ink on her fingers from the envelopes she was addressing. Archer felt exhausted. The doctor had questioned him closely and then the police had been suspicious and asked him tricky questions as though they suspected that he had slipped into the house and held Pokorny's head under water while his wife was away. Two reporters had appeared and Archer heard Mrs. Pokorny say clearly and loudly over and over again that they had killed her husband. Arche had been in the bedroom talking to a slow-moving detective who made little marks in a notebook while listening to Archer, so he didn't hear exactly what Mrs. Pokorny had told the reporters, but he thought he heard his name mentioned once or twice and when he finally got out of the house one of the reporters, who smelled from gin and cocktail onions, had walked two blocks with him pretending to be solicitous and trying to pump him.

"I don't know anything," Archer had said again and again. "I don't know why he did it. Ask Mrs. Pokorny."

"Mrs. Pokorny has her own theory, Mr. Archer," the reporter said. "She has her views of your place in the picture and I think our readers would like to have your side of it, too. We want to be fair to everybody involved," the reporter said, trying to look fair, upholding the best interests of impartial journalism, trotting alongside Archer because he was walking so fast. "She has some very harsh things to say, Mr. Archer," said the reporter mournfully, "some pretty strong accusations, and I think all parties involved ought to have a chance to speak for themselves before the story is printed."

"I am not involved," Archer said, wondering how far from the truth he was. "I knew. He worked for me. We were friendly. I happened to drop in. That's all. I am not interested in getting into a debate with Mrs. Pokorny." He waved to a cruising taxi and jumped in, as the reporter leaned into the cab, making it smell like a crowded bar, saying. "Just one short statement of the other side of the case, Mr. Archer. Just one sentence . . ."

Archer started pulling the door shut, pressing it against the reporter, and the man fell back, shaking his head in regret at the unco-operativeness of the public in the search for front-page truth.

When he came heavily into the bedroom, Archer could tell from Kitty's first glance that she was disturbed about something, too. He prayed that she would wait until morning. He took off his jacket, threw it down and slumped into a chair, overacting his weariness a little in an attempt to make Kitty hold whatever was bothering her for a better time.

But Kitty was not to be put off. Keeping her head bent and not looking at Archer as she scribbled on an envelope, she said, "I made out a lot of checks. If you'll sign them and put them back in the envelopes, I'll mail them tomorrow morning."

"OK," Archer said, rubbing the top of his head slowly.

"I've been looking through the stubs," Kitty said. "There's some very strange things in this checkbook."

"Are there?"

"I thought you told me we ought to economize."

"Well, so we should. Do you object to that?"

"I agree. I agree completely," Kitty spoke very quickly, running the words together in little spasms. Archer recognized the signs. Kitty was suspicious and preparing to be angry. "I've cut down on a lot of things. I haven't bought any clothes for myself or Jane in months. I changed markets because Cucitti's is five cents more a pound on butter than anybody else."

"That's fine," Archer said warily, not understanding what Kitty was doing. "That must be quite a saving each month. Probably three, four dollars."

"Three, four dollars," Kitty said flatly. "I'm glad to see you're so concerned."

"Please, Kitty . . ." Archer stood up and began to take off his tie. "Couldn't we talk about this some other time? I'm awfully tired tonight."

"I don't want to talk about it some other time. I'm doing the bills tonight and I want to talk about this tonight."

Archer went into the closet and hung up his coat and tie. The closet smelled of tobacco and cedarwood and Archer remembered the steamy, close smell of the Pokorny bathroom.

"You don't seem to be worried at all about money these days," Kitty was saying, addressing the closet. "Large-handed would be a nice way of putting it. Debonair."

Archer came out of the closet and looked at himself in the mirror over the bureau. His face looked exhausted, long lines falling away from his mouth, and his eyes looked as though he hadn't slept well in weeks. Irritated with the way he looked, he turned back, leaning against the bureau and facing Kitty. "What's the matter, darling?" he asked gently.

Kitty riffled through the checkbook. "Check number 35," she read. "To Woodrow Burke. Three hundred dollars. Do you remember that?"

Archer sighed. He went over to the chair and sank into it, stretching his legs. "I remember it," he said.

"Do you have to sigh like that?" Kitty asked, her voice high and tense.

"No," Archer said. "Forgive me."

"Why did you give Woodrow Burke three hundred dollars?"

"He asked me for it. He's out of a job. He's broke."

"There're a lot of people who are out of jobs," Kitty said. "Do you plan to give them all three hundred dollars?"

"Oh, Kitty . . ."

"Check number 47," Kitty read. "To Alice Weller. One hundred dollars. I suppose she's out of a job, too."

"As a matter of fact, she is."

"As a matter of fact," Kitty repeated. She has a very irritating way of arguing, Archer decided.

"That big, gushing slob of a woman," Kitty said. "And I've been worrying about saving five cents a pound on butter."

Archer stared coldly at Kitty, hating her lack of charity. From time to time, in arguments, this trait came out in Kitty, but only when she was angry, and she was always repentant later for the things she said and Archer made a point of forgetting those ugly disclosures as soon after as he could. "Kitty," Archer said, "this is my business. I don't want to talk about it tonight. I'll tell you about it some other time."

Kitty riffled the checkbook. "Two hundred dollars this morning," she said. "To cash. Have you got the money now?"

"No."

"I suppose you gave that away to somebody who was out of a job, too."

"I did."

"I suppose that's your business, too?"

"Yes," Archer said flatly, "it is."

"Will it be your business when we haven't got a cent to our names, the way it was when we first got to New York," Kitty asked, "or will it be my business, too?"

"Kitty, darling," Archer said wearily, "why don't we go to sleep now? I've had a terrible day and I don't feel like talking any more. Tomorrow . . ."

"I want to know what's happening," Kitty said. "You're throwing our money away like a drunken sailor. I know I told you you didn't have to tell me anything—but it's getting unbearable. Every time I talk to you or ask you a question, I can see you figuring out how to avoid talking to me . . . I haven't felt I was really married to you for a month. Don't shake your head. It's true," Kitty wailed. "It's true. Don't try to deny it. It's not a marriage any more. You've put me outside. I wish I wasn't going to have this child! I didn't want it! You wanted it, not me, and now look what's happening . . ."

Archer got up and went over to the bed. He sat down and put his arms around Kitty. She wasn't crying. She pulled away from him fiercely.

"Listen, Kitty," he said softly, "I gave that two hundred dollars to Manfred Pokorny to try to save his life. Listen carefully, darling. When I went over to his house tonight, he was dead."

Kitty sat absolutely still. Then she turned her head and stared, frozen, at Archer.

"What?" she whispered finally.

"He killed himself. While we were eating dinner. While I was walking across town to see him. I didn't take a taxi because it was such a nice night." Saying it hurt. He had avoided phrasing it for himself before this.

Kitty suddenly put her arms around him and held him, hard. "I'm sorry. Oh, dearest," she whispered, "I'm so sorry."

Archer kissed her cheek. "I don't want to talk about it now," he said. "If you don't mind."

"Of course not." Kitty began to shiver violently. Gently, Archer took her arms down and said, "Get under the covers. You're freezing. Try to sleep."

Kitty nodded, her eyes wide, staring, frightened. She

lay back and Archer wrapped the blankets around her. She didn't stop shivering and the silk coverlet rippled over her body. Archer gathered together the scattered bills, the canceled checks, the envelopes with Kitty's child-like scrawl on them, and put them on her desk. Then he went over and kissed her forehead.

"I'm going downstairs for awhile," he said. "Don't worry."

Kitty didn't say anything.

He put out the lights and went out. He descended the steps slowly and went into his study. The whole house seemed sentimentally neat and cosy after the Pokornys' apartment. Chintz, shining brass student lamps, flowers in bowls, gay striped draperies, polished wood, none of the garish disorder of the composer's home. If anything tragic happened here, Archer thought, looking around him, it would seem out of place.

On his desk there was the album of records of Pokorny's quartet. After Archer had come back from the bank that morning, he had taken it off the shelf, intending to play it, to make up for the sense of guilt he had had when Pokorny had asked him how he liked the piece and he had lied and said that he liked it very much. But the telephone had begun to ring before he could put it on the machine and he hadn't had time to listen to it.

Archer picked up the album. The one piece of music of Pokorny's that had been recorded in this country, he remembered. Pokorny's contribution to the culture of America. Three records, on both sides, from a man who was dead at the age of fifty. *Suburban Themes,* the album said. Probably some clever young man at the recording company had suggested the title. It didn't sound like Pokorny.

Archer went over to the phonograph and put the records on. He turned the dials down low, so that the sound wouldn't disturb Kitty upstairs. Then he sat down in an easy-chair, facing the machine.

The music was gay, small, clever, full of charming,

unpretentious passages. You could imagine children dancing to it and grownups smiling a little as they heard it. There was no trouble in the music. It was pure and bubbling, even rather elegant, and the last movement was serene and evening-like, nothing big, no grand sunsets, no clouds in the sky, no fear of the night, just people meeting each other at suburban stations, after the day's work was over, kissing each other placidly, turning on the car headlights and carefully going up small hillside roads to comfortable houses and family dinners. Somewhere in Pokorny there had hidden a lyrical householder who worked in a small garden and went sleepily to bed at ten-thirty, surrounded by children.

The music came to an end. Archer sat for a moment in the silence, broken only by the minute swishing of the circling turntable. Then he got up and put the records on once more and listened again to the dead man's music.

20

You could look around the studio and see who was going to the funeral by picking out the dark suits and black ties. Pokorny had, as a last awkward and troublesome gesture, chosen to be buried on a Thursday, in the middle of rehearsal. There was only time for one preliminary reading of the script in the morning, with everyone sitting in a semicircle on collapsible chairs, and the grave color made a wintry pattern among the dresses of the women and the slacks and corduroy jackets of the younger actors. Barbante, Archer noted, Levy, O'Neill, and, surprisingly, Brewer, the engineer, were dressed in honor of the corpse. None of the women was going, Archer saw from their costumes, but, then, none of them had had anything to do with the composer. Vic had on a gray flannel suit with a red tie. Vic hadn't known Pokorny well, but he had spoken to him more often than Brewer, and had frequently told Archer how much he liked Pokorny's music. Archer had taken it for granted that Vic would go to the funeral and he found himself staring at Vic's colorful tie during the reading and concentrating on it to the point of missing a half page of dialogue at a time. At least, Archer thought unreasonably, taking his eyes away from Vic, he might have worn a plain tie today.

When the reading was over, Archer stood up. "There'll be a break now," he said, "until one o'clock, so that anybody who wishes can attend the funeral of Manfred Pokorny, who used to do the music for this show."

The cast stood up soberly, without the customary joking and conversation that ordinarily came at a recess in rehearsal. Everyone looked solemn and reserved, giving Pokorny a polite farewell by speaking in near whispers for a minute or so as they filed out of the studio.

"Clement," Brewer said, "could you wait for me for five minutes? I have to go upstairs. Then I'd like to ride down with you."

Archer nodded. "I'll wait for you here." Brewer went out, looking like a lumberjack dressed for church in his blue suit.

Archer drifted over toward Vic, who was reading a newspaper. "Vic," Archer said, "aren't you coming with us?"

Vic looked up from the paper. "I don't think so," he said. "Funerals lost their charm for me during the war. I don't get any message from cadavers any more." He grinned crookedly up at Archer. "Too much of a good thing, I guess. Make my apologies to the survivors for me."

"Still," Archer said quietly, "I think you ought to go."

"I'm not dressed for the occasion," Vic said, touching his tie.

"We can stop in on the way downtown," said Archer, "and buy you a black tie."

Vic shook his head. "I'll be honest," he said. "I could be dressed like an undertaker and I still wouldn't go."

"Out of respect for Pokorny," Archer said stubbornly. "Out of respect to his friends."

"Respect for what?" Vic asked derisively. "A hundred and sixty pounds of dead meat. And I don't respect Pokorny. He was a gutless little man and he blew up the first time anybody took the trouble to poke him. As for his friends . . ." Vic laughed harshly. "They're feeling mournful and guilty and they think going down and sitting for an hour while somebody moons over the corpse is going to give them back that bright, innocent, empty-boweled feeling. Well, I don't feel guilty and I have too many other things to be mournful about. And when I die, I hope somebody has the sense to throw me into a wagon quietly and dump me somewhere with the other garbage." He smiled mirthlessly at Archer. "Getting my message, Jack?" he asked.

"Sure," Archer said, unpleasantly. He started to turn away to talk to Barbante, who was sitting three seats away, his head thrown back, his eyes closed, his short legs stretched out in front of him. Barbante hadn't said a word all morning. As usual, in the morning, he seemed sleepy.

"Did you see this?" Vic carelessly offered Archer the newspaper he was holding. It was a so-called liberal paper that wound back and forth across the Communist Party line on most issues. The paper was folded back to the page on which the columnists held forth. "This feller," Vic said, tapping a column with his finger, "is taking a bite out of your ass this fine morning."

"What?" Archer took the paper and stared at the column. He saw his name several times scattered throughout the piece, but for the moment he somehow couldn't start to read it.

"J. F. Roberts," Vic said. "He does think pieces for unthinking readers. He doesn't like you this morning at all. You're the vanguard of Fascism, he says; you killed the musician. He's been talking to Mrs. Pokorny, and she seems pretty peevish."

Vic lit a cigarette and watched Archer closely as he read the column. The whole thing was in there. Mrs. Pokorny had obviously not held back anything. The column was written in harsh newspaper prose, and Archer and the Immigration Department shared honors in it for dogging Pokorny to death. Reading it, Archer could not help but feel how righteous the columnist made the piece sound. If it had been anyone but himself, he realized, he would have approved of the column completely. The columnist heaped scorn on the Immigration Department for wishing to exile a man who twenty-seven years ago in a foreign country had flirted with the Communists for only two months. The arguments, Archer realized, were exactly the ones that he himself had used to defend Pokorny. As for Archer, the columnist contemptuously dismissed him as a timid hack so eager to keep his job and do the bidding of his masters that he leaped at their slightest signal and committed artistic murder at a snap of the corporate fingers. The entire article, Archer realized dully, was written in exactly the same exasperated and belligerent tone as the articles in *Blueprint* on the other side of the question. Style, he thought, is interchangeable on political questions. Political articles these days, he decided, all sound as though they had been dictated by Mrs. Pokorny or an opposed twin.

Archer read slowly. It was difficult to go through the untruths that were impossible to contradict, the facts that were slightly and fatally twisted, the biting epithets that were attached to his name, the reasonable-sounding half-truths that were so false and so damning. Mrs. Pokorny, Archer saw, had also revealed that Archer had tried to persuade her to disguise the fact that Pokorny had killed himself and there was a literal and quite accurate account of his conversation with her about the pills and the robe. God, Archer thought, she must have a notebook on her at all times. In print this way, with the shadow of the dead men hovering over the page, Archer's action, which he had attempted almost automatically and out of a protective instinct for the composer and his wife, now seemed like the most callous maneuvering and concealment. If it was about anyone else, Archer thought, I'd think he was the most despicable coward in the world.

His hands were shaking when he finished the article. The columnist promised to supply new and equally damning evidence the next day. Suddenly, staring at the page, Archer hated the sight of his name in print. Clement Archer, Clement Archer . . . The name had a tainted ring to it after its use ten times in ten paragraphs. Archer blinked, checking himself consciously from blurting out what he felt. He handed the paper back to Vic. He tried to smile. "This fellow," he said, "really lays it on, doesn't he?"

"Great little old circulation builder," Vic said carelessly, taking the paper. "You still going to the funeral?"

Archer hesitated. Everybody at the funeral would probably have read the piece. They would be friends and relatives of the dead man and in the moment of grief and anger almost certainly would share Mrs. Pokorny's estimate of Archer's share in the tragedy. And there would undoubtedly be photographers there from the newspapers to catch the look of guilt on Archer's face as he confronted the widow. I wish I was sick, Archer thought. I wish I was sick in bed with the doctor in the room telling me it would kill me to go out today.

"Yes," Archer said to Vic. "Yes, I'm going to the funeral."

"You don't like to let yourself off anything, do you?" Vic said. Somehow he sounded cold and unfriendly and Archer wondered if he believed what was in the paper this morning, too. Vic stood up. "I'm going to get my hair cut," he said. "See you at one. Do you want this?" He waved the newspaper a little.

"No, thanks."

Vic nodded and tossed the paper onto a chair. Then he strolled out, a tall, youthful man in a fine tweed suit, heading for the barber who would clip his thick, blond hair close around his well-shaped head, so that he would look like a gentleman who had been graduated not too long before from a good college, a man who was too lucky to have to attend funerals.

While the door was still open, Woodrow Burke came in. He saw Archer and waved and came over quickly. The ex-commentator was fatter than ever and his collar was too tight for him now, giving his face a pale, strangled look. In America, Archer thought, adversity adds weight. The highest standard of living in the world, operating to put double chins on the country's failures. Burke had a copy of the newspaper under his arm and Archer thought that he could tell from the expression on Burke's face that the commentator had read the column. But at least he wasn't drunk.

"Good morning, soldier," Burke said. He didn't offer to shake hands. He just stood in front of Archer, fat, rumpled, pale, his hair thinning, pretending he wasn't a failure, pretending he didn't have a hangover, pretending his suit wasn't too tight for him. "How're things?"

"Greater," Archer said. "How'd they happen to let you in?"

"They told me there was going to be a break for a couple of hours and there're still one or two of the guards around here who remember when I was a big shot, so they passed me in. Do you mind?"

Archer shook his head. "Delighted," he said. "Always pleased to see old friends and debtors."

"Oh." Burke smiled fleshily. "I guess I had that coming. I never wrote and thanked you for the check, did I?"

"I don't seem to recall that you did," Archer said slowly. He wanted to get away from Burke. It made him nervous to talk to a man with that paper folded under his arm, with the name Clement Archer, Clement Archer, all over the inside page.

"Regrets," Burke said. "I must mend my manners. I meant to. I really did. I even wrote myself a memorandum." He dug in his pocket and got out a crumpled piece of paper. He smoothed the paper out, his hands shaking minutely, and peered at it. "Here," he said, thrusting it at Archer. "See for yourself. My intentions were of the best."

Archer took the paper. "Write Archer this week," he read. "Bread and butter note." Archer rolled the slip into a ball and flipped it at a wastebasket ten feet away. It didn't go in. "Thanks," Archer said. "I'll file it away to remind me of you."

"Look," Burke said, "I didn't come up here to talk about that. I forgot and I'm sorry and I apologize and I don't want you to hold it against me. I'm working on something that's very important for you and just because I forget things these days and you're sore at me, I don't want you to . . ."

"I'm not sore at you," Archer said. "Forget it. I haven't got much time now, Burke. This is burying day for radio musicians and I've got to go to the funeral. So if you'll call me some other time, I'll try to . . ."

"Don't brush me off, Archer," Burke said, his tone half-pleading, half-pugnacious. "I've read this little hymn of hate this morning . . ." He waved the newspaper. "And I happen to know that worse is coming from the other side, and you'd better start to worry about building character. Fast. And I want to help you. You've got to believe me, Clem."

"What do you mean—worse is coming from the other side?" Archer tried to smile. "What're they going to do—say that I murdered my mother with an axe?"

"Something along those lines," Burke said. "I've got an advance copy here." He dug in his inside pocket and brought forth a thick mess of papers, old envelopes, bills, newspaper clippings. He sorted through them with his thick, shaky hands. "Friend of mine who's a press agent at a night club. Gets the dope early. They're going to hang you with a nice thick rope . . . God damn it," he muttered petulantly, "I could have sworn I had it on me." He went swiftly through the sheaf of papers again, not finding what he was looking for. "Well, I don't have it," he said, stuffing the papers back, making a big bulge in the front of his jacket. "But they have you listed as belonging to everything but the Sicilian national guard. Listen to me, Clem . . ." He stood close to Archer, holding onto his sleeve, peering earnestly at him, his eyes yellowed and opaque from ten years' drinking. "Tomorrow it's going out that you're a Red, a Red sympathizer, a defender of Reds, and it'll be all over town, and unless you do something about it, you won't be able to get a job sweeping out the men's room on the 22nd floor."

Archer chuckled. He didn't mean to, and it surprised him. "Don't they read the newspapers?" he asked. "Don't they read that I'm in the vanguard of Fascism and that I'm a tool of the big corporations?"

"They don't read anything but old letterheads and inscribed copies of *Mein Kampf*," Burke said bitterly. "Ask me. I'm the boy who knows. Nobody would listen to me a year ago, when they pinched me out of the line. Maybe they'll listen now. People've been yellow and they're paying for it now. They didn't defend me or the others when we got the boot to the seat of the trousers. They just pretended it had nothing to do with them and prayed they wouldn't get it next if they kept their mouths shut. Well, they got it next, and you're getting it next, because those're the tactics, soldier, defeat the buggers in detail, make them commit themselves piecemeal, never let them fight in mass."

"Burke," Archer said wearily, "will you forget for a moment that you were once a military commentator and talk in something that sounds like English? What're you driving at?"

Burke looked offended. "Sorry if my vocabulary doesn't please you," he said stiffly. "What I'm trying to say is that this is the time for everybody to get together and fight for everybody's life. Actors, writers, directors, commentators. And now is the time. Pokorny's suicide makes a perfect peg for it. Poor little jerk of a man lying in a pool of blood because those bastards on

Blueprint did a job on him. It'll give a focus to the whole thing and people who wouldn't lift a finger otherwise'll be shocked enough for a day or two to rally round. What I came here to say, Clement," Burke said, "is that there's going to be a meeting tomorrow night after the theatre, so that actors who're playing in shows can get to it. A protest meeting against the blacklist and everything it stands for. All shades of political opinion. Figure out some way of protecting artists and semiartists like you and me—" Burke smiled bleakly "—from being pushed over the cliff. And we want you to make a speech."

"Wait a minute," said Archer. "Before you go on I want to make something clear to you. I'm absolutely opposed to the Communists. You still want me?"

"I have some interesting news for you," Burke said. He was trying to smile, but his lips were trembling. "I'm not a Communist. That's for your private information. And I hate the bastards. That's for anyone's information. And I don't know whether you believe me or not and I don't care. And you can say anything you want in your speech. Just be there. Present yourself. Just tell what happened to you. Tell what happened to the people on your program. If you don't want to say anything else, just tell the group how competent or incompetent Vic Herres and Stanley Atlas and Alice Weller are, and what sweet music that poor dead jerk used to write before he took the pills."

"Hold it," Archer said sharply. "What's this about Herres and Weller? Who brought their names into this?"

"Tomorrow, son," Burke said. "In the same article in which they give you the low-level bombardment. It's all-out now, and the shelters're all full. Well?" Burke stepped back and cocked his head, narrowing his eyes to look at Archer.

"Who else is speaking," Archer said, "from this program?"

"I asked O'Neill. He's going to let me know tonight.

Don't worry," Burke said. "You'll have plenty of company. In the last year there've been two hundred people canned. Bank accounts're dropping fast enough all around town so that people're just about ready to open their mouths."

"If I made a speech," Archer said, "who'd have to approve it?"

"Nobody. You won't have to show it to anyone. Well?"

Archer hesitated. He looked around the room. O'Neill had just come back and was standing against the far wall, watching Burke and himself. O'Neill looked like a detective in his dark-blue suit and his black tie.

"Give me your number," Archer said. "I'll let you know tomorrow."

Burke sighed. "What do you expect?" he asked. "Do you think you'll see a vision tonight?" But he wrote out his number on a scrap of paper and gave it to Archer. He started to leave, then turned back, embarrassedly. "What I need," he said, "is a drink. And I happen to be a little strapped. Do you think . . ."

"Sorry," Archer said. "Three hundred is a nice even number. Let's leave it at that."

Burke smiled unhappily. "I don't blame you," he said. "Don't think I blame you a bit. Don't believe anything you read in the newspapers."

He waved his hand and went out. Why is it, Archer thought, watching the door close, that so many people you feel you ought to help are so objectionable? Maybe, he thought, when I get to the point that Burke's at now, I'll be just as objectionable, too.

Brewer came in, putting on his overcoat, and they all went downstairs—Archer, Barbante, O'Neill, Levy and Brewer—and got into a cab after O'Neill gave the address of the undertaker on Second Avenue. The cab was crowded with the five men in their bulky coats and they talked desultorily about everything but Pokorny or the article about Archer in the newspaper. Archer felt that they looked like a group of men taking an afternoon off from the office to go to the races.

The undertaker's chapel was in a small store on the corner of a busy block on Second Avenue in the Twenties. There was an Italian grocery store beside it, with long cheeses hanging in the window. Three news photographers waited outside the entrance to the chapel and they took Archer's picture and O'Neill's picture as the two men got out of the cab and crossed the sidewalk.

Inside there were only about twenty or twenty-five people, sitting on folding chairs facing the casket. They were whispering quietly and they all hushed for a long moment and turned in their chairs as Archer came in with the others. There was no expression on their faces. Most of them seemed to be refugees, with clothes that looked as though they had been bought in second-hand shops in foreign countries and Archer got the impression that they were all huddling together as though they thought they could hide better in a group than singly. There were some flowers, looking sadly pure and spring-like in the drab room, and sending a disturbing fragrance into the dank air, mixing with the strong smell of incense that the undertaker used to disguise the odor of previous deaths.

Archer and the other men from the program sat down as unobtrusively as possible in the rear row of seats. He didn't know what to do with his hat. Some of the mourners were wearing theirs, but others were bareheaded. There didn't seem to be a rabbi present, or if there was, he was not dressed in any ceremonial clothes. Archer didn't want to offend the religious sensibilities of the group, whatever they were, but he felt uncomfortable with his hat on when almost half the other men were bare-headed. With a sudden gesture, he took it off and put it on his knees. Brewer, sitting next to him, watched him, then carefully followed his example.

Mrs. Pokorny was standing with two men near the casket and she seemed to be arguing with them, although their voices were kept low and Archer couldn't hear what they were saying. Mrs. Pokorny had on a black dress but it was covered with a grayish cloth coat, obviously the only one she had. Her face, Archer decided, looked no better or worse than it ever had. It was not a face for grief and the lines of anger that were always present there were not intensified by the happenings of the last three days. She had not looked up when Archer entered.

Suddenly, as though exasperated with the arguments of the two men, who were smaller and slighter than she, and over whom she towered menacingly, Mrs. Pokorny strode down the side of the room, trying to shake them off. But they followed her and the little group came to an uneasy halt in the back of the room, close enough so that Archer could hear snatches of what they were saying.

". . . I repeat," Mrs. Pokorny was saying, "he doesn't need any religious services."

"But, Madam," the shorter of the two men said, pleadingly, "he was a Jew, a prayer must be said for him." The man had a frail, wan, studious face, like a mathematics professor. He was about fifty years old and he had an accent. "I don't think it's right, at a time like this, Madam," the man said insistently, "to deny the comforts of religion. I took the liberty of asking Rabbi Feldman here to officiate and he is ready and . . ."

"My dear Mrs. Pokorny," the rabbi said, "out of a sense of respect, as a comfort to his friends, as an appeal to God for the soul of your husband . . ." The rabbi was young and had a Boston accent, flat and almost

Irish-sounding. "A Jew should not be buried without the traditional prayers. For three thousand years . . ."

"He wasn't a Jew," Mrs. Pokorny said.

"Mrs. Pokorny . . ." the little man said faintly, spreading his hands. "I knew him ever since he was a schoolboy in Vienna."

"I deny he was a Jew," Mrs. Pokorny said, dwarfing the two men in their dark hats." "He wasn't anything. He didn't believe in your God or anybody's God, and neither do I, and I don't want your mumbling and your superstition at a time like this."

"I don't believe it, Mrs. Pokorny," the frail little man said quietly. "He believed in God. I know he did. We had many talks, before your marriage . . ."

Archer sat rigidly, embarrassed, wishing he hadn't come.

"Now, I've had enough of this," Mrs. Pokorny said loudly. The mourners all heard, but sat stiffly, their heads pointed toward the casket, desperately attempting to pretend that nothing was happening behind them. "There's going to be a speech by a mutual friend and I've agreed to let one of Manfred's friends play a number on the violin. That's enough."

Once more she walked away from the two men and sat down in the front row, her head outlined against the casket. The two men looked at each other and the rabbi shrugged. "Later we will get together ten friends," he said softly, "and say a prayer by ourselves, all the same." He patted the little man's arm, and they both found seats and sat down.

A bare-headed man of about forty stood up and faced the mourners. He had a red face, as though he worked in the weather year in and year out, and he was larger than most of the other people present. He looked like a longshoreman, Archer decided, and when he spoke, in a hoarse voice that sounded as though it had cracked many years before, shouting against the wind, the impression was strengthened. This one, Ar-

cher decided, is a member of Mrs. Pokorny's team, and
he isn't too friendly toward God, either.

"Ladies and gentlemen," the man said in his hoarse
riverside voice, "and friends of our dead friend. We're
here to pay our respects to a martyr in the struggle
for freedom and peace."

Oh, no, Archer thought, shocked, it's not going to
be like that! Even Mrs. Pokorny wouldn't do that.
They're not going to parade the poor, forlorn, chubby,
meaningless little corpse and pretend he was a hero of
the revolution!

"But first," the longshoreman said in the tones of an
orator who has quelled many a union meeting and
street-corner demonstration, "we will hear a selection
on the violin, one that our dear departed friend personally wrote in better days and which his loving and
courageous wife has chosen because her husband would
have wanted to hear it one more time before he left
us. It will be played," the man said, like a practiced
master of ceremonies, "by an old and close comrade of
the departed, Mr. Ely Rose."

Mr. Rose stood up, wearing a hat and fumbling with
a violin case. He opened the case and put it down carefully on the floor. Then he tuned the violin nervously,
his long fingers fiddling swiftly with the pegs and getting sharp, twanging, off-tune notes from the instrument.

Archer closed his eyes in embarrassment for a moment. When he opened them again, Mr. Rose was beginning to play. The music was nondescript, slow, sorrowful, without climaxes, fitting for funerals, and Mr.
Rose played with too much feeling, bending his body,
closing his eyes, the bow sweeping up past the brim of
his hat, his fingers quivering on the strings, making a
long, vibrating, sentimental moviehouse tremolo of
every passage. Archer never felt that he knew enough
about music to criticize anybody, but he was sure Mr.
Rose was a bad violinist. Archer looked over at Levy.
Levy was sitting bolt upright, his handsome, long nose

wrinkled, his eyes squinted shut as though he were suffering from some inner pain, and Archer knew that he was right about the violinist.

Mr. Rose finished. Tears were streaming down his cheeks. He almost bowed, then sat down abruptly, holding the violin pressed to his cheeks. Some of the women among the mourners were sobbing and some of the men were pushing at their eyes with handkerchiefs.

The longshoreman stepped forward and began to speak. After the first few sentences, Archer didn't bother to follow him. Pokorny, it appeared, had been sacrificed to the warmongers because of his courageous efforts in the cause of peace and freedom. Peace and freedom were mentioned often, as though the longshoreman were discussing his private property. There was also a protracted comparison between America today and Germany in 1932, with references to artists, Jews and union leaders. The lying and bloodthirsty press also came in for its share of attention. Actually, Archer thought, half listening and resentful, a great deal of what this fellow is saying has elements of truth in it—in a way Pokorny *is* a victim of the warscare; in a way there are disturbing similarities between pre-Hitler Germany and America today; orthodoxy *is* at a premium and deviations from a narrowing and intolerant standard are being savagely punished —but the clichés that the speaker was using and the rhetorical, practiced emphasis of his delivery, with its echoes of many identical speeches on other occasions, made it impossible to listen reasonably or be moved or persuaded. Also, picking Pokorny's inoffensive corpse as a rostrum for political fulminations was hateful to Archer. And to make such a baleful speech to the huddled two dozen elderly exiles who had come softly and tragically to say farewell to one of their number who had thought he had escaped and hadn't —God, Archer thought, the Communists don't understand anything because they are not human.

The speaker neared the end of his peroration in a

thunder of warnings and boasts about the hidden strength of the working class. Archer looked over at Mrs. Pokorny. She was staring at the speaker, her face proud, defiant, exalted, as before her eyes she could see her husband, dead, being transformed into a shining symbol which the living, stubborn, shabby flesh never would permit.

The speaker stopped and there was a sigh from the mourners. By now, everyone had stopped crying. The body could not be viewed, because there had been an autopsy and the top of the skull had been removed to get at the brain. The speaker went over to Mrs. Pokorny and she looked up at him fiercely, clutching his hand, saying, "Thank you, Frank. It was wonderful."

The undertaker's men came in and rolled the casket out a side door and the mourners stood around in little groups, murmuring softly, dissatisfied, unfulfilled by this curious service, wishing that someone had called on God, that some ritual had been observed to bind Pokorny with the three thousand years and the unnumbered dead that were behind them all.

"Let's get out of here," Levy was muttering angrily. "Fast!"

"Don't you want to go over and say something to the widow?" Archer asked.

"No." Levy said. "I'll wait for you outside."

But the others went over. Archer hung back while Barbante and O'Neill and Brewer shook Mrs. Pokorny's hand and said the polite things. When Archer approached her, he held out his hand. "I'm terribly sorry," he said.

Mrs. Pokorny looked up at him, granite-faced. She didn't put out her hand. "This is the one, Frank," she said to the man who had made the speech.

Frank shook his head mournfully. "Man, man," he said, "will you never learn? Will you have to wait until you're behind the wire?"

Archer flushed. All around him, the mourners, who seemed bowed and tiny next to him, were watching him curiously, suspiciously. He dropped his hand and went out onto Second Avenue.

"What I need," he said, as he joined the others, "is a drink."

There was a bar on the next block and silently they all started to walk toward it, through the housewives doing their morning shopping and the children staring gravely out of their carriages. As they crossed the street, the hearse passed them, and two limousines filled with mourners. Eight people, Archer counted, going a little too fast in the 1940-model Cadillacs to watch the casket being lowered into the grave among the crowded monuments on Long Island.

"God damn it," Barbante said, in a low, strangled voice. He was standing on the corner, his hands rigidly at his sides, staring after the funeral procession disappearing briskly among the beer and laundry trucks. "God damn everybody!"

"Sssh. That's all right, Dom," Brewer said soothingly, putting his hand on Barbante's arm.

But Barbante ignored him. His voice rose suddenly to a wild shout and his mouth moved in a tortured grimace as though he were in pain. "Pokorny was right," he said. "He's the only sensible man on Manhattan Island this minute. And they're moving him off at forty miles an hour. The only thing is to die. Why wait, boys, why wait? If I had the guts I'd buy a hundred pills this morning." He looked crazily up at the sky. "If I saw them up there with the bomb," he shouted, as the housewives moved their children uneasily around him, "I'd yell to them, here I am, drop it right here."

"Come on, Dom," Archer said quietly, embarrassed by the sight of the debonair and foppish man waving his arms and screaming on the street corner. "Let's have a couple of drinks and calm down a little." He went over and took Barbante's other arm. Barbante pulled away.

"God damn you," Barbante said. "God damn everybody."

He walked away.

After awhile they went into the bar. They had two drinks and then went uptown to finish the rehearsal.

21

Kitty was seated at the table reading the newspaper when Archer came down the next morning for breakfast. He had slept late, in a drugged stupor, after the funeral and the long rehearsal and the show. And there had been a sorrowful scene with Kitty, who had read the columnist's attack on him and had waited up for him to ask him about it.

Now Kitty was sitting at the table, sipping a glass of milk with her breakfast toast, reading the morning newspaper which she had propped up against the coffee pot. She looked tired, as though the night's sleep had not refreshed her. It was a gray day and the light in the room was dead and colorless. Archer, dressed in pajamas and a robe, went over behind her and bent over and kissed her cheek. She put her hand up and held his head close to hers for a moment. Over her shoulder, Archer saw that she had the paper opened to the page on which there was the story of Pokorny's funeral the day before. There was a picture of Barbante, O'Neill and himself going into the funeral parlor. There had been a similar picture in the evening papers the night before and a tabloid had run a glaring headline on the third page under the picture,

"Friends Honor Red Suicide." Kitty was reading the New York *Times*, and the accompanying article was sober and conservative and full of "it is allegeds" and "It was reporteds." The word Red was not used in the article and there was a pathetic, short list of the conductors and orchestras which had played Pokorny's works in America. The Duluth Philharmonic Society, Archer read, the Santa Monica Symphony. The picture was just as bad, though, Archer decided, staring at it. He looked puffy and frightened and his hat was pulled down too far in front, making it seem almost as if he had been trying to disguise himself.

He didn't say anything about the article. He kissed Kitty's face again, lightly, and she dropped her hand. He went around to his place and sat down and drank his orange juice.

"Want part of the paper, darling?" Kitty asked.

"No, thanks." How wonderful it would be, he thought, to be someplace where no paper reached you until it was six months old.

He ate lightly, not relishing his food, eating out of habit, listening to the rustle of the paper as Kitty turned the pages to the advertisements for dresses.

The phone rang. Kitty looked up, but Archer was on his feet. "I'll answer it," he said. "I'm finished anyway."

It was O'Neill. "Clem," O'Neill said, his voice sounding urgent and baffled at the same time, "you've got to get up to the office right away."

"What's the matter now?" Archer asked, sighing. "This is Friday and I have a million things to do."

"I'm sorry, Clem," O'Neill said. "But you have to come. It's Barbante. He's here now and . . ."

"What's he doing up so early? Is he sick?"

"He was waiting for me when I came in. He says he's quitting. Today. You've got to talk to him."

Archer sighed again. "OK," he said. "Hold him there. I'll be there in a half hour."

He hung up and went back to the dining room. Kitty looked up at him questioningly.

"I have to go uptown," Archer said. Standing, he took a last sip of the coffee. It was cold.

"Why?" Kitty asked.

"Nothing important," Archer said vaguely, starting out of the room. "Barbante is being foolish . . ."

"Clement," Kitty said quietly, "you're going to remember what we talked about, aren't you? I'm in on everything from now on . . ."

"I remember," Archer said. "You're in on everything." He smiled sourly. "You'll probably be good and sorry."

"No, I won't," Kitty said. "Never for a minute."

"OK," Archer said, waving, as he started out of the room, "you'll get a full report each night at taps. Satisfied?" He grinned at her from the doorway.

Kitty nodded. "Satisfied," she said.

Archer dressed quickly, putting on his overcoat as he ran down the outside steps to the street. He walked to the corner, looking for a cab. The newsstand on the corner had a fresh pile of newspapers, and after a moment's hesitation, Archer bought a copy of the paper in which he had been attacked the day before. Might as well see what the bastard has to say about me today, he thought. Looking at the papers spread over the stand, with iron weights on them to keep them from being blown away by the wind, Archer realized that his name was prominent in every one of them. Five million people, he realized, smelling the faint aroma of fresh ink that came from the stand, are reading my name today. Clement Archer, Clement Archer, finally famous after a lifetime of obscurity, well known for one day at the age of forty-five, because of the death of a ninth-rate Viennese musician.

There was a cab parked across the street at a hack stand and he was just about to hail it when another cab swerved in toward him and the driver opened the door. Archer got in and was about to give the driver the address when the driver of the parked cab jumped out of his machine and shouted belligerently across the street, "What's going on here? What the hell do you think I park on this corner for? Why don't you use the local people, for Christ's sake?"

"Stuff it, bud," the driver of Archer's cab shouted back. "You don't own the streets." He jerked in the gear shift and the cab spurted up the avenue. Archer looked out the back window. The other man was standing impotently in the gutter, waving his fist angrily, shouting unheard curses over the noise of the traffic. How can a man be so furious, Archer wondered, so early in the morning?

He settled back in his seat and opened the newspaper to the page of columns. He saw his name in the first paragraph and took a deep breath. For a moment, he glanced out of the window at the crowded street.

"Those hack-stand guys," the driver said. "They think they own the cement. Just because they're too lazy to cruise. I'll tell you something. When I take a cab I make it a point never to take one from a stand." The man had a harsh, angry New York voice and he drove the machine as though he had a grudge against it. He was a thin man with gray hair showing under his cap, uneven against his wrinkled neck.

There ought to be a law, Archer thought, looking down at the newspaper which was shaking with the motion of the cab, to make all cab drivers keep their mouths shut while on duty. They're worse than barbers.

Today, he saw, the columnist had decided to be philosophically analytical about Archer. "What sort of man is it," Archer read in the second paragraph, "who is chosen these days to do the dirty work for the yahoos of reaction?" Yahoos of reaction, Archer thought wearily, must they write like that?

"The history of the insignificant hack, Clement Archer," the piece went on, "is a neat case in point. We've done a little research on the frightened little man who tried to hush up the death of a great artist and there are some interesting facts that have come to light."

A great artist, Archer thought dully, staring at the page. Death has promoted Pokorny quickly.

"A nondescript man who wandered from profession to profession," the columnist continued, somehow making a change of jobs sound like a criminal offense, "Archer pretended, in private conversation at least, to be a liberal when it was fashionable and safe, only to jump to the other side at the first crack of his masters' whip. Not content with sending a victim of Hitler's to his grave, this fearful gentleman also lined himself up with the other racist heroes by firing that gifted and beloved Negro comedian, Stanley Atlas, as his very first obedient move. For anyone who happens to believe that Archer was forced into this action, we have absolute proof that Archer has an ironclad contract with the Hutt and Bookstaver Agency which puts ALL HIRING AND FIRING completely in his power."

Archer sighed. It was all so nearly true. He *did* have the contract, although he would have been fired and paid off if he had attempted to enforce it, and naturally the columnist wouldn't know about that and if he did would not mention it. And Atlas *was* gifted, and possibly beloved, especially by those who had never met him.

"Hack-stand cabbies," the driver said loudly, over the traffic turmoil. "They cost me thirty-six hundred dollars. I hate them all."

Archer kept quiet, hoping that the man would be discouraged. But he wasn't. "I had a collision," he went on, hunched angrily over his wheel. "With a trolley car. In Brooklyn. Right in front of a stand. Five cabs. The drivers all there, standing in front of the first cab beating their gums. The trolley was beating the light, those trolleys think the sun rises and sets on them, nobody else has a right to breathe. I was going with the green, and this God-damn trolley just plows into me. Wreckage. I was scattered for fifty yards. I was laid out in the street like icing. There wasn't enough left of the cab to make a kiddie car. I was blood all over. If you want I could still show you some of the scars. They thought I was dead when the wagon came for me, the doctor was surprised I could breathe, he told me later. My own cab, all paid for. I was in traction eleven weeks and it was summertime, too. I thought my leg was going to drop off. The trolley company sent a man from the insurance, he made me an offer. Four hundred and fifty dollars. For the cab and the personal damages. I spit in his face. If I could've moved I'd have choked him with my bare hands."

The driver honked his horn and jerked the car fiercely, hurling it between two trucks. Occupied, he didn't talk for several moments, and Archer went back to the column.

"But timidity is this gentleman's banner," Archer read, "and he sails under the flag of surrender. He gave up being a teacher, he gave up being a writer, and he gave up being an artist, a liberal and a friend. I do not wish to be uncharitable. In 1942, I have learned, he was rejected by the Army. Since that time, he has taken up Yogi, trying to escape from his sense of failure in deep breathing, vegetarianism and half-baked mysticism. A fellow devotee of Indian culture, a man with whom Archer engages in the weird Oriental rites, is at the moment circulating an appeal for a million names in an effort to present to the UN a motion to outlaw all slaughter of animals for food. This gentleman, whose name I am at present withholding to spare him embarrassment at his place of business, has assured me that Mr. Archer shares his sentiments and has offered to add his name to the petition."

Archer felt himself beginning to sweat in the cold taxi, as he read on. "Ordinarily," the columnist went on, "these high jinks would be dismissed as the harmless if distasteful aberrations of a foolish bookworm. But if the believer in Yogi and the crusader against meat suddenly turns up doing the sinister hatchet-work of the Imperialist warloards, it is the duty of any honest journalist to print the facts. The fact is that the man who was chosen to put the finger on honest and talented artists is an unstable dabbler in outlandish religions who was found unfit to serve his country in time of war."

Archer dropped the paper to the floor, unable to read any more. He felt dazed and helpless. Where did he get this information? Archer thought heavily. Who could have told him these sad and ludicrous secrets? Why does he want to print them? What did I ever do to him to make him hate me this much?

"So I went into court," the cabbie said, glancing over his shoulder to fix Archer's attention. "The lawyer said I had a open and shut case against the company. He subpoenaed the five cabbies as witnesses and we asked for a hundred thousand dollars. And what do you think happened? You guessed it, brother. The company got to those five bastards. Gave them ten bucks a day to testify against me. I got balls. Eleven weeks in traction in the hospital and I was still on a cane in the courtroom and I didn't get the sweat off the judge's left nut. In 1936. In Brooklyn. It convinced me," the cabbie said powerfully. "Since that day I volunteer every chance I get for jury duty. I served nine times already. And every time a hackie comes up in front of me, I give it to him between the eyes. No matter he's right or he's wrong, no matter if he got hit and got both his legs fractured by a truck going the wrong way on a one-way street—I find against him. With satisfaction. I hate every hackie who ever lived."

"Shut up," Archer said thickly.

"What's that, brother?" The driver turned around in surprise.

"I said shut up and drive. That's all."

"Christ," the driver said obscurely, "you're one of those." He mumbled for the rest of the trip, but not loud enough for Archer to hear him, and he ddin't say thank you, even though Archer gave him a quarter tip.

Those are the people who read the newspapers, Archer thought, as he went into the huge gray building where O'Neill and Barbante were waiting for him. Those're the people who make up the juries and hand out justice without fear or favor. God, what chance does a man have any more?

Barbante was standing at the window of O'Neill's office when Archer came in. The writer needed a shave and he looked as though he had slept in his suit. There were cigarette ashes on his jacket and he was playing with the Venetian blinds on the window, flicking them up and down in jittery, clicking little movements. O'Neill was seated at his desk, doggedly trying to read a script. They weren't talking and it looked as though they had said everything they possibly could say to each other long ago.

"Welcome," said O'Neill grimly, "to Playland." He stood up and made sure the door was closed.

"Good morning, Dom," said Archer quietly. On the way up in the elevator he had made a conscious effort to compose himself. I must behave, he had decided, as though that piece had never come out in the paper and as though no one had ever read it.

"First of all, Clement," Barbante faced slowly around from the window, "I want you to understand that I didn't ask to have you come up here. You didn't have to disturb yourself on my account."

"OK," O'Neill said. "It was my idea. OK."

"I made up my mind," Barbante said, his voice lacking its usual deep timbre and sounding with the first tones of age that Archer had ever noticed in the writer. "I made up my mind to quit last night at exactly ten forty-three in the men's room of Twenty-One."

"Forgive me, boys," Archer said, taking off his coat and throwing it over a chair. "I came in late and I don't know the plot."

"I met Lloyd Hutt over a basin," Barbante said flatly. "He was washing his hands and he was dressed in a becoming shade of blue and I made up my mind."

"What're you talking about, Dom?" Archer asked, trying to be patient, wondering if Barbante had read the paper that morning.

"He was leaning over, being sanitary, and he saw me in the mirror," Barbante said, "and he said, 'What the hell is the matter with you anyway, Barbante? I thought I told you to stay away from that funeral.' "

"What?" Archer asked, puzzled. "Did he?"

"It's my fault," O'Neill said. O'Neill looked stubborn and frightened, sitting behind his desk. "Hutt told me to pass the word around that he didn't want anybody from the program to be seen at the funeral."

Archer took his eyes off Barbante and stared at O'Neill. "But you went yourself," Archer said, feeling that there was a misunderstanding here that would never be unraveled.

"So I did." O'Neill sounded defensive.

"I didn't hear you tell anyone to stay away from the funeral."

"Didn't you?" O'Neill asked flatly. "That's queer. Because I never did say it."

"Insubordination," Barbante said. "There will be a court-martial of trusted lieutenants in the morning for the crime of affection for the dead."

Archer began to understand and pity O'Neill and like him more than he had ever liked him before. "What the hell," Archer said to Barbante, "you're not going to quit because Hutt shot off his mouth a little, are you? You went, it's over, Pokorny's buried, and there's nothing Hutt or anybody else can do about it."

"Oh, yes, I'm going to quit," Barbante said in a

curious singsong. Archer suddenly realized that the man was drunk. "My golden typewriter is withdrawn from the service."

"It's breach of contract, Dom," O'Neill said warningly. "And don't think Hutt won't use it against you. He'll keep you from working anywhere else in radio, or maybe anywhere else in anything."

"I had a vision among the handbowls," Barbante said. "I suddenly saw that I couldn't live if I couldn't go to funerals of my choice. If that's the only way you can sell liniment and foot powder these days, I'm not interested any more."

"In a way," O'Neill said pleadingly, "you can't blame Hutt. He's splitting a gut trying to save the program and it's marked lousy in every paper in town this morning with all our pictures and Pokorny being called the Red composer of University Town and juicy excerpts from that bastard's funeral oration in black type getting a big play from the hyenas. If I had known we were going to get a performance like that, I don't think I would've gone, either."

"Emmet," Barbante said gently, "don't lie. Please— you did a nice thing—don't piss on it now."

"I'm not lying," O'Neill shouted. "I mean it. I went to say good-bye to a poor slob who'd had some bad breaks. I didn't think I was going to May Day at the Kremlin."

"Save it," Barbante said, "for your interview with Hutt. You'll need every alibi you can lay your hands on."

"Oh, shut up," O'Neill said. "I'm tired of you."

"Cut it out," Archer said authoritatively. "We're not going to get anywhere by yelling at each other. Dom," he said, "I don't want you to quit. We're tottering as it is. There's nobody else who can write this program at the moment and by the time we work in a new man, even if we can find one, we'll be off the air. You'll be responsible for putting fifty people out of work."

"Sorry, Clem," Barbante said. "Every man for himself from here on in. Maybe next week there'll be another funeral I'd want to attend that Hutt didn't approve of. Maybe you'll die, or my father, or Joe Stalin, and I'd get the itch to go even if Hutt thought it was bad for drugs."

"Will you for Christ's sake stop talking about funerals?" O'Neill shouted.

"Freedom of speech, press, religion, and lamentation," Barbante said stubbornly. "The Barbante bill of rights. No death without mourners. For the new Atlantic Charter."

"What're you going to do?" Archer asked, hoping to lead Barbante into more reasonable fields.

"I'm glad you asked that question, Mr. Archer." Barbante smiled theatrically, like a lecturer. "I'm retiring to California to take up two projects that have long been dear to me. I'm going back to my father's ranch and I'm going to get married and write a book entitled *The Dialectics of Atheism.*" He nodded, smiling insanely.

"Well," O'Neill said heavily to Archer, "you see what I've been getting since nine o'clock this morning."

"I wrote a letter to the *Times* last night," Barbante said, "outlining my main points. A trial balloon. You might be interested in the opening sentence, O'Neill—'The time has come to consider the abolition of religion before it abolishes us.' "

O'Neill put his head in his hands and groaned. "That's great," he said. "That's all we need now. We'll all be lynched."

"Don't worry," Archer said curtly, wondering how he could get Barbante out of the room. "He didn't write anything. He's kidding."

"Oh, no, I'm not." Barbante smiled like a lunatic child. "I wrote it. Four pages. Closely reasoned, as they say in legal circles."

"When that comes out," O'Neill said, looking up, "you won't have to quit. You'll be busy running."

"Don't be silly, Emmet," Archer said testily. "Even if he wrote it, nobody'll print it."

"Maybe I'll have it privately printed," Barbante said dreamily, "and dropped over Radio City from an airplane. A new use for airpower. The attack of reason. Don't be alarmed, O'Neill. It's not Communist propaganda. The Communists're the worst of all, because in this day and age they're the most religious of all. Faith —faith is the most destructive element because it can't permit dissent or deviation. So the Communists kill the non-Communists or the almost Communists or the doubtful Communists, just the way the Jews killed the Christians and the Christians killed the Jews, and the Catholics killed the Protestants and the Protestants killed the Catholics, and the Crusaders killed the Mohammedans and the Mohammedans killed the Hindus. And right here in this country—the Puritans cut the ears off Quakers and nailed them to the church doors. Faith in a god or faith in a state or a system of government frightens me and if you had any sense it would frighten you, because one way or another you will be asked to die for it, either fighting against it or defending it. The only way out, the only way we have a chance to survive, is not to believe in anything. Not our god or our ideas or our people or our anything. The important thing is not to feel too strongly about anything, not have any belief that can be insulted or endangered or that has to be defended . . ."

"Oh, God," O'Neill said, "do I have to listen to this?"

"I'm sorry," Barbante said mildly. "I thought Clement asked me what I intended to do from now on."

"Dom," Archer asked gently, "when was the last time you had any sleep?"

Barbante smiled weakly. Then he put his hand over his eyes. "Three, four days ago," he said in a whisper. "I don't know. You think I'm a little crazy, don't you, Clem?" he asked slyly.

"Maybe a little." Archer nodded.

"You're right." Barbante chuckled weirdly. "I think you're absolutely right. And if I stayed in this town, in this sinkhole, they'd cart me away in a straitjacket and they'd be giving me the electric-shock treatment morning, noon and night." Suddenly he was pleading with Archer. "I have to quit. You see that, don't you, Clem? I can't go through three more days like this again, can I? A man has to be sure he's got something left, something besides the gold cigarette cases and the nice fat check every Friday. How about you, Clem?" Barbante moved away from the window toward Archer. He didn't walk steadily. He stood close to Archer, short, dulleyed, creased, smelling stale and liquorish and unperfumed. "What've you got left, Clem? Take stock. Take that good old half-century inventory, Clem. What've you got on the shelves this year, Clem, besides footpowder and penicillin, Clem?"

"You said you were going to get married," Archer said. He didn't want to talk about himself this morning. "Who's the lady?"

Barbante looked sly and amused. He put his finger beside his nose and squinted craftily. "Haven't decided yet. Circling over the field. Observing the candidates, lying in bed having their breakfasts now, twitching their long, pretty, unsuspecting legs. Got to get something that fits the terrain. California type that can survive in a dry country. Careful choice necessary for experiment in godless monogamy. We're introducing Brahma bulls. From India. Can live on dew and sagebrush, and even so, an extra hundred pounds of meat in one year. Circling, circling . . ." Barbante waved his hand, his fingers pointing down, in a round, insane gesture. "Circling over the pretty little bedrooms."

"The hell with it," O'Neill said. "I'm going to tell Hutt we don't want Barbante any more. He's had it."

"Barbante's had it," the writer chanted, moving back toward the window. "Excellent phrase. Descriptive. Slang from World War Number Fourteen. In which we fought. Except me. Except Clem. Except good old Yogi Clem." He winked intimately at Archer. "Secret, Clem. Secret between you, me, and anybody with the price of a nickel newspaper."

"I'm sorry, Clem," O'Neill said soberly. "That son-ofabitch Roberts . . ."

"Forget it," Archer said curtly, feeling, This is the first time. I have to get used to it. I have to practice not showing anything.

"Don't worry, Clem," Barbante said, "the scientists're at work. Machines to do the work of a thousand men. A thousand scriptwriters. Probably one in the patent office right now. Call up International Business Machines and they probably can deliver one this afternoon. Plug it into the wall and watch the lights blink on and off and take out the next ten copies of University Town two minutes later. Perfect. Untouched by human hand. No trouble with the mechanism that a screw-driver can't fix. Machine guaranteed to believe in God, not stay up late at night, not have any political opinions, not get on any blacklists, never want to go to anybody's funeral."

"Oh, God," O'Neill said, "we're back on that again."

The door opened and Hutt came in without knocking. He looked fresh, as though he had just had a cold shower, and his suit was wonderfully pressed. Whenever Hutt came into a room, Archer realized, you always were struck by the thought that here was a man who was at least ten years older than he looked.

"Good morning, gentlemen," Hutt said. O'Neill stood up and Hutt waved graciously at him to sit down. "It's good of you to arrive so promptly." He smiled gently at Barbante and Archer as he seated himself on the edge of O'Neill's desk.

His ears have stopped peeling, Archer noticed.

"The well-pressed tycoon," Barbante said. "Tell me, Mr. Hutt, who is your tailor?"

Hutt glanced sharply at Barbante, then at O'Neill.

O'Neill shook his head. "Not a chance," O'Neill said.

"Have you talked to him, Archer?" Hutt asked.

Archer nodded. "I'm afraid O'Neill's right."

"Barbante's had it," the writer said. "We took a vote."

"Perhaps you'd like to think it over for another day," Hutt said, his voice friendly. "Calmly."

"Haven't got the time to think anything over calmly," said Barbante. "I'm busy circling." He chuckled.

Hutt looked puzzled for a moment, then shrugged, and turned to O'Neill and Archer. "How many scripts ahead are we?" he asked.

"Two," said Archer.

"Posthumous Productions, Incorporated," said Barbante gravely. "Additional dialogue by departed writer."

"Perhaps," Hutt said easily, still friendly, to Barbante, "you'd like to go back to your place and rest, Dom. You look all done in."

Barbante shook his head stubbornly. "I like it here. I'm interested in the grownups' conversation."

Hutt examined Barbante coldly, his pale-blue eyes taking in the untidy hair, the rumpled suit stained with cigarette ash, the purplish beard on the pale chin. Then he turned his back on Barbante. "Archer," he said mildly, "there seems to have been some confusion about my instructions yesterday about the funeral."

"There wasn't any confusion, Lloyd," O'Neill said in a low voice. "I didn't tell him."

Hutt nodded agreeably. "Not your confusion, then, Archer. O'Neill's confusion. You've seen the papers, I suppose."

"Yes," Archer said.

"We've gotten thirty-seven telephone calls already," Hutt said, without heat, "from church groups, veterans' organizations, patriotic individuals, demanding that O'Neill and you and Barbante and Levy and Brewer be dropped from the program immediately.

"Advertise me," Barbante said. "In the interests of

better public relations. Announce that Barbante has patriotically and individually dropped himself."

Hutt ignored him. "What's more," Hutt said, "calls have been coming into the sponsor's office, and even to his home, although he has an unlisted number. I don't mind telling you gentlemen that Mr. Sandler is getting rather restive, to put it as mildly as I know how." Hutt smiled, a businesslike, board-meeting smile.

"Church groups," Barbante mumbled. "Cut the Quakers' ears off and nail them to the bronze doors."

Hutt glanced at Barbante puzzledly. "What's he talking about?"

O'Neill shrugged. "He's off on a private tear. He can't explain it and I'm sure I can't. We could've saved ourselves a lot of grief if we'd sent him to a psychiatrist for the last two years and charged it up to entertainment."

"I was born and brought up a Roman Catholic, gentlemen," Barbante said, "and I played third base for the Church of the Good Shepherd until they found a boy who could hit curve-ball pitching."

"I'm sure it comes as no surprise to you gentlemen," Hutt addressed O'Neill and Archer again, "that the sponsor is seriously considering dropping the program entirely. I must say, too, in his defense, that I can't really blame him."

There was quiet in the room while nobody blamed the sponsor.

"I won't disguise the fact that we're hanging by a thin thread." Hutt said. There's a man, Archer thought irreverently, who will take any cliché head-on, asking and giving no quarter. "There's a good possibility that unless we take things in hand immediately," Hutt went on, "the option on the program will not be taken up when the time comes next month. I won't deny that I'm worried," Hutt said confidently, "but I don't think we're beaten yet." He smiled around the room, putting them all graciously on the same team. "If we work together, we can salvage the program and perhaps even

come out better than we ever were. First, I've arranged
a press conferenc up here this afternoon at three o'clock,
and I want everybody who is connected with the program—and that means everybody—actors, musicians,
engineers, sound men—to be here and answer any
questions any reporter asks, answer candidly and
with perfect frankness. I've already sent telegrams to
all the people who work on the program, even bit-part
actors who perhaps only appear two or three times a
year for us. I've invited Connors, the editor of *Blueprint,* who's coming as a personal favor to me, and
he's indicated that he is going to ask a certain number
of our people directly whether they are Communists or
not. You're one of them, Archer," Hutt said, smiling
deprecatingly, as though it was a childish joke that he
was reporting. "It seems," Hutt said softly, "that the
word has gone round that you were fighting our little
private cleansing operation and they've been looking
into your background rather intensively." Hutt shook
his head sadly. "Connors was good enough to show me
what they've picked up. I must say, Archer," Hutt said
tolerantly, "you seemed to have signed your name to
a grotesque list of things."

"Like what?" Archer asked stonily.

Hutt looked surprised. "Do I have to tell you?"

"I'm afraid you do," Archer said. "My memory is
failing me."

"It goes all the way back to the time you were teaching in college. But really, now," Hutt laughed softly, I
don't have to tell *you.*"

"What did I do in college?" Archer asked. "I really
want to know."

"Well, for one thing . . ." Hutt shrugged, as though
half good-naturedly giving into Archer's whim. "You
were one of the founders of a chapter of some college
instructors' union. And then you were chairman at a
meeting called together by the American Student Union
to hear a Communist candidate for office in 1935."

1935, Archer thought desperately, trying to reach

back into his memory, what did I do in 1935? He remembered nothing.

"The American Student Union, as you know, of
course," Hutt said, "is on the Attorney-General's list of
subversive organizations."

"I don't know of course," Archer said. "And I'm
damn sure it wasn't on any list in 1935. The list didn't
come out till 1947."

"Now, Archer." Hutt shook his head, mildly reprov-
ing. "That's mere verbal juggling." He smiled again.
"And then you seemed to sign your name to every
piece of paper that had the word Spanish on it between
the years of 1936 and 1940. Good Lord, man, it looks
as though you were trying to win the Spanish war
single-handed right in Ohio." He laughed generously,
showing Archer that he understood the immature en-
thusiasms of youthful history instructors. "And then, it
seems you contributed to Russian War Relief in 1942."

"I won't even comment on that," Archer said. "You'll
probably find fifty senators on the same list."

"Conceded," Hutt said reasonably. "But it sounds
unpleasant these days just the same, doesn't it? And it
has been declared subversive."

"I guarantee," Archer said, "not to relieve the Russians in any future wars. Does that make everybody
happy?"

"Actually, Archer," Hutt said pleasantly, "you happen to be in a quite fortunate position. Through no
fault of your own, and at the moment, I'm sure you
don't appreciate it fully . . ." He chuckled. "But the
columnist on that Red sheet who's been after you the
last couple of days has done you a world of good,
actually."

"What?" Archer asked, bewildered. "What do you
mean?"

"An attack from that quarter is enormously wholesome," Hutt said sonorously, "and reassures people who
have been entertaining serious doubts about your re-

liability. And some of the phrases he's used, although they're the most exaggerated nonsense, like 'vanguard of Fascism' and 'hatchet-man for the imperialist warmongers' have the effect of giving you almost a clean bill of health, all by themselves. Almost, I said." Hutt pointed his finger warningly. "Almost. Of course," he said sympathetically, "some of the other things must be rather embarrassing and I'm terribly sorry they had to be printed. The absurd bit about the Yogi exercises and the information about your being rejected by the Army."

"Loony," Barbante said at the window. "Cracked as an old jug. Our Clem. On a clear day you can see his brain parting at the seams."

Hutt glanced sharply at Barbante, then decided to ignore him. "But then you've got to expect vulgarities like that," Hutt said to Archer, "from gentlemen of that persuasion."

Persuasion, Archer thought dazedly. What does he mean by that? Does he mean Roberts' religion?

"Still," Hutt said expansively, "I'm sure that if you answer all the questions put to you this afternoon by the gentlemen of the press, and answer them candidly and frankly, as I said, and as I am sure you can and will, we'll find that you will be completely rehabilitated in the public mind by the time our next program goes on the air. And anything I may have said previously to you, in a moment of exasperation—" Hutt waved his large pretty hands magnanimously "—anything to the effect that your usefulness was at an end or any hint that perhaps we would have to come to a parting of the ways, I'm sure both you and I will be able to forgive and forget."

He smiled, friendly, dapper, in control, maintaining the perfect, cool, superior, almost cordial relationship of employer and employee.

"Barbante," he said, standing up and taking a step toward the writer, speaking in the hushed, sedative tones of a male nurse, "even though for the moment you no longer happen to be associated with us, I think it would be a nice gesture on your part if you would be present at the conference this afternoon, although of course there is no hint of any accusation against you." He chuckled paternally. "You never seemed to have signed anything at all."

"I was too busy," Barbante said soberly, "following girls down Madison Avenue."

Hutt smiled, the male nurse humoring the patient. "Of course you did go to the funeral yesterday," he said, "and there might be a question or two on that score, but I'm sure there'll be no real difficulty."

Even as involved as he was with his own dazed reactions to Hutt's speech, Archer knew that Hutt shouldn't have used the word, "funeral." From the look on O'Neill's face Archer recognized that O'Neill was of the same opinion. Archer saw Barbante growing tense. His head rocked a little from side to side and he flicked the Venetian blinds in a rapid, irregular, tinny rhythm. But for the moment, he didn't reply. Hutt looked at him curiously, frowning slightly, then turned back to Archer. "Oh," he said, as though he had just remembered, "one more thing. Word has reached me that tonight there is to be a meeting at the St. Regis Hotel, a meeting called and paid for by Communists in radio, television and the theatre, to protest the so-called blacklist. Word has reached me, also, that several people from our program have been invited to attend. Naturally," he said carelessly, "I expect everyone in this room to leave it severely alone."

"Can't go to funerals," Barbante muttered, walking unsteadily toward O'Neill's desk. "Can't go to the St. Regis. Can't go to the potty, because Lloyd Hutt says no."

"Barbante," Hutt said sharply, "since you've decided you no longer wish to work for us, I think you can be excused from this conference."

Barbante stared at him drunkenly, thick-eyed. "The

man in the Bronzini tie," he said. Then he came over to Archer. "Clem," he said, "a woman I never met coined a phrase. Name of La Pasionaria. Spanish lady. Red as the Russian flag, I wouldn't be surprised. During that little old war you tried to win with your signature in Ohio, Clem. Eloquent old bag. Made a speech. Know what she said?" He peered owlishly at Archer, who was standing now, near the door. "I'll tell you what she said—'You can die on your feet,' the lady said, 'or you can live on your knees.' Wartime choice. Oratory. Heard round the world. OK, while it lasted, Clem. Old-fashioned. Romantic. Other times, other choices. Not up to date. Shows signs of wear and tear, obso—" He stumbled on the word. "Obsolescence. Needs modernizing and I'm the boy to do it. With special permission of the copyright owner. Got it all brushed up for Mr. Hutt and 1950. Still preserve original form, original concision. Still preserve important element of choice. Here it is, the latest model—" He peered around him triumphantly. "You can die on your feet," he said loudly, thinking hard, "or you can die on your knees. Hear me, Clem?" He touched Archer's shoulder, briefly. "OK, OK," he said pettishly, "I'm going."

He went out, walking carefully.

There was silence in the room for a moment and then Hutt said, "Well, I'm glad we got rid of him." Then, more softly, to Archer, "Well, I don't think there's anything more we have to discuss at the moment, Archer. I won't keep you any longer. I'll see you up here this afternoon at three. We're using the Board of Directors' room because we expect a lot of people."

"No," Archer said, and he listened carefully to the words that were coming out of his mouth, as though they were surprising him, too. "No, you won't see me up here this afternoon."

"What's that?" Hutt asked.

Archer saw O'Neill slowly lower his head and look down at the desk in front of him.

"I won't be here this afternoon," Archer said evenly. "I'm not coming to your party. I'm busy. I have to prepare the speech I'm going to make at the St. Regis." He picked up his hat and coat, throwing his coat over his arm. He felt very calm.

"Archer . . ." Hutt began. Then he stopped. His shoulders drooped and his mouth twitched and he looked older and more human than he had five minutes before and for a moment Archer was sure there was something baffled and frightened and pleading in the well-kept, controlled, handsome face. Then Archer went out.

"O'Neill," he heard Hutt's voice saying wearily, as he went into the outer office, "if you'll be so good as to close the door, there are one or two things we have to talk about . . ."

Archer went downstairs and called the number Burke had given him and told him he would be at the St. Regis early.

22

He wanted to be alone for awhile, so he walked all the way downtown, even though the weather was threatening and it was cold and it looked like snow. He tried to think of what he wanted to say at the meeting that night, but all he could think of were sentences that began, "It is guaranteed in the First Amendment," and "As the Bill of Rights puts it," and "In the words of Voltaire . . ."

Archer walked down Fifth Avenue, past the department stores, with their windows full of dresses, coats and furs, and the women rushing in and out of the doors, their faces lit with the light of purchase. It is the new profession for the female sex, he thought—buying. If you wanted to set up an exhibit to show modern American women in their natural habitat, engaged in their most characteristic function, he thought, like the tableaux in the Museum of Natural History in which stuffed bears are shown against a background of caves, opening up honeycombs, you would have to set up a stuffed woman, slender, high-heeled, rouged, waved, hot-eyed, buying a cocktail dress in a department store. In the background, behind the salesgirls and the racks and shelves, there would be bombs bursting, cities crumbling, scientists measuring the half-life of tritium and radio-active cobalt. The garment would be democratically medium-priced and the salesgirl would be just as pretty as the customer and, to the naked eye at least, just as well dressed, to show that the benefits of a free society extended from one end of the economic spectrum to the others. Eat, drink and acquire, because tomorrow the city may no longer be here or the price of rayon may go up.

He moved into the zone of Oriental rugs and Chinese objets d'art. The men who went in and out of the stores seemed dispirited and beaten, as though they were trying, without success, to hide from themselves the fact that no one bought Oriental rugs any more and that the Chinese had long ago given up making vases, ivory fans and plump glazed horses in favor of the more interesting business of destroying one another.

The men and women who hurried past him on the avenue looked sullen and cold, as though they thought the bitter weather was a personal attack against them, unjustly delivered by a malicious and powerful enemy. Today, Archer thought, regarding the city, everyone looks as though he would rather be somewhere else.

Washington Square was better because there were children there. They slept in carriages and they chased puppies on the dead grass and they played ball against the monument, unaware that the weather was bitter or that they would soon become adults who would feel the cold and be doomed to stand in shops and try to sell things that no one wanted any more. Washington Square was one of Archer's favorite walks, but on one side workmen were tearing down a handsome old building, and it stood in jagged ruins, as though it had been prematurely bombed. And on the other side, New York University had spilled over into the beautiful row of mansions, and when you walked past you saw fluorescent lighting and people typing at crowded desks in lovely, high-ceilinged rooms where ladies and gentlemen should have been balancing teacups and speaking in deliberate sentences. Grace, Archer thought, is being superseded by ruins and institutions. Private sweetness is giving way to public need, or at least to what the public thought it needed.

In five years' time, Archer thought, the only people who will have the heart to walk in Washington Square will be law students and accountants.

He decided to go home and try to write the speech he had to deliver that night. Maybe, he thought, putting it on paper would make it easier. As he walked toward his house he hoped that Kitty was out. It would be good to have the house all to himself with no questions to be answered, no disturbing domestic noises except the distant humming of Gloria in the kitchen.

But when he opened the door, Archer heard voices from his study. As he put away his hat and coat he listened. Nancy and Kitty. He was surprised. Nancy seldom came down during the day and Kitty hadn't said anything about expecting her. He toyed with the idea of stealing upstairs quietly and working in the bedroom, but the phone began to ring in the hall and as he picked it up, he saw Kitty coming out of the study to answer it. He waved to her and she stopped, waiting to see if the call was for her. "Hello," Archer said into the phone.

"I want to speak to Clement Archer." It was a man's voice, rough and harsh.

"Speaking."

"You God-damn Jew-loving Red sonofabitch," the man said evenly. "Why don't you leave the country before we carry you out?"

Archer hung up. He looked reflectively at the instrument, then smiled at Kitty.

"Who was that?" Kitty asked.

"Wrong number," Archer said. He put his arm around Kitty and tried to get her to walk with him toward the study. But Kitty didn't move.

"Was it another one of those calls?" Kitty asked.

"Which calls, darling?"

"There've been nearly a dozen of them this morning," Kitty said. She talked swiftly, but Archer could see she was making an effort to be calm. "Men and women. Cursing you and me, too. Threats."

I mustn't be angry, Archer thought. That's what they want.

"Yes," he said gently. "I'm afraid it was."

"Don't you think we ought to do something about it, Clement?" Archer realized Kitty was frightened. "Call the police?"

Archer grinned. "What would you suggest they do—arrest everyone who has a nickel in his possession? Don't worry, Kitty . . ." He propelled her gently toward the study. "Nobody's been killed yet by telephone. It's probably just a couple of cranks with nothing to do and some loose change in their pockets."

"It's scary," Kitty said. "Right in your own home. That's why I called Nancy and asked her to come down. She says they've been calling Vic, too."

"I must ring my broker," Archer said, determined not to take it seriously, "and tell him to buy a hundred shares of telephone stock for me this afternoon. Hi, Nancy," he said, as he and Kitty went into the study. He kissed Nancy. She was standing against the desk. She had on a trim black suit over a white lace blouse. She was wearing a nice perfume, too. Archer sniffed deeply. "My," he said, "you smell delicious."

They all sat down, Kitty on the couch beside him, holding his hand.

"How're things uptown this bright morning?" Archer asked.

"Confused," said Nancy. "The kids're staying home from school today and our nurse left and . . ."

"What's the matter?" Archer asked. "They sick?"

"No." Nancy shook her head. She was wearing a little hat with a veil that was modeled on a bullfighter's

hat and she looked as though she ought to be going to
an elegant restaurant for lunch. "Our calls started to
come in early. Five-thirty. Then every fifteen minutes
from then on. I told Vic to have the company disconnect the phone, but he says he likes to hear what his
public has to say. He just stands there and chuckles
and calls them the most horrible names back over the
phone."

"That's an idea," Archer said. "The technique of
counter-terror. Tell them they don't fool us, they're
Jew-lovers, too."

"People're insane," Nancy said. "Just because you
went to that funeral yesterday. And Vic didn't even
go."

"It wasn't just because of the funeral, baby," Archer
said quietly. "And people aren't insane. They're just
horrible."

"That awful magazine," Nancy said, sighing. "Did
you see the last issue?"

Archer shook his head. "I made a decision this
week. No reading matter that has been written later
than the eighteenth century."

"I saw it," Kitty said. "Those people ought to be
put in jail."

Archer grinned and patted her hand. Nice, simple
Kitty, who still thought she lived in a world in which
you could call the police.

"Somebody sent a copy to Miss Tully, our nurse,"
Nancy said, "and she came in and told me she was
going to quit. She wouldn't even stay overnight. She's
been with us five years and she wept when she said
good-bye to the boys, but she said she couldn't stay in
the house of a man who was an enemy of the Church.
She's very devout. The kids howled bloody murder and
she must have used five handkerchiefs mopping her own
tears, but she wouldn't even take two weeks' pay as a
bonus from Vic. She said it was dirty money. Happy
days in the nursery," Nancy said grimly. "After I leave

here I have an appointment at an agency to interview some more nurses. That aren't so politically sensitive, I hope. Anyway, we decided to keep the kids home from school today. I was afraid somebody might annoy them on the way. Vic says there's nothing to worry about and he was all for sending them along as though nothing was happening, but I feel better with them in the house. I must confess I don't take those calls as calmly as Vic does. Those people sound . . ." She hesitated. "Demented."

"I'm sure there's something that could be done," Kitty said firmly. "Even if you had to go to the Mayor. It can't be legal to call up a perfect stranger in his own house and call him the foulest words anyone could imagine. You have no idea, Clement . . ." She turned to Archer, her lips trembling, "Some of the things they've called me over the phone this morning when I told them I was Mrs. Archer."

"You stay away from the phone from now on, baby," Archer said. "I'll answer it or get Gloria." He grinned. "I'll tell Gloria she's free to say anything that comes into her head. They'll think twice before calling again."

"I think we all ought to go away someplace," Kitty said. "To the country. Away from phones. Away from these horrible people. Clement . . ." She appealed to him, holding his hand, "Can't we get into Vic's car tomorrow and go out to Connecticut and find a little hotel or even a house? It's out of season and I'm sure you could get one for almost nothing for a month or two."

"There's a little question of work, darling," Archer said lightly. He felt guilty and cowardly because the idea attracted him so much.

"You could come in on Thursdays," Kitty said. "Or even two or three days a week. And the rest of the time you could rest and forget about this. You look terribly tired, Clement, and you're sleeping so badly. I hear you moving around and groaning in your sleep all night long."

"Vic'll be able to spend a nice long spell in the country," Nancy said grimly. "They dropped him yesterday from Griffith Theatre." Griffith Theatre was the other program that Vic did regularly. "And he hasn't been offered a new job in three weeks."

"We'll see," Archer said. "Maybe it'll all blow over by tomorrow."

Gloria came into the room. "Mis' Archer," she said, "the laundryman is here in the kitchen. He says he ain't responsible for putting those holes in the curtains. He wants to talk to you."

Kitty stood up, moving slowly. "All right," she said. "I'll talk to him."

Nancy and Archer watched Kitty walk heavily and ungracefully after Gloria. Archer rubbed the top of his head thoughtfully.

Nancy lit a cigarette, pushing up her veil to smoke it. "Sorry you came to the Big City, Professor?" she asked. "Do you find yourself longing for the simple, uncomplicated academic life?"

Archer smiled wearily. "I understand," he said, "that many colleges are now equipped with telephones, too."

"Are you going to the meeting at the St. Regis tonight?" Nancy was flipping the pages of a magazine, not looking at Archer.

"I believe I am," Archer said slowly.

"You going to make a speech?"

Archer nodded. "By popular demand."

"What're you going to say?"

Archer shrugged. "Who knows? The usual platitudes, I suppose. The same thing that everybody else'll say. Freedom of opinion, no censorship by accusation or by pressure groups. The same boring guff. What can you say? I suppose the important thing isn't that you say anything particular but that you're there." He went over to the desk and filled a pipe. Nancy stood up, dropping the magazine. She pulled her skirt into place with deft, womanly little movements of her hands.

Archer regarded her with pleasure. She looked pretty this afternoon, not worn and hungry as she had looked on the night of Jane's play.

"That's quite a hat, Nancy," Archer said, smiling.

"Clement," Nancy said absently, ignoring the compliment, "do you think it'll do any good?"

"What?"

"The meeting."

Archer shrugged and lit his pipe. "Who knows? Who knows if anything will do any good? Maybe the only thing that would do any good would be if a hole opened up and Russia fell into it. Still, you've got to do something."

"Isn't it possible that it'll do a lot of harm?" Nancy asked quietly, staring at Archer. "The meeting, I mean. Won't the people who make speeches be attacked more bitterly than ever?"

Archer puffed on his pipe. "Probably," he said. "It sounds likely."

"Mightn't it be wiser," Nancy asked, "just to keep quiet? Lie low for awhile. Not give them any more targets to shoot at."

Archer looked sharply at Nancy. "I don't know," he said, wondering what Nancy was aiming at, whether she was speaking for herself or whether she and Vic had decided on this together. "I'm a new boy in this league. I'm just an amateur victim. I haven't got the fine points of martyrdom under control yet."

Nancy took a step toward him. "Don't be angry with me, Clement," she pleaded.

Archer smiled. "I haven't been angry with you one minute," he said, "since the day you slipped Vic's flask out from under the blanket in 1935. I wouldn't know how to be angry with you if I wanted to."

Nancy smiled, too, but it was nervous and hurried and polite. "They wouldn't be after you at all," she said, "if you hadn't tried to help Vic."

Now, Archer thought, I have to be very careful. "I

tried to help a lot of people, Nancy," he said softly, remembering Weller and Motherwell and Atlas and Pokorny. "With varying success. Some of the recipients of my charity," he said harshly, "are already six feet underground and others may be observed at this very moment hurrying with old wedding rings to the nearest pawnshops."

"But you went all out for Vic," Nancy said stubbornly, almost as if she were accusing him. "You risked your job for him. You were going to quit if they fired Vic, weren't you?"

"I don't know, Nancy, darling," Archer said wearily, leaning back against the desk. "It was so long ago, when I was a brave and ignorant young man."

"I know," Nancy said. "I know all about it."

"Maybe it wasn't for Vic," Archer said. "Maybe it was for what they call in literary saloons a principle. A medium-sized, old-fashioned principle."

Nancy came close to him. He could smell her perfume, fresh and not cloying, and see the small lines around her eyes. Her eyes were blue-gray, still very clear and almost childishly bright and wide open. "Clement," Nancy said softly, "I wanted to tell you how grateful I am."

"And all that," Archer said nervously, not wishing to be thanked.

"All right." Nancy smiled, recognizing Archer's self-consciousness. "I won't praise you. I won't tell you that you're a lovely friend and the perfect godfather and that if you only had hair you'd be too good to be true . . ."

"Nancy, darling . . ." Archer put the pipe into his mouth defensively. "The old man is in pain."

"But I have one thing to say," Nancy said, growing very grave again. "About tonight. You've done enough. I don't want you to be hurt. Not for Vic or for me or for anyone else. Think hard, Clement. Tonight may turn out to be very bad. Awful. It may take years to recover from. Or maybe you'll never be able to re-cover from it. Think of yourself. Please. If you think you have to go for your own reasons, OK. But not for Vic. Do you hear me, Clement? *Not for Vic.*"

Archer stared down at her for a moment, puzzled. Without taking his eyes from the youngish, delicately lined, intense face so close to his, he put his pipe down behind him. Then he took her softly in his arms and kissed her. She was rigid next to him, and her arms around him gripped him with convulsive force.

He kissed her cheek gently again, holding her light-ly. There was the sound of Kitty's slow, heavy foot-steps and Kitty came into the room.

Archer patted Nancy's shoulder, then dropped his arms. "You still smell delicious," he said, smiling.

The phone rang when they were all in the hall, say-ing good-bye. Archer picked it up, watching the two women at the open door.

"Archer?" A voice asked.

"Yes. Who is this?"

"None of your God-damn business," the voice said. "It won't be long now, brother, that's all I wanted to say . . ."

Archer made himself smile because the two women had stopped talking and were watching him.

"We're going to get you and every bastard like you," the voice said, not very loud, not very excited, sounding almost as if the man were slightly bored with what he was saying, as though he had said it many times before. "Watch out now, brother, because we . . ."

Archer hung up. "The man from the telephone com-pany," he said, going over to the door. "He wants to know if the reception is clear."

The women didn't say anything. He stood with his arm around Kitty at the open door, watching Nancy go down the steps, slender, wonderfully pretty and youthful-looking at this distance in her silly, charming hat. Cassandra, he thought, half-humorously, still puzzling over the veiled warning Nancy had given him. Cassandra in silk stockings and a funny hat, going off to hire a children's nurse after her obscure prophecy. Was Cassandra pretty, too, and what occupied her time between warnings?

The telephone was ringing, and he closed the door and went back into the hall with Kitty. He picked up the phone and by the tone of the voice which asked for Clement Archer he knew what it was. He put the phone down on the table and watched it placidly as louder and louder noises came from it.

"At a distance of four feet," he said mildly to Kitty, who was looking frightened again, "it's no worse than a bad cold."

He let the voice shout away, not hearing any of the words, just getting an impression of senseless truculence and exasperation from the instrument. Kitty passed him, almost running, as though even that undistinguishable small flood of mechanical sound was too much for her to bear. Archer watched Kitty disappear into the living room. The man on the phone must have been shouting at the top of his voice, because now and then Archer could just make out words like "Communist" and "bastard." I wonder, Archer thought, what the fellow who is monitoring this phone is going to make out of this day's conversation. If he's a well-brought-up young man with a distaste for profanity and blasphemy, he's going to have a bad hour or two.

The voice stopped and there was a click on the phone. Archer picked it up and listened for the dial tone. Then he called the operator and asked for the business office.

A crisp, pleasant young woman's voice spoke in the name of the telephone company, eager for service.

"I'd like to disconnect this phone temporarily," Archer said, after giving his name and number. "I'm going out of town."

"Yes, Mr. Archer," the voice said. "When would you like us to cut the service?"

"Immediately," Archer said. "As soon as I hang up."

"Would you like us to have the calls transferred to another number," the young lady asked, "so that you can get any messages?"

"No, thank you," Archer said. "I don't expect any messages."

"When would you like us to resume service?" the young lady asked.

Never, Archer thought. In the year 2000. On the first date that civilization sets in. "I'll call you," Archer said. "I'll let you know."

"Thank you, Mr. Archer. Have a pleasant trip."

"Thanks." Archer hung up. Did she say that, he wondered idly, out of the goodness of her own heart or is it something she's told to do by the company in the interests of better relations with the subscribers?

He went into the living room. Kitty was carrying a large wooden armchair across the floor to a spot near the window. It was heavy and she had to carry it very high to avoid knocking over a vase of flowers that was on a coffee table. She was panting and her face was strained.

"What're you doing, Kitty?" Archer went over and tried to take the chair from her.

"Oh, no," Kitty said. "Leave it alone. I want to do this myself."

Archer fell back a little. "What're you moving the chair for?" he asked again, feeling puzzled and helpless.

"I want to change this room around," Kitty said. She put the chair down near the window and stepped back several feet and regarded it critically. "I'm bored with the way this room looks." She picked the chair up again and carried it to a position in front of the other window. Archer watched silently while she made two more trips across the room for an end table and a lamp. She bent to get the lamp plug out of the wall socket and had to push herself up laboriously to stand erect again and he could hear her breath coming short and hard.

"You shouldn't tire yourself, darling," Archer said carefully. He didn't like the intense, distant expression in Kitty's face as she bustled about, her full skirt swinging, bumping clumsily into tables and the backs of chairs. Kitty didn't answer him. She didn't seem even to have heard him.

"I told the telephone company to disconnect the phone," Archer said, trying to gain her attention. "We won't be bothered by those hoodlums any more."

"That's fine," Kitty said, painfully sinking to her knees to put the plug into the new socket. "Now we're completely cut off from everything. Modern living."

Archer stared at her. When she sounds like that, he thought, there's no sense in talking to her. He started into the study, but at the door, he couldn't resist trying one more time. "Kitty, darling," he said plaintively, "I wish you'd leave the room alone. I think it looks great just as it is."

Kitty was carrying a screen now to put behind the armchair. "Don't you have some work to do?" she asked.

"Yes."

"Well, you take care of your department and let me take care of my department, please." Her tone was sharp, annoyed, unreasonable, and she kept fiddling with the screen, moving it a few inches one way, then another, never looking over at Archer. Archer shrugged and went into the study, closing the door behind him.

There was still a faint fragrance from Nancy's perfume in the study and Archer decided not to light a pipe for a moment, so that he could enjoy it. On the other side of the door, he could hear Kitty moving furniture around. The sounds were sudden and nervous, as though Kitty was jerking irritably at things that were too heavy for her.

Archer sat down at his desk and got out some sheets of paper. He decided against using the typewriter. This should be simple and personal, he thought. Somehow, using pencil and writing by hand seemed more personal.

"Ladies and gentlemen," he wrote. He stopped and closed his eyes, trying to imagine what the room in the St. Regis would be like that night, and who would be there. There would undoubtedly be some ladies and gentlemen, among the others. There would also be thieves, plagiarists, gossips, Communists, non-Communists, anti-Communists, Fascists, nymphomaniacs, drunkards, pederasts, and several persons who, everyone in the room would know, were certain to be committed for the rest of their lives to lunatic asylums within the next few years. All these would be sitting there, waiting to be convinced—of what? Many of them would gladly stand by and watch various other of the assembled artists put to death. The only thing that linked them was that they made their livings from the radio, television and the theatre.

Archer opened his eyes. He put a neat pencil line under the words Ladies and Gentlemen. For emphasis.

He began to write, slowly at first, then more fluently as the arguments developed in his mind.

"As I look around me," he wrote, already envisioning himself standing on a platform in a crowded room, "I am struck by one fact—how different everyone in the room here is from everybody else. This is a more or less typical American group, so there is bound to be a typically American difference of opinion and belief represented here. All shades of political thought are collected here and I am sure that at election time every conceivable party finds support from certain sections of this audience. There are Communists here and there are Fascists here, although I trust there are very few of either of these persuasions; and there are Democrats, Republicans, Socialists, prohibitionists and single-taxers. The divisions among us are easy to find. What we have to find here tonight is the tie that has collected us in this room and which unites us."

There was a muffled, sliding sound from the living room, and Archer frowned as he heard it, thinking of Kitty, restless and unhappy, pushing too-heavy furniture from place to place. He reread what he had written and decided it was too stilted. The best thing, he decided, would be to jot down the topics he wanted to cover, with a phrase here or there for further guidance, and speak extemporaneously from his notes when the time came.

"One link," he wrote. "All artists. Some craft as Melville. Duse. Stanislavski. Examples of repression other times. Dostoyevsky. D. H. Lawrence. Obscenity. Different issue. Vindictiveness of penalty. Victor Hugo. Published from exile. Worse now. Concept of limitless punishment. . . ."

He wrote slowly and neatly in his orderly handwriting, numbering topics, Roman numeral One, Roman numeral Two, sub-heading A, sub-sub-heading arabic one, dimly conscious as he was working of how many times in the past, when he was preparing his lectures in college, he had sat like this in a quiet room, writing, "Causes of the French Revolution, Roman numeral One, Literary. Sub-heading A, Rousseau. Influence of. Sub-heading B. Voltaire. Roman numeral Two. Political. Luxury of Court. Excessive Taxes. *Lettres de cachet . . ."*

He worked methodically, enjoying his trained academic ability for organization, remembering the quiet pleasure of distant afternoons. One thing is different, he thought wryly, as he glanced over the long yellow pages. At the end of those lectures I didn't have to tell the student to *do* anything. I didn't have to advise them to find a barricade or put their heads under the guillotine. The advantages of history, past, to history, present.

There was a crash from the living room, and the

tinkle of glass. Archer jumped up and ran over to the door and threw it open. Kitty was standing in the middle of the room, looking down at a lamp that lay broken into dozens of pieces on the floor.

The room looked torn apart. Chairs were piled together at one side, the couch was out from the wall at a crazy angle, end tables were scattered haphazardly around, the rug showed flattened, lighter patches where pieces of furniture had been standing for years. Kitty stood in the middle of the confusion, staring down at the pieces of broken glass, saying, "Damn, oh, damn." She was flushed an alarming red and her hair was disarranged, with tendrils of it plastered to her forehead, where she was perspiring.

"Here," Archer said, going over to her, "you sit down. I'll pick this up."

"Leave me alone," Kitty said. She got down heavily on one knee and began to pile the bits of jagged milky glass together. "I'm doing this."

"I'll help you," Archer said, bending and carefully picking up some of the larger portions of the glass.

"I don't need any help," Kitty said loudly. "I don't want your help. Go back to your work." She lifted her head and stared angrily at him, collecting the wrecked pieces of the glass together without looking at what she was doing.

"Now, Kitty," Archer said gently. "I know you're upset but there's no reason . . ."

"Oh!" Kitty cried out. She looked down at her hand. A long, thin seam appeared pink on the palm, then turned red, then the blood began to seep out of it and run down her wrist. She held her hand up stupidly like a child who has been hurt, but hasn't decided yet how badly.

"Here," Archer said quietly. He stood up and helped her to her feet. "Let's fix that. Sit down and hold your hand up so it won't bleed too much. I'll get some bandage."

Kitty sat down obediently on a wooden chair next to a table that was standing out in the middle of the room. Archer put her elbow on the table and she sat there, with her hand pointed up, the blood running in a thin stream down her arm, which was bare now that the loose sleeve of her dress had fallen back. The blood was coming slowly and spreading out into little new streams like the tributaries of a river on the map.

"Oh," Kitty said, "I'm so silly. I'm so damned silly."

Archer hurried upstairs to the bathroom and filled a basin with water and found the iodine and some bandage. When he got down to the living room again, Kitty was sitting as he had left her, resting her elbow on the table, looking curiously at the palm of her hand and the slowly lengthening red streaks down her arm. She didn't say anything as Archer gently washed the blood away and she didn't even wince when he put the iodine on the long, shallow cut. He bandaged the hand swiftly and made a neat bow to hold it in place.

"Now," he said, "will you sit still?"

"Look at this room," Kitty said. She almost smiled. "We look as though we've had two different sets of movers in here with two different sets of instructions. One to move us in, the other to move us out."

"I'll tell Gloria to put everything back where it was. You go up and lie down."

"I had to do something," Kitty said, turning her head away from him. She didn't move her hand. She kept it in the same position, like a child proud of her bandage. "I couldn't sit still in here today, expecting the phone to ring, then remembering that it was turned off and that nobody could reach us."

"Don't worry about it," Archer said. "In one day you'll probably get to love not having a phone." He leaned over and kissed her cheek lightly. Her skin was warm and damp.

"You put on such a lovely bandage," Kitty said

gravely. "And you were so fast and efficient. And you didn't yell at me at all."

"You were very brave," Archer said, smiling, "during the entire operation."

Suddenly Kitty shivered, as though she had a chill. "I don't want to be brave," she whispered. "I never want to be brave." She stood up and touched Archer's arm with her bandaged hand. "Clement," she said, in a very low voice, "you're not going to that meeting tonight, are you?"

Archer hesitated. "Let's not talk about it right now, darling."

"When should we talk about it?" Archer was surprised at the violence in Kitty's voice. "After we're on relief?"

"We won't be on relief," he said softly.

"Grow up," Kitty said harshly. "Come out of the nursery. For once in your life, look at things realistically. What do you think is going to happen to you after you stand up in public tonight and defend Communists? Do you think the National Broadcasting Company will pin a medal on you and sign you to a ninety-nine-year contract?"

Kitty was holding tightly onto his arms now. He pulled away gently and she released him. He turned and walked back into his study. He couldn't stand the disordered living room any more, with the piled chairs and the pale spots showing on the carpet and the broken lamp all over the floor. He hoped Kitty wouldn't follow him. For her sake, he didn't want to hear what she was thinking. All during their married life she had taken chances with him unhesitatingly and he had always congratulated himself on having a wife with that kind of trust and blind courage. He despised timid women who drained the courage out of their husbands, and he'd told it to her again and again. In the study, he went over to the desk and picked up the pages on which he had been writing his speech. His hands shook a little as he tried to read them, and he didn't turn around when he heard Kitty follow him into the room.

"Oh, no, you don't," Kitty said, close behind him. "You can't hide this time." She came around to the other side of the desk and faced him. "What's that you're so interested in—the speech you're going to make? Do you want to make sure that you're making it strong enough, so that if there's the slightest chance for us now, you can ruin it?"

"Kitty," Archer said, with a firmness he didn't feel, "I'm afraid I'll have to ask you to leave me alone today. I . . ."

With a sudden, fierce movement, Kitty leaned over and ripped the pages out of his hand.

"I want to read this," she said.

"Give it back to me, Kitty!"

"I'm interested in my husband's literary production," Kitty said, backing off a little, as though she were afraid Archer would wrestle with her for the sheets of paper. "That's reasonable enough, isn't it? You were always after me to read those miserable plays of yours and tell you what I thought of them. Why do you want to change now?"

Archer was silent for a moment as they stared at each other. Then he shrugged. "All right," he said wearily. "Read it if you want to. I don't care." He went over and sat down heavily in the easy chair, watching Kitty.

Suspiciously, as though she still didn't quite trust him not to leap up and reclaim the papers, Kitty began to read. "Oh, God," she muttered, going through the first page rapidly and turning to the next one. "Oh, good God, you're insane."

She didn't go through all the papers. She glanced quickly at Archer, to make sure he was not prepared to move, then ripped the papers in half, then in half again, then into smaller and smaller pieces. Archer started out of his chair, than sank back, waiting for her to finish.

She was panting and the bandage on her hand was giving her trouble and she looked clumsy tearing at the obstinate paper. Finally, she dropped the ragged shreds on the floor. Then she stared at Archer, fearful and defiant. "That's what I think of it," she said loudly. "That's my candid opinion."

"All right," Archer said patiently. "Now we don't have to discuss it any further."

"You hate me," Kitty said.

"I don't hate you at all."

"Yes, you do," she said. "You want to destroy me."

"Oh, Kitty," Archer said, "don't be a fool."

"You want to destroy me," Kitty chanted in a singsong, "and you want to destroy our home. And I won't let you."

"That's nonsense."

"They call me up and they call me a bitch and a whore," Kitty said, "and words I couldn't even repeat to you now, because of what you've been doing. What do you think they'll call me if you get up and talk like that to all those Communists?"

"They're not all Communists," Archer said wearily. "They're everybody."

"Do you believe that? Are you simple enough to believe that? Why're you so anxious to ruin yourself?" Kitty demanded. "What's the secret? What've they got on you?"

"There's a certain principle at stake," Archer began, unpleasantly aware that he was sounding like a professor, "and it's just my bad luck that I'm involved in it . . ."

"Isn't there a principle about protecting your wife and your children, too?" Kitty asked shrilly. "Or is that too unimportant for noble artists like you? Artists," she said sardonically. "God, you make me laugh with your artists! Actors who couldn't get a job with the third road show of *Tobacco Road*. Writers who write advertisements for laxatives as long as they're paid seventy-five dollars a week for it! Melville! Duse! Don't you know how funny you sound? And that's what you're willing to throw away your whole life for! Come back to earth! Don't you know we'll be out in the street in six months if you make that speech? What'll you pay the rent with—your principles? What'll you feed the baby with—the approval of the Communist Internationale? What's the matter—are you bored with living like a decent human being, now that you've finally done it for a few years? Or do you think that you're so handsome and brilliant and desirable that people will be dying to have you somewhere else after the radio industry is through with you?"

"If you knew how ugly you looked," Archer said, and regretting it as he said it and knowing that it was true, "when you talk like that, you'd stop right now and leave me alone."

"I don't care how I look," Kitty wailed. She moved forward to the desk and leaned on it, her face distorted. "I don't care what you think of me. I don't care if you never talk to me again as long as I live. I'm not going to be poor again, I'm not going to start all over again at my age, wondering where I can find the money to have the baby's tonsils out and how I can stall the butcher another month. I've had those pleasures! I'm too old for them now! And I don't care what you think. I don't care what idiotic, woolly principles you've cooked up in that crazy head of yours. I have one principle—Me. Me and Jane and the child. And I'm not going to have the child in the public ward at Bellevue, either. I want a private room and a decent doctor and the bills all paid on the fifth of the month and a feeling that there's some sense to going through the agony again, that there's some chance for me and the baby when it's over . . ."

She stopped, breathing heavily, momentarily exhausted.

Why did she have to do that? Archer thought, exhausted himself. Why did she have to talk like that?

"Are you through now?" he asked.

"No, I'm not." Kitty came around the desk and stood over him. "I know why you're doing this. You don't fool me for a minute."

"Why?" Archer was surprised to realize that he was honestly curious.

"Your good friends Victor and Nancy Herres," Kitty said loudly.

"What?" Archer looked up at her puzzledly.

"What? What?" Kitty mimicked him sardonically. "The man doesn't know what his wife is talking about."

"Kitty," Archer said warningly, "you'd better stop now. You've said enough." He wanted to tell her that they had to live with each other for the rest of their lives and that she had to leave some foundations left, some remnants of affection and honor.

But Kitty was rushing on. "That's the whole reason. Don't think I don't see it. Vic got himself in trouble and naturally you had to get on your white horse and charge to his rescue."

"Supposing that were true," Archer said, trying to be reasonable, "supposing that was the real reason—don't you think I *should* go to his rescue?"

"No."

"Kitty . . ."

"He got into the trouble without your help. Let him get out the same way. Times're tough," Kitty said harshly. "Every man for himself."

"I hate that," Archer said coldly. "I hate you for saying it."

"Of course you do," Kitty said. "I knew you would. Because you're in love with Vic Herres and you're in love with Nancy Herres and you're in love with Johnny Herres and with Clement Herres and the ground Vic Herres walks on and the chair he sits in and every random thought that goes through Vic Herres' head."

"This is hopeless," Archer said. He started to get up. Kitty leaned forward and pushed him sharply and he fell back into the chair, with her standing over him.

He realized how silly this would look to anyone else, the small, frail, pregnant woman with the bandaged hand knocking a huge, wide-shouldered man back into a chair and looming over him threateningly. He almost laughed.

"No, you don't," Kitty said wildly. "I want you to hear this. I've been thinking this a long time and you might as well hear it now. It's sick. It's psychopathic. A middle-aged man tagging after another man like a little puppy, calling him up all the time like a kid calling up his girl, running to him with your troubles, bringing gifts to his children, mooning over his wife . . ."

"Kitty!" Archer said sharply.

"I see you, I see you," Kitty shouted. "Talking to her for hours in corners at parties, sharing God knows what secrets, kissing her every chance you get. You never kiss anybody else, you're so fastidious. You haven't kissed me on the mouth for years . . ."

That's true, Archer thought dully, that much is true. Is it possible?

"When you're home alone with me," Kitty poured on, "you never say a word, you sit and read and mumble when I ask you a question. And when we go out with other people you're bored and you expect them to consider themselves real lucky if you condescend to speak three sentences an evening to them. But when you're with Vic or Nancy, you're a torrent of wit, the smile never comes off your face, you never want to go home, you pull out all your tricks as though you were afraid if you didn't keep charming them, they'd lock you out in the cold. And when their kid has measles you never give it a thought, you go plunging into the room, never thinking what would happen if you caught it or if you passed it on to me with the child inside me. No, you have to show the Herreses how brave and daring you are, how delightful, how faithful."

Oh, that, Archer thought. That's why she was so angry that day; she was saving up all this.

"And you're not satisfied just to adore," Kitty swept

on frantically, all barriers far behind her, "you have to *be* like your hero. You ape him, the way he talks, the way he walks, the way he wears his hat. I don't have my own husband any more, I have a carbon copy of another man, and I'm disgusted with it. And now," she said, "here's your final great chance. The final identification. You can suffer for his sins. How could I expect you to pass up an opportunity like that?"

"That's enough," Archer said thickly. "I can't stand any more." He got up. This time, Kitty stepped back without interfering.

"I'm going to tell you something," she said, suddenly calm and very cold. "I hate Vic Herres. And I hate that sly, secret little wife of his. He's cold and conceited and he doesn't care if you or anybody else lives or dies. You amuse him, because you pay him homage. He enjoys you because he can maneuver you. It's a game for him. He said, 'Come to New York,' and you gave up a perfectly good job and a nice house and you came to New York. He said, 'Write for the radio,' so you wrote for the radio. He said, 'Now is the time for all brave men to go to war,' because he was young and they were going to take him anyway, so you tried to go to war. He said, 'Now be a director,' because that would make it easier for him, it meant he had a sure, easy job, with no trouble and no criticism as long as you worked, so you because a director. Now he's in trouble and they're attacking him, so he says to you, 'Defend me, there's a principle at stake.' He and his wife have locked me away from you for ten years. I haven't been a wife. I've been a witness to a sick mass love affair."

"Shut up!" Archer whispered.

"I'm going to tell you something," Kitty said. "When Vic Herres went off to war, I prayed he would be killed." She said it calmly, standing in the middle of the room, crossing her arms in front of her, triumphant, desolate, lonely, discharged.

Archer put his hand in front of his eyes. He couldn't

bear looking at Kitty. How did it happen, he thought confusedly, at what point did it begin to happen, how could that delightful, brave, loving girl turn into this? How do we live in the same house now?

Blindly, he left the room. He picked up his hat and coat and plunged out into the street, leaving Kitty standing wearily near the desk, her face collapsed and passionless, picking absently at her bandaged hand, as though the blood were beginning to run again under the layers of gauze.

23

It was after eleven when he got to the St. Regis and he went up in the elevator with two ruddy country types in evening clothes who sounded as if they had been graduated from Princeton in 1911, and who would never be accused of anything.

The small banquet room was quite full, but the meeting hadn't begun yet. People were standing together in little groups and the room was full of the nervous, intense bursts of conversation, punctuated with high, musical woman's laughter that you always heard when you got actors and actresses together. Most of them were standing up, or kneeling with one knee on the little gilt chairs. People in the theatre or its associated professions, Archer remembered, regarding the room, always sit down reluctantly, as though they feared to lose the precious mobility on which success or failure for life might at any one moment depend.

Many of the women wore glasses. The frames were all colors, very thick, bright red and blue and gold-filigreed in the season's style. There was a great variety of shapes, too, curious bows and flattened triangles and tilting harlequin designs. Somehow, Archer thought, displeased with the thick blue and red shadows the glasses threw on the pretty, cosmetic faces, it makes them look as though they are all suffering from an obscure nervous epidemic. Near-sightedness in 1950 has become over-fashionable. There must soon be a swing of the style pendulum toward normal sight.

"Hi, soldier," a voice said behind him. "I was waiting for you."

Archer turned and saw Burke coming toward him. He decided to tell Burke, very soon, to stop calling him soldier. Also, he remembered, to tell Barbante to stop calling him amigo. Except that Barbante would shortly be 3000 miles away. Well, he'd write him.

"The speakers're sitting on the platform." Burke took his elbow and began guiding him down the side of the room. "We're just about ready to begin. We've got a good house tonight." Burke sounded like a complacent company manager with a hit. "You going to dazzle the folks with your oratory?"

"I'm all prepared," Archer said, unpleasantly conscious of the over-firm grasp on his elbow, "to recite the 'Communist Manifesto' from memory and selected excerpts from the writings of Leon Trotsky."

Burke laughed appreciatively. He had had his suit pressed, but it was still too small for him, and his face had the stiff, impatient expression of a man whose belt is too tight around his waist. He had just shaved, too closely, and there were little flecks of blood on his collar from the spots where he had nicked himself. There was a thick layer of talcum powder over his purplish beard and he looked like a man who expected to have his picture taken.

Archer stepped up to the low dais. Lewis, a director who kept introducing motions in praise of the Soviet Union at Guild meetings, was seated there, mumbling to himself as he thumbed through some notes on white cards. He looked up when Archer passed him. "Hello," he said. His tone was unfriendly and he bent over his cards again immediately. A little thin man by the name of Kramer was seated just behind the lectern. He was an agent who called everybody honey and who wore checked tweed jackets that made him look like a midget pretending to be an Irish horse owner. The jackets were so warm that there was a constant thin film of sweat on Kramer's forehead when he was indoors. He was always smiling because in this business you never knew who was going to be famous next week. Along with the soft, horse-owner jackets he wore thick, gold, knobby cuff links. He had high blood pressure and he had eaten rice for a year. Just now he was putting two magnesia tablets in his mouth, because he had belched four times in the last ten minutes.

Archer glanced around him uneasily.

"Woodie," he asked, "is this all you have?"

Burke looked nervous. "We're going to throw the meeting open to discussion from the floor," he said. "We expect a lot of help from the floor when things warm up a little."

"Where's O'Neill?" Archer asked. "I thought you said you'd asked O'Neill."

"O'Neill," Burke said bitterly, "has retreated to previously prepared positions. That eighteen thousand dollars a year began to look awfully sweet to O'Neill as H Hour approached."

"I would be most grateful," Archer said, "if you'd be good enough to translate."

Burke blinked angrily. "You know damn well what I mean. O'Neill fiddled for a while, then turned me down. He suddenly found out he was an agency man."

Archer was sorry for O'Neill, and disappointed.

"I can't blame him," he said.

"I can," said Burke. He looked around the room. People were still standing in shrill little clusters and more people were coming in through the door. "I'll give them another minute," he said, "before blowing the whistle."

Archer sat down, leaving three empty chairs between

Lewis and himself. He put on his glasses and stared out at the audience. He spotted Nancy near the door, off by herself, unprofessionally seated. At that distance she looked pale and haggard, but it may have been the lighting. Archer couldn't find Vic. In the first row, Frances Motherwell was sitting reading a newspaper, not paying any attention to what was going on around her. In the next row two young radio writers sat down and stared longingly at her legs. Alice Weller was seated halfway back smiling tremulously up at him. He smiled falsely at her, noting that Atlas had not come and that Roberts, the columist who had attacked him and whom he recognized from his photographs, was a grinning, soft-looking, plump little man with thick glasses.

Slowly, Archer let his eyes sweep over the room. There were many people whom he could identify. They had been on his programs or they had come up to O'Neill's office about one thing or another when he was there or he had met them over a space of ten years in bars or at parties. There were many Communists there. I know I shouldn't say that, or even think it, Archer thought. They've never told me and I really couldn't swear that I know for sure. And until they admit it or it's proven in a court of law, it's dangerous and unfair to label them. And, officially, it was entirely possible that many of them really didn't belong. But he'd listened to them argue, the long, pointless, boring, bitter, half-drunken arguments of the last five years, replete with the stock phrases—"imperialist aggression," "Wall Street money-lenders," "the people's democracy of Czechoslovakia," "Tito, the betrayer of the working class . . ." They might just as well wear buttons and wave the red flag, no matter what they belonged to. And some of them were very pleasant men, soft-spoken, witty, talented, friendly, with bright children and charming wives. And he'd gone to ball games with them and played tennis with them, had exchanged Christmas cards with them, and had dinner at their apartments, and had spent agreeable evenings with them when not one word had been spoken about politics for hours at a time. And, he recognized, there were puzzled people there, people who argued one way one day and another the next, because they had read a different magazine the day before, and there were people who had changed, in 1945 or 1946, or 1947, people who suddenly discovered they couldn't stomach what had happened to Benes or what the secretary of the Communist Party had said at his trial. And there were the girls. There were the virtuous girls who had married idealistic young men who had drifted into Communism because they were so appalled by the behavior of the anti-Communists. And then the girls, married, like good wives who loyally interest themselves in their husband's hobbies, had made out the invitation lists and prepared the canapés for the parties in which money was raised for the defense of indicted union leaders and at which petitions were drawn up criticizing decisions of the Supreme Court. And then there were the loose girls, on the hunt for men, who had found an exhilaratingly free and busy social life and an abundance of invitations to bed at the endless, happily confused functions that the Party and its sympathizers were always giving. And there were the lonely spinsters, of that special type which is to be found in the theatre, almost pretty, almost desirable, almost talented, but domed to celibacy by the severity of the competition in this, their chosen field, who gladly gave themselves to good works instead of a man. And good works in this era, Archer thought sadly, are now shown to skirt the edge of treachery. But now, faced with this accusation and righteously conscious of their own virtue, how could these deprived, busy women be expected to admit that?

What do you do with the women who signed petitions and raised money for refugees who later turned out to be Russian spies, the women who had aimlessly advanced the Revolution because they were afraid of having dinner alone that night?

"Ladies and gentlemen," Burke was saying, standing at the lectern and banging on it with a gavel, "ladies and gentlemen. . . ."

Reluctantly, people began to sit down, their conversation dying slowly, with little new waves of last-minute noise, as though everyone there was certain that what they would hear from the platform would be less interesting and amusing than what he himself was saying to his neighbor.

"Ladies and gentlemen," Burke said, when the hum had almost subsided, "I want to thank you for coming tonight. And I want to thank you for this magnificent turnout in defense of a free press, a free theatre, a free radio. . . ."

The room was three-quarters full. Perhaps two hundred people, Archer figured roughly. How many people were there who made their living out of the theatre and the radio? Five thousand? Ten thousand? And in the room how many were FBI agents, investigators, reporters? Did 200 out of 10,000 really seem magnificent to Burke for this particular cause?

Burke's tone, as usual, was pugnacious and threatening, in his well-known commentator manner. If he were to recite the "Ode to a Nightingale," Archer thought idly, he would make it sound like the summation of the district attorney in a murder case.

"I have been chosen to be chairman of this meeting," Burke was saying, "because I have the dubious distinction of being the first victim of the latter-day Thuggees of Madison Avenue. I've been out of work for a year," Burke said accusingly, making everybody feel vaguely guilty, "and I've had time to reflect on the issues and the strategy. They used me as a test case and when they saw it worked so easily they had a little celebration and raised the black flag and moved in on the main body of the fleet."

Now, Archer thought wearily, we have moved out of the trenches and engaged in a naval action.

"The main body of the fleet," Burke said harshly, "is you. Everyone of you sitting here. And everyone who writes or acts for a living who is too lazy or too pleasure-loving or too gutless to show up here tonight and fight for himself." He peered furiously over the lectern, making his audience move uncomfortably in their chairs, as though somehow they were responsible for the sloth and luxury and cowardice of the absent artists. "I've been warning you people for a year now," Burke went on, "every chance I've had. . . ."

That's no lie, Archer thought, remembering Burke's tireless alcoholic tirades. Cato, over a thousand double Scotches, saying that Carthage must be destroyed.

"And none of you listened," Burke said scornfully. "You were doing OK. You thought, The hell with Burke. What's one commentator more or less? So you let them move their big guns up without firing a shot at them, and now they're spraying the rear positions with HE and stink bombs and you're all getting it now and you finally're yelling for support. Well, now it may be too late," Burke said with glum satisfaction, "but maybe we can put up enough of a show to force them to negotiate for terms. Right now, they're calling for unconditional surrender. They've got us on the run and they're pouring it onto us on land, sea and air, and they're advancing at will because so far they haven't even been annoyed by snipers anywhere they've gone. They've got the zones of occupation all marked out, and the gauleiters've all been picked and are ready to go to work."

Burke was enjoying himself, Archer realized, as he painted this dire picture. He had suffered alone so long that he was greeting the new legion of recruits to misery with shouts of hoarse and mournful delight."

"Before I go any further," Burke said, glaring out at the brightly lit room, "I want to say something personal." He paused for effect, rocking a little, both hands gripping the lectern dramatically. "I am not a Communist," he said slowly, "and I never have been a Communist and I never expect to be a Communist."

Lord, Archer thought wearily, the formula has reached the status of a set art form now, like a sonnet, from long use and repetition.

There was silence in the room. Archer looked over at Lewis, on the other side of Burke. Lewis had his hand up over his face and was making a disgusted grimace.

"What's more," Burke said, "I am unalterably opposed to the Communists."

Somebody applauded in the back of the room. The single, persistent clapping sounded theatrical and embarrassing. Then, from different sections of the room, there came a curious little noise. Archer frowned, trying to place it. Then he recognized what it was. People were hissing softly.

"OK, OK," Burke said. "I knew this was going to make me unpopular. But that's the way I feel and you might as well know it. I've been registering as a Democrat since 1936, and that's what I am, and I see no reason for pretending to hide it. And if all the Communists in this country felt the same way about what they believed in and came right out and said it publicly, we'd be a damn sight better off right now."

What a strange man, Archer thought, half-admiringly, he enjoys the process of getting people to dislike him.

"But there's another side to me," Burke said, reveling in this opportunity for self-expression after the long silence that had been imposed upon him since he lost his program. "I hate the other side even worse than the Communists. I hate the Nazis and the Fascists and the concentration-camp boys and the crematorium-builders, and I suspect that if we scratched around a little we'd find out that those're exactly the people who have been making all this fuss in the radio business and getting people kicked out of their jobs in the name of one hundred percent Americanism. So what I propose is that we do a little investigating on our own hook. Let's raise some money and get our Guilds to chip in and hire a couple of detectives ourselves. Instead of screaming about how pure we are, let's get in and slug it out with the bastards on their own terms. Let's see some of the skeletons in *their* closet, for a change. We're in a fight and we're getting our eyes gouged out. Let's stop calling for the referee and do a little eye-gouging ourselves."

Archer sighed. Woodie, he thought, I have left you long ago. Burke was a victim of his vocabulary. Everything was an ambush, a landing, a prizefight, and he never could appeal to a man who thought in less primitive terms.

"I'll tell you what we'll find," Burke was shouting. "And I'll bet my last dollar on it. Let's look and see where the money comes from and we'll find it's been handed in by ex-Christian Fronters, by patriots who were chummy with Goering in 1940, by money-boys who had a nice deal on with Mussolini when that looked like the winning side. If they come out with the news that we sent our old fur coats to the Russians in 1941 let's tell the world that they had dinner with the German consul the same year."

Burke's law, Archer thought. Everybody is as evil as everybody else. All parties are totally guilty. Pragmatic morality for the last half of the century. Archer began to feel sorry that he had come this evening.

"Attack," Burke said belligerently, echoing dozens of press conferences with divsional commanders. "Attack them where they live. Stop defending yourselves, because that way you always give them choice of weapons and choice of ground, and you'll be licked every time. Seize the initiative," he growled, once more the man who had jumped from burning planes and entered cities with the first patrols. "Club them so hard and so often they'll be too busy to club you. Thank you."

Burke sat down, full of loathing and malice toward all. There was a half-hearted attempt at applause, which died down almost immediately. Two more speeches like that, Archer thought, and you won't be able to get a majority of this meeting to agree that this is Friday night.

Burke stood up, remembering that he was the master of ceremonies.

"Now," he said mildly, "in case there's anybody here who still doesn't believe what's happening in the radio industry, anybody who thinks that it's just a couple of cranks and crackpots who couldn't get jobs anyway who are cooking this up, we're going to hear from a man who's on the inside and who's seen it happening and who's brave enough to tell about it. You all know Joe Kramer. He's sold some of the biggest shows on the air and he's been peddling actors and writers since Maude Adams hung up her cleats, and he's in and out of everybody's office ten times a day and he can tell you from the other side of the fence just what we're all facing today. Joe Kramer."

There was a surprisingly strong burst of applause, because the audience wanted to applaud someone and it was impossible to applaud Burke. Kramer got up, his forehead moist, his jacket rippling richly. He looked flustered because this was the first time in his life that anybody had ever applauded him.

"Boys and girls," Kramer said, his voice high and shrill and professionally friendly, "I'm very happy to be here tonight."

Why? Archer thought. Why should anyone be happy to be here tonight? Kramer, whose profession it was to please everyone at all times, would undoubtedly say he was happy to be here tonight at an execution.

"I'm not going to say that I approve of everything I've heard here on this platform," Kramer said cautiously, keeping his lines open in all directions, "although I have the deepest admiration for Woodie Burke, whose work we all know and respect and who was one of the most popular commentators on the air until recently. I don't approve, as I said, and I don't disapprove. That's not my line. What I know about politics you could put in a chorus girl's g-string and it wouldn't raise a lump. As far as I know, Warren G. Harding was the greatest President we ever had and Russia is the place we get borscht from and plays that haven't made a nickel for anyone since 1910. All I'm interested in, boys and girls, is stealing actors from other agents and trying to keep other agents from stealing actors from me." He grinned, to show that this was a joke, and he was rewarded by a laugh from his audience. "Also," he said, "I'm interested in getting a couple of more bucks a week for my clients and getting my ten percent and keeping everybody happy. But Woodie here is a client of mine. . . ." Kramer turned toward Burke and made a small bow of gratitude and deference, "and he asked me to come and talk to you boys and girls and here I am."

Kramer took out an enormous handkerchief from his breast pocket and wiped his brow delicately. "First of all," he said, "I want to tell you boys and girls something you ought to know. There *is* a black list. . . ."

There was a burst of ironic laughter from the audience and Kramer looked flustered for a moment and confused, as though he hadn't realized that he had told a joke. Then he grinned, a little uneasily. "What I mean," he said, "is that you hear a lot of denials all over the industry. You can't pin down any agency head or network official and get him to come right out and admit it. In Woodie's case, for example . . ." Again his voice slurred affectionately as it passed over his client's name, "Woodie's rating was 10 point 5, when option time came up, and you all know what that means. Woodie was ahead of every other commentator in the country, and to tell you the truth, I was contemplating going in and asking for more money from the agency.

But then the option was dropped. Just like that. Just a note from the agency, which will be nameless, because there is no sense in dragging in the names of people who have been good friends for a long time. I couldn't believe my eyes," Kramer said dramatically. "Then, when I started to try to find out what was happening, I got the brush. Just the brush. First the program director was in conference, then the vice-president was leaving for California, then finally, two weeks later, when I insisted on getting in, they told me go see the network man. Then, at the network, they gave me the shuffle. Nobody would take responsibility and I spent six weeks going from office to office and finally they admitted they wouldn't sell the time for Woodie, they didn't think he was important enough for that time. A man with a Hooper of 10 point 5!" Kramer said wonderingly. "Not important enough for a fifteen-minute spot at six o'clock weekdays! Then, at last I got it from somebody at the agency whose name I am not at liberty to divulge. He told me they'd been receiving protests, twenty or thirty calls a day. They checked with the phone company once and they found out that all the calls on one particular day came from the same phone booth in Long Island City. And all the calls said the same thing. They said Woodie, who you have just heard say he is opposed to the Communists and who has a personal letter of commendation for patriotic service from the War Department, they said that Woodie was a Red and that unless he was put off the air, they would boycott the sponsor's product. And the network was getting the same calls, too. The man at the agency who told me all this also told me that if I ever repeated this he would say I was lying and that he had never said anything of the kind. And since that time, boys and girls, I have met resistance on a lot of people that I used to be able to sell for the biggest programs in the country just by lifting the telephone and making a two-minute call. I never get the real reason. Just the same runaround. Just that the agency is looking for another type of show or another type of character. But I know and you know what the answer is, when big personalities who have been at the top for ten years, drawing top money, suddenly don't fit specifications any more. And there doesn't seem to be just one set list. Some agencies're a little more lenient than others. They'll hire people that can't get jobs with the firm down the hall. But there's a certain group of people, and I won't mince words, who might just as well move to Nebraska and start raising corn, because the only way they can get into any radio or television program is by writing in for tickets."

The room was very quiet. Kramer mopped his forehead and went on earnestly. "Boys and girls," he said, "I'm going to tell you frankly right here in this public meeting just what I tell to my clients in the privacy of my own office. Something practical. What I tell them is simple, 'Son,' I tell them, 'you go through your books and you find out what organizations you ever belonged to, all the way back to the Pontiac Athletic and Social Club when you were ten years old, and you sit down and write a letter and keep a copy and have it registered and send in your resignation. And if the organization folded up twenty years ago, that makes no difference. Write that letter. And if anybody asks you to join any new organizations, run like a thief. And that goes for the YMCA or Young Republicans for Taft or anything that has the word Freedom in the title and I don't care who's the president or on the board of directors, Eisenhower or Winston Churchill or anybody. A lot of people aren't working today because they sent twenty bucks somewhere because Mrs. Eleanor Roosevelt, the great American, wrote them a letter ten years ago and asked them for a contribution. It doesn't make any difference to that feller in Long Island City with a pocketful of nickels whether a five-star general or an ambassador to England sat next to you on the platform that night. He's out to get your job and he knows how to do it and he's doing it. Face the facts. You're an artist. Leave politics to the politicians or you'll fry. And if they put a piece of paper in front of your nose and you have to swear you're not a Communist and you hate the Communists worse than polio, you sign it, and sign it ten times a day, if that's what they want.'"

Kramer was sweating profusely now and his face was an alarming high-blood-pressure scarlet. "That's what I tell my clients," he said, "in the privacy of my office because I want to keep them alive and I want to keep myself alive. And I'm going to tell you something else. If they don't agree to do what I say, no matter how big they are, and how much I like them personally, I shake their hands and I say, 'Get yourself another boy from now on, son. I don't handle you any more.'" He nodded soberly at the gathering. "Boys and girls," he said earnestly, pleading for purity and ten percent, "I know the public pulse and I love you all, even the ones who make fun of me and call me a bloodsucker and a parasite. I love everyone who gets up on a stage or in front of a mike and reads a line or sings a song and makes people laugh or cry. I know it sounds corny, but it's the truth, and I don't want to see you murdered. So remember what I said. Resign, disaffiliate, quit. Entertain. Let the Supreme Court worry about the Bill of Rights. Thank you." Kramer bowed stiffly and walked briskly, in short, nervous steps, on his shoes with the built-up heels, over to his chair, and sat down.

After a while, there was a slow, dispirited scattering of applause. Most of the audience merely sat pensively, staring down at their hands.

Even if you agreed with him, Archer thought, Kramer had hardly voiced a doctrine that could be greeted with wild enthusiasm. Resign, Disaffiliate, Quit, Entertain. Archer remembered photographs taken outside Tripoli during the war. Pictures of shell-torn buildings of Italian colonists on whose walls Mussolini had painted another slogan. *Credere, Ubbidire, Combattere*. Believe, Obey, Fight. The Italian had said nothing about entertaining. He had missed out on an interesting modern imperative, probably because he was new at the game and hadn't had time to work his philosophy out fully.

Burke was walking thoughtfully up to the lectern as the applause died down.

"Clem . . ." Kramer leaned across an empty chair toward Archer, the color in his face slowly receding. "Clem," he asked anxiously, "how did you like it?"

Archer thought for a moment. "Joe," he said gently, "I feel like crying."

"Didn't you like it?" Kramer asked, hurt.

"I didn't say I didn't like it. I just said I feel like crying."

"Thank you, Joe Kramer," his client was saying over the lectern, "for being good enough to come here and give us your views."

The audience sat sullenly, not thankful for Joe Kramer's tweedy views. They moved uneasily, thinking, no doubt, of all of the organizations they had ever belonged to and the difficulty of resigning from them.

"Now," Burke said, "we are going to hear from a man who has spent a good many years directing radio shows and who is most active in the Radio Directors' Guild, on whose board of directors he has served for some time. Mr. Marvin Lewis."

Lewis stood up portentously, ignoring the applause. He had a surly, handsome, aggrieved face, and was known to use a heavy, sarcastic tongue on actors who displeased him. He was bulky and healthy and careless about his clothes, as befitted an artist. He walked slowly over to the lectern, staring pugnaciously down at the notes in his hand. He put the cards down on the lectern and took a heavy pair of glasses out of his pocket and held them in his hand like a weapon, while the room settled uneasily into silence. The door opened at the back and a woman came in hesitantly. Silently accusing her for her tardiness, Lewis waited until she had seated herself in the last row. Archer blinked his eyes as he realized that it was Kitty, slow-moving and clumsy, looking very large in front in the coat. Now, he wondered, why did she have to come here tonight?

"I'm going to warn you people," Lewis said, without preliminary, his voice loud and threatening, "that I am not going to be polite. The time is past for politeness." He jammed his glasses on his head, as though he were pulling down the visor of a helmet before battle. "I'm not interested in good manners and if anybody here is touchy, I advise him to leave now."

He glared around the room, waiting for the touchy members of the audience to file out. Everyone sat very still.

"We're here to accomplish something tonight," Lewis said loudly, "and the only way we'll do it is by coming out with the truth. The truth is, I don't like what I've heard on this platform tonight and I don't like the people who are sitting up here with me."

The room was absolutely still and Archer could feel the embarrassment coming up from the audience toward the platform. An ingenious opening, he thought professionally, calculated to hold the audience and create suspense.

"We are all in this together," Lewis said, whipping off his glasses and shaking them threateningly, "and our only chance is if we all pull together and what I've heard up here is divisive and inflammatory propaganda and weak-kneed invitations to surrender completely to the enemy. If the other side had selected the speakers themselves, they couldn't have picked more useful specimens." He slammed on his glasses again, glaring disdainfully out across the room. "First you've heard a gentleman declare that he was not a Communist and that he opposed the Communists. And this from a

man who by his own admission was the first sufferer
for his so-called liberal activities. Who asked him for
this indecent incantation? What purpose does he think
he is serving by it? Does he think that he is defending
the right of free speech this way, or the right of holding private political beliefs, or the right of artists to
express opposing points of view to the public? Or does
he think he can save his skin by sacrificing others and
forcing others to join the diseased scramble to announce
a timid and frightened loyalty? And loyalty to what?
To the Constitution of the United States, to the concepts of individual conscience and the right to disagree or to the narrow and intolerant doctrine of hatred
and fear which is sweeping the country today and which
will lead us all into war and total silence? And does
he really think he can save his skin by this shameful
abnegation? Does he think that because of his confession on the rack tonight, his illustrious agent will be
received with open arms tomorrow and told that his
client will be taken back, at an increase in price, as a
high priest of the true faith? You know and I know,
even if he and his agent don't, that he hasn't got a
chance. He has been disposed of because he dared to
offend by dishing out a little mild pablum about individual liberty a year ago, and he will remain disposed
of until there is such a sweeping, furious movement of
revulsion against the reactionary masters of the industry that they have to take him back along with all the
others. And if there is not this mass, sweeping revulsion, I say that the time will come, and damn soon
at that, when Woodrow Burke will find himself in a
concentration camp side by side with just the people
he is so ready to sacrifice tonight. And he can say he is
opposed to the Communists seven nights a week, and
no one will listen to him and no one will care and he
won't get out one minute sooner."

Archer glanced over at Burke. The commentator was
sitting on the edge of his chair, hunched over, his mouth

open as though he were on the point of shouting, his
fists opening and closing slowly.

"And if anyone is thinking that this prophecy is the
result of my disordered imagination," Lewis was saying,
"with no basis in fact, let him remember the fate of
people like Woodrow Burke, the fine, self-serving,
liberal gentlemen, just a few years ago in a country
called Germany. Let Mr. Burke reflect for a moment
on what happened to the gentlemen of his stripe there
who made professions like his, who fought the Nazis'
battles for them on the pages of newspapers and on
the air, who destroyed the unity of the forces opposing
Hitler in 1931 and 32."

Germany, Germany, Archer thought, everybody uses
Germany to prove everything.

"We have all been put in this boat together by our
enemies," Lewis said with grim triumph, "whether we
like it or not. Now we either row together or we go
on the rocks. It is as simple as that. As for our commercial friend here . . ." Lewis bowed ironically in
the direction of Kramer, who was sweating and looking
unpopular. "I don't think in a gathering like this it is
necessary to spend too much time examining his arguments. Mr. Kramer, by his own proud admission, is
interested only in the dollar . . ."

"Now, Marvin, honey," Kramer whispered faintly,
using his handkerchief on his forehead.

"Mr. Kramer," Lewis went on, ignoring the agent,
"will do anything for the dollar and in the privacy of
his office advises his clients to do anything for the
dollar—resign from everything, maintain total silence,
shout the war cries obediently when they are called
for, give up all the rights and opinions of American
citizens. For his ten percent, Mr. Kramer would have all
artists, whom he professes to love so dearly, eagerly
enlist in a new disenfranchised slave class. If anyone
here shares these feudal views on the function of the

artist, I advise him to go home now. Nothing I have to say here will be of any interest to him."

Nobody in the audience moved, presumably because they were not concerned with money at all.

"As for the other speaker on this platform," Lewis went on, taking his glasses off again, "Mr. Clement Archer . . ."

He speaks my name, Archer noted, almost amused, as if I were a newly discovered minor disease.

"I asked to be allowed to address you," Lewis said, without looking at Archer, "after he had spoken, but for reasons best known to the chairman of this meeting Mr. Archer was scheduled as the last speaker. Without mincing words, I have to say that I regard it as unfortunate, to put it politely, that Mr. Archer is here tonight and I invite him publicly, right now, to put on his hat and coat and leave this meeting, which he has clearly demonstrated he has not earned the right to address."

That man, Archer thought calmly, has by now invited a great number of people to leave in the interests of unity. Then he blinked. After a moment of hesitation, applause was breaking out in various portions of the room, heavy, disciplined, ominous-sounding. They decided, Archer realized painfully, they decided in advance to do this to me. He stared out across the room stubbornly, trying to distinguish and remember the people who were applauding. Why did Kitty come? he thought, why did she have to be here for this?"

Lewis put up his hand and the applause stopped dead. Archer rubbed the top of his head and made himself keep his eyes up.

"No doubt," Lewis was saying, "you have all read the excellent series of articles by that brilliant columnist, Mr. J. F. Roberts, on the subject of Mr. Clement Archer and I shall not go into the propriety of having as a speaker at a meeting like this a gentleman who, using the power of his position, has picked on Negro and Jewish artists as the first objects of his discrimination and who has been largely responsible for the suicide of a man of talent who was a friend of many in this room."

What I should do, Archer thought, making himself sit completely immobile, is get up and try to kill him with my bare hands.

"I regret that these things had to be said tonight," Lewis said severely and righteously, "but the ground had to be cleared and the issues had to be exposed before we could begin to do anything constructive. Now," he said, lapsing gratefully into the jargon of political oratory, "we have to decide what must be done to defend ourselves, to defend the traditions of our crafts, and the traditions of our country. Whatever his private reasons for advancing it, Woodrow Burke's plan, as far as it goes, has some solid merit to it."

Archer tried to recall what Burke's plan had been and couldn't remember. He felt fuzzy and was sorry he had drunk so much that day.

"I think," Lewis said, self-confidently, "that the idea of getting the various guilds to contribute to a war chest and hire investigators to find out just what sinister influences are behind the editors of *Blueprint* is an excellent one."

What happens, Archer thought stubbornly, if the investigators find nothing? Or find that all the influences behind the magazine are innocent, patriotic, above suspicion? Do we get our money back?

"But that's only part of what must be done," Lewis went on. "And only a small part. We must conduct a triple campaign. By all means let us expose the forces lined up against us for what they are. But at the same time, let us present our case to the public, the case of free citizens and free artists who are fighting for everyone's freedom. Let us take out full-page advertisements in the newspapers, let us turn out millions of pamphlets, let us buy radio time ourselves showing what the danger is, who the real enemies are, what the opposition against us consists of. And, practically, let us all call emergency meetings of our guilds and get the membership to announce that so long as any agency or network is guilty of using a blacklist, no writer or actor or director or musician or engineer will take the job of any person who has been dropped because of his political beliefs."

This time the applause was spontaneous and full. Lewis looked over the meeting, somberly gratified, allowing the applause to run itself out.

"They need us," he declared loudly, as if he were shouting to comrades on a barricade. "They won't be able to stay on the air half an hour without us. Let's give them a taste of how powerful we can be, united and unafraid, when we're challenged, and I guarantee you that one month from today there will not be a single murmur about political blacklists. And to show you that I am in earnest and not just making a gesture, I hereby pledge five hundred dollars to a strike fund, if it comes to that, or any other fund that is necessary. And I also pledge that I will not take any offer, no matter how promising, from any agency or network against which there is any suspicion of blacklisting."

There was a great deal of applause at this, and from various portions of the room, voices called out, "I pledge a hundred," and, "I pledge fifty." Archer watched curiously, recognizing rehearsal, and wondered what Burke, as chairman of the meeting, was going to do to handle the cleverly stage-managed stampede.

Lewis turned and sat down, putting his glasses in his pocket and tapping his little white cards neatly against the palm of his hand, for use, perhaps at other meetings.

Burke walked slowly to the lectern. His face was

white and angry and he was making an obvious effort to control himself with parliamentary dignity.

"Thank you, Mr. Lewis," he said coldly, when the commotion had subsided, "for your views. If you don't mind, I'd like to reserve motions like that for the end of the meeting, when all the speakers have been heard from and there has been a chance for discussion from the floor."

Lewis shrugged, suggesting wearily that he had been prepared for just such cowardly hedging, but he didn't protest.

"Ladies and gentlemen," Burke said to the audience, "I am not going to try to defend the next speaker, as he is known to most of you, and should need no defense." He waited, but there was no demonstration of any kind from the audience. "Mr. Clement Archer."

Burke's eyes were glittering as he shook Archer's hand ostentatiously.

Archer looked out over the room. The faces seemed blurred by hostility. Is it possible, he thought dully, that all these years, while I have worked with these people and traveled among them, they have been secretly hating me? Far off at the back of the room, Kitty's face was a pale, withdrawn triangle.

"Ladies and gentlemen," Archer said. His throat was dry and his lips were twitching and it was difficult to speak. "I had a speech prepared for tonight, but . . ."

There was a noise from the back of the room and Archer stopped, puzzled, until he realized that people were calling, "Louder. Louder. We can't hear you."

"I said that I had a speech prepared," Archer said, more clearly, "but I'm not going to make it. Everybody here seems to have a definite plan about what to do. I don't. I'm groping. I'm not certain about how to proceed. I'm not certain even that anything we decide on here tonight," he said, speaking more strongly now, "and anything we do after tonight will be of any value. I'm in doubt and maybe you don't want to hear

at this time from doubters. But I'm sure about one or
two things and I'll tell you what they are first. First of
all, I want to tell you what I know about the people
on my program who are under attack. Manfred Pokorny,
Alice Weller, Stanley Atlas, Frances Motherwell, and
Victor Herres." As he spoke the names it seemed to
Archer that he had been involved with them all his
life, as though he were the prisoner of those names
and he would never escape them. "Since they are all
artists—" (Was a past tense necessary for Pokorny and
would anyone check him on this?) "—the most important information about them concerns the quality of
their work. And here I am on firm ground. I have
worked with all of them over a period of years and I
can say, unhesitatingly, that their work was good, and
in some cases brilliant." (Alice. Was he being absolutely candid about Alice and could he be challenged
on that?) "As a man who is responsible for putting on
a show every week, I naturally prefer to be able to
choose performers, if only on the grounds of con-
venience, without having to inquire into anything but
their talent. Until now, in this country at least, that has
been the only basis on which artists have been judged
and I am sure we are the better for it. Some of the greatest works of art have been produced by some of the
greatest scoundrels of history. Artists in general are not
the most stable citizens of any society and their behavior often does not conform to the accepted legal and
moral codes of their times. Still, I hear no one cam-
paigning to have the Sistine Chapel whitewashed because of the rumors about Michelangelo's sexual behavior and there is no movement on foot to have
Francois Villon's poems burned because he wound up
on the scaffold as a common thief. Nor are Dostoyevsky's novels attacked because he confessed to raping a
ten-year-old girl." Archer closed his eyes momentarily
and remembered the yellow pages on which he had
written that afternoon, and remembered Kitty tearing

them clumsily, with her bandaged hand, and shouting, "Artists! God, you make me laugh with your artists!" He wondered what Kitty was thinking now, listening to him in the back of the room. "Are we to be stricter with our contemporaries," he asked, "merely because they are alive? Will it be a good bargain to shut down on future Dostoyevskys and Villons in exchange for political conformity? I know it must sound grandiose to use names like that in addressing a meeting of people who write and act in soap operas and televised vaudeville performances. But the principle is the same and I'm afraid it's indivisible. By accident, or by clever design, the dwarfs in the company of art are being forced to do the fighting to save the giants."

Archer was aware of hurt, angry, vain faces staring up at him at this unpleasant description, but he went on stubbornly, feeling himself grow less and less nervous. "It doesn't make it any easier," he said, "that among the people we have to defend are those who would mercilessly shut down any voice of which they did not approve, and who have, in a large measure, provoked this action against us and who have supplied ammunition and techniques to the censors and book-burners and who have done as much as anyone else to create the atmosphere in this country which tolerates repression. Many of you, I know, do not believe this and despise me for saying it. I myself did not believe it for a long time and I have to force myself to believe it now, because it makes me face up to a despairing, quarrelsome and perhaps violent future. Many of you think of yourselves as innocent and persecuted. Persecuted you may be, but you are not innocent."

Ostentatiously, a woman in a large-brimmed, black hat stood up in the middle of the room, put on her fur coat and walked down the middle aisle toward the door, her heels making a loud tapping in the still room. Archer waited until she went out. Then he went on.

"It may seem strange to you," he said, "that a man like me, who is himself under attack, chooses to speak like this. From the material that has been published about me I see that a fairly good case could be made out for those gentlemen who prefer to call me a fellow-traveler. In the 1930s and during the war years, I joined several organizations and supported several causes which were also supported by the Communists. At the risk of damaging myself even more than I have up till now, I am going to confess that I knew perfectly well that I was allying myself at that time with them. But naively, or accurately, I believed that it was not I who was traveling with them, but they who were traveling with me. Today that does not seem terribly intelligent, but try to remember the different climate of that time, when Nazism was on the march, when there was no talk of world revolution or Russian aggression, when our Government not only tolerated but encouraged collaboration with Communism all over the world. What's more, I make no apologies for what I did and thought in those days, and I suspect the rectitude of the men who would punish me now for those long-ago thoughts and actions. No matter how many lists are published, I refuse to believe that attempting to save the republican Government of Spain, for example, from Franco and Mussolini and Hitler was a subversive act or contrary to the best interests of the American people. And no matter what happens in the future I will never be convinced that sending old clothes or penicillin to Russia at the time of Stalingrad was anything but necessary and sensible behavior."

There was applause somewhere in the room, the first overt reaction since he had started speaking. The applause caught on and spread over the room. Archer stared soberly at the audience, wondering how much of the applause was ironic or window-dressing or relief.

"Now things have changed," Archer said. "Mr. Lewis will undoubtedly say that it is *I* who have changed, out of cowardice or a desire to be comfortable, or because I read the wrong newspapers. Others will say that the Communists have not really changed, they have only been more completely revealed. I suspect that all of these things are partially true. Still, we won't solve the problem by imposing silence on all who oppose us or allowing ourselves to be silenced because our opinions happen to be unpopular. As matters are going now, I could not be surprised to see everyone in this room, myself included, clapped into jail within the next few years. I hope you will believe me," Archer said, smiling for the first time, "when I tell you I do not think this country will be better off on that day. This would seem to put me in agreement with Mr. Lewis, who said that now we are all in the same boat and that we had better row together to save ourselves. Actually, we are not in a position to think of rowing at the moment. The best we can do is bail together and hope to keep afloat. When the time comes to row I have a notion Mr. Lewis and I will insist upon rowing in different directions. In talking of Mr. Burke, Mr. Lewis said that he will find himself in a concentration camp even if he says he is opposed to the Communists seven nights a week. Mr. Lewis obviously implied by that that Mr. Burke was wasting his breath and would be more useful if he kept his opinions to himself. I happen to disagree. If, along with Mr. Burke and Mr. Lewis, and whatever Communists, non-Communists, radicals, liberals and cranks are inaccurately collected in that doleful time, I am put behind wire, I will feel much better if I know I am there for my own reasons and not for anyone else's. We are not in the same situation, regardless of how hard the Communists and their opponents try to include us. The sheriff who is caught in the same jail with a suspected murderer and who fights to defend him against a lynch mob is not of the suspect's party. And even if the mob kills him on its way to the cell, or swings him up on the same tree they use for the alleged criminal, he must insist with his last breath on his separateness and on his difference in function . . . There is a reverse side to this proposition, too. At the risk of incurring Mr. Lewis's further displeasure, I must say that I am opposed to the Communists, here and abroad. The great majority of Americans join with me in this opposition. Most of these people are, I am convinced, decent and honorable. There are some, though, the shrillest of all, who use their anti-Communism to cloak bigotry, a lust for war, an approval of dictatorship, a hatred of all liberalism, all progress, all freedom of expression. They are the lynch mob and it is as necessary for me to denounce them and disassociate myself from their principles as it is for me to disassociate myself from the principles of the accused man they are out to hang. As a law-abiding citizen, I am committed to defending the rights of the accused to a proper trial and a proper hanging if he is guilty and a proper exoneration if he is innocent. But I insist on believing that accusation is not evidence, criticism is not heresy, an advocacy of change is not treason, a search for peaceful settlement is not subversive. The courts are slowly making firm ground for us all to stand on in these matters and I will be content to abide by their decisions, even if I feel they are too strict or influenced unduly by the fearful temper of the times. We have a history in this country of righting wrongs and reversing immoral legal decisions and I refuse to be stampeded into premature punishment by cynical and disingenuous attacks on the reputations of people who may have campaigned at one time or another for the forty-hour week or the policy of flying the UN flag over public-school buildings or even for the outlawing of the atom bomb. It was just such attacks on people who worked on my program that have led me to appear here tonight. Partly out of curiosity and partly from a desire to keep a program that I had worked on for more than four years from disintegrating, I spent some time in investigating

the politics of accused actors and musicians. Some
spoke candidly, others properly told me to mind my
own business. And regardless of my agreement or disagreement with any of them or my approval or disapproval of their politics, I came to the conclusion
that none of them in their positions on University Town
represented a threat to what we call the American system or had committed acts which merited punishment,
especially the severe and vindictive punishment of
being deprived forever of their means of livelihood."

Archer looked out over the blur of faces uncertainly.
There were other things he wanted to say, but they
were elusive, complicated, contradictory, and he
couldn't find words for them. He wanted to say that
loyalty—loyalty to anyone or any cause should not be
pushed to the extreme limits of its logical end. He
wanted to say that he was baffled and that he mistrusted anyone who was not baffled. He wanted to say,
Be merciful—merciful toward past malice and future
errors. He wanted to warn against Lewis and his plan
for a counter blacklist, first of all because it wouldn't
work, since people were not fanatics and trimmed to
survive and also because there were many actors who
certainly would not sacrifice themselves to salvage a
known Communist's job, even if it meant destroying
their guilds in the process. And he wanted to warn
against Lewis' happy assumption of the opposition's
ugliest tactic, because regardless of their motives, they
would all come out the uglier for it.

But he didn't say any of these things. He looked out
wearily at the divided faces, the faces that were set
against him, the faces that seemed to approve, the waiting, balancing faces, and said, "I told you in the beginning I didn't have a plan, that I'm groping. I'm afraid
I haven't been very helpful and many of you probably
feel that I've been wasting your time. I think I'm
clear by now about the way I feel, but I know I'm
uncertain about what to do about it. I'm afraid I have

to join with Mr. Lewis in saying that I don't like any
of the speeches I heard up here tonight, including his
and probably including mine. I hope there will be
better speeches and better plans brought forth from
the floor and I shall sit down now and listen expectantly.
Thank you."

He sat down, feeling tired and disappointed with his
performance, although the applause was surprisingly
warm. It was all so inconclusive, Archer thought. I'm
too reasonable for oratory and my energy is too low.
Fifteen years ago I might have conceivably made a
fiery speech, full of emotion and stirring calls for action, on this subject. But, then, nobody asked me to debate this subject fifteen years ago.

Frances Motherwell was standing at her seat in the
front row, holding up her hand. At other points in the
room, people were raising their hands, too, asking for
the floor.

"Mr. Chairman," Frances said loudly and clearly,
"Mr. Chairman."

"Miss Frances Motherwell," Burke said, motioning
to her to come up to the dais. She walked swiftly
toward the lectern, in her provocative, energetic way,
her skirt swinging lightly around her legs. She stepped
up gracefully, youthful, desirable, beautifully dressed,
the lipstick bright on her mouth, her large eyes cleverly
shadowed with a line of mascara on the lids. She carefully avoided looking at Archer as she stood a little
to one side of the lectern, resting one hand on it, her
other hand on her hip, her body athletic and full under
the expensive dress, her legs long and shining rising
from high-heeled, black suede shoes. The room was
very still, the women watching her warily and with despair, the men with obscure, unpolitical uneasiness. She
stood silently for a moment, staring out, making her impression. She was hatless and her hair was very smooth,
caught in back by a narrow black bow and she looked
as girls in small towns hope they can one day look
when they come to the city and conquer it.

The comrades had chosen their opening speaker shrewdly, Archer guessed, getting sex, respectability, talent, wealth, and a gown from a French collection in one glittering and dangerous package. The monolithic approach toward life—in which all aspects, qualities, abilities were always turned into weapons for the cause. Archer stirred uncomfortably, looking at the tense, perfect profile.

"Ladies and gentlemen," Frances said finally, in her husky, disturbing voice, which carired easily to the back of the room without any effort on her part. "I have listened with great interest to what's been said here tonight. Especially to the opinions of Mr. Archer, who was kind enough to vouch for my abilities as an actress, and who was also kind enough not to mention anything about my politics. Mr. Archer happens to know a great deal about my politics, because a little more than a month ago he asked me and I told him."

Archer watched her intently, feeling himself grow tense, conscious of the effort that was necessary to sit there quietly and without moving. This is going to be bad, he thought, staring at the handsome, wild face, this is going to be very bad.

"What I told him was simple and explicit," Frances went on evenly, her diction clear and professional, her voice vibrating with the curious overtone of excitement that had contributed so much to her success. "And I will repeat it here and now."

Suddenly Archer felt himself grow calm, because it was going to be much worse than he had ever imagined and there was nothing to be done about it any more.

"What I said," Frances continued, her long, fine hand dropping off her hip and slowly and lightly caressing her silk flank, "was that I joined the Communist Party in 1945."

She paused and Archer was conscious of the heavy, unnatural silence of two hundred people sitting in one room without movement, without a sigh, a whisper, a cough.

"For your benefit," Frances said huskily and quietly, staring out over the meeting, "I will say that I am still a member tonight, although when this is over, I am going home and writing in my resignation." She threw back her head, and her hair, in its little bow, flicked on the back of her neck in a pretty, girlish movement. Her chin was up and her eyes were shining and she looked defiant and exalted. God, Archer thought, she must have turned religious. That was bound to be next on the list. And of course, she would pick an occasion like this, public, emotional and tense, for her announcement. Her hunger for drama and attention, her stage-center nerves, could never be satisfied by private renunciation. Archer remembered stories about Frances suddenly and without warning turning on the lover-of-the-moment at parties and breaking off with him for a real or fancied misdemeanor, humiliating him with savage intimacies and witty and vicious truths and half-truths while the other guests fell painfully silent around her and her stricken gallant. Now, in giving up a political party, she was keeping to the old compulsive pattern of the public tirade she had until now reserved only for the gentlemen who had rashly visited her bed.

Curiously, Archer turned to look at the rows of people in front of him. Many of them, he realized, must be feeling their hearts sink within them as they waited for the revelations in the husky, quivering voice. But the faces were grave and thoughtful and there was no telling, at this distance, who expected to be cut down next.

"The reason for my resigning is a simple one," Frances was saying, "and Mr. Clement Archer is connected to it. After I told Mr. Archer that I was a member of the Party, I was called before the leader of my group and harangued. I was told that if I ever admitted membership again I would be dropped in the interests of Party discipline. If I was asked about what I had told Mr. Archer by any committee or in any court of law, I was to deny everything, even if it meant being indicted for perjury. I was told point-blank that I was engaged in a conspiracy and that conspirators did not expose themselves and if I had ever thought anything else, it was now time for me to rid myself of such romantic, girlish notions. I was told that I had been under suspicion for a long time in the Party, that I was considered unstable, and that was why no work of any real importance had ever been entrusted to me." Her voice was bitter and Archer could see that she was still suffering from the blows to her vanity that these revelations had dealt her. If she had been treated more tactfully, Archer thought idly, she'd never be up here tonight.

"I walked away from that meeting," Frances said, "thinking hard. I had never believed that I was a member of a conspiracy and I thought that the writers and politicians who said that were pimps and prostitutes of reaction . . ."

Whatever else she had broken away from, Archer thought, she still carries the vocabulary with her.

"Suddenly the blinders fell off," Frances said. "The people whom I had admired, the men who I thought were working for freedom, justice, peace . . . Those words." For the first time she turned and looked at Archer, and she smiled. He remembered her saying the same words about her dead young man in England. "That was all hogwash." She turned back to her audience. "I saw what they were really like. I remembered how pleased they were when people got hurt on a picket line, when companies closed down and threw men out of work. They're interested in trouble, in bloodshed, in unhappiness, that's the only climate they can work in and they know it and if they don't find it, they make it. They *have* to conspire, because they're misfits, neurotics, lunatics, and if they had to work in the light of day, everyone would be able to tell in ten minutes how ridiculous and incompetent and dangerous they are."

We have now reached the point, Archer thought calmly, at which the mad call each other mad.

"I'm a lot of things, I suppose," Frances went on, her voice challenging and high and filled with the delight of talking about herself, "and many of you here probably have told each other some pretty sharp things about me. But there's one thing I'm not and never could be. And that's a conspirator. And certainly not a conspirator against my own country. I don't do anything in secret." She grinned, as though a vulgar joke about herself had fleetingly crossed her mind. Then her face grew grave and she spoke seriously, using her talent to sound sincere and repentant. "After I decided that," she said, "I had to go on to the next step. Was I to keep quiet about what I had seen and heard, what I had learned? Was I going to stand off and watch the machinations, watch people being deluded and used and disillusioned, watch the country being weakened and divided, and never open my mouth? Or was I going to make up for my error and my stubbornness and do my share in repairing the damage to which I had contributed?" Swiftly, with the merest flicker of her eyes and re-arrangement of her position, she changed to a woman who had accepted matyrdom for a noble cause. "It would have been much more pleasant to keep quiet. And it would have been easy. No one demanded anything of me. Only my conscience . . ."

Archer closed his eyes momentarily, embarrassed. Frances, darling, he thought, you should have gotten someone else to write your lines tonight . . .

"I've stayed up night after night, wrestling with myself," Frances said, looking like a woman who slept ten hours a night and who had her face massaged five times a week. "And finally, I knew what I had to do. I had to come here tonight and tell what I knew. As a warning, as an example. Now," she said briskly, cleverly

switching from the almost religious level on which she
had been working to a conversational and friendly, almost gossipy tone, "now we can go on to more specific
things. Mr. Archer, for example. I don't know why
Mr. Archer has chosen to be so discreet about my
affiliations," Frances said, "but I have my suspicions.
Mr. Archer is quite a mysterious figure and it's a little
difficult to make a coherent pattern out of what he
says and what he does. I used to think he was quite
a simpleminded and rather bumbling fellow. But things
I have learned about him in the last few weeks, plus the
speech tonight in which he successfully said one thing
while proposing another, have given me new respect
for him. Respect for his cleverness if not for his candor.
My politics were not the only thing Mr. Archer has
taken pains to hide. He has also hidden the fact that
the program for which he was responsible was written for four years by a man who is an avowed and
militant atheist. A man whom he approved of so much
that he permitted him to be seen in every night club
in town with his eighteen-year-old daughter."

"Now, Frances." Archer stood up, trying to keep his
voice from being thick. "I think that's enough of that."

"Mr. Chairman," Frances said to Burke, "I understood the floor was mine."

"Sit down, Clem," Burke whispered, pulling at his
sleeve. "You'll only make it worse if you argue with
her."

Slowly Archer sat down. He hated Frances, mostly
because she was so plainly enjoying herself.

"Among other things that Mr. Archer conveniently
neglected to mention," Frances went on, the melodious,
nervous voice dominating the room, "was his curious
generosity. Mr. Archer, because of certain activities,
has for some time been under surveillance and investigation and several interesting items have come to light.
For example, Mr. Archer not long ago gave as a loan
or a disguised gift, a check for three hundred dollars

to the chairman of this meeting, Mr. Woodrow Burke, and I have seen a photostat of that check. He also gave a check to Mrs. Alice Weller, who was a principal speaker at a congress which our own State Department condemned as subversive and opposed to the interests of our country. Whether he donated this money out of sympathy for the lady's political views or out of gentlemanly tenderness, I have no way of judging."

Poor Alice, Archer thought, sitting out there in the middle of the room, dowdy, inefficient, remembering that it was Frances herself who had trapped her into sponsoring the congress, knowing that in the spate of accusations no one would take the time to ask her for the accurate history of the affair or even listen to her explanations. Probably, Archer thought, staring fascinated at the slender, fashionable figure five feet away from him, probably by now Frances doesn't even remember it or has come to believe she was in no way involved with it.

"I have also seen the photostat copy of that particular check," Frances was saying. She laughed, a high, jumpy giggle. Somehow, that short, almost-deranged burst of disconnected laughter made Frances seem more dangerous than ever. A woman who laughs like that, at a time like this, Archer thought, is beyond reach.

"And on the day before Mr. Pokorny, who did the music for Mr. Archer's show, was scheduled to go down to answer charges that he had perjured himself to enter this country from Mexico," Frances said, "Mr. Archer took Mr. Pokorny to his bank and withdrew two hundred dollars from his account and handed it over to Mr. Pokorny. And I have seen a sworn affidavit from the teller in the bank to this effect."

Archer closed his eyes. He couldn't bear to look at the pretty, triumphant, expensive figure on the platform anymore. And I thought they were only tapping my phone, he thought, only my phone.

"Mr. Pokorny," Frances said, "in case anyone here is in doubt, was an admitted member of the Austrian Communist Party and was married to a high-ranking official of the American Communist Party and was due to be deported by the Government as an undesirable alien and if anyone wishes proof of any of these things I am prepared to furnish it."

Unlucky Pokorny, lying in the crowded Long Island cemetery, Archer thought, he will be forever remembered not by his excellent, modest music but by his shabby brush with the officials of the Immigration Department and by his connection with his impossible wife.

"Isn't it strange," Frances asked, her voice mischievous, almost coquetting, "that Mr. Archer, who has told you so righteously that he is opposed to Communists, should confine his charitable impulses so strictly to ladies and gentlemen who are, to put it as delicately as possible, so far to the left of center?"

Archer opened his eyes, feeling himself begin to sweat. The Red Cross, he thought dazedly, the Community Chest, the Urban League, should I tell them about the checks to them? And will anybody listen?

"What's more," Frances moved away from the lectern, going downstage to be closer to her audience for the big scene, "Mr. Archer, in his attempt to keep his friends snugly placed on his program, took the trouble to go down to Philadelphia and vouch to the sponsor of the program that Mr. Victor Herres, whom he has known intimately for fifteen years, is not a Communist, pledging this on his honor. This was very loyal and comradely and had the desired effect. To this day, Vic Herres has not missed a single program. Unfortunately, this charming guarantee was not true. I know it," Frances said, "and eight or nine of you in this room know it. And we know it for a very simple reason. We know it because Vic Herres was the leader of the Communist cell to which we all belonged." Again there was that high, disturbing giggle. "Those of us who were privileged to know these two gentlemen," Frances said softly, "know that they took great pleasure in each other's company and were seen together almost daily. I will not try to examine here the probability that a grown, intelligent man, a man who has taught history at a college, would not understand the politics of a friend whom he has seen almost every day for fifteen years."

Vic, Archer thought, Vic. Why wasn't he here tonight? Did he know she was going to say these things? Is that why?

There was a stir in the back of the room and Archer saw Kitty standing up and moving, head bent, eyes down, awkward and unsteady, toward the door. He wanted to call to her, cry, "Don't go, dearest, don't leave now . . ." But Kitty never looked back. She went out, the door sliding silently shut behind her, only Nancy, from across the room, looking up and noticing her exit.

Where is she going tonight? Archer thought wildly. Will I ever see her again?

"A good friend of mine," Frances said into the aching silence of the room, "who is interested in these matters has given me all this information . . ."

Who? Archer wondered desperately. O'Neill? Hutt? Miss Walsh? Old man Sandler? An FBI agent? Vic? Vic?

"There is just one more tasty little nugget," Frances said, "that I think you ought to know about. Mr. Archer, who has assured us that he is such a staunch democrat and patriot, in 1946 signed his name to a nominating petition for a Communist candidate for the State Legislature and I have seen the petition and I can produce a copy of it for any one of you who wishes to see it with his own eyes."

Archer shook his head slowly, as though to clear it. For a moment he almost believed her, almost believed he had signed what she said he'd signed, acted for the motives she described, plotted as cunningly as she charged.

"In the light of all this," Frances said challengingly, "it may strike some of you as queer that the Communists have chosen to attack the man who has fought so well for them. Mr. Roberts, who is sitting there in the third row, smiling up at me, and who so faithfully writes what he is told, has said some very harsh things about Mr. Archer. And Mr. Lewis . . ." She turned and bowed pleasantly in Lewis's direction. "Mr. Lewis, who I am happy to acknowledge as a former colleague of mine, continued the attack on this platform tonight."

Lewis, who had his legs crossed, recrossed them and stared expressionlessly out at the audience.

"It is a very clever tactic," Frances said, "and one worthy of the people who engineered it. By accusing him themselves, the Communists cleared Mr. Archer of suspicion, giving a great deal more weight to his arguments in their behalf."

Oh, God, Archer thought, weirdly amused despite himself. We have reached that stage now. If you are praised you're guilty, if you have been attacked, you're more guilty. Suddenly he stood up. He couldn't tolerate the hot, close room any more, or the trained, sensual, flickering voice. Ponderously, moving carefully, conscious that everyone was watching him intently, Archer stepped down from the platform, and not looking at anyone in the room, walked down the center aisle to the door. He went through the door, closing it politely behind him.

He got his coat, remembering to tip the attendant, to whom weddings, reunions and meetings in which people were destroyed forever merely meant a certain number of quarters in the saucer on the small table in front of the cloakroom.

It was cooler out in the corridor where Archer waited for the elevator and he could feel the sweat that had run down from his armpits grow cold under his shirt. There were women's steps behind him, hurried and vaguely familiar, but he didn't turn around.

"Clement," Nancy said, "do you mind if I go with you."

Archer looked at her. Her face was strained and flushed, and she was fighting to keep her lips from quivering. There was a smell of liquor on her breath, mingling with her perfume. He took her arm and helped her into the elevator when it came.

24

Outside the hotel, they walked east toward the river along the cold, deserted street. They didn't talk for a long time. They crossed several avenues, waiting for taxis that rushed past them, taking people to night clubs. They reached a block with bare trees shaking uneasily in the wind and Archer felt that it was familiar and that he should remember some significant fact about these rows of pleasant houses. Then he realized that it was the street on which Frances Motherwell lived and he remembered the long climb up the steps to her apartment, and the striped draperies and the blobby modern painting and the chocolate walls and Frances telling him about the boy in the Air Force who went to bed with an English girl after dancing with Frances and pretended he had Frances in his arms. Archer also remembered the other boy who had died. Saint Hank, he remembered, from California, who had made a Communist of her and who could be held responsible, in the military cemetery in Metz, for what had happened tonight.

"She's crazy, you know," Archer said. "She's going to wind up making speeches to the other inmates about visions of the dead and about how the guards rape her every Tuesday night."

They walked in silence again, crossing still another avenue, where whores walked their dogs, avoiding policemen, looking for the winter trade.

"Vic didn't come tonight, did he?" Archer asked in the darkness, midway between one lamppost and the next. "I looked, but I didn't see him."

"No," Nancy said gently. "He didn't come. I don't know where he is. He started to get drunk about six o'clock and all of a sudden he just put on his coat and went out."

Archer nodded. He could feel Nancy's hand light on his arm. "Nancy," he said flatly, "am I in love with you? Are you in love with me? *Were* you ever?"

Nancy didn't answer for a long time. "I suppose so," she said wearily. "For a moment or two here and there through the years. I suppose there have been times when I wanted to be with you, when I thought that if I said the proper word, you would tell me you wanted me."

Archer nodded. "That's what Kitty told me this afternoon," he said. Every charge, he thought despairingly, can be proved to be almost true.

"It's not strange," Nancy said. "If a man and a woman see each other so often, if they admire each other, they can't help speculating how it would be, and half-want it, almost tell themselves they should reach out for it. I wouldn't ever do anything about it, and I know you wouldn't either, and I knew it would pass over quickly. The imagination finally invents every possible situation, I guess. You can't help it and most of the time it doesn't do any harm. Kitty hates me, doesn't she?"

"That's what she said this afternoon."

"What do you think she'll say tomorrow afternoon?" Nancy's voice had a sharp edge of bitterness now.

"Nancy . . ."

"Yes?"

"Did Vic know what Motherwell was going to say tonight? Is that why he wouldn't come?"

There was a tiny pause. "No," Nancy said, and her voice was so low that Archer could hardly hear her. "That wasn't why he didn't come."

"Nancy . . ."

"Yes?"

"It's true, isn't it? What that girl said?"

Again there was the pause. "Yes," Nancy whispered. "It's true."

They crossed under the el. Far off, a train made a small, wandering, diminishing noise, going downtown over the lighted bars and the locked shops.

"I've argued with him and argued with him," Nancy said tonelessly. "It doesn't do any good. I've never won an argument from him yet, except the time I insisted on coming to New York. I don't have any hope for him, Clement, and you shouldn't either. I love him and I think I would throw myself off the bridge it he left me, but I don't have any hope for him."

They were walking past garages now, bleakly lighted, and cluttered antique shops. Before she was pregnant, Archer remembered, Kitty spent many afternoons in this neighborhood, to come home excited about the purchase of a Norman commode or a pair of gilt sconces.

"Do you want to know why Vic got drunk and didn't show up at the meeting?" Nancy asked harshly.

"If you want to tell me."

"I want to tell you," Nancy said. "It's about time you knew all about your friend Victor."

"Maybe I know enough," Archer said.

"You don't," Nancy said. "And you deserve to know the whole thing. There was a conference this afternoon at our house. To decide how this meeting tonight was to be handled. They always do that. They always plan everything out. Frances Motherwell was there and Marvin Lewis and that Roberts, that columnist—and some others. Do you want to hear their names?"

"No," Archer said, feeling that he didn't want to hear

anything more, but knowing that he couldn't stop Nancy now.

"I eavesdropped," Nancy said. "After nine years of meetings I finally eavesdropped on one of them. I've been fighting with Vic so much about what they've been doing to you, I decided I had to hear just what went on. I couldn't hear everything. But I heard enough. Enough. You know, it was Vic who told Roberts all that stuff about you—about the terms of your contract and the Army and that silly Yogi thing that made you look so foolish."

Archer stared down the dark street. A pair of headlights was coming slowly toward them. "Why?" he asked. "Why did he want to do that?"

"Why?" Nancy repeated violently. "Why? Because he's fanatic, because he would sacrifice me and Johnny and young Clem and himself and anybody else if he was told it was for the cause, because he's out of his mind, because he thinks he's so reasonable and a reasonable man gives up little things like a friend or a wife for the future of the world. Because they decided you were a convenient point of attack. You were vulnerable and you couldn't fight back very hard because you weren't important and because they could ring in the Jews and the Negroes neat and easy around you, and because you were the one who went and told Pokorny he was fired and he killed himself and people pitied him. And they figured your program was really finished no matter what happened, anyway. And they knew what sort of man you were and they knew that you wouldn't let it make any difference, that you'd still fight their battle for them just the same. You were perfect for them and your good friend Vic is so God-damn logical and disciplined and cold as ice. I'll tell you something you don't know about your friend. When that man was arrested for giving away atomic secrets to the Russians, he said he would do the same thing if he had the chance. I tried to warn you about going to this meeting tonight, but then I didn't have the guts and then Kitty came in just when . . ." Nancy stopped. She was crying and she couldn't talk through her sobs. Archer put his arms around her and for a moment they stood that way, under the light of a lamppost, looking like two lovers saying good night before parting in the dark winter night.

"Then, after those people left the house this afternoon," she said, fighting down her sobs, "I told him he had to go to you and warn you not to speak tonight, not to come. We had a terrible fight and I said a lot of the things I'm saying now. He yelled at me and he said he should have married someone like Frances Motherwell." Suddenly she began to laugh. She laughed louder and louder, shaking in his arms, the tears gleaming on her cheeks. "Oh, God, I wish he had been there for that performance tonight! His sainted Motherwell, spilling everything she knew, and a lot of things she never knew, at the top of her pretty voice, after sitting there so hot and revolutionary and such a fine, upstanding conspirator all afternoon! Oh, God, it would have been almost worth it just to see his face as it came tumbling out!"

Then she began to sob again. Archer held her, feeling lonely and helpless and blank, feeling that many years had gone past without profit.

"Don't see him again, Clement, dear," Nancy whispered up into his face, close to him. "Forget him. Write him off. Don't see me. Wipe us all out. Please."

"What are you going to do?"

Slowly, the sobs stopped and Nancy pulled away. She rubbed her eyes with the back of her hand, like a little girl. "I'm going to go and look for him," she said quietly, "and bring him home and put him to bed and hold him in my arms and comfort him, because he'll never be happy again as long as he lives."

She turned and started running toward the distant avenue, a small, surprisingly nimble figure in a fur coat, running with a quick, urgent clatter of high heels on the cold pavement, running past the shabby stone houses shut against night and winter and betrayal.

Archer watched the figure growing smaller and smaller and saw her hail a taxi at the corner and get in. Then the taxi spurted across the intersection, with the red light shining intense and useless against traffic that would not appear on the streets for seven more hours. Then the taxi was gone and Archer never saw Nancy again.

He walked back to Third Avenue and got a taxi under the el and sat in the back, carefully not thinking about anything, until he got home.

When he opened the front door, he saw Kitty's coat thrown across a chair. He heard someone moving around in his study and he went in. Jane was there, walking slowly back and forth in front of the window, smoking a cigarette. She had never smoked in the house before and for a moment, before he spoke to her, Archer wondered what the innovation meant.

"Hello, Jane," he said. "What're you doing home?"

Jane wheeled around as though he had frightened her. "Oh," she said. "Daddy." Her voice was flat and without spirit and she seemed to realize it herself because she threw away the cigarette and made herself smile and said, "People're beginning to arrive at all hours in this house, aren't they? Mother just got in, too." She came over and kissed him. She held him just a little tighter and a little longer than ordinarily before she stepped back.

Archer scrutinized her. She seemed tired and there was a mottled look to the skin under her eyes. "What's up, Jane?" Archer asked, seating himself. "I thought you were going away for the week-end."

"Oh." Jane shrugged and went back to the window and Archer had the feeling that she was trying to keep her face turned from him as much as she could. "I changed my mind. Week-ends in the winter get to be a bore in the country."

"Come on, baby," Archer said gently. "What hurts?"

"Nothing hurts," Jane said. Then she smiled. "OK, something hurts a little. Man by the name of Barbante went off and got himself married today."

"Oh," Archer said noncommittally. "He told me he had something like that on his mind. I thought he was drunk."

"He wasn't drunk," Jane said ruefully. "He married a twenty-eight-year-old lady he's known since the end of the war." For a moment, Jane's lips trembled, but she bent over to light a cigarette, and when she raised her her head again, her mouth was under control. "He's a funny man," she said lightly. "He took the trouble to send me a lot of letters up there at school this last month. Seventeen letters," she said with childish precision.

"He's a fool," Archer said, furious with the seventeen letters and feeling that without reading them he could accurately tell his daughter what was in them.

"Oh, don't be mean to the poor man," Jane said. "He has his points. I never took him seriously, but I won't deny he was a nice man to go out with. He—he made me feel—" she searched for the true and accurate word. "He made me feel slender."

Archer tried to keep back the smile and half-succeeded.

"But I suppose in a little while," Jane said, staring out between the curtains at the dark backyards, "he'd have turned out to be like all the rest. Weary-making." She shrugged. "You told him he was too old for me, didn't you, Dad?"

"Yes."

Jane nodded. "He was supposed to come out on Sunday and drive me back to school," she said. "Then he called up and said he couldn't drive me back, he had to get married. I guess it's childish—but I always feel real mean when anybody breaks a date with me." She turned and faced Archer. "You look solemn, darling," she said. "Please don't look solemn on my account."

Archer stood up and went over and kissed her forehead. "From now on," he said, "whenever I think of you, there will be a wide smile on my face. Because you're going to turn into a very good type." Jane's lips trembled again and the tears came into her eyes, but they just glistened there.

"Now," Archer said, "I'm going to bed. Coming upstairs?"

"Not just now," Jane said softly, smoking furiously. I'm not tired. I'll just sit down here for awhile and think about twenty-eight-year-old women." She managed a quivery smile for her father as he waved to her and went out of the room.

He left her there, faced with what would probably be the first sleepless night of her life, a night in which she would have to chew and digest her first major defeat, a night in which she would have to take a long step toward maturity. But as he went up the stairs, Archer felt curiously light-hearted. Part of it was relief that Barbante was now safely out of the way, but the greater part came from the new feeling of pride and confidence that Jane had given him.

Only one bed was turned down in the bedroom and Archer guessed that Kitty was sleeping in the spare room. For a moment, he thought of going in and saying good night to her. Then he sighed and began to get undressed. It can wait till morning, he thought.

He was asleep two minutes after he turned out the light.

25

There was a bell ringing somewhere and he woke up and reached for the phone on the table next to the bed.

"Hello," he said, but there was no sound in the receiver. Then he remembered that the phone had been disconnected. The bell rang again and he realized it was downstairs, at the front door. He looked at the clock. It was only eight o'clock. He felt exhausted, as though he had run a great distance the night before. He closed his eyes, hoping someone else would open the door or that whoever was there would go away. But the bell rang again and he got up. The other bed was still made up. Kitty hadn't slept in it. Bruisedly, he put on his robe and fumbled into slippers. He walked downstairs heavily, annoyed at the insistent clamor.

He opened the door. There was an old man there in a torn army overcoat and a cap. It was raining out and the old man was purple with cold and his cap was soaked.

"Western Union," the man mumbled, thrusting out an envelope. "Sign here."

Archer signed. He searched aimlessly in the pocket of the robe for a tip. There was a handkerchief in the pocket and a half-used book of matches. "Sorry," he said to the old man. The old man smiled sadly and skeptically, accustomed to ingratitude, and hunched off into the rain. Archer closed the door. He went into the living room and turned on a lamp, because all the curtains were drawn. He sat down slowly in an armchair and stared at the yellow envelope. Then he tore it open, his fingers clumsy with sleep, and unfolded the message.

CANNOT REACH YOU ON PHONE.
URGENT YOU BE IN MY OFFICE NINE O'CLOCK THIS MORNING. URGENT. O'NEILL.

Archer let the telegram drop to the floor. He sat with his legs stretched out for five minutes or so, too tired to move. Then he heaved himself up slowly and went upstairs, avoiding looking at himself in the hall mirror. His legs felt old and uncertain on the steps and he had a thick taste in his mouth. Upstairs, he looked along the hall to Jane's room. The door was closed now. He thought of going in to the guest room and talking to Kitty, and hesitated, his hand on the curve of the banister. Just say good morning, he thought, say I'm sorry, say it is too late for us now to be enemies, say, I am going to have breakfast, will you join me for a cup of coffee? Then he shook his head. It will have to wait, he thought. It's too bad, but it will have to wait.

He went to the bathroom and shaved carelessly, cutting himself, because his skin was tight and flaky. He remembered the flecks of blood on Burke's collar the night before and Burke's loud, accusing voice. He took a shower, his face stinging where the soap got into the cuts under his chin. His stomach felt tight and knotted, even in the shower. When this is over, he thought, I ought to go to a doctor.

He dressed quickly, putting on the same clothes he had worn the night before because he didn't feel like making any decisions about what shirt, what tie, what suit to wear. While he was knotting his tie before the mirror, Kitty came in. She was fully dressed. He took one look at her, then glanced away. He couldn't bear the way she looked.

"I have to go up to O'Neill's office," Archer said, conscious of his wife standing behind him. "I just got a telegram. I don't think it'll take very long. I'll be back soon. Then we can settle whatever has to be settled." He didn't like the way that sounded. Dry, cold, antagonistic, without pity or love or hope. But he was too tired to choose the proper words.

"We don't have to settle anything," Kitty said. She sounded exhausted. "Everything's settled."

Archer didn't reply. He put on his jacket, flattening down the collar.

"That suit's all creased," Kitty said. "You look awful."

Archer looked in his wallet. There was enough there for a taxi.

"I'll make you breakfast," Kitty said.

"I haven't got time."

"You can't go out without breakfast," Kitty said stubbornly.

"I said I haven't got time." He turned and faced her. There were big dark rings under her eyes, making them look enormous and desperate, and the bones of her face seemed to be pushing out of her skin.

She stared at him for a moment, then walked clumsily over to the bed and sat down, her head bent, her hands hanging limply down. Archer took a step and kissed the top of her head. Her hair smelled stale and dry. She made no move and he left her sitting like that.

He bought a newspaper at the corner and went into a drugstore for coffee. The coffee was hot and he could only drink it in tiny sips as he glanced through the paper. There was no story about the meeting the night before. Or he couldn't find it. He was too impatient to go methodically through the thick paper. The casual readers of the *Times* were treated that morning to news of an airplane disaster in which thirty-eight people had died and to an exchange of discourtesies in the UN between the Americans and the Russians on the subject of China.

He finished his coffee and went outside and hailed a taxi. The taxi skidded to a halt at the curb, but as he took a step toward it, a plump woman with an umbrella dashed past him and reached the door and flung it open. "Be a gentleman!" the woman said, snapping her umbrella shut and waving it in his face. Her voice was triumphant and menacing and she nimbly threw herself into the cab and slammed the door. Archer watched the cab pull away, throwing water from its tires, and he was very wet by the time he found another cab.

The pretty girls in the outer office smiled deliciously at him when he came in and offered him melodious soprano good mornings, as though nothing had happened to them or to him, as though youth and sex, commerce and high income were permanent and irrevocable. But O'Neill's face reflected a different climate. He was alone in his office, standing at the window, staring out, sagging in his colthes. When he turned to greet Archer he didn't smile and his eyes were weary and clouded. He shook hands silently. For a moment they stood in the middle of the office, looking at each other uncomfortably.

"I'm sorry, Clem," O'Neill said. "Terribly sorry."

"Forget it." Archer shrugged. "Hazards of the trade." He took off his wet overcoat and threw it over a chair. The rain had soaked through at the shoulders and his jacket was damp and warm.

"They're waiting for us," O'Neill said. "Hutt and Sandler. In Hutt's office. Do you want to ask me any questions?"

"No."

O'Neill hesitated, as though he wanted to say something. Then he shook his head slightly and went over to the door and opened it. "Let's go then," he said.

They walked through the mingled smells of perfume and typists' toilet water in the large outer office to Miss Walsh's desk at the far end. Miss Walsh looked up at them with sallow hostility. "Go right in," she said. "He's waiting."

There was a pile of rumpled newspapers on the floor at Sandler's feet, where he sat in a leather chair, facing the door impatiently. Hutt was sitting at his desk, working on a script with a blue pencil. Neither of the men rose when O'Neill and Archer came in.

"Good morning," Hutt said, in his near-whisper. "Will you close the door, please, Emmet?"

O'Neill closed the door. Hutt let them stand there one moment too long, then said, "Find yourselves chairs." He put down his blue pencil and pushed the script he had been working on to one side.

Archer sat down on a straight wooden chair, facing Sandler. O'Neill remained standing along the wall, bulky and pale.

"Did you see these, Archer?" Sandler asked, kicking at the newspapers on the floor.

"I only read the *Times*," Archer said.

"Well, you should've invested a few more nickels," said Sandler harshly. "Your name's all over every other paper in town."

"You didn't get a very good press this morning," Hutt said.

"No?" Archer asked mildly.

"No."

"No," Sandler said. "And neither did I. And neither did the Company."

"I'm sorry," Archer said.

"You're sorry." Sandler snorted and learned forward angrily. His face was set, his opaque blue eyes that Archer saw now were so much like Hutt's, cold and angry. He was making an obvious effort to control his temper. "This is a hell of a time to be sorry."

"What do you want me to say to that?"

"Don't be impudent," Sandler snapped. "I didn't get up at five o'clock in the morning and travel ninety miles to listen to impudence." His lips were pale and thin and the white, preserved, sharp teeth seemed to bite at every word. "What the hell did you think you were doing, Archer?"

For a fraction of a second Archer thought of trying to explain. Then he looked at the shut, furious face of the old man and Hutt's pale, frigid eyes, and he knew there was no use. "I don't think," he said wearily, not wanting to fight either, "that there's much sense in going over all that again."

"Let me tell you some of the things that have been happening in the last few days," Sandler said. "In case you're not up on current events. My God-damn phone's been ringing twenty-four hours a day. In my office. At my home. And lunatics have been unloading the most vicious kind of filth on me, on my wife, on my secretary, my maid, on anybody who picks up a phone. Four goons followed my son into a parking lot last night and beat him up so bad he had to have six stitches over his eye. My butler quit. Every mail I . . . What the hell are you smiling at?"

Archer hadn't realized he was smiling. "I guess," he said mildly, "because it strikes me as a little funny that a butler gives his notice these days because his employer is charged with being sympathetic to Communism."

"Well, stop smiling," Sandler said loudly. "It isn't so God-damn funny. My wife is almost hysterical and I'm going to have to pack her off to Arizona until this blows over. If it ever blows over. And what's more, cancellations have started to come in for orders from all over the country. Firms we've been doing business with for twenty years. And God knows where it will end. And you did it, Mr. Archer, you did it."

"I can't really accept that," Archer said, not because he felt there was any possibility of convincing the old man, but to break up his crescendo of rage. "I didn't call your home or your office. I didn't threaten your wife. I didn't cut your son's eye. I haven't canceled any orders. People're tired and worried and afraid these days, and violent and bigoted. That's not my fault."

"I say you did it, Archer," Sandler said stubbornly, "no matter how many speeches you make on the world situation. And I don't want any more speeches from you, either. I listened to one too many and I ought to have my tail booted for it and I've had enough. You did something to me that nobody's ever done in forty years and got away with. You lied to me and you pretended to be loyal and you hid information from me and you played on my sympathies in the most cynical and insidious manner and you're not going to get away with it."

"I didn't lie to you," Archer said, feeling himself grow angry and trying to keep the anger down. "And I didn't hide any information."

Sandler laughed sourly. It was an ugly, menacing sound. "Did you or did you not guarantee to me that a man who had been your friend for fifteen years was not a Communist?"

"I did. But . . ."

Sandler leaned over and picked up a newspaper from the floor. He threw it at Archer. It fluttered loosely, pages falling out and floating to the carpet. "Read that," Sandler said. Archer didn't pick up the paper. "Go ahead," Sandler said hoarsely. "Go ahead and read it. Read about your friend."

"I don't have to read it," Archer said. "I know what's in it."

"Oh," Sandler shouted, "now you say you know what's in it. But you didn't know when you came down to Philadelphia? You didn't know anything about a man you'd practically lived with for fifteen years?"

"I didn't know he was a Communist."

"Do you expect me to believe that?" He waited for Archer to answer him, but Archer didn't say anything. "And now," Sandler went on, his voice calmer now, but cold and incisive, "and now what do you know about him?"

"I know what I heard last night," Archer said.

"Uhuh," Sandler nodded, as though he had suddenly decided to be reasonable. "And I suppose you only know what you heard last night about that Barbante, that writer. Your daughter's friend. I suppose you had no notion that the man who was writing your scripts for four years was an out-and-out atheist."

Archer sighed. "What's that got to do with it?" he asked. "We certainly never attacked religion on our program."

"Never attacked religion on our program." Sandler mimicked him, in falsetto. "That was nice of you. That was very considerate. Listen, Archer. I live in a devout community. I believe in God. I believe in people going to church and fighting to preserve their religion. I'm the president of my synagogue. I'm the chairman of a half-dozen inter-religious charities. I have meetings with priests and rabbis and ministers every week of the year. What do you think they're going to say to me at the next meeting when I get up to address them and they know that I've been paying a man seven hundred dollars a week who's out to destroy them? What do you think the Jew-haters're going to be able to say about that?"

That, too, Archer thought exhaustedly.

"What're you trying to do to me?" Sandler shouted, his voice surprisingly strong and young and malevolent. "What the hell did I ever do to you to put me through this?" Sandler stood up and strode over to Archer and stood over him, almost as though he were on the verge of hitting him. He was breathing hard and his face was flushed now and Archer thought of heart failure and sudden strokes. He looked up at the old man curiously, wondering if he really would try to hit him.

"Aah." Sandler turned away and walked slowly toward Hutt's desk. He seemed tired now, as though he had suddenly realized that he was an old man and that he had been up since five o'clock that morning and that he had already traveled a long distance that day. "What's the sense in talking to you?" He leaned against the desk, facing Archer, with Hutt behind him, immobile, watchful, expressionless. "You're lost, Archer. You're a clumsy, foolish, untrustworthy man and you're going to pay for it now. The program's finished. As of this minute, Hutt."

"Yes, sir," Hutt said.

"We'll advertise in the magazines from now on," Sandler said. "If we have anything left to advertise. How much longer does Archer's contract have to go?"

"Seven weeks," Hutt said promptly.

"Don't pay him," Sandler said. "Let him sue, if he wants to. We'll drag him through every court in the country if that's what he wants. But not a penny."

"Yes, sir," Hutt said. He picked up his blue pencil and stared at it.

"That's all," Sandler said heavily. "I've got to go. I have a date in Philadelphia."

He picked up his coat. Hutt stood up and helped him on with it. Sandler put on his hat carelessly, its brim up all around, giving him a rakish, Western air. He didn't thank Hutt. He looked once more at Archer, puzzled, reflective. Then he walked out slowly, shuffling along the carpet. He didn't close the door behind him and Archer had a glimpse of Miss Walsh outside, smiling sharply at her desk, before O'Neill, who hadn't moved during the entire scene, went over and shut the door.

Hutt sat down behind his desk again, playing with the blue pencil. "Well," he said, "that's that. You heard what he said, Archer."

"I heard."

"Are you going to sue?"

"I'll let you know," Archer said. He knew he wasn't going to sue, but, maliciously, he wanted Hutt to worry about it.

"We'll kill you," Hutt said calmly, twirling the pencil in both his hands. With a gesture of his head he indicated the newspapers on the floor. "Those'll seem like love notes in comparison by the time we get through with you."

"You don't need me anymore, do you, Lloyd?" O'Neill said, starting toward the door. He looked tortured and pent-up, and Archer knew that he didn't want to have to listen anymore. "I have a desk full of work and . . ."

"Stay here, Emmet," Hutt said. "I'd like you to listen to what I have to say to Mr. Archer. It might be instructive."

O'Neill dropped his hand from the doorknob and went back to his station along the wall.

"I warned you," Hutt said to Archer, and there was the flicker of triumph in his voice. "I warned you a long time ago not to fight me. You should have listened to me."

Archer stood up. "I think I'll go now," he said quietly.

"You're finished, Archer," Hutt said, whispering. "I told you you would be and I'm glad to see it happened so soon. It's going to cost me a considerable amount of money, but it's worth it. I don't begrudge a penny of it. Before you leave I'd like to tell you that I had a good deal to do with what happened to you last night."

Archer stopped at the door, puzzled at what Hutt had said. "What do you mean by that?" he asked.

"When you went down to see Mr. Sandler in Philadelphia," Hutt said, "breaking one of the oldest and strictest rules of this organization, I decided it was about time I found out more about you. In self-defense. You've had two detectives investigating you for more than a month, at my own expense, and I must say I feel it was money well spent."

The telephone tap, Archer thought. That's where it came from. Incongruously, he felt a sense of relief. At least it wasn't the Government.

"You miserable sonofabitch," Archer said clearly.

Hutt shrugged and even smiled a little, mechanically, although he flushed. "I ignore that, Archer," he said, "because you're of no importance to me any more. I tried to save you. I gave you a lot of time and I used all the arguments and all the eloquence I was capable of. They weren't wasted, though." He smiled more widely, his wedge-face splitting frostily. "I got them in good order, trying them out on you, and when I had to use them again, they worked charmingly. Frances Motherwell was not quite as deaf to the claims of patriotism and reason as you were and from all reports she put on a very good performance last night, didn't she?"

"I suppose," Archer said, "you're proud of that dirty scene you put her up to last night."

"I told you you can't make me angry, Archer," Hutt said. "This was something that had to be done publicly, without warning, and without giving anyone any chance to wriggle quietly away. For educational purposes. From now on, people who work for me will be very careful about what they say or whom they endorse or how they oppose me. And Frances Motherwell was ripe anyway. She comes of an excellent family. She's fundamentally a decent, honest girl. She was ready to leave her old friends, anyway. She told me herself she was disgusted with them. If you'd had any sense you would have expected something like this. After all, she told you herself that she was a Communist. Did any of the others ever do that? Of course not. She's a straightforward American girl and it was only a question of time before she'd turn away in disgust from the Oriental plotting she saw all around her."

"She's a straightforward psychopath," Archer said, "and she'll probably wind up in a straitjacket, getting the shock treatment three times a year. And I wouldn't be a bit surprised if you'll find yourself keeping her company on the next table."

Hutt chuckled. "I'll tell her that," he said. "I'm having lunch with her this afternoon to celebrate. I expect it to be a very merry lunch. Because we really accomplished something last night. We really hurt you, all you soft-headed orators with your shady friends skulking behind you. All your wild-eyed, filthy immigrant friends whose families haven't been here long enough to learn to speak the language without degrading it, all you misfits and spies and conspirators trying to drag their betters down to their own stinking level." Hutt stood up. His face was very red now and his eyes were almost colorless and raging as he gave up all control over himself. "And don't think I'm stopping here," he whispered. "I'm going to drive everyone of you out of the industry, out of the city, out of the country, if I can. I'm going to tell you something. Three men put up the money to start *Blueprint* and I was one of the three, and I never made a better investment in my whole life. We'll starve you out and we'll raise the country against you, and we'll hound you and defame you and we won't stop until you're all behind bars or swinging from trees, as you ought to be."

Archer sprang across the room and hit him. He only hit him once, because O'Neill grabbed him and held him.

"Stop it, Clem!" O'Neill whispered. "Don't be a Goddamn fool."

Hutt didn't do anything. He didn't fall back. He didn't even put his hand up to his face, which had grown pale, except for the mark high on the cheek where Archer's clumsy blow had landed. It was the first time Archer had hit anybody since he was fifteen years old. He was ashamed of himself for the outburst and dissatisfied that it had been so ineffectual. "Let go," he said thickly to O'Neill. "It's OK."

Cautiously O'Neill released him. Hutt was staring at him, breathing heavily, his eyelids narrowed, as though his mind was racing over the possibility of doing further harm.

"I'll take you out of here," O'Neill said. "Come on."

Archer walked slowly across the room toward the door, stepping on the newspapers that were strewn over the carpet. O'Neill held onto his elbow as they went past the desks, with the pretty, busy girls, the sound of typewriters, the fragrance of perfumes. In O'Neill's office, Archer put on his coat in silence. It was still wet. He and O'Neill refused to look squarely at each other.

"Everything," O'Neill said after a moment, looking down at his shoes, "everything turns out to be a lot dirtier than anybody ever expected, doesn't it?"

Archer didn't answer. There was a mirror on one wall and he went over and looked at his face. It was just his face. There was no sign of what he had gone through. Curiously, he was a little disappointed. He didn't know what he had expected to find, but he felt that something should be different. He shrugged under the wet cloth of his coat.

"Well," he said, "I've got to be going."

"I'll give you a call," O'Neill said. "We'll go out for a drink."

"Sure."

The phone rang and O'Neill picked it up. "O'Neill speaking," he said. He looked at Archer. "It's for you," he said. He handed Archer the phone.

"Hello," Archer said.

"Daddy." It was Jane's voice, and she sounded frightened and hurried. "Is that you, Daddy?"

"Yes, Jane," Archer said. "What's the matter?"

"I'm calling from the corner," Jane said. "The phone in the house doesn't work any more."

"Yes, Jane," Archer said impatiently. "What do you want?"

"You'd better come right home, Daddy," said Jane. "Mother's not feeling very well and she asked me to call you."

"What's the matter?"

"I don't know exactly. She won't tell me. She just said to call you. I think . . ." Jane's voice broke a little and she hesitated. "I think it's started. I think it's labor . . . Gloria's been in there and she says there's some bleeding . . ."

Archer tried to speak, but his mouth was dry and he couldn't seem to get anything out.

"Daddy," Jane said, "are you still there?"

"Listen, Jane," Archer said, wetting his lips and his tongue. "When you hang up there, call the phone company and tell them we want the service connected immediately. Tell them it's an emergency and they have to do it right away. Have you got that?"

"Yes."

"Then call the doctor and tell him to come right down."

"Yes, Daddy."

"When you speak to the doctor ask him if there's anything that you can do before he gets down," Archer sadi. "Then go home and see if you can help your mother . . ."

"Daddy . . ." Jane's voice was hesitant and strange. "Something funny's happening. Mother doesn't want me in the house."

"What?" Archer asked incredulously.

"She's not angry at me or anything," Jane said swiftly. "She just says she doesn't want me around now. For this. She says this is private. Between you and her, she says. It's awfully queer . . ." Archer could tell that Jane was struggling to keep from crying in the telephone booth. "Cathy Rooks invited me up to her place for the weekend and Mother made me promise I'd go. I didn't know what to do. Mother was so—so determined. She said she wanted me out of the house

before you came home. Everything's so upset. What should I do, Daddy?"

Archer sighed. "Darling," he said wearily, "I guess you'd better do whatever your mother wants just now."

"Will you call me?" Jane asked. "Will you let me know when she wants to see me again?"

"Of course."

Jane was frankly crying now, the anguish remote and mechanized over the wire. "Is it my fault, Daddy?" she sobbed. "Is this happening account of me?"

"No," Archer said. "Never think that. Now, listen, baby." He was conscious of O'Neill staring at him, puzzled and apprehensive. "You go home," Archer said into the phone, "and tell Mother I'll be there in fifteen minutes. And tell her . . ." He hesitated. He wanted to give Jane a message that would tide Kitty over the next quarter hour, a word, two words, a sentence that would carry reassurance, love, confidence. Jane waited at the other end of the line, but no words came. "Just tell her," Archer said lamely, "not to worry. I'll be right home."

He hung up. "I've got to get out of here," he said. He started out of the office toward the elevators. O'Neill trailed beside him.

"What's the matter, Clem?" O'Neill asked.

"Kitty. It looks as though labor may have begun already." Archer rang for the elevator.

"Oh, Christ," O'Neill said. "Wait a second. I'll get my coat and go down with you."

"Thanks," Archer said. "It's not necessary. I'll be able to handle it."

O'Neill hesitated. "Will you call me if you need anything?" he asked.

Archer looked gravely at him. Then he said something he was going to regret for a long time. "Just what do you mean by anything?" he asked.

O'Neill took a step back. Then the elevator came and Archer got in and the door slid shut, blotting out O'Neill's baffled, shamed, rejected face.

26

He sat in the ambulance, going uptown. It was dark by now. Kitty had said she was feeling better when Archer got home from O'Neill's office, and the bleeding hadn't been bad until about six o'clock. The doctor, who hadn't been able to come in person, had told Archer over the phone that it probably was only false labor and merely to keep Kitty quiet and give her a couple of sleeping pills. But then the bleeding had begun again, and regular pains, although not too severe and not too closely spaced, and Archer had called for the ambulance and phoned the doctor's office (he was still out) and left word, rather roughly, that they were going to the hospital immediately and that he wanted the doctor to put in an appearance in the next half-hour.

The interior of the ambulance was dim, and Kitty was almost buried under the blankets. The two large, gentle attendants had wrapped her head in a wool scarf, so that only the pale, small glimmer of her face, occasionally reflecting the lights of a shop window, could be seen. Archer remembered a black puppy he had had when he was ten years old. His mother, who was a fanatic on the subject of cleanliness, whether for small boys or small dogs, used to wash the puppy in the tub, then wrap him in towels and old blankets, leaving only his mournful, soap-betrayed muzzle sticking out, and put him on a chair to dry. The puppy, Archer remembered, had had distemper later in the summer and had to be killed.

"Really, Clement," Kitty said, her voice dreamy from the sleeping pills, "we didn't have to go to the hospital. I feel fine. Really I do. And we didn't have to take an ambulance. It's so expensive and there're so many nicer ways of spending the money."

"How do you feel, Kitty?"

"Fine. Honest. A little sleepy, that's all, only I don't want to sleep. Clement . . ."

"Yes?"

"Are we passing red lights?"

"Yes."

"That's nice. I know how you always yearn to pass red lights. You're so impatient." She chuckled. "You always cheat a little, when you're driving. You never *quite* wait for them to change. Did you have dinner?"

"Not yet."

"You can have dinner at the hospital. You can even have a drink. It's a very fancy hospital. I inquired especially. They'll even send up a Martini. Do you feel like a Martini?"

"I think it'd be tempting fate to ask a hospital bartender to make a Martini," Archer said.

Kitty moved under the blankets and she closed her eyes and the lines of pain bit around her mouth. It took nearly a minute; then she was all right again.

"You feel so important riding in an ambulance," she said. "What're the initials they used for big shots in the war?"

"VIP," Archer said. "Very Important Personage."

"VIP Kitty Archer," she murmured. "Passing all the red lights." She was silent for a moment and he thought she was falling asleep again. "Clement," she said.

"Yes?"

"Is it still raining out?"

"No. It's turning cold."

"Did you ever ride in an ambulance before?"

"No."

"VIP. You're not worrying, are you?"

"Of course not."

"There's really no reason to worry. A lot of women go through this in the sixth month. A little bleeding, a few pains. Just a warning to take things easy. You mustn't worry."

"I'm not at all worried."

"I'm going to hold on, you know," Kitty said. "I'm absolutely sure."

"Of course."

"And it's going to be a boy. I've told you that, haven't I?"

"Yes."

"You've always wanted a son. You never said it, but I knew. We'll start a whole new life with a son. Would you like to move to the country? Someplace where there are a lot of fields and he can run around and not worry about traffic or about having his mother watch him all the time? I think it's about time we moved to the country, don't you?"

"Yes," Archer said.

"New York . . ." Kitty's voice almost trailed away. "New York's nice, but it's sort of all used up, isn't it?"

"Kitty, darling, why don't you try to sleep? Then when you wake up you'll . . ."

"What street are we on, Clement?"

Archer looked out the wide, clean window over Kitty's head. "Sixty-seventh street."

"We're going so slow. It's taking so long." There was the grimace of pain again, and the twitching under the blankets. She sighed once, then opened her eyes again. "Look away, Clement," Kitty said. "Please. When that happens."

"I didn't see anything," Archer said.

They rode in silence for awhile. The driver wasn't using the siren now and there was only the muted, careful hum of the tires in the ambulance, and the slight creaking of the jump seat on which Archer was sitting, near Kitty's head.

"You know what would be nice, Clement?"

"What?"

"If Jane would get married and come and live near us. In a house in the country. A nice man that we all could like," Kitty murmured. "And we would have time to get to be friends again. There are so many things I never had time to tell her . . ."

Archer closed his eyes momentarily. Jane had been gone when he got home that morning, and they hadn't mentioned her name all day.

"You don't mind that I sent her away, do you, Clement?" Kitty asked.

"Of course not."

"You understand, don't you?" Kitty pleaded. "This is just between you and me. I—I didn't want us to be—divided—at a time like this. It's—it's more like when we were young, this way, when you took me to the hospital when I had Jane—what kind of car was it we had then?"

"An Essex." Archer said. "A 1928 Essex."

"It worked out so well, then," Kitty said, ramblingly. "It was so easy . . . And there was no family, nobody else, just you and me. For luck. Am I superstitious, darling?"

Archer made himself smile at her. "Yes, dear," he said.

"Just you and me," Kitty said. "The Essex had plaid seat covers. It smelled of apples, because we'd brought home a basket of apples from my mother's place the week before." She looked around her vaguely, her head moving uncertainly in its swathing of wool. "A 1950 ambulance," she said, "going uptown. Oh, I give you so much trouble," she whispered. "So damn much trouble."

"Sssh. Sssh." Archer put out his hand and touched her forehead. It was hot and dry. They rode that way until they reached the hospital.

"The chances are three to one that she'll abort," Dr. Graves was saying judiciously, making Kitty sound like a bomber turning home before reaching the target because of engine failure. Graves and Archer were walking slowly down the corridor after the doctor had examined Kitty. Graves hadn't been able to come for almost two hours, but he had left word to have Kitty given morphine to quiet her. Unfortunately, the morphine had made Kitty vomit again and again, and the pains were coming more and more regularly now and with greater severity. "These things happen, Mr. Archer," Graves said, professionally resigned. "There is always a certain irreducible percentage of cases."

"Why?" Archer asked. He didn't like the plump, self-satisfied man and his complacence about making Kitty an irreducible percentage. "Why does it happen?"

Graves spread his soft, clean, delivery-room hands in an almost religious gesture of wonderment. "The way of Nature," he said devoutly. "The mysterious intention of God."

"If it's all the same to you," Archer said sharply, "I don't like to hear about the mysterious intention of God from doctors. I prefer hearing about the certain remedies of science."

Graves looked at him obliquely, and Archer could almost sense the doctor pigeonholing him in the category of nervous and irascible relatives of the patient who are likely to blame the physician and who have to be treated delicately but with firmness. "Technically," Graves said, his little mustache moving deliberately over the words, "there is no reason why labor should have been premature. Mrs. Archer is fundamentally healthy and normally formed. Of course, she is no longer young . . ." His glance was almost accusing, or as accusing as Dr. Graves, who had a polite and expensive practice and a large office on Park Avenue, would permit it to be. Somehow he made Archer feel as though wanting another child was a bestial and depraved desire for a man his age.

"But one never knows," Graves said. They were standing at the elevator now, and there was just the slightest rumor of polite impatience in Graves's stance, as though there were many children who were delaying being born because he had to stand here and talk to Archer. "The emotional state has a great deal to do with it. Has Mrs. Archer been emotionally disturbed recently?"

Now, what does he expect me to say to that? Archer thought. "Yes," he said.

Graves nodded. "The way I prefer to look at it," he said, well-rehearsed, "is, if it happens, it is probably all for the best. There is an imperfection perhaps, an improper development, an indication of future malfunction, that Nature, in her wisdom, tries to reject. That is not to say," he added hastily, "that we will not do everything in our power to prolong the pregnancy. But if it happens . . ." He shrugged with plump resignation. "Perhaps in the long run it is something to be thankful for."

You be thankful, you scientific, pious old lady, Archer thought. It's not your child, it's not your wife, you don't have to go home with her to the empty house.

"What are the chances," Archer asked, noticing that Graves was inching imperceptibly up to the elevator button, "what are the chances of the child's surviving?"

"If it is born tonight?"

"If it's born tonight."

Graves shook his head. "I don't want to raise your hopes, Mr. Archer. It is my policy to be as candid as possible at all times. This is only the beginning of the sixth month, and it is really little more than an embryo at this stage, and most likely terribly small. Of course, there have been instances, but I would say the chances are a thousand to one. It will not really be viable, Mr. Archer."

The elevator door opened and a tall, blonde girl, whose time was obviously imminent, got out of the elevator with her husband. They were a handsome couple, both of them well dressed, and they were holding hands and smiling. They walked slowly down the corridor, the girl's head proudly thrown back. She walked gracefully on long legs, even though she was very large, and the expression on her face was serene and confident.

That's the way it should be, Archer thought jealously. You should be young and beautiful and be absolutely certain that everything would go neatly, by the calendar, without terror or loss.

"I have to go now," Graves said. "I expect a delivery upstairs very soon. I'll be in the hospital all night." He moved plumply into the elevator, which had been waiting for him, and went off behind the silently closing door, to his place of business on the upper floor.

God, Archer thought, standing there, not wanting to go back to Kitty's room, how did we ever pick this one?

He walked slowly down the corridor, smelling the hospital odors, the flowers, the roses and carnations and medicines, mingling in the dimly lit, severe perspectives of the hall.

Kitty's face above the blanket was flushed and feverish and her eyes were dilated and dark from the morphine and her hair was tangled and drenched with sweat. But she smiled when Archer came into the room, and her voice was clear and cheerful as she asked, "What did old Nature Boy have to say?"

"Everything's fine," Archer said, sitting down in the chair next to the bed. "The chances're very good. You ought to sleep and try to keep quiet," he said.

"I can't sleep." Kitty chuckled. "Isn't it just like me?" she asked. "Allergic to morphine. The one lady in the whole world who can't be doped. Are you ashamed of being married to a freak?"

"That's all right," Archer said, making himself match the mood she was desperately trying to maintain. "As long as we don't tell our friends."

"Friends . . ." Kitty moved her head drowsily from side to side on the creased pillow.

That's one subject we won't talk about, Archer thought grimly. "I've told the office," he said hastily, "to keep trying to get a private night nurse, and they said there's still a chance."

"I don't need a private nurse," Kitty said. "I'm fine. And the floor nurses are awfully nice. Miss Kennedy told me all about the Army, in between throw-up periods. She was a lieutenant in the Army and she was in a hospital on the Riviera. She used to go swimming on the beach at Cannes. I'd love to see her in a French bathing suit." Kitty chuckled again. "She has a face like the Palisades and she's built like a restaurant icebox."

Then the pains came. Kitty turned her face away, arching agonizedly in the bed, the muscles in her throat showing rigid and sharp. She moaned softly and Archer held her hand and she clutched it hard, her nails biting into his skin. Then it was over and she settled back, spent, into the pillow, her body slowly relaxing into the bed.

"It's going to be all right," she said, looking straight up at the ceiling. "I promise you. I solemnly promise you. I'm going to hold on. I only have one thing in the whole world that I have to do now and that's hold on. All I have to do is concentrate and I'm going to do it. I promise."

In a strange way, Archer realized, Kitty was welcoming the pain, welcoming the problem and the challenge, because, for the time being, at least, it blotted out the necessity of thinking about or resolving all the other things. With a shock he understood that he was welcoming it, immersing himself in it, for the same reasons.

Kitty moved in the bed, making herself more comfortable as her strength returned once more. "Clement," she said, "did you call Jane? And tell her I was all right?"

"Yes," said Archer.

"She's really a very nice girl, isn't she, Clement?" Kitty said, pleading.

"Yes," Archer said.

Then Kitty screamed. She put her hands over her head and gripped the narrow pipes of the bedstead and screamed wildly and continuously and Archer knew that it had started and that there was no going back now.

He rang for the nurse and went to the door and threw it open. Kitty's scream reverberated down the empty corridor. Archer expected to see people come running out of the doors at the noise, but nothing happened. No door opened. Patients and visitors remained privately enclosed, thinking, Of course. That is what you expect to hear in a hospital. Then Miss Kennedy turned a corner far down the hall and walked swiftly and bulkily on her silent white shoes toward the scream.

"It's beginning," Archer said, and Miss Kennedy nodded and went in, closing the door, leaving Archer outside. The scream died down. A moment later a large, pudgy intern came down the hall, almost trotting, his stethoscope swinging around his neck. Without speaking to Archer he went into the room. Five minutes later an attendant appeared, pushing a rolling stretcher, moving deliberately. Right behind him came Dr. Graves, with his coat off and his sleeves rolled back. They went in together with the stretcher, leaving the door open, and Archer watched Miss Kennedy and the intern pick up Kitty and place her on the stretcher. Archer went into the room as they were wrapping the blankets around Kitty.

"Doctor," he said to Graves, who was standing to one side, looking down calmly at Kitty's sweating red face. "Doctor, is there an incubator ready?"

"What?"

"I said is there an incubator ready?"

"Oh." Graves turned to Archer. "I told you there wasn't one chance in a thousand . . ."

The intern looked up sharply. Archer was surprised at the hatred that showed in his face. He ripped the telephone off its base. "Give me the premature nursery," he said. He was from Georgia, and he said, "premachuah nursera." "Hello," he said, "this is Dr. Fredericks. We're taking a patient up to the delivery room right now. I want a Davidson incubator up there immediately, all ready." He put the phone down and stared with loathing at Graves for a moment. Graves seemed flustered and started out of the room. "I have to get prepared," he said.

Graves led the procession down the hall, the stretcher rolling silently with Miss Kennedy and the intern pushing it and Archer walking by its side. Kitty turned her head to look at Archer. "I can't," she whispered. "I just can't this time, darling. Forgive me. Please forgive me."

"Sssh, Kitty. Don't worry," Archer said. For the first time it occurred to him that Kitty might die.

She only screamed once more before they got into the elevator.

Upstairs, they rolled the stretcher swiftly to the delivery-room door. They tried to get it through, but the stretcher was too wide. It bumped against the door frame and Kitty moaned.

"God damn it," the intern said savagely to the attendant. "Where did you get this one?"

"I just picked the first one that was handy," the attendant said aggrievedly. "How was I supposed to know it wouldn't . . ."

"Jeepers," Kitty said, and even her voice sounded childish and small. "Jeepers, this is awful." Then her voice changed and was hoarse and angry. "Christ," she said, "what's taking so long?"

"We'll have to wait, Mrs. Archer," Dr. Graves said, "until we get another stretcher downstairs and . . ."

"Christ," Kitty said, trying to sit up, "the hell with a stretcher. I'll walk in."

"We'll do better than that," the intern said. "I'll carry you in."

"I think," Dr. Graves said formally, "that it would be wiser to . . ."

"You," the intern said to Graves. "You get in there and get ready."

Graves looked as though he was going to protest. Then, with dignity, he went into the delivery room.

"Mrs. Archer . . ." The intern bent over Kitty, his voice very soft and Southern. "Do you trust me to pick you up and carry you in my arms?"

Kitty nodded. The intern threw back the blankets and put his arms under Kitty's head and thighs. Watching him, Archer felt helpless and in the way. The intern straightened up easily, picking Kitty up as though she were weightless. Miss Kennedy held the door open and he started in. Archer started to follow him.

The intern stopped, holding Kitty high in his arms. "This is as far as you go," he said harshly to Archer. "You stay out of here."

He went through the doorway. There was a bright light beyond. Kitty's eyes over his shoulder were frightened and pleading as she looked at Archer. Suddenly she smiled. She raised her hand and blew a kiss. Archer remembered to smile back. He felt proud of Kitty and he wanted to cry. Then Miss Kennedy let the door swing shut and Archer was alone in the hall with the attendant. The attendant piled the blankets on the stretcher and rolled it down the hall toward the elevator. After a moment, Archer followed him. His mind was blank. All he could think of was, That fat Georgia boy is going to be a first-rate doctor some day.

Kitty didn't come down for a long time and Archer sat in her room, trying to read a newspaper, listening to the dying sounds of the hospital as the visitors left and the patients settled down for the night. There was an account of a basketball game that had been played the night before and Archer read it four times. A man named Klipstein, who was six feet, eight inches tall had scored thirty-nine points. Everything is changing, Archer thought. When I went to school nobody was six feet, eight inches tall and nobody ever scored thirty-nine points. There was an article about the H bomb, too, and Archer read that very carefully, too, although not as carefully as he had read about Mr. Klipstein. The author of the article disclosed that actually the H bomb would cause only ten times the destruction of the A bomb, and would be very expensive to produce and might turn out to be uneconomic, as there were very few targets big enough to make it worthwhile. The author sounded vaguely regretful about that and as though he blamed the Russians for not being enterprising enough to build adequate targets for the Air Force. He also said it was a triumph of American science.

American science wasn't being so triumphant upstairs, though, Archer thought. They could extract explosives of godlike violence from the elements of the air, but they couldn't manage to secure a child in its mother's womb for just the twenty days more that would mean the difference between life and death. Archer went back and read about Mr. Klipstein again and wondered how tall Mr. Klipstein had been at birth.

The door opened and a little woman in a gray hospital uniform came in with a box of flowers.

"Mrs. Archer?" she asked uncertainly.

"She's not here at the moment," Archer said, conscious of the fact that it sounded foolishly ordinary and polite, as though Kitty had just stepped out to mail a letter or get her hair washed.

"These flowers just came," the woman said. She had a piping, childlike voice and she was very frail in the bleak cotton smock, and she looked as though she had never been able to get past being sixteen years old, although her hair was graying and her hands were rough with work. "Do you want me to put them in a vase?"

"Thank you," Archer said.

He watched her as she got a vase from the bathroom and started putting the flowers in. They were roses, intensely red, on long stems, not quite open. Archer looked at the card. "When you need me," the card said. "O'Neill."

Archer put the card in his pocket.

"Ah," the little woman said, "aren't they beautiful? They remind me of the day I got married." She spread the flowers with fluttery little aimless movements of her small, worn hands. "I wore flowers that color." She looked at Archer brightly and vacantly. "My parents didn't want me to get married," she said. "But I said, I will elope, and they had to give their permission. I wore a maroon taffeta dress, with flowers like that . . ." She waved toward the roses. "To my wedidng. I did not wear a veil. It was a spring wedding. It was the most beautiful dress I ever had."

"How long have you been married?" Archer asked.

"Twelve years," the woman said dreamily, "but I remember every detail."

"What does your husband do?"

The woman moved her head in a regretful little nod. "Nothing much," she said. Her voice was flat now, without the color that it had when she spoke about her wedding. "He was wounded seven times and he just got out of the veterans' hospital. He thinks he is going to get a job. Wounded seven times. If I was him, I'd just quit, but he thinks he's going to get a job." She stepped back and looked at the roses again. "Ah, what beautiful flowers," she said, her voice sounding like the wedding again. She peered around the room. "Are there any dirty dishes?" she asked.

"No," Archer said.

"Good night," she said, and she shuffled out.

The fragrance of the roses was very heavy in the small room, oppressively sweet. Archer sat there staring at them, trying not to think of what was happening upstairs. Again he thought of the possibility that Kitty might die. How many women died in childbirth? You were always reading the statistics somewhere and you always forgot them. Was it one out of a hundred? Out of a thousand. Ten thousand? You knew other statistics. You knew that a certain basketball player was six feet, eight inches tall, you knew that the H bomb would devastate an area exactly ten times the diameter of the area that an A bomb would level, but vital information, like what chance your wife had to live or die, you forgot.

Without emotion, he thought of what it would be like to live without Kitty. Even if you could pay the rent, which was unlikely, you wouldn't stay in the big house, rattling around in all those rooms, thinking of the woman who had belonged to you who had lived there and who had gone from you. You would take a room somewhere and you would eat in restaurants most of the time and you wouldn't have that feeling of irritation at the beginning of each month when the bills came in and you saw how much your wife spent on clothes and furniture. You would probably have a certain small vogue as an available extra man at dinner parties, because you were acceptable-looking and didn't talk badly, and some of the women you knew would try to get you married off to their friends, and you could sleep with anyone you wanted and were good enough to get. Examining himself, Archer realized that he had felt a little tingle of excitement at the thought. I should be disgusted with myself, he thought. At a time like this.

"She can't die," he said aloud. "She won't die."

You would look younger and feel older, as men without wives did, and you would invent reasons for not going home at night for just one more hour, and you would remember Kitty when she was nineteen and beautiful and you would keep remembering the day you got married and the night Jane was born, and all the bad times would be forgotten and all the good times blurred and rolled together, so that Kitty would always seem young and gay and full of laughter, and you would have a tendency to weep on holidays and wonder where your life had gone to.

He couldn't sit in the small, over-fragrant room any more, staring at the neatly made bed that was waiting for his wife. He got up and went out into the corridor. He looked at his watch. It wasn't midnight yet, and it seemed to him that he had been in the hospital all his life.

He walked down the dark corridor toward the spot of light near the elevator where a nurse sat at a desk, making notations on charts. She looked up and smiled at him and he managed a smile in return. Above her head little green lights winked on and off mysteriously. The nurse paid no attention to the lights.

There was a little waiting room with two stiff couches across from the elevator, and Archer went in there and sat down. He put out the light and sat in the darkness, rubbing his eyes.

The telephone rang on the nurse's desk, and he heard her say, "Yes, Doctor, he's here. Yes, I'll tell him." Then the nurse came into the dark room and said, tentatively, "Mr. Archer . . ."

"Yes?" Archer reached over and switched on the light. The nurse was young and pretty, with a soft red mouth, and she had a vulnerable, gentle way of smiling that didn't fit with her cap and uniform.

"That was Dr. Graves on the phone," she said. "Mrs. Archer has just given birth. To a little boy. She's fine, the doctor said."

"How's the child?" Archer said, thinking, A boy. Kitty kept saying it was going to be a boy.

"He didn't say anything about the child," the nurse said softly. "He's coming right down. He said he'll tell you himself."

"Thanks," Archer said. "Thanks very much." He was conscious that he must look unkempt, in the same clothes that he'd been wearing for two days, and that he needed a shave and that his face must be sagging and old-looking after the long, hideous day. He wondered what this pretty young girl must think about men, after seeing them in this place in the hours of the night, torn and dishonored by pain or shabby anxiety. Could she go out gaily with them, dance, laugh at their jokes, touch their bodies tenderly in lovemaking with the memories of all the nights in the dark, anguished corridor constantly with her? Some day, he thought, I must talk to a nurse.

"Can I get you anything?" she was saying. "A glass of milk? A cup of coffee?"

"Thank you," Archer said. "Not at the moment."

She went back to her desk and Archer stood brushing his clothes, arranging a stolid front to present to Graves.

Graves had his business suit on when he got off the elevator. He looked fresh and executive-like. First he shook Archer's hand, looking at him soberly.

"Well?" Archer asked.

"Mrs. Archer is fine. She'll be down in a half hour or so. We used a spinal and she's conscious. She's a little tired, of course, but she came through splendidly. Splendidly," he repeated. "She had a very easy time," he said. He sounded as if he were congratulating himself.

"And the child?" Archer asked.

Graves shook his head. Archer decided he didn't like the way Graves shook his head. It was practiced, and denoted restrained, rehearsed, quiet, gentlemanly regret, like the performance of an actor who has been on the stage a long time and has studied his craft conscientiously but who is fundamentally without talent. You knew what he was driving at, but you didn't believe him. "The child is very small," Graves said. "As I predicted."

"Is he alive?"

"As of this moment," Graves said. "Yes. We didn't weigh him, we put him into the incubator immediately, but I doubt if he weighs as much as two pounds. He's breathing, but that's about all just now. I wouldn't raise our hopes too high."

"Did Mrs. Archer see him?"

"I don't think so," Graves said. "At the moment of delivery we gave her some gas. Just enough to put her out for a minute or two. Do you want to see the child?"

"No." It was spoken before he thought about it. He felt confused and hurt and he knew he didn't want to expose himself to any more pain that night.

"I think you ought to go up and take a look," Graves said, surprisingly insistent. "You'll feel better about it later. No matter what happens. Take my word for it, Mr. Archer."

"All right." Archer started out of the room. There were tears in his eyes and he didn't want the doctor to see them.

They went up to the top floor in the elevator without speaking. In the premature nursery, there were two incubators. A fat old white-haired nurse was seated between them, looking in through the plastic sides.

"Mrs. Grogan," Dr. Graves said, "this is the father of the Archer baby."

Mrs. Grogan smiled. She had no teeth and her mouth collapsed around her gums. "Here he is," she said, with a brogue. "The poor wee thing."

Archer looked down. It was small and crumpled and scarlet and the clamp on the umbilical cord looked cruelly surgical. Archer flushed. For a queer moment, standing there before these two strangers, he knew he felt ashamed, responsible for the struggling, freakishly tiny, inadequate creature in the plastic box, living on oxygen.

"He's perfectly formed," Mrs. Grogan said, "in every detail."

"He's breathing, though." Archer looked for a moment more, then stepped back.

"He's breathing now," Mrs. Grogan said. She shook her head. "But I'm fearful it's going to be too much for the poor lad. He's sorrowfully small, you know."

"Yes." Archer looked at the other incubator. There was a little girl there who looked gigantic and powerfully alive compared to his son. "How about that one?"

"Oh, that one," Mrs. Grogan said gaily. "That one will be ready for the world in no time. She's a darling."

"She had four weeks more," Graves said, "four very important weeks."

Four weeks, Archer thought.

"Of course," Mrs. Grogan said, "I've seen them this size before and they've lived to marry and raise a family. But it's a miracle when it happens. But at least you've had the pleasure of seeing him alive. You'll be thankful in days to come."

Archer turned and went out of the room. The corridor seemed very cold after the moist warmth of the nursery. Graves came out and said, "They've probably got Mrs. Archer back in her room by now."

Archer nodded and walked back to the elevator.

Miss Kennedy was in the room with Kitty when Archer got there. The nurse was making last little arrangements, filling the vacuum jug with fresh water and putting it on the bedside table and placing the electric plug with the call-button on it near Kitty's head, beside the pillow. The room was quiet, lit by the light of one lamp, with only a cold whisper of wind coming in through the slightly raised window, and Miss Kennedy moved in accurate silence about her tasks and greeted Archer only with a little nod when he came in. Kitty was lying still, stretched out, her head thrown back on the flat pillow and her eyes closed and Archer thought that she was asleep. But she turned her head and opened her eyes when she heard Archer's step. Archer went over and stared down at her. Kitty looked queerly young, childish and exhausted, and Archer remembered photographs he had seen during the war of boys who had just come out after many days of combat. Kitty had been where he could never go and she had fought a battle he could never fight. He sank to the bed and put his arms around her, clutching her tightly. Kitty's arms went around him and he could feel her silent tears against his cheeks and he began to weep.

Miss Kennedy went softly out of the room, closing the door behind her.

"Clement . . ." Kitty whispered, holding him. "Clement."

For Kitty's sake, Archer struggled to stop crying.

"It's all right," he said senselessly. "It's all right."

"I couldn't do it," Kitty wept. "I tried so hard. I swear I did. But I just couldn't do it. I let you down."

"You mustn't say that."

"I did. The one last thing you wanted from me. The one thing you depended on me for."

"Kitty, please, don't talk like that." He held her closer, trying to smother her self-accusation.

"I've been so bad, so selfish." Kitty wrenched her head away and whispered into the pillow. "And I've been punished. Only you've been punished, too."

"Nobody's been punished, darling. You mustn't think that. It's an accident, that's all."

"It's not an accident. It's a judgment . . ."

"Kitty . . ." Archer rocked her in his tight arms, not wanting to hear any of this.

"A judgment because I've been a useless wife. These last months, when they've been torturing you so—I didn't help. I made it worse. I joined them, I tortured you, too. I was frivolous and I was mean and I only thought about myself. All those things I said about you and Vic and Nancy. How could I say them? How can you bear to live with me any more?"

She took her arms away from Archer's shoulders and let them fall limp behind her head. Archer lowered her gently onto the pillow and stood up. He turned away and wiped his eyes. Kitty had never seen him cry before and he felt embarrassed, as though he had exposed a shameful secret about himself that he had cunningly hidden for twenty years.

"What's happened to me?" Kitty whispered, staring up at the ceiling. "How did I get so bad? I used to be so proud of myself, I used to think I was so strong, I used to think I was a protection for you, that I paid my way, that we had a real marriage, you and I . . ."

Archer put his handkerchief away. He stopped crying suddenly. His nose felt as though he had a cold. "We do have a real marriage," he said. He sat down in the chair beside the bed and rested his hand under Kitty's head, low down, feeling the damp hair and the warm, firm skin on the back of her neck. "You mustn't ever think anything else."

"And the way I fought you," Kitty went on, disregarding his attempt to comfort her. "When you were in the worst trouble of your life. When you had to act the way you did, because that's the sort of man you are and that's why I love you. And I yelled at you like the worst kind of money-loving, comfort-loving bitch . . ."

"Kitty . . ." Archer pleaded. "Not tonight. Wait . . ."

"And I was so wrong about Jane," Kitty went on inexorably. "I was so offhand and modern and superior. I was too lazy to see what was happening, I was too busy making myself comfortable, I didn't want to bother . . . I let her slide away. I let her hurt herself and get beaten and shamed . . ."

"You're being too harsh with yourself," Archer said, believing that what he was saying was half true. "It's only because you're exhausted and you've been through so much tonight."

"No good as a mother," Kitty whispered. "No good as a wife. All the time I was up there in that room, waiting, I kept thinking of what I said a month ago . . . I said, 'I hope he comes out in seven months, I'm getting so tired of carrying him around.' Do you remember?"

"You never said anything like that," Archer said, although he remembered when she had said it and remembered the slight superstitious twinge of fear he had felt when he'd heard it.

"Oh, yes, I did," Kitty said. Her voice turned into a flat sing-song. "I said it and you remember it, because I remember the look in your eye when I did. Well, I got my wish. Better than my wish. I was tired, I said. I was annoyed at the inconvenience. Oh, God, what sort of woman am I?"

"Look," Archer said, "we're going to forget everything you said and everything I said and all the mistakes we've made and all the chances we've muffed. And we're going to start over again . . ."

"I'm not going to forget anything," Kitty said. "And neither are you. Why don't you leave me? I'm no good for you, nobody'll blame you if you just put on your hat and coat and go right now."

"Kitty, darling," Archer said desperately, "I'm going to call Miss Kennedy and tell her to give you some dope and let you sleep for awhile."

"You can't call Miss Kennedy," Kitty said in the toneless singsong. "She's gone off duty. She's going to church. Clement . . ." Kitty's face was distorted with grief. "Clement, she said she was going to pray for our son."

He put his arms around her again, letting her weep, kissing her cheek. She cried for a long time before she grew quiet and then she was very sleepy and she said in a small, but clear and surprisingly calm voice, "I'm all right now, darling. Why don't you go out and get some air and a drink and something to eat?"

Then she fell asleep.

Archer stood up. He felt broken and unsteady and it was hard for him to believe that he had ever slept in his whole life. Kitty's mouth was open, and she was snoring softly, the sound hoarse and domestic in the strange, cold room. As he watched his wife sleep, he wondered how much of what she had said was true, how much of what had happened to them was really a judgment. But on whom, he thought, who has been judged?

He took his hat and coat off the rack carefully and went silently out of the room, closing the door gently on the soft, defeated, snoring noise within. As he walked down the dark corridor, surrounded by the convalescing, the delivered, the doubtful, the dying, he remembered that Kitty hadn't asked him whether he had seen their son, whether he was dead or alive.

The night was cold and Archer put up the collar of his coat as he walked down the empty street toward the river. A drink would have been good, but he didn't want to see people, he didn't want to hear saloon laughter or jukebox music.

The river slid past blackly, looking wintry and dangerous, and there were only occasional cars rushing home in a quick flare of headlights along the highway. Downstream, bulking out of the night, punctuated by weak, irregular patterns of light, were the islands on which were the hospitals and the prisons. Upriver were the swinging, mathematically spaced lights of the great bridge, unsubstantial in the darkness. There was no moon, but the stars were bright and frosty in the cold darkness of the sky.

The biting air was insistent against Archer's face, waking him up, but making him feel a little lightheaded, as he stared out over the water and smelled the brackish tidal salt of the river.

I should go to sleep, he thought. Tomorrow's another day. Not correct. It was past midnight. Today's another day. He turned around and looked at the hospital behind him. It was almost completely dark. Only here and there a light shone, people refusing to die in the dark, nurses having coffee, doctors probing pain with experienced fingers, saying, This will wait till morning. And in a room high up on top of the building, Mrs. Grogan, without teeth, watching the two incubators, waiting placidly, because it was her job and that's how she earned her ten dollars a day and bought her tea and her chop and her cotton stockings, waiting placidly, as she had done how many times before in her cheerful, kind-hearted way, for a small, inadequate, hurried heart to stop beating. All sorts of strange jobs in the world and all sorts of ordinary people to fill them. Mrs. Grogan, keeping an eye on the oxygen gauge, comfortably sucking her toothless gums, on the death watch for infants. Thinking what, under her thin gray hair? *You're well out of it, lad, and don't let anyone tell you different. Listen to an old lady who's been through it all. There's nothing to it, lad, only disappointment and leavetakings, and people telling you one thing and meaning another, and fight, fight, fight all the long days of your life. You're not missing much, lad, and that's a fact. And from what I read in the papers, we're all to be blown up any day now, in one thorough explosion, and left to rot in the rubble with our bones turning to water and our blood thinning to acid and giving off signals like a radio station and the signals always saying the same thing, good-bye, good-bye. And here you are dying comfortably in a nice warm box, and not old enough to regret any of it, and there'll be many on that day who'll envy you tonight.*

Archer turned his back on the hospital. Down the

river, on the Queens side, among the factory-stacks, an
enormous sign wrote a message across the sky in electric
red letters. PEPSI-COLA. Look past the borders of
the city at death-time, look for comfort and omens, and
see the cryptic, shining words of the oracle, steadfast
in mists and storms, saying PEPSI-COLA.

Archer stared out across the river, conscious of the
cold and the silence and emptiness of the streets around
him, and it made him remember that other night, such a
short time ago, when he and Vic had walked side by
side along Madison Avenue after the program was over
and they were both feeling good, and the night was
promising, and the evening's first drink was waiting for
them in the warm bar.

Where had that feeling gone? What had happened to
that promise? That night he had chuckled at Pokorny
because he was so comically over-serious, and how
comic was Pokorny tonight? And he had kissed Alice
Weller and congratulated her and assured her she would
work again, and on what grounds could he congratulate
her now? And he had criticized Barbante for using too
much perfume and had joked about his passion for
women, and where was the joke now and was he expected to laugh at it tonight? He had been annoyed with
Atlas because Atlas was independent and scornful and
only Atlas had really survived. And Atlas had survived
because he was suspicious and despairing from the beginning and had built a defense for himself out of a
protective combination of shrewdness and loathing.
Perhaps there were lessons to be learned from Atlas,
but who could learn them?

And Vic . . . Fifteen years. The lanky student with
the black eye and the bruised nose and the pretty girl in
the summery classroom. The ferocious boy on the football field, playing with that curious mixture of violence
and disinterest, disdainful of the praise or friendship
of his fellows, coldly unmoved by the pleas of the coach
or the dislike of his classmates, making his own rules

as he went along, arrogantly, confidently, not taking anybody else's advice or, at least when he was young, serving anyone else's system of values. The gay, inventive, useful, inevitably successful man. *You're not satisfied just to adore,* Kitty said. *You have to be like your hero. You ape him, the way he talks, the way he walks, the way he wears his hat. I don't have my own husband any more. I have a carbon copy of another man, and I'm disgusted with it. And now, here's your final great chance. The final identification. You can suffer for his sins. How could I expect you to pass up an opportunity like that?*

Fifteen years. Ending in an overheated banquet room in a fancy hotel with a cleverly dressed, beautiful, neurotic girl making this year's confession of sin and turning this year's version of state's evidence. Ending in the embrace under the lamppost, and the tears, and Nancy's voice saying, *Forget him. Write him off. Wipe us all out. Please.*

Very early, Hutt had warned him. *Nobody can stand investigation. Nobody,* Hutt had said. *If you think you can you must have led your life in deep freeze for the last twenty years.* Well, he hadn't listened, and the investigation had taken place, and it had turned out that Hutt had been right. His life hadn't been led in deep freeze, and bit by bit it had been shattered. He was defamed and jobless. His wife had lost his son, who might be dying at this moment in the dark building behind him. She had also lost her own respect for herself, because she had proved jealous and ordinary at the climactic moment of their time together and both she and Archer knew that however good their life together might be from now on, it would be a patched life and not whole and complete as it had been before. As for Vic . . . Investigation had proved him a liar and a betrayer of trust, and there went another fifteen years.

If he had done what he wanted to do that day in Hutt's office, Archer thought, if he had resigned immediately, none of this would have happened. He'd be out of work, but he was out of work now, and he would still have a complete wife, a friend. His wife would still have been frail and undependable, his friend untrue— but he wouldn't know about it. He was forty-five—the necessary illusions might very possibly have stood up the twenty or twenty-five years more that he had to live. Perhaps he had known all this subconsciously and the immediate, almost instinctive gesture of resignation had been a reflex, not so much of courage and loyalty as a panicky and disguised attempt at self-preservation. Perhaps he had known, deep down, that he was surrounded by people who were not what they seemed, that he was committed to loyalties and concepts that could not bear investigation, that the structure of the world he had built for himself had depended equivocally on his own naïveté and that when that naïveté was destroyed by fact, the structure on which he rested would be shattered along with it.

Perhaps, Hutt had said, *perhaps we have to resign ourselves to an unhappy fact. Perhaps we live in a time in which there are no correct solutions to any problem. Perhaps every act we make must turn out to be wrong.* You couldn't afford to believe this—but could you afford not to believe it?

And Barbante had taken it another step. *You can die on your feet, or you can die on your knees,* Barbante had said, drunk and desolate in Hutt's office. Surprisingly, thinking of it now, Archer felt that there was more hope in Barbante's formulation. At least it included the notion of moral choice and hidden in it there was a conception of dignity and the possibility of right through tragic action that was missing from Hutt's program. The only trouble was that it was an action that had to be performed in the dark, in a twisting, deceptive, obscure medium, with the horizon, in momentary glimpses, always at a different and surprising angle. There is an activity in which I can profitably engage myself in the next twenty years, Archer thought with a queer sense of triumph at having reached this far. I can devote myself to discovering at every moment just how vertical I am. I can commit myself to the single task of keeping my knees from touching the ground.

He felt cold now. The wind was stronger and bit at his face and his hands were stiff in his pockets. He turned and walked away from the river toward the hospital. He looked up at the top floor and wondered numbly and without emotion if his son was still alive. He thought of the warm, moist room and the shapeless old lady between the plastic boxes, and the struggling, desperate, overreached heart. Curiously, he put his hand under his coat and through his shirt to the skin of his chest. His hand was cold on the skin, but under it his own heart beat steadily and prosaically. If only there were some way, he thought, to give a fraction of this strength, a share of this reliable, unthinking movement, to the crumpled small form on the top floor. If only there were some way to subtract a day of his own heart's beating, a month, and add it to his son's. If Graves would work on something like that, he thought grimly, instead of resigning so gracefully to the mysterious intentions of God . . .

Archer took his hand out from under his coat and walked slowly up the hospital steps. Most of the lights had been put out in the downstairs hall and at first Archer didn't see the man who was slumped in a chair in a corner. But then the man stood up and started toward Archer and came under a light and Archer saw that it was Vic.

Archer stopped, waiting. Vic came over slowly, shambling, walking in a way that Archer hadn't seen before. He had a queer, diagonal small grin on his mouth and it looked as though it had been set there a long time.

"Hi," Vic said, stopping a few feet away.

"Hello, Vic," Archer said. He didn't offer to shake hands.

"How is it?" Vic asked.

"Kitty's OK," Archer said, wondering what OK meant. "The kid is still alive. Or he was still alive the last time I asked."

Vic nodded soberly. "I hope . . ." he began. Then he stopped, self-consciously. He looked very tired and he kept his coat collar turned up, as though he was cold, even in the warm hallway. "Give my love to Kitty," he said.

"I will."

"I don't suppose she'd want to see me."

"I don't suppose she would," Archer said.

Vic nodded again. "I wanted to tell you something," he said. "Something that's probably been puzzling you." He waited, but Archer didn't speak. "About that petition," Vic said. "The one you were supposed to have signed."

Archer tried to remember. He knew there was something about a petition that had seemed important at one time, but it was so long ago, an dso many things had happened since then, and whatever it was, it no longer was even important enough to remember.

"The one Frances Motherwell spoke about at the meeting," Vic explained patiently.

"Oh, yes," Archer said.

"You never signed that," said Vic.

"I know."

"I did," Vic said. "I forged your name."

"OK," Archer said disinterestedly. He wanted to get upstairs and ask about the child.

"We needed a certain number," Vic said, "and it was beginning to get awfully hard to dig up names."

"OK."

"If you want," Vic said, "if you think it will help, I'll announce it. I'll send a note to the papers saying it was me all along."

"Forget it," Archer said. He felt uncomfortable and he realized that what he was uncomfortable about was seeing Vic standing there so strangely contrite and beaten. It wasn't like Vic and he didn't want to see it.

"Nancy told me she gave you the gory details about me," Vic said. "You know the worst."

"Yes."

"In case you're interested," Vic said, still with that queer, slit grin, "I'm not ashamed of any of it."

"OK," Archer said. "You're not ashamed."

"I'm only sorry about one thing."

"What's that?"

"I behaved like a fool about Frances Motherwell."

"I imagine you did."

"Not the way you think." Vic chuckled softly. "Not politically. Sexually. Learned a lesson. Sex is politics, too. Just like economics, art, war. I underestimated the role of the bedroom in the advance of the Revolution. The lady took a liking to me. Four years ago. Always be careful when one of those girls with eyes that pop just a little out of their head begin to yearn over you. First I pretended I was too modest to understand what she was hinting. Then she stopped hinting. Did you know there's a whole new breed of woman loose in America, who drink four Martinis and go up to a man at a party and say, 'I'm going to make a pass at you'?" Herres shook his head ruefully. "Result of advanced higher education for girls; the progressive feminization of the male sex brought about by luxurious living; the alarming increase in homosexuality among artists and college graduates . . . I don't know. I behaved in an urbane manner," Herres said, laughing a little. "Or as urbane as I could be in a situation like that. I explained I had a pathologic addiction to monogamy. I pretended that I was flattered and that perhaps some other time, if I ever got into trouble with my wife . . . I tried to turn the talk to nobler topics like the drama and the organization of sharecroppers in Tennessee and she'd just laugh, that wild, curdled laugh of hers, and tell me she'd get me in due time. I got to hate the sight of her, but I had to pretend I thought she was fine, and of course in the Party I couldn't let feelings like that influence me. Then recently she took to writing me the most obscene and specific invitations and calling me up in the middle of night, dead drunk, crying and using words over the phone that you'd be embarrassed to hear in a Marseilles whorehouse. Finally, I made the big blunder. I gave it to her. I told her what I thought of her. Big mistake to do with any woman. But with someone like Motherwell, whom you have to depend on—fatal." He shrugged. "I told her I didn't like promiscuous women." He grinned. "That isn't even absolutely true. There're some promiscuous women I like very much. Salt of the earth. Merry, useful citizens, easing the burden of being alive in an intolerable civilization. But I didn't like her. I told her to climb up out of the gutter. I told her she ought to go to an analyst. I told her she ought to get married and have five kids. I told her she disgusted me. For the first time in many years, I indulged myself in an emotional attitude. And I'm paying for it. The wages of virtue," Vic said, smiling queerly, "is death. Beware of the puritan within. I made the virgin's error—I overestimated the value of chastity and the lady got up in meeting and paid me off in another coin. If I'd been a little more realistic I'd've visited that little chocolate-colored apartment a couple of afternoons a month and put a blindfold on and screwed like a patriot for the International. And Frances Motherwell would still be a silent, satisfied worker for the Cause. Oh, I forget," Vic said, his eyes amused, though his voice was sober. "You don't like me to use language like that."

"All right," Archer said. "Now I have the full and glorious history of Frances Motherwell, who doesn't interest me very much any more. Now, how about you and me?"

"What about you and me?"

"The stuff to Roberts," Archer said. "The lie before I went to Philadelphia. The attack on me at the meeting. You helped plan that, too, didn't you?"

"Yes," Vic said. He looked vaguely around him at the dim hospital lobby, with the low gleam of subdued lights cold off the marble walls. "There was nothing personal in that."

"Oh, God," said Archer. "Nothing personal."

"No," Vic said. "There was a certain situation that had to be handled. A particular tactic was called for. In a war, when a commander has to expose certain elements of his troops to being cut off and decimated, or allow some civilians who happen to be on the ground to be hurt, that doesn't mean that it's a personal transaction between him and them. It was just bad luck. You were exposed and in the line of fire and you had to get hit. That's all."

"That's all," Archer said. "Just as a point of interest —nobody told me it was a war."

"Read the papers, brother," Vic said softly. "The communiqués are on every page."

"I'm a funny man," Archer said ignoring Vic. "I believe that whatever two human beings do to each other, and certainly whatever two people who are friends do to each other, is personal."

"You're a funny man," Vic said gravely. "You said so yourself."

"And if anybody believes in something that prevents him from treating me personally, and that means taking into account the necessity of telling me the truth, the necessity of behaving honorably," Archer said, "I can't accept him as my friend. I don't want to see him any more. Ever."

"Honorable," Vic said. "Slippery word. Subject to a variety of interpretations."

"I don't think so."

"Time changes a word like that," Vic said. "Geography. Law. Ultimate aims. The weather. Everything. It's like love. You get into bed with an eighteen-year-old girl in Connecticut and it's love. You do the same thing in California and it's statutory rape." He grinned. "You start a revolution in America in 1776 and you happen to win, so you're an honorable fellow. Father, I chopped down the cherry tree, oh, what a bright boy am I. Talk about the same thing in 1950 and hanging's too good for you. You think I betrayed you, don't you?"

"Yes," said Archer.

"Another word. Betrayal. Treason. In a more general sense you think I'm a traitor, too, don't you? Or at least potentially?"

"Yes," Archer said slowly. "I do. Nancy told me that when that man was arrested for giving away atomic secrets to the Russians, you said you'd do the same thing if you had the chance."

"Nancy talks too much," Vic said harshly. "But she wasn't lying. Why not? Listen—during the war, when a German turned against the Nazis and helped us, you thought he was a noble fellow, indeed, didn't you? Remember all the pretty articles that were written about it—the higher call, the duty to humanity above the narrow duty to your country, the necessity for private revolt to save the very people you were revolting against. All that? Well, I fell for it. I'm a big man," he said mockingly, "for the higher duty. I'm busy trying to save America from itself. And if I have to lie a little here and there for it, and if I have to say one thing when I mean another, and not advertise everything that comes into my mind in the New York *Times,* I don't mind that at all. The guys who sneaked across the German lines with maps of Nazi artillery positions didn't announce what they were doing over a public-address system, either. Were they dishonorable because they crossed the lines at night?"

"That was Germany under Hitler," Archer said. "In America it's a different . . ."

"Different. Different!" Vic said sardonically. "America is immune to everything, including Fascism and the common cough, because God loves us so much. Let me tell you something about America. We're the most dangerous people in the world because we're mediocre. Mediocre, hysterical and vain. We're worse than the worst religious fanatics. We can't bear the thought that anybody anywhere else might be more advanced or more intelligent or better organized or be closer to the true faith than we are—and we're ready to knock down a hundred cities in one night to stifle our own doubts. We're the ruin-bringers. We lick our chops, waiting for the moment to start the planes off the runways. All over the world when people hear the word America, they spit. We call it freedom and we'll stuff it down their throats like hot lead if we have to. Our idea of freedom includes two hundred million radioactive corpses. And what do you think it's going to be like here? There'll be plenty of the free dead here, too, because the rest of the world will see to that. And the ones that aren't produced by foreigners'll be supplied by the domestic trade. Look at the newspapers, listen to the radio—everybody in this country is slavering to get his hands at the throat of his neighbor. Give us two, three years of another war and we'll blow up here like a firecracker. The whites'll kill the blacks, the Protestants the Catholics, the Catholics anybody they can lay their hands on, the rich'll machine-gun the poor, the poor'll turn Fifth Avenue red with blood, if there's still a Fifth Avenue left that anybody can find. Everybody in this country hates everybody else. All you have to do is follow one political campaign to know that. And there'll be a big sigh of relief when the killing season is officially introduced . . . And if I have to do a little lying to my poor old history professor now and then in an attempt to postpone all this, let the angels punish me in heaven for it. Nobody who ever accomplished anything ever behaved like a boy scout on Sunday. Look for your scrupulous friends on the losing side of everything. Morality—morality is what the conqueror imposes upon the conquered to make sure they both remain exactly that. Don't think I'm taken in by the lies," Vic went on stubbornly. "Not the Chamber of Commerce lies or the Hitler lies or Hutt's lies or *Pravda's* lies. I don't believe we're all brave, free, friendly patriots here and that everything will always be just dandy as long as we salute the flag and pay our income tax on time. And I don't believe that Russia is full of merry, singing peasants and the Kremlin is full of saints and that nobody gets killed in the Soviet Union and nobody gets tortured and nobody gets his face pushed in when he happens to say something unpopular. But I say that it's coming to a showdown and when that time comes, it's going to be worse here and I'm betting that the Russians'll be at least fifty-one percent right. And I'll bet that when that time comes you'll have to be on our side."

"You should have been at the meeting Friday night," Archer said. "I made an interesting little lecture on just that subject. I'm going to be on my own side."

Vic made an impatient gesture. "I heard about your speech. It wasn't a lecture. It was a suicide note. You're so God-damn anxious to be pure that you're making it absolutely certain that you'll be cut down without the slightest effort. Because nobody on either side'll raise a finger to help you. It's going to take a new invention to service people like you, Clement. A cellophane wall. So that when you go to your martyrdom, the firing parties of both sides can hit you at the same time. You've outdated the opaque, non-transparent wall for execution purposes, Clem, and you'll be remembered for your contribution." He grinned coldly in the shadowy marble hall. "And you've done it the old-fashioned way," he went on. "With all the old ingredients. Honor. Loyalty. Literal truth. You'd've been a big success in the fifteenth century, but this year, kid, you're just a joke. You're hundreds of years behind the times and the worst of it is that you're proud of it. And the sad part of it is that there're so many like you. You want all the benefits of the twentieth century, you want to ride in cars and fly in the air and have an easy, modern, up-to-date, latest-model conscience, but you can't grind a cylinder or put in a rivet or do any of the dirty work that has to be done to keep people from starving or wars from breaking out. You're great on results but when it comes to the techniques you suddenly discover your mother won't let you get your pretty clothes dirty playing with the grease and the heavy machinery."

"You're so proud of yourself," Archer said. "You're so sure that you're right."

"Well," Vic said, leaning easily against the wall, his hat tilted down over his eyes, "I am. Why deny it?"

"What if the people you say you're working for, the people you say you want to keep from starving, to keep from getting killed in wars, what if they don't want you? What if they reject you, the way you *are* being rejected? What do you do then?"

Vic shrugged carelessly. "Screw them," he said. "One hundred million slobs. What do they know? They're stunned from reading their idiotic newspapers and going to their movies and listening to their politicians and preachers. Leave them alone and they wouldn't know enough to come in out of the rain. You ignore what they tell you and save them despite themselves. Then ten years later they're screaming your name in ecstasy and they're ready to tear anyone apart who dares to hint you can't piss to windward."

Archer shook his head. "Vic . . . Vic," he said softly. "Do you remember back in school, when you quit the football team . . ."

Vic grinned. "That idiot Samson."

"Remember I told you you were suffering from the sin of pride and maybe that was the worst sin of all . . ."

"You were a little stuffy in those days, Professor," Vic said, smiling. "The cloistered atmosphere. Big improvement noticeable in recent years."

"God help us," Archer said, "if you ever have your way."

"Don't worry, pal," Vic said. "We'll all be dead first."

"Vic," Archer asked, "why did you come up here tonight?"

Vic sighed. He suddenly looked very tired. "I don't know why," he said. "Maybe because we've known each other a long time. I don't know. Maybe I came to tell you a joke." He grinned weakly. "You know what started me on my fall from grace? You. The first time I ever read Karl Marx it was in the copy of *Das Kapital* you loaned me from your own library in 1935." He chuckled emptily. "Don't worry," he said, "wild Congressmen couldn't drag it out of me. Come up to my house some time," he said carelessly. "I'll lend *you* a book." He peered closely at Archer. "You've got a very funny look on your face, dear boy," he said.

"Now listen to me," Archer said. "I don't ever want to see you again. But you represent fifteen years of my life. You, Kitty, Nancy . . . Jane. A third of my life. I can't let myself feel that I was wrong all that time. I've got to make myself remember what I believed about you for many years—that you were an extraordinary man—that you were valuable human material. And, for my own sake, no matter what you've done, I can't believe now that all that fundamental stuff is gone. Tonight," Archer said, talking slowly and painstakingly, conscious of the set, crooked, meaningless grin on Vic's heavily shadowed face, "tonight I had to examine myself very carefully. I found out that I was paying for a lot of things. I was paying for being naive and ignorant and lazy. I was paying for all the years I was too timid to examine myself closely. Vic, examine yourself tonight, too, examine what you've been doing, what you're going to do from now on. Are you going to move away from the magnificent boy you were or are you going to try to move back to him? Because what you are now is no good. You're corrupt and you corrupt everything you touch. And that's the worst of it.

You use people's best impulses, their charity, their desire to see justice done, to betray them, just the way the Nazis used people's worst impulses, their cruelty and greed, to betray *them*. You've put a look of suspicion on the face of every decent man in the country. Stand up to yourself. Is that what you want? Is it too late to change?"

"Repent, ye sinners," Vic said, "because everybody's doing it this year at all the best parties. You make me feel sorry for you. Because you're trying so hard to make yourself believe I'm a villain, and you can't manage it. Because, deep down, you have to ask yourself— what's he doing it for? What's in it for Vic Herres? Am I getting rich out of it? No. I'm losing everything, and you know it, and I don't give a damn. Do I expect medals, honors, prizes from it?" Vic laughed sardonically. "I'll be lucky if I stay out of jail six more months. What do I want? Power?" Vic grinned. "How much power do you think the Communists're going to have in this country in the next ten, twenty years? Is it revenge I'm after? For what? Ever since I was a kid America's flopped on the bed for me and spread its legs and said, 'Do it again, baby, do it just the same way to me again.' Do you think I want revenge for that?" He chuckled harshly. "So you're down to the bedrock horror about me. The one thing you can't bear to believe. That I'm doing all this not for myself, because I got mine, but for the hundred million poor, tortured, screaming, beat-up, shot-up, scared, bomb-happy slobs out there . . ." He made a stiff, awkward flinging gesture toward the city, toward the dark, stretching country outside the hospital. "I despise them, but I feel responsible for them and I want them to live a little happier and die a little later. And that's my villainy, and maybe they'll hang me for it in the end, but you'll never get it out of your craw. And finally, it'll poison you, because you'll never be able to digest it."

Archer looked at him hazily, as though Vic was far

away, obscured in mist. Virtue, he thought thickly, everyone is so certain of his virtue. Vic, Hutt, Sandler, Motherwell. The torturers of the Inquisition were also sure of their virtue, applying the fire, smelling the searing flesh, tearing the breasts and testicles, *their* vision of the ultimate good always there beyond the screams and the devoured bone, breaking how many bodies for the soul's salvation, enlisting recruits for heaven at the stake, confident, serene, impervious, unmoved by agony, confident in their bloodstained dungeons that they were in the service of the angels. Only the angels change. The inquisitors are always present. Always grinning, their certain, dedicated, fanged grin, always pitiless, always inhuman, always armed, always to be fought. Sometimes to be beaten, sometimes to be lost to, but always to be fought. . . .

"All right," Archer said. We're not through with each other. Because I'm going to fight you. From now on, everything you do, every word you say, I'm going to challenge. Me. Personally. Privately, publicly. I don't know how I'm going to do it, but I'm going to do it. Maybe it took me a long time to wake up, but I'm awake now, and watch out for me. I'm going to be dangerous to you and everyone like you, at home and abroad. You educated me and the process hurt, but I thank you for it. You've made me real useful and I'm going to use myself to destroy you. Every disguise you put on, I'm going to rip off, because you finally took me backstage and showed me how you did it. Every time you open your mouth I'm going to pin the lie on your lips. And in the end, if it comes to it, I swear to God I'll pick up a gun and kill you. Remember. Now get out of here." He walked around Vic and rang for the elevator. Down below, in the shaft, there was an iron clanking.

Vic turned and they faced each other. There was no grin now and he seemed weary and regretful, no longer like a young man, not quite so impervious. "I never thought you'd say anything like that," Vic said.

"I said it." Archer stared at Vic, far away in the distant mist.

"Look me up," Vic said. "Twenty years from now."

Archer said nothing.

They were silent for a moment, listening to the low whine of the mounting elevator. They stood there, not quite looking at each other, with nothing to say to each other.

"Well," Vic said, and Archer could see that he was trying to smile, "good-bye, dear boy."

"Good-bye, Vic," Archer said. They didn't shake hands and Archer watched Vic walk slowly across the lobby toward the door. He had his hands in his pockets and his head was bent and his shoulders seemed tired. Then, halfway across the lobby he suddenly straightened up, throwing his shoulders back, and crossed the rest of the distance quickly, with the easy, jaunty, pleasantly arrogant stride that Archer remembered so well. Then he threw open the door and went out into the darkness.

Behind Archer, the door of the elevator slid open and he went in and said, "Fourth floor, please."

The soft-faced nurse was at the desk, with the green lights winking on and off above her head. "Mr. Archer," she said, as he passed her, and he stopped. She stood up and came out from behind the desk. "We were trying to find you," she said softly, and Archer knew what she was going to say. "The little boy died," she said. "At one thirty-two."

"At one thirty-two?" Archer repeated insanely.

"I'm terribly sorry," the girl whispered.

Archer nodded and walked down the dark corridor toward Kitty's room.

There was no light on in the room, but there was a glow from the street lamps that filtered through the window. The window was open a little and Archer could hear the river wind going softly past the building.

"Clement?" It was a low whisper out of the deeper darkness of the bed.

"Yes, Kitty." Archer worked carefully at keeping his voice ordinary and cheerful. He took off his hat and went over to the bed and sat down on it without taking his coat off. He could see the pale blur of Kitty's face on the pillow and ghostly tiny reflections of light in her wide-open eyes. He didn't put out his hand to touch her because his hands were still cold. "How are you, darling?" he asked.

"I heard," Kitty said, but her voice was even. "I called the nursery and they told me."

"Yes, Kitty."

"I'm not going to cry. I'm all done crying," Kitty said.

"You ought to try to sleep."

"Later. Did you have a drink?"

"No. I . . . I just took a little walk."

"It's cold out, isn't it?"

"Yes."

"I can tell from the way your coat feels. It's windy out, too, isn't it?"

"Not too bad," Archer said.

"The wind sounds funny in this room," Kitty said. "It sounds like nurses walking outside the window." She lay silent for a moment. "Clement," she said, her voice sounding childish and tired in the darkness, "Clement, are we all right?"

"Yes, Kitty," Archer said gravely.

"You're not just saying it—because this is a bad night."

"I'm not just saying it."

"If you're disappointed in me, if you feel you can't go on with me after what I've done, you can tell me," Kitty whispered. "You don't have to pamper me any more."

Archer put his arms around her and pulled her toward him, holding her tight, kissing her throat, in a tangle of blankets and hospital nightgown.

"I'm so glad," Kitty whispered. "I'm so glad."

Holding her, feeling dry, helpless tears somewhere deep in his throat, feeling the frail, drained, exhausted, loved body through the clumsy material of his coat, Archer was filled with a bursting sense of relief, of reunion, of unreasonable hope. This has survived, he thought confusedly, this good, precious, battered, necessary thing has survived, so I shall survive.

"I'm going to be better from now on," Kitty said softly into his ear, and she put up her hand to stroke the back of his head. "Now I know what I have to guard against in myself. Before this I was so proud, I thought I was so strong, I thought that I would always do the right thing automatically. Now I know—nothing's automatic. There are horrible places in me, horrible streaks, and I have to fight them, fight them, every minute. Darling, we're going to try again," she whispered, "aren't we? We're going to try everything again?"

He kissed her. "Yes, Kitty," he said. "Everything again." He let her down gently to the pillow. Her eyes were shining in the darkness.

"Clement," she said drowsily, "will you watch me fall asleep?"

"Yes, Kitty."

"Good night," she said, almost inaudibly.

"Good night, dearest."

Archer moved silently over to the window. In a moment, he heard Kitty's even breathing. He looked out the window. The city fell away from him in the darkness, waiting for the first and final siren. Softly, Archer closed the window and pulled down the shade. Then he sat down and watched his wife, deep in her healing sleep in the quiet room.